I0747049

<u>**Praise for Minerva Spencer & S.M. LaViolette's**</u>

"Spencer creates characters worth rooting for. Readers will be eager to see Phoebe's sisters find their own matches next."

-Publishers Weekly on **PHOEBE**

<u>**THE BOXING BARONESS**</u>

"Swooningly romantic, sizzling sensual…superbly realized."

–Booklist **STARRED REVIEW**

A *Library Journal* **Best Book of 2022**

A Publishers Marketplace Buzz Books Romance Selection

"Fans of historical romances with strong female characters in non-traditional roles and the men who aren't afraid to love them won't be disappointed by this series starter."

–Library Journal **STARRED REVIEW**

"Spencer (*Notorious*) launches her Wicked Women of Whitechapel Regency series with an outstanding romance based in part on a real historical figure. . . This is sure to wow!"

-Publishers Weekly **STARRED REVIEW**

<u>**THE DUELING DUCHESS:**</u>

"Another carefully calibrated mix of steamy passion, delectably dry humor, and daringly original characters."

—Booklist **STARRED REVIEW**

VERDICT: Readers who enjoyed *The Boxing Baroness* won't want to miss Spencer's sequel.

–Library Journal **STARRED REVIEW**

A *Library Journal* **Best Book of 2023**

"[A] pitch perfect Regency …. Readers will be hooked. "

(THE MUSIC OF LOVE)

★*Publishers Weekly STARRED REVIEW*

"Lovers of historical romance will be hooked on this twisty story of revenge, redemption, and reversal of fortunes."

Publishers Weekly, STARRED review of THE FOOTMAN.

"Fans will be delighted."

Publishers Weekly on THE POSTILION

NOTORIOUS

"Brilliantly crafted…an irresistible cocktail of smart characterization, sophisticated sensuality, and sharp wit." ★*Booklist STARRED REVIEW*

"Sparkling…impossible not to love."—Popsugar

"Realistically transforming the Regency equivalent of a mean girl into a relatable, all-too-human heroine is no easy feat, but Spencer (Outrageous, 2021) succeeds on every level. Lightly dusted with wintery holiday charm, graced with an absolutely endearing, beetle-obsessed hero and a fully rendered cast of supporting characters and spiked with smoldering sensuality and wry wit, the latest in Spencer's Rebels of the Ton series is sublimely satisfying."

—Booklist STARRED review of INFAMOUS

"Perfect for fans of Bridgerton, *Infamous* is also a charming story for Christmas. In fact, I enjoyed Infamous so much that when I was halfway through it, I ordered the author's first novel, Dangerous. I look forward to reading much more of Minerva Spencer's work."

—THE HISTORICAL NOVEL SOCIETY on INFAMOUS

"LaViolette keeps the tension high, delivering dark eroticism and emotional depth in equal measure. Readers will be hooked."

-PUBLISHERS WEEKLY on HIS HARLOT

"LaViolette's clever, inventive plot makes room for some kinky erotic scenes as her well-shaded characters explore their sexualities. Fans of erotic romance will find much to love."

This book is dedicated to the queen of gothic romance, Victoria Holt, whose novel *The Devil on Horseback*, is the book that made me love romance.

Aurelia

The Bellamy Sisters
Book 4

Minerva Spencer

writing as
S.M. LAVIOLETTE

Author's Note
The Isle of Crewe is a product of my imagination, not a real island in the
Hebrides.

Chapter 1

The Isle of Crewe

Off the coast of Scotland

Roland Montgomery, the eighth Earl of Crewe, had just come to the tricky section of his upcoming presentation for the Royal Society, about sexual dimorphism among the *selasphorus rufus* of *Las Floridas*, when somebody knocked loudly on the library door.

"It had better be damned important!" he bellowed.

Everyone—family and servants—knew Roland was not to be disturbed when he was in the library, which also served as his workroom.

His cousin, Arthur Montgomery, opened the door halfway and hovered on the threshold. "I'm terribly sorry to interrupt you, Crewe, but I'm afraid there is a problem."

Roland scowled and gestured for him to enter. "What has my daughter done now?"

"Why do you immediately assume that Celsa has done something bad?"

"When is it ever anything else?" Roland slumped in his chair and waved his hand in a *get on with it* gesture.

"Well, as it happens, you are right." Arthur ignored Roland's unamused bark of laughter and went on, "Celsa has been, er, naughty. She locked Miss Hatchet in the dungeon."

Roland groaned and let his head fall back. "Bloody hell! How long?"

"The woman says it was almost six hours. I'm afraid she is a bit, er, hysterical."

Roland muttered a string of curses that made the other man recoil. It always astounded him how he and Arthur had been as close as brothers as boys and worked together as men, and yet Arthur had somehow ended up possessing the worldview of a rural vicar.

"I managed to calm down Miss Hatchet," Arthur said.

"Thank Christ for your God-given abilities," he said, ignoring Arthur's wince at his blasphemy.

Just like every other woman on the island, the fussy governess was three-quarters in love with Roland's angelically handsome cousin. Not that Arthur ever took advantage of any of the dozens of women who threw themselves at him.

Arthur's milk-pale cheeks darkened. "I did not say anything inappropriate to her, Crewe."

"I know that, you gudgeon." Although Roland couldn't help thinking it would be better if Arthur *did* step out of line occasionally. But he knew from experience that his puritanical cousin would not thank him for the suggestion.

He massaged the back of his neck as he considered the problem of Celsa and her ninth governess. "Did you convince the woman to stay? Or do we need to hire another one?"

"She agreed to another month after I promised to ensure that Celsa behaves."

"How? By murdering her?"

"She's not a bad girl—"

"She's a bloody demon, Arthur. Only you would think the little monster can be tamed."

Arthur gave him *that* look, the same one he'd used throughout the years whenever he had felt it was his duty to serve as Roland's moral compass. "She is only misbehaving because she craves your attention."

"Then perhaps it is time I give her the same sort of *attention* my father gave the two of us when we were lads and misbehaved."

Arthur gasped. "You cannot whip a girl!"

"Oh, I *could*—trust me—but I would never be able to bear the looks of reproach you'd turn on me afterward," he said, only partly in jest. If there was one thing Arthur did excellently, it was to make Roland feel guilty for his bad behavior.

"Can't you just spend some time with her?" Arthur asked quietly.

"I see her every evening at dinner."

"You know I mean more than that. If you would just—"

"I am not a nursemaid, Arthur. I engage a governess and pay her a bloody fortune to live on this island and keep my daughter occupied. And what does Celsa do but torment and persecute the woman."

"Without her mother, the only parent Celsa has is you."

"She has *you*. You are more a father to her than I've ever been."

Arthur's flush stained his cheeks, and he said stiffly, "I hope you don't think I try to usurp your—"

"Don't be a fool. I am grateful for what you do with her—for everything you do."

Arthur looked away, visibly embarrassed. "Oh, nonsense. Without you, I'd have nothing."

Roland waved away the other man's protest, which was one he'd heard many times in the past and was just as untrue now as it had always been. "I will hear no more of that from you."

Arthur tried to protest, but Roland silenced him with a glare.

"So, you want me to do *something* with the brat? What? She has no interest in the natural world, no desire to apply herself to any subject—art, literature, or science—and she has alienated every other child her age on the island with her willful, often malicious, behavior."

Arthur looked pained. "She misbehaves because it is the only way she can gain your attention. There is one area in which she shines, and that is anything to do with horses."

"She is an excellent equestrienne," Roland admitted.

"Perhaps you could take her with you when you visit your tenants? It would be good for her to start taking up such duties. Especially since she is probably going to inherit them," he added in a much quieter voice.

Arthur was probably right about that; Roland had no intention of marrying and producing any more children, which meant that Celsa would be mistress of everything once he died.

"I will think about it," Roland said, finished with the subject. "Now that you are here, I wanted to talk to you about another matter."

"Oh?"

"It is about Sadie Roy and her daughter, Dora."

Arthur's angelic features hardened. "What about them?"

"I understand that you told Sadie she would need to leave her cottage if her daughter refused to marry before her child is born."

"She came running to you, did she?"

"No, Arthur, she did *not* come running to me."

"Then who told—oh, I know." He gave Roland a look of disdain and mild revulsion. "It was Mary Neel, wasn't it? I saw you ride out late last night. You went to her again."

The fact that Roland felt a stab of guilt—albeit very mild—at his cousin's glare was a testament to the other man's ability.

"Have you been spying on me, Arthur?"

"I most certainly have *not*."

Roland suspected his virtuous cousin was telling a fib. Arthur's chambers did not look out in the direction of the stables, so he would have needed to make an effort to see Roland leave the castle.

Rather than point that out, Roland said, "Yes, I saw Mary last night. What of it?"

"You must know that everyone on the island is aware that she is your— your—"

"Occasional bed partner?" Roland suggested when Arthur seemed to have frozen.

"I was going to say *whore*."

The amusement Roland had been feeling dissipated. "Do not refer to her that way again, Arthur."

Arthur's flush deepened at Roland's cold tone. "You are right; that was unchristian. *However,* do you really believe your behavior is decent, Crewe?"

"Not that this is any of your damned affair, Arthur, but I am an unmarried man of legal age and free to put my cock in whomever I choose—so long as my partner is willing."

Arthur's pale cheeks went wild with color and his lips pursed in an expression of distaste at Roland's crudity. "Yes, but it is copulation outside the bounds of matrimony and it sets a bad example for your people."

It was an argument Arthur had put forth often over the years and Roland found it just as unpersuasive as it had always been.

"Fortunately, I have never set myself up as a beacon of virtue for others to emulate, Arthur. Nor have I sought to define what constitutes appropriate moral rectitude—or lack thereof—for anyone on this island. But it sounds to me as if you would like to be judge, jury, and executioner in matters of right and wrong on Crewe."

"I don't. It is just—I only meant—"

"I find it astounding that you think to cast Sadie from her cottage because her daughter has fallen pregnant outside of wedlock." It was also bloody ironic, given Arthur's patrimony, but Roland kept that to himself. He might be an immoral womanizer, but he tried not to be a vicious arse.

"The girl refused to tell me who the father of her child was," Arthur said, his expression so prim that Roland wanted to kick the man.

"I. Don't. Care."

Arthur recoiled at his angry tone, his lips parting in shock.

Roland lowered his voice and said, "I do not understand your rigidly unrealistic attitude toward sex. It is a favorite pastime of *all* creatures—both humans and animals—and because people are flawed, they will invariably make errors in judgment. Sadie and her daughter will have to live with Dora's decision."

"You are mistaking the point, Crewe."

"What is the point?" Roland asked wearily.

"You are the Laird of Crewe. The people look to you for spiritual leadership and—"

Roland had to laugh. "I bloody well hope not! They have a vicar to see to those needs, Arthur. I am their landlord, not their confessor. Not only is that a position I do not wish to fill, but it is one I am singularly ill-suited for, as I'm sure you will agree. Now," he said when the other man opened his mouth to argue, "I have sent word to Sadie assuring her that the cottage is hers for as long as she wants it."

"But—"

"No. You will not interfere with them. I am adamant on the subject."

Arthur gave an exasperated huff. "Why do you continue to indulge that woman, Crewe? She has taken egregious advantage of you over and over again, and all because you shared her bed many years ago." Arthur's face purpled with anger. Or perhaps embarrassment. "People talk about—"

"I do not care if people talk," Roland said. "One of the benefits of being wealthy and powerful is that I don't have to care. As for Sadie and my indulgence, that is my affair and this will be the last time you raise the subject with me." He locked eyes with his cousin, irked by the righteous indignation in Arthur's celestial blue gaze. "I am no man—or woman's—conscience, Arthur. And neither are you. Do not make decisions like this again; it is not your place. Understood?"

Knots ran up and down the other man's jaw and for a moment he thought Arthur would rebel against Roland's authority as leader of their family. If he did, it would be the first time in twenty years.

But after a long, tense moment Arthur nodded. "I will abide by your wishes on the matter."

"Good. Let that be an end to it." Roland glanced out the window. "I daresay my new artist will be staying over in Balcrewe tonight if it keeps blowing like this."

"Old Em swears the weather will calm later in the day, so your Miss Burton will be here for dinner.

"If Old Em predicts it, then it must be so," Roland scoffed, although it was true that the crone—who had been ancient even when Roland's father had been a boy—had an uncanny ability when it came to predicting the weather.

"I still do not understand why you hired a woman artist," Arthur said.

"Because she was the best out of all the candidates who applied."

Arthur looked unconvinced.

Roland gave the man an exasperated look. "I can see why you would think a man is a better pugilist or farm laborer than a woman, but painting does not require superior muscle, Arthur. Surely you don't believe men are inherently better artists than women?"

"No, of course not," Arthur said, although Roland thought he sounded less than convincing. "I—well, it's just that females should be home, raising children and tending to a husband's needs, not galivanting about and taking jobs that men should have."

"You did not raise this objection when we hired a governess."

Arthur's mouth dropped open and for a moment he looked like a stymied carp. "No," he finally admitted. "But that is…different."

"Why?"

"Because the position of governess is an accepted one for a spinster. But painting—especially scientific illustration—is rightfully a male purview. Why, just imagine some of the specimens she might be called upon to examine?" Arthur's cheeks pinkened and he leaned toward Roland. "She will have seen, erm, the private parts of animals." His eyebrows threatened to launch off his forehead as he hissed, "She might even have studied *human* anatomy, Crewe!"

Roland laughed.

"Oh, you *would* find that amusing," Arthur said in disgust. "But the mere fact that a female would presume to engage in such an activity shows a lamentable independence that is unbecoming in a woman." He paused, took a deep breath, and then said, "Not to mention that having an unmarried woman in a bachelor household adds unwanted complications."

It amused Roland how careful Arthur was to tiptoe around the subject of women who displayed *lamentable independence*. Roland's deceased wife, Jane, had epitomized *lamentable independence*. At least to Arthur.

Roland had always enjoyed his wife's ability to hold her own in the male-dominated field of botany. And he had also respected the fact that she had insisted on accompanying him on all his expeditions, no matter how dangerous.

Jane hadn't just been a damned fine botanist, she had also been one of the most beautiful, overtly sexual, women Roland had ever met. Needless to say, Jane and Arthur had hated each other at first sight.

Roland had to admit that Arthur had a point when he mentioned women causing *unwanted complications* among a group that otherwise consisted of men.

If Jane had been meek and mild, her appearance might not have been a problem. But she'd had a fierce temperament to go along with her exceptional beauty. And she had also brimmed with mischief. Indeed, Jane had adored the sexual tension her presence had created on Roland's expeditions and had enjoyed exacerbating it, bedding more than a few men, behavior which had nearly driven Arthur mad on the one journey he had made with them—Jane's last, as it happened.

It had been Jane's infidelity that had probably led—at least indirectly—to her death on their trip to Las Floridas. If she hadn't been fucking one of the luggage bearers that night, she might have had a chance to shoot the panther that had killed both her and her lover.

When Roland had tried to save his wife, the cat had turned on him, leaving him blind in one eye, hideously scarred, and without the full use of his dominant arm.

He didn't care about his appearance. Indeed, it was just as well that matchmaking mamas and their daughters found his scarred, one-eyed face hideous. But he missed his glorious bitch of a wife a great deal. Roland had never loved Jane—nor she, him—but she had been his closest friend and confidant for years.

It had not been a perfect marriage, or even a very good one, but then Roland was the sort of man who should never have married in the first place. He certainly had no intention of ever doing so again. Not when his first wife had run off with her lover and his second had died with another man in her bed. Or tent, rather.

Roland did not blame either woman. He had neglected poor Rebecca, his first wife, in favor of his studies, and he had argued and fought nonstop with Jane. The only times he and Jane had *not* argued had been when they'd been working or engaging in vigorous bouts of post-argument coitus.

Marriage just was not right for him—and it had been hell on his wives—and he'd made a terrible husband.

"I'm sorry," Arthur said, his subdued voice breaking into Roland's thoughts. "I didn't mean to remind you of Jane. I know you—"

"There is nothing to apologize for," Roland said, despising the soft, pitying look his cousin got in his eyes whenever anyone mentioned his dead wife. "However, I fail to see a correlation between my dead wife and the artist I've engaged. A woman on an expedition with fifty men is one thing. A woman on an island where at least half the population is female, is another matter entirely."

Arthur sighed. "Yes, I suppose that is true."

Once again, Roland changed the subject. "Do you think you can persuade Miss Hatchet to stay longer than a month? Hatchet!" he snorted and shook his head. "What an unfortunate name. Especially when she looks rather like one, and possesses a personality to match."

"That is unkind, Crewe." Arthur gave him a chastising look, reminding Roland that it had been Arthur who'd hired Miss Hatchet and he frequently sang the woman's praises.

"Yes, you are right—it was not a nice thing to say," he agreed. "So, do you think you might convince her to stay?"

Arthur chewed his lip, the action making him look like a pensive angel. All he lacked was wings and a harp to complete the picture. "I might be able to prevail upon her if Celsa can behave for—"

"So the answer is *no* in other words."

Arthur sighed. "Probably not. Especially as Celsa seems to have taken a particular dislike to the poor woman for some inexplicable reason."

Disliking the prudish, sanctimonious governess was a subject Roland and his daughter were of one mind about.

But just because he didn't like Miss Hatchet didn't mean he condoned tormenting her. Celsa needed to learn that being cruel to people who could not fight back—like one's employees—was unacceptable.

"Would you like me to begin searching for a new governess?" Arthur asked.

Roland was beginning to wonder if the governesses themselves might bear some responsibility for the difficulties with Celsa. He had allowed his cousin to manage the hiring of the women and they had, to a one, been rigid, humorless, and self-righteous. At first, Roland had assumed that was the nature of governesses—creatures he'd heretofore known nothing about—but now he suspected the women reflected Arthur's own beliefs.

"I might interview a few candidates myself this time," he said.

Arthur's expression hardened and he swelled with indignation. "If you don't trust me with the decision, then you are more than welcome—"

"I trust your judgment," Roland lied. "But I'm actually considering other solutions than another governess."

"Such as?

"Sending her away to school."

"She is only four and ten!"

"Soon to be five-and-ten."

"It is too young."

"My father sent us away when I was nine and you were one-and-ten," he reminded his cousin.

"Yes. And it was hellish. Without you to protect me it would have been even worse. Poor Celsa won't have anyone."

It was true that Arthur had had a dreadful time at Eton. He'd been tall—almost as tall as Roland—but skinny and so pretty that he'd been teased relentlessly.

Roland, who'd possessed the demeanor of a badger as a lad—and some would argue still did—had protected his more retiring cousin whenever he could. But there had been times when Roland hadn't been there to save him.

"Perhaps girls are not as vicious as boys," Roland said.

Arthur gave him a look of disbelief.

Roland laughed and held up his hands. "Yes, you are right: that was an idiotic thing to say." Especially as they'd just finished discussing his dead wife Jane, who could be twice as vicious as any man he had ever met.

"Celsa needs to get at least a few years of, er, *finishing*, before she is launched into society," Roland pointed out. "I think school is an excellent notion."

"A year should be ample. That means you don't need to send her until she is seventeen."

Roland was amused by his cousin's protective instincts toward his daughter. He strongly doubted Celsa would be an underdog if she were to go off to school. It was far more likely that she would end up at the top of the pecking order.

Arthur gestured to the journal article Roland had been working on before he'd been interrupted. "How is that progressing?" he asked, clearly wanting to leave the subject of sending Celsa to school behind.

Roland held up his left hand to show the tremor in his injured arm, which still functioned but was very weak. "I have to take frequent breaks to rest my hand. Also, my handwriting is worse than ever; you will need to re-write everything in your handsome copperplate."

"It shakes far less than it did a year ago," Arthur said, ever the optimist.

"Yes, but it is easily fatigued and the tremor gets worse the longer I use it." He flexed his fingers and stared at the black scars on the back of his hand—scars that went all the way up his arm. "It was wishful thinking to believe I could help with any of the paintings. I suspect I will never have the control over my fingers that is necessary to paint, or even sketch. Miss Burton will have to do the bulk of it."

"And you believe she is up to the task?"

"I certainly hope so," Roland said, and then cleared his throat and turned back to the pages on his desk, picking up his quill.

"You are eager to get back to work," Arthur said, getting to his feet.

Roland did not deny it.

"I shall see you at dinner," Arthur said.

But Roland had already stopped listening.

Chapter 2

L ady Aurelia Bellamy sat in the coffee room in the Laughing Hen Inn and public house and stared out the window at her future home.

Even from three miles away, Castle Crewe dominated the horizon, perched as it was on the highest point of the Isle of Crewe.

The guidebook Aurelia had consulted said the castle had been the stronghold of the Lairds of Crewe for over seven hundred years. It was an imposing fortification that was made even more daunting by its black walls. The black color was the result of a particular variant of lichen. Legend had it that the black edifice had so daunted several waves of invaders that they had changed their minds about assaulting the island. And so the lichen had been allowed to proliferate even though it slowly eroded the stone. Still, with walls that were several feet thick, the intimidation value had been considered well worth the gradual erosion.

And *that* was where she would be living for the next year.

With the infamous Earl of Crewe.

Although she had been secretly illustrating for scientists all over Britain for five years, this trip to the Isle of Crewe was the first time she had ever traveled to a client's estate to do the work. Indeed, in the past her clients had believed her to be Albert Burton rather than Aurelia Bellamy. So, this was also her first job under her real name. Well, half her real name. To spare her family any shame, she had given the Earl of Crewe the fictitious surname *Burton*.

Not that taking such an alias had been enough to appease her mother.

"If you leave now to work for the Earl of Crewe you will no longer have a mother, a family, or a home, Aurelia. I will tell people that you died and I only have five children."

The Countess of Addiscombe's words were still ringing in Aurelia's head even a week after her mother had flung them at her.

Although the countess had never been warm or affectionate, Aurelia hadn't believed she was cold enough to disown one of her children merely for trying to earn a living—especially given that everyone in their family, the countess included, might soon be bereft of a hearth and home thanks to the earl's reckless gambling.

She sighed, shook away the unpleasant thought, and took a sip of tea, turning her thoughts to the job that was awaiting her.

Lord Crewe had engaged her to paint flora and fauna from *Las Floridas*, the Spanish colony that bordered the English settlements in America. He was the first Englishman to explore the interior of the Spanish possession and it was said that the specimens he'd brought back were unlike any ever seen.

He was selling subscriptions for a two-volume work that would be published the following year, and Aurelia's paintings would be the basis for many of the plates. It was truly the opportunity of a lifetime and she had traveled six long, hellish days in a public coach to get there. And yet it seemed the last three miles—from the village of Balcrewe to the Isle of Crewe—might be the hardest, thanks to the weather.

"Miss Burton?"

She turned to find the publican, Mr. Anderson, smiling at her.

"Have you found somebody to row me across?" she asked, laying her napkin down beside her empty teacup and saucer.

"Me son will take ye, but the billows be too rough just yet," he said, gesturing to the window.

Aurelia assumed he meant the whitecaps on the water between the mainland and the island.

"How long will I have to wait?" she asked.

"If they get worse, mayhap until tomorrow. But don't ye worry, Lord Crewe has already instructed me to have a room for you."

Aurelia digested that unwelcome piece of information.

"Would ye care to go up to yer room and rest a while?" he offered.

She had just spent six days crammed into a carriage, the last thing she wanted was to stay indoors.

"I believe I will take a walk—not too far, so I will be at hand if the crossing becomes possible," she assured him.

"Aye, there be a nice path that runs just north to Andrew's Cove. Right pretty it be." He glanced out the window again. "I reckon the wind might be dyin' down. Come back in an hour and we'll see."

As Aurelia strode toward the path he had indicated, she pondered what she had learned thus far about Lord Crewe from Mr. Anderson and his wife as the two had lingered after serving Aurelia her tea.

Mrs. Anderson had been visibly delighted to be the first person in Balcrewe to meet Aurelia and assured her that the entire village was agog to see *the lady artist*.

While neither of the Andersons had been openly critical of the earl—whom they'd said owned not only the Isle of Crewe but also most of Balcrewe, including the land their pub sat on—they had not hesitated to pass along scandalous tidbits about their laird.

They had made numerous unsubtle references to the earl's popularity among neighborhood widows and passed along observations about how Lord Crewe's distinctive features could be seen on more than a few children in the area, both those born in *and* out of wedlock.

And then they had moved on to the earl's wives…

"Mind you, the master isnae the only one that gets up to mischief," Mrs. Anderson had murmured.

"No, indeed," Mr. Anderson had chimed in with a chuckle.

"How do you mean?" Aurelia had asked to the delight of her hosts.

"The first Lady Crewe done up and run away from the master less than two years after they wed," Mrs. Anderson said in a low voice, although Aurelia had been the only guest in the tearoom at that time.

"Now, now, we don't know that, Mother," her husband chastised, and then said to Aurelia, "The countess's boat washed up on Crewe a week or two after her ladyship disappeared. Nobody knows where she was headed or if she ever got there." He shrugged. "Could be Davy Jones got 'er."

"You mean she died?" Aurelia had asked.

Mr. Anderson had merely looked mysterious.

But his wife had said, "But many do say she run off with her lover."

"Aye, aye. So they do," the innkeeper had muttered, but then his eyes had sharpened. "As for the *second* Lady Crewe…"

He and his wife had both chuckled, the expression in their eyes so avid that Aurelia had felt a fleeting pang of shame for encouraging their gossip.

"A right beauty the second ladyship were," the innkeeper said, his eyes glazing fondly at the memory.

Mrs. Anderson had rolled her eyes at her husband and leaned close to Aurelia to hiss, "A she-rake, is what she were."

Mr. Anderson chuckled. "Aye, and a merry chase she did run him."

"A merry chase they led each other," his wife corrected.

Aurelia had seen, by the sly look in both the Andersons' eyes as they'd regarded her, that they believed the job title *female artist* was merely another euphemism for mistress. She had no doubt the garrulous innkeeper and his wife would soon be spreading gossip about Aurelia—if they weren't already.

She could have told the Andersons that she had no intention of becoming Lord Crewe's latest conquest. While she was not opposed to women engaging in amorous liaisons if that was their choice, she *was* opposed to engaging in an amorous liaison with an employer so influential in the scientific community that he could destroy her reputation with only a few words.

Too much rested on the success of this position for her to jeopardize it. She hoped that Lord Crewe would recommend her to his associates at the Royal Society if he—

"Give that back!"

Aurelia spun around at the anguished female cry, which was loud enough that it could be heard over the wind and surf.

A cluster of five young men were facing a fissure in the cliffside, one of them waving something—a satchel?—over his head in a mocking fashion while his mates laughed and jeered.

"Give it back or I will—I will report you." It was the same female voice as before, but Aurelia still could not see who it belonged to.

"Come an' get it, if ye want it, traitor!" one of the men yelled back.

"Aye! Report us all ye like, ye Boney-loving tart!" shouted another.

And then one of the gang threw a rock.

A pained female scream shattered the air and Aurelia's feet were in motion before her mind had even decided.

"You there!" she yelled before she reached the ruffians. "What are you doing?"

The surprise on the youths' faces—for that is what they were, the eldest probably no older than six-and-ten—would have been comical if not for the fact that boys in a gang could be more vicious than a pack of wolves.

The lead boy threw out his shoulders and swaggered toward Aurelia as she stormed toward them. He was holding the kind of leather bag a messenger might use, meant to be slung crosswise over the torso.

"What is that in your hands?" she asked.

"Why should I tell you?" he demanded sullenly.

"The bag is *mine*!" A young woman emerged from a deep crevice in the cliff. Although her clothing looked well made, it was torn in several places and her long, almost black hair was half-up and half-down. Blood trickled down one cheek.

"You are hurt," Aurelia said. "What happened?"

But all the woman's attention was on the boy with the satchel. "Give me back my bag!"

The boys who'd initially backed away when Aurelia ran up to them now crowded closer, their courage bolstered by their leader.

"You want it? Come an' take it," the leader taunted.

The others chuckled, an ugly avidity in their eyes.

Aurelia reached out to take the girl's upper arm. "Come with me now," she said in a low, firm voice.

"I'm not going anywhere without my—"

A rock flew, narrowly missing Aurelia's shoulder.

"What on earth do you think you are doing?" she shouted, fear making her voice shrill.

They ignored her, their hungry eyes on the other woman as two of them bent to pick up more rocks.

"We've no scrap with ye," the leader said to Aurelia, not taking his gaze from his quarry. "It's the traitor's get we want."

The others chimed in:

"Aye, the traitor!"

"She'll get what she deserves!"

"We'll not leave wi'out 'er!"

"Get gone and ye'll nae get hurt," the leader said, stalking toward the other woman, his minions on his heels.

Aurelia stood her ground, even though her knees were shaking. "I will report you. You will all go to—"

"None around here care about the likes of her! Now, step away or—"

"What on earth is going on?" a deep masculine voice demanded.

The boys turned. Rather than sneering or taunting, they immediately doffed their hats.

"We ain't doin' nothin', Sir Gideon," the leader said, no longer swaggering.

A horse and rider came into view, the man's garments elegant and his mount obviously expensive. "What are the five of you up to, Barry?"

"They were attacking this young woman," Aurelia said, before any of them could answer.

The man—Sir Gideon, she assumed—turned toward her, his dark brown eyes striking against his pale, handsome face. His gaze flickered to the woman beside Aurelia.

"What happened, Miss Clifford? Your cheek is bleeding."

"I am fine, Sir Gideon."

"She is *not* fine," Aurelia said. "These—these *ruffians* were throwing stones at her and took her bag. They should be made to answer for their actions."

Miss Clifford shook her head. "I just want my bag and I shall be on my way."

Sir Gideon turned to Barry. "Is that her satchel?"

The boy eyed him sullenly. "Aye."

"Give it back to her."

"We jest wanted to check it for secrets. What if she's sellin' things to the Frenchies?"

Sir Gideon gave him an exasperated look. "You fool! Give it back to her. *Now.*"

The boy scowled. "Here's yer bag." He hurled the satchel hard enough that the woman had to step back or risk getting hit in the head with it.

Sir Gideon's jaw tightened. "Lord Crewe will hear about this, Barry."

The name *Crewe* seemed to inject a chill into the air and several of the boys began to slink away.

"We din't mean nuthin'," Barry whined.

Sir Gideon ignored him. "All of you—get out of here."

The boys scattered.

Aurelia turned to the other woman, who was going through her bag."

"Is anything missing?" Aurelia asked.

Miss Clifford heaved a sigh of relief. "Thankfully, no."

"You should come to the inn and I will see to the cut on your face," Aurelia said.

"Thank you for your help Miss—"

"Burton."

The other woman's eyes widened. "Oh. You are Lord Crewe's lady artist."

"I am," she said, amused that everyone in the county appeared to know who she was.

"You were very brave to help me." She smiled, but the expression was tinged with weariness.

"I could hardly walk away."

Miss Clifford gave a bitter laugh. "Most other people would." She turned toward Sir Gideon, who'd dismounted and walked his horse closer. "Thank you, Sir Gideon. I feel as if you are always rescuing one of us."

"I am terribly sorry that you and your sisters have needed so much rescuing since moving to our area. I must apologize for the ugliness you have all faced."

Miss Clifford gave him a tired smile. "My sisters have already left for London, so it will only be me in need of rescuing for the foreseeable future." She nodded at them. "Thank you both. I'm afraid that I must get back to work." She inclined her head and then hurried out of the shallow rock shelter and out of Aurelia's sight.

Aurelia turned to Sir Gideon. "What in the world was that all about?"

"Miss Clifford is one of the daughters of Randolph de Clyfford, the last Earl of Daventry."

It took a few seconds for Aurelia to place the name. "Goodness! The one who—"

"Yes, the one who stood accused of treason and took his own life rather than face his punishment," Sir Gideon finished for her, his expression one of distaste.

"I thought Daventry's seat was in Lincolnshire?"

"When he was attained, all that property went back to the Crown. His daughters changed the spelling of their last name to distance themselves from their father and came all the way up here to seek shelter with Miss Pomeroy— their former governess—but a few months ago she suddenly took ill, so now they are alone. It sounds like only Miss Larissa Clifford has stayed. I daresay they have all gone off to find whatever work they can, the poor things. They certainly had a rough time of it in Balcrewe, I'm ashamed to say."

The story of the treasonous Earl of Daventry had been on the front page of every newspaper for months. Lord Daventry had sold secrets to the French and the evidence against him had been damning. His wife had died of an overdose of laudanum a few days before her husband had hanged himself in his gaol cell.

The newspapers had made much of Daventry's five daughters, who had been turned out of their family home with little more than the clothing on their backs.

The girls' horrible situation served to put Aurelia's life in perspective. Her father was an inveterate gambler who'd lost everything at the card tables, but at least he wasn't a traitor to King and country.

"My heart goes out to them," Aurelia said.

"Yes, the sins of the father are indeed visited on the children in this situation." He seemed to shake himself. "I am Gideon Talbot, by the way." He executed a graceful bow.

"Aurelia Burton," she said absently, still rattled.

"It was very brave what you did—but foolish," he chided gently. "When a gang's blood is up the situation can quickly devolve into violence."

"I know you are right, but I just couldn't stand by and let them hurt her."

"I will report them to Lord Crewe. I hate to say it, but I am glad to hear the women are leaving. Even if these boys are punished, I'm afraid it will probably not be the last instance of unpleasantness against them."

Aurelia knew he was right. If the Clifford women had moved to Little Sissingdon, the village where she had grown up, the people there would have been every bit as vicious toward the children of an infamous traitor. After all, everyone knew at least one person who'd died during the interminable war with the French.

"You were out walking when you encountered the ruffians?" Sir Gideon asked.

"Yes. I am waiting for Mr. Anderson's son to row me across to Crewe. He said the water was too rough, but I can't help feeling that his son is just not available right now."

Sir Gideon chuckled. "Yes, poor Anderson has a devil of a time with that boy." He glanced at the ocean. "There is a little chop to the water, but it would not be dangerous to cross right now." He paused, smiled at her, and then said, "I know this will sound terribly forward, but might I row you over to Crewe?"

"Oh," Aurelia said, surprised by the offer. "That is kind, but I should hate to impose."

"I need to talk to Crewe about the situation with Miss Clifford, so I will be going in any event."

Aurelia smiled. "Then I accept your generous offer, Sir Gideon. Er, when would you like to go?"

"Why don't we head to the pier now? I keep a skiff there."

Aurelia nodded and they fell into step alongside each other, Sir Gideon leading his horse beside him.

After a moment, he glanced at her. "Did you meet Lord Crewe when you applied for the position?"

"No, it was all done through the post."

"Ah."

"Ah?" Aurelia repeated.

"He is a forceful person. The island is his own personal fiefdom. To a lesser extent, so is Balcrewe, as he owns most of the land the village is on and much more besides. But on the mainland, there are magistrates and justices of the peace and so forth. Not on The Isle. Although it is only three miles away, it is hundreds of years back in time."

Aurelia digested what he'd said, which largely fit with what the Andersons had implied with their gossip.

"I'm not trying to worry you," he said. "Just to prepare you for a rather different…environment on Crewe."

"You know the earl well?"

"We are acquaintances at best. He is older than me by twelve years and has spent very little of his time in the area until these past two years, after he was injured in America."

Aurelia had read of Lord Crewe's injury—the entire country had—and knew that his wife had been killed at the same time, both victims of a panther attack.

"You are going to talk to Lord Crewe about the attack on Miss Clifford, but didn't you say there were authorities here on the mainland?"

"There are. But the earl is the landlord for most of the people in these parts, so I want him to know what is transpiring on his property."

"What do you think he will do?"

Sir Gideon's expression turned wry. "Nobody can ever guess what the earl might do in any given situation. The only thing one can be certain about is that whatever he does, it will be exactly what he wants."

The more Aurelia heard about her new employer, the more she wondered what she had got herself into.

***

Roland had put Arthur's interruption behind him and was making strides on his article when there was yet another knock on his door.

He flung down his quill and spattered the scattered parchment with ink. "Damnation!" he muttered, hastily blotting up the mess with his handkerchief. "What in the name of God did she do now, Arthur?" he shouted.

The door opened and Beekman, his butler, entered. "I beg your pardon, sir."

"Oh. It's you. What do you want?" he barked.

"Miss Burton has arrived, my lord," Beekman said, immune to Roland's odious temper.

He glanced at the clock and saw it was later than he thought. He would get no more work done today. "Well, show her up, Beekman."

"Sir Gideon is with her."

Roland frowned. "Talbot? Why the devil is he here?"

"He rowed her over, my lord. He asked that he might have a word."

He considered putting the man off, but Sir Gideon Talbot could be persistent, so he might as well get it over with. "Yes, go ahead and show them both up."

"Shall I have tea sent up, sir?"

The last thing Roland wanted to do was spend a tedious half-hour over tea and crumpets with Sir Gideon Talbot. "Not now. Wait until after I've sent Talbot on his way."

"Very good, sir," Beekman said, exhibiting no surprise at all at his employer's rudeness.

Once the door closed Roland removed his glasses and went to the mirror over the fireplace to check his appearance. He had no ink stains on his face but his overlong hair looked as if a very small farmer had made tiny haycocks all over his head. When he worked, he had a tendency to run his fingers through his hair and smear ink all over everything.

On one memorable occasion, he'd delivered a talk at the Royal Society with black smudges on his chin and the end of his sizeable nose. Even among a group of men notorious for their lack of sartorial awareness, he had been a figure of amusement.

A few moments later the door opened and he turned to find Gideon Talbot standing beside an exceedingly lovely young woman.

Roland was momentarily poleaxed. He hadn't thought much about his new artist other than to assume that she would be an elderly woman. That assessment had been based on the quality of her illustrations, which were superlative. The ability to breathe life into stuffed or bottled specimens was difficult work and a rare skill.

The woman currently hovering in the doorway was not old. Indeed, she could not be any more than four-or-five-and-twenty, although she was garbed in rather matronly clothing, as if she believed it would distract people from her expressive hazel eyes, exquisite facial features, and shapely figure.

"Hallo Crewe," Talbot said in his sunny, cheery way, pulling Roland from his gawking.

Roland forced a smile, still not taking his gaze from the woman. "Good afternoon, Talbot. Welcome to Crewe, Miss Burton."

"My lord." She dropped a graceful curtsey.

Beautiful *and* graceful. She only needed to add sexually promiscuous to that list and Arthur would be apoplectic when he saw her.

"You are probably wondering how I was fortunate enough to deliver your newest employee," Talbot said once the two had taken seats in front of Roland's desk.

"I was, rather." It was a struggle to wrench his gaze from Miss Burton, but the flags on her cheeks told Roland that his blatant ogling had been noted, so he forced himself to turn to Talbot.

"Were you aware of who was living with Judith Pomeroy?" Talbot asked.

Roland's brow knitted at the bizarre segue. "Daventry's daughters. Why?"

"Formerly Daventry," Talbot corrected, as if the entire nation wasn't aware of the attainder of the peer—something that had only happened a handful of times in the last five hundred years, as far as Roland knew.

"What of it?" he asked, his gaze sliding again to Miss Burton.

She was gazing at the handsome paragon beside her, no doubt admiring his perfect profile. He could not blame her; there was no denying the baronet was far more appealing to look at than Roland.

"A group of young men accosted Miss Larissa Clifford this morning. Fortunately, Miss Burton stopped them before they could do too much harm."

Roland's eyes—both the one that worked and the other that was hidden beneath the black leather eye patch—widened. "Did you, indeed, Miss Burton?"

"I only made them pause their abuse," she demurred. "Sir Gideon was the real hero."

Talbot murmured something suitably modest and flashed his white teeth, which were as perfect as the rest of him.

Roland absently tongued his chipped canine as he watched the handsome pair smile at each other. Why did he find their mutual appreciation so damned annoying?

"Do you know the names of the men?" Roland asked, having had enough of their mating dance.

Talbot pulled his gaze from Miss Burton with visible effort and took a piece of paper from his coat pocket and handed it to him.

Roland studied the short list. He recognized the surnames but did not know the lads themselves. He glanced up. "I will look into the matter tomorrow."

"It is unlikely that Miss Clifford will wish to pursue any action against the men," Talbot said.

"I wouldn't be surprised. Fortunately, bringing charges is not the only weapon in my arsenal. Based on the surnames, at least three of these lads live in my cottages. I will speak to their fathers and make them aware of my displeasure and how that might lead to the revocation of their leases, or a precipitous rise in rents." Roland smiled. "I daresay that will do something to encourage good behavior."

Talbot's expression was one of mild disapproval. The handsome baronet was the white knight to Roland's black prince. They didn't know each other well, but what Roland did know of Sir Gideon was that he was universally adored.

Roland doubted there were too many who felt that way about him.

"Was that all you wished to see me about? Or was there something else?" Roland asked.

Talbot was nonplussed by Roland's obvious dismissal, but he rallied quickly. "No—no, that was all. Oh, actually, there was one more thing." He turned to Miss Burton. "Might I have the sketch?"

Miss Burton looked at Roland.

Roland raised his eyebrows. "Yes?"

"Er, I made a sketch of Sir Gideon as he was rowing me over to Crewe and would like to give it to him as a *thank you*. Might I have some cardstock to protect it? So it doesn't become damaged."

Roland stared at her just long enough to make her cheeks flush a delightful pink and then inclined his head toward the north wall, where he had a small work area beneath the window. "You will find what you need on those shelves."

She stood and Roland appreciated the back view of her, which was every bit as delightful as the front.

He heard a throat clearing and turned to see Sir Gideon regarding him with a stern look.

Roland was amused, rather than annoyed, that the man had the stones to chastise him under his own roof.

Miss Burton came hurrying back with two stiff pieces of cardstock. She fumbled in her satchel and took out a sketchpad. Her fingers shook as she flipped through it and then tore out a page.

"Let me see," Roland said.

Miss Burton blinked at his peremptory tone, but obediently crossed the few feet between them and handed him the sketch.

The woman had masterfully captured the essence of Talbot, the sea, and a miniature collection of buildings in the distance that was undisputably Balcrewe. And she had done it all with shockingly few lines. She was a very fine artist, indeed.

Roland looked up as he handed the sketch back to her. "How much are you charging him for it?"

Her jaw dropped and Roland laughed. "I am just teasing. Talbot can pay me directly seeing as you are currently in my employ."

Neither of the two laughed.

Miss Burton deftly packaged the sketch and gave it to Talbot.

"Thank you," Sir Gideon said, his smile far too friendly for Roland's liking.

Roland cleared his throat, shattering their moment of intimacy. "Thank you again, Talbot."

Talbot gave Roland a wry smirk before saying to the woman, "It was truly a pleasure, Miss Burton. I do hope you will visit Talbot House whenever you are at liberty to do so."

"I certainly shall."

Talbot turned to Roland. "You needn't bestir yourself, Crewe," he said, the words ironic given that Roland had made no effort to stand and had no intention to do so. "I know the way out."

Good. Use it.

Roland waited until the door closed before he turned to Miss Burton. "Alone at last."

27

Aurelia: Book 4 of The Bellamy Sisters

Chapter 3

I t took Aurelia less than a minute to understand why Sir Gideon and the Andersons had given her such odd looks as they had attempted to describe the Laird of Crewe. The earl was, quite frankly, a force of nature.

Sir Gideon was an extremely handsome man, but he had paled into insignificance while sitting in the same room with the scarred earl. Lord Crewe seemed to draw all the light in the room toward him, his presence somehow more… substantial.

It wasn't just his imposing person that made one notice him—although he was physically impressive—but also the aura of utter confidence, or arrogance, maybe, of a man accustomed to dominion over all he surveyed.

He was very tall—certainly over six feet—and appeared even taller given his lean build. Before being mauled by a panther he would have been a very attractive, classically handsome man. Aurelia suspected that many women would find him even more compelling now, with the arresting scarring over the left side of his face and the stark black leather patch covering his eye.

His overlong hair was sun-bleached to a corn silk blond, and his remaining eye glittered like a pale blue sapphire in his darkly tanned face. The expression in that eye was intelligent and uncomfortably knowing. Aurelia had never met anyone who made her feel so unsophisticated and uncertain.

Although he wore the clothing of a country gentleman, his black clawhammer and snug breeches had the sort of stylish cut that one only found in foreign tailoring, the garments molding lovingly to his broad shoulders and powerful thighs.

The scar on his face was truly horrific and she hated to think of the pain he must have endured. The claws of the beast that had mauled him had not only sliced the flesh, but pieces must have been torn away. There were three deep, jagged gouges and a fourth that was less pronounced. The uppermost claw must have raked directly over his eye before slashing his eyebrow. Scars pulled at his lips, the side of his nose, and skimmed over his chin, coming dangerously close to the veins in his throat.

For all its savagery, there was a primitive beauty to the marking.

Only when he cleared his throat did Aurelia realize that she had been taking an extremely detailed and impertinent inventory of her new employer.

She lifted her gaze to meet his.

He smiled and something about the seemingly pleasant expression struck her as… dangerous.

Aurelia had no reason to make such a judgment, and yet she felt the truth of it in her bones. Not that he was a physical threat, of course, but she knew without saying that he would be a menace to her peace of mind.

"I'm sorry you were witness to such senseless violence on your first day in Balcrewe, Miss Burton."

"You can hardly be held accountable for that, my lord."

"Of course I can," he said, more than a bit imperiously. "Balcrewe is as much my demesne as this island is."

Well, Aurelia had been warned about his feudal characteristics. "Everyone else I encountered was very civil."

"Including Talbot." His expression was one of sly amusement, either at the way she'd ignored his chest-thumping comment, or he was making some point about her unorthodox arrival in the company of Sir Gideon."

"Yes, Sir Gideon was very kind."

His lips pulled up on the unscarred side, exposing a few teeth, one a prominent canine. "And yet sassenachs are always saying we Scots are surly and inhospitable."

"I find sweeping generalizations both banal and unreliable. As such, I strive to avoid them."

Rather than look annoyed at her not-so-subtle chiding, an expression that could best be described as *unholy glee* flickered across his face. "Do you indeed? My, my. What a sensible young woman you are."

Aurelia's face became uncomfortably hot at what she was certain was mockery.

He smiled, evidently finding even her silence humorous, and then picked up a piece of parchment from the desk. "I recently had a very interesting letter from Sir Ian Rowan."

Aurelia had done work for Sir Ian on more than one occasion, but always under her male nom de plume. "I see," she said, although she did not see at all.

"When I told him that I'd engaged you he was most effusive in praising the work you did for him."

"That is very kind of him." Aurelia wondered if the earl had also shared the fact that she was not *Albert* Burton, but *Aurelia* Burton.

"Never fear, I referred to you as *Albert*. Who you decide to tell about your gender is your affair," he said, reading her thoughts far too accurately for her comfort. "Although I don't suppose it can stay a secret for long with so many people in the area knowing about you."

"I assumed when I took this position that I would no longer use a male alias for my future work." She hesitated. "That is… if you do not have any objection to me signing my work as *Aurelia Burton*."

"None at all," he said, studying her with an intensity she suspected he normally reserved for flora and fauna specimens. "I must admit that you are something of a surprise, Miss Burton."

"How so, my lord?" she asked, her voice becoming colder as it always did when she was at her most nervous and vulnerable.

"Not only are you a great deal younger than I expected—"

"I am of legal age and hardly a child."

"No, you are hardly a child," he agreed.

Why was it that everything the man said sounded like a double entendre?

"I can tell from your accent that you are gently born," the earl went on.

"Does that present a problem for you, my lord?"

"A problem? No. But you must be aware that living in my house for the next year—with no chaperone—will likely cause the sort of speculation that will have a negative effect on your future."

"By *future* I assume you mean my marital prospects."

He gave her an almost gentle smile. "Among other things. I'm afraid that your reputation cannot benefit by living in proximity to me, Miss Burton."

"I am devoted to my work and do not aspire to marriage. So preserving my reputation is not a priority for me."

"And your father approves of your decision to work here?"

"My father is dead." As useless as her father was, Aurelia still felt a twinge of guilt at killing him off so heartlessly, but she wanted to present herself as an adult, not a girl still under her parents' protection. "As for my mother," she said, before the earl could ask, "she has been bedbound for years."

"She might be bedridden, but she must have an opinion about her unwed daughter taking a position in the house of a widower?"

"I have already given the matter of my reputation adequate, and final, consideration," she said. "Unless you believe it has any bearing on my ability to work, I have nothing else to say on the subject."

Lord Crewe laughed, evidently delighted. "And now I have been put in my place."

Aurelia didn't dispute that.

"Very well. I will not broach the topic again. Instead, let us discuss my expectations. First, all the paintings need to be presented to my engraver in Edinburgh no later than a year from now, where they will be used to make plates using etching, engraving, and aquatint. In addition to my specimens, you will be working on my deceased wife's samples."

Aurelia searched his face for any sign of grief as he talked about his countess.

She found none.

"I have sold subscriptions for a two-volume work comprised of flora and fauna. The projected release date for the first volume is two years from now."

"And how many drawings do you anticipate requiring?"

"Two-hundred-and-twenty-three."

Aurelia goggled.

He laughed. "Never fear, Miss Burton, you do not need to draw even half that many. My wife was more efficient than I am and immortalized many of her discoveries whilst we were on the expedition. There are perhaps forty of hers that still need to be completed, the specimens well-preserved thanks to Lady Crewe's proprietary solution. The liquid does a fair job of maintaining the integrity of most specimens, but of course, the colors have suffered. You will have access to her journals, which contain excellent color charts and superlative descriptions to help you along. As you complete your work, we will send the publisher new batches. Ideally, I would like to have the last batch of paintings to him by the end of this coming January, but we have until March."

Aurelia would have her plate full, but the schedule was not impossible. "May I ask who has done your paintings in the past?"

"I did."

It wasn't so surprising. Many naturalists—not just his deceased wife—learned to draw and paint well as they frequently had no other way to capture what they saw on their expeditions.

He stood and went to one of the many bookshelves. When he returned, he handed her an elegant leather and gilt portfolio. "Go ahead—open it."

Aurelia unwrapped the leather cord and unfolded the wings.

When she removed the protective sheet of onionskin she gasped at the vivid lime-yellow bird, labeled *Turaco* in exquisite copperplate.

"You are an artist, my lord. Why do you need me?"

"Was."

"I beg your pardon?"

"I *was* an artist." He raised his left hand, the tremor in it was slight, but still visible. "I can manage the less detailed work, but I will never again paint anything like that which you are holding."

The stab of sympathy she felt at his confession was visceral and nausea bloomed inside her belly at the thought of what he had lost. What would she do if she could no longer paint or draw? Aurelia shied away from the thought. It would be a sort of death.

It would be devastating.

She turned back to the paintings, the vivid birds so masterfully depicted that they appeared as if they might fly off the paper at any moment.

"You have incorporated watercolor, pastel, graphite, oil paint, and chalk," she murmured enviously. "I'm afraid my own are rather mundane by comparison."

"Not at all. The watercolor samples you submitted were excellent, by far the best of any I received."

Aurelia warmed at his praise; her gaze caught by the last painting. "Oh, this is a lovely bird. What is it?" She held up the portfolio so he could see.

"Ah, yes—*saucerottia cyanifrons*, more familiarly referred to as a hummingbird. That is an indigo-capped from New Granada. They are small, approximately the size of some of the species of hawkmoths we have here. Indeed, you might mistake one for the other when they are in flight."

"Magnificent." She carefully replaced the paintings and closed the portfolio.

"I have hundreds of sketches in addition to all the taxidermy samples I've collected. There are drawings for everything in my journals, some more detailed than others." His mouth pulled down at the corners. "While many of the taxidermied samples are well-preserved it is a constant battle to keep them so. In addition to the usual vermin—mice, rats—there are numerous insects that love to feast on them, so it is probably wise if you begin with those."

Aurelia nodded.

"The specimen room is extremely chilly and windowless, but most of the smaller samples are in glass cases, so you may take them to a more well-illuminated location. I have instructed my butler to show you the rooms that have the best natural light and you may take whichever you please as your workroom."

"Thank you."

"As far as supplies go, there are a good many paints, pastels, and so forth in the—"

The door to the library flew open and a tall, blond, and extremely handsome man hovered on the threshold. "Crewe! I wanted to be here when you welcomed Miss Burton." His blue eyes, a brighter blue than his lordships, slid from Lord Crewe to Aurelia and he gave a start of surprise at the sight of her. He quickly recovered, however, and a smile curved his full, shapely lips as he strode into the room. "Welcome to Crewe, Miss Burton."

"This is my cousin, Arthur Montgomery," the earl said dryly. "He is so eager to meet you that he has overlooked an introduction."

Mr. Montgomery laughed as he took the chair beside her. "You will think my manners savage," he said, smiling at Aurelia. "It is a pleasure to meet you."

Like his cousin, Mr. Montgomery was very tall and fair, but where Lord Crewe was lean with chiseled features this man was far softer in appearance, and all angelic sweetness.

"Your work is superb Miss Burton," Mr. Montgomery said. "I look forward to your rendition of *my* work."

"You are a naturalist, as well?" Aurelia asked.

"No, no, not at all. My interest lies in taxidermy."

"Arthur was with Lady Crewe and I on our last expedition," the earl explained. "He is an expert taxidermist."

Mr. Montgomery smiled at his cousin, giving Aurelia his profile, which was as perfect as his face. "I had wanted to accompany Crewe for years, but the time never seemed right." His full lips suddenly pulled down at the corners. "I was there when Lady Crewe's death and my cousin's injury occurred, so I was able to help out when it came to preserving some of their work."

"Arthur's assistance was priceless and he took prodigious care of me when I was wounded," Lord Crewe said.

The other man blushed. "I was pleased to be of use."

Again, the door opened, and this time it was a maid bearing a large tray.

"Ah, excellent," the earl said. "Let us have some tea and then you can go to your rooms and relax before dinner. Put the tray on low table, Sally," he instructed the maid, and then turned his disconcerting gaze back to Aurelia, his eye glinting with humor, which appeared to be his default expression. "Will you pour, Miss Burton?" he asked, his tone almost… caressing.

"Of course," Aurelia murmured, grateful for something to occupy her hands while his smile and attention muddled her wits.

Chapter 4

Aurelia hadn't really known what sort of reception she would receive at Castle Crewe—she was just an employee, after all—but she had never hoped for luxury such as this.

Her chambers were situated in one of the newer extensions of the castle, which must have been added in the mid-to-late seventeenth century.

The bedchamber was huge with an adjacent dressing room that held a second fireplace, the sort of room conceived with entertainment in mind, during a time when many aristocrats invited guests to enjoy their toilette.

The bed was a masterpiece of Restoration excess and required a wooden stepstool with three steps to climb up to the mattress. It was a guest's room, not that of an upper servant like a governess or tutor.

The room occupied a corner so the view was spectacular and she could see Balcrewe which was huddled against the cliffs and hugging the small bay. To the north she could see Andrew's Cove and the section of beach where the boys had attacked Miss Clifford.

And down below, in that cavernous library, is a man who unsettled you more than anyone you have ever met. And also fascinated you more…

Aurelia disliked admitting it, but the accusation was true. This position was supposed to be the one that established her in the world of scientific illustration. Her name would be on the artwork in Lord Crewe's books. It was the opportunity of a lifetime.

It was *not* the time to become infatuated. Especially with a sophisticated, jaded, and experienced rake like Lord Crewe, who would not be interested in a naïve rustic like herself, in any case.

Her instant fascination for him was disquieting. Aurelia would need to avoid him as much as possible. That shouldn't be terribly difficult as painting was a relatively solitary activity. She wouldn't need to consult him about much if she had access to his journals.

Aurelia firmly thrust the earl from her mind and turned to the lovely, but far too large, armoire—one of *four* in the dressing room—and began to unpack her bags.

There certainly wasn't much. She had given her books to her sisters, along with most of her other trinkets. Although she had been the only Bellamy daughter to have a Season and the wardrobe to go with it, over the years she had refashioned many of her garments for her younger sisters. It hadn't seemed fair that she was the only one with ball gowns and carriage gowns and so on. And thus, she'd created small, but respectable, wardrobes for the others while retaining ample clothing for her own needs. Not that any of them had needed fancy clothing these past few years, buried as they'd been in the country. But it was nice to know she could clothe herself decently to dine at a lord's table.

Once she'd slipped on her primrose evening gown, she sat at the dressing table and unplaited her hair. Her fingers worked without thought as her mind returned to Lord Crewe's library earlier. Aside from the effect of the man himself, the knowledge that there were hundreds of paintings to be made excited her. There would be work for months—almost a year! And his terms in the letter had been generous. After only five or six months she should have enough money to afford a deposit on a modest property for her siblings if they were to lose their home. No longer would she be dependent on her father.

Yes, taking this position had been an excellent decision. Her mother might have disowned her, her reputation was already beyond redemption, and working alongside an infamous rake would be fraught with temptation, but she would finally stand on her own two feet.

A knock on the door pulled her from her pleasurable thoughts and a maid opened the door. "My name is Ruby, Miss Burton. I'm here to show you to the dining room when you are ready."

Aurelia paid attention to her surroundings as she followed Ruby. Having grown up in an ancient house, Aurelia was accustomed to grandeur and wealth, but this was a castle, not just built for habitation, but for defense and to demonstrate the power of the lord who occupied it.

As magnificent as the winding stone staircase and ancient corridors were, the building was not comfortable and the wrap she wore could not cut the gusts that all but howled through the corridors.

Ruby stopped in front of massive wooden doors, the thick timbers held together by age-blackened metal straps and nail heads the size of large coins. She opened the right-side door and Aurelia entered a room that might have come out of a Shakespearean play. The rough-hewn wood table that sprawled beneath an exquisitely timbered ceiling could have easily seated twenty, but only four places had been set at the end.

Four?

Aurelia wondered who the fourth would be.

"His lordship will be down soon, miss. He and Mr. Montgomery would have been here already but for—" Ruby broke off and bit her lower lip. "If that will be all, miss?"

"Of course. Thank you, Ruby." Aurelia wondered what the girl had been about to say.

In addition to the long table, there were massive fireplaces at both ends of the chamber. Fires were blazing in each, but even that was not enough to cut the chill.

Aurelia had just made a circuit of the room when the door opened.

"Good evening, Miss Burton," Lord Crewe said as he entered, his blond hair a dark gold, as if he had just come from his bath. Aurelia was relieved that she'd dressed in her nicest gown as he was garbed in elegant evening clothes, his black coat and pantaloons bearing the same imprint of foreignness as his daytime apparel.

Behind him came the butler, carrying a tray with glasses and a decanter.

"Dinner will be ten minutes late this evening," the earl said, nodding his dismissal to his servant, his mouth tightening ever so slightly as he removed the stopper and poured two glasses without asking her if she wanted one. He handed her one and then drank deeply from his own glass before seeming to pull his thoughts together and smile at her. "How is your room? Do you have everything you need?"

"It is lovely and luxurious and the views are superlative. The entire structure is… awe-inspiring."

"I am pleased you like my castle." He gestured toward the chairs and settees that sat in front of one of the fireplaces.

Once they were both seated, he said, "So, tell me about your journey all the way from—what was the name of your village again?"

"Little Sissingdon."

"Little Sissingdon. Hmm, I seem to have heard of it before. Who is the local lord?"

"The Earl of Addiscombe." She cleared her throat. "Do you know him?"

"Not personally, but I've heard of him. A great friend of our Regent in his wilder days, if I recall correctly. A bit of a gambler."

"Yes, that is what I've heard."

"You lived with your mother there?"

"Yes, my lord."

"No swain?"

Aurelia's jaw fell.

He gave her one of his disarming smiles. "I'm sorry, is that too personal? I was just wondering how a woman who looks like you has managed to remain unmarried."

"Er, thank you, I think. But no, I have no swain. I have been too busy trying to establish myself as a painter to think much about marriage." That was mostly the truth. She didn't need to tell him that given her family's poverty and her lack of a dowry suitors had not exactly been lining up to marry her or her sisters.

"Your time has certainly been well spent, Miss Burton. Your skill is outstanding, especially for one so young. That is why I assumed you were older. You must have done a great deal of sketching and painting."

"There is little else to do in the country."

He laughed. "Plenty of people find other, less commendable, ways of spending their time."

Aurelia wondered if he was including himself in that group.

"I daresay your services will be very much in demand in the years to come." He took a drink and then raised an eyebrow. "Is going to the homes of your employers something you intend to make a habit of?"

Really! The man did pry. "I will do whatever is necessary for my work."

"Ah, now you are telling me with that chiding look and slightly scolding tone of yours to keep my big proboscis out of your affairs."

"I did not mean—"

"No, no, do not apologize." He chuckled. "Put me in my place! Somebody needs to. I can be damnably nosey and have lost what little couth I might have once possessed after spending so much time in far-flung, uncivilized parts of the world." He swirled the ruby liquid in his glass, eying her as if he might see the contents of her head if he looked hard enough. "I thought your drawing of Talbot was excellent."

Aurelia blinked at the sudden change in subject. "Thank you," she said after a short pause.

"Perhaps I will ask you to make one of me, Miss Burton."

Aurelia suspected that she would make plenty of sketches of this man in the months to come, but she had no intention of admitting such a thing. She also had no intention of having him sit for a portrait. Being closeted in a room with the clearly devious, mischievous earl while he slowly and expertly reduced her to a babbling fool was not part of Aurelia's plans.

Instead, she said, "I am not a portraitist, my lord."

Lord Crewe smiled at her not-very-subtle evasion. "One should always embrace an opportunity to learn new skills, Miss Burton."

Thankfully the door opened and Mr. Montgomery joined them before his lordship could pursue the subject.

Mr. Montgomery's cheeks were flushed, as if he'd been running. "So sorry I'm late, Crewe, Miss Burton."

"I thought you were bringing her?" Lord Crewe barked, his smile of only a few seconds earlier nowhere in evidence.

"Er, I thought she might dine in her room tonight given that—"

"Damnation, Arthur!" The earl set his glass down so hard Aurelia was surprised it did not shatter. "I told you—and her—that I wanted her here."

Mr. Montgomery cleared his throat and his celestial blue eyes slid to Aurelia and then back to his cousin, and then he raised his eyebrows.

Lord Crewe made an exasperated noise and turned back to Aurelia. "Excuse my language, Miss Burton." He strode to the door, flung it open, and then spoke with somebody who must have been waiting outside.

Mr. Montgomery poured himself a glass and Aurelia could not help noticing that his hands shook when he lifted the decanter.

The earl strode back to his seat and picked up his glass. "Where did you learn to paint, Miss Burton?" he asked, his expression no longer annoyed, but politely interested.

"I was fortunate to have a governess who'd been trained by a drawing master in her youth. Once she had imparted all she knew, she advised me to hone my skills by looking at as much art as possible to keep learning."

"You must peruse my gallery," Lord Crewe said.

"Indeed, it is as excellent a collection as you will find anywhere in Scotland," Mr. Montgomery chimed in.

"Miss Burton is an Englishwoman, Arthur. To impress her, you must say my collection is as good as any in *England.*"

"I am sure there are many excellent collections in Scotland," Aurelia said, exasperated by his references to the Scotland-England divide. "We are all one nation now, my lord. We have been for quite some time."

Lord Crewe laughed.

"Do you really believe the divisions between us are so great?" Aurelia couldn't help asking.

"Oh, Miss Burton! I do hope you did not say such inflammatory things during your brief time on the mainland. If so, we should prepare ourselves to be invaded by boats bearing pitchfork-wielding villagers who demand that I hand you over."

Aurelia pursed her lips and gave the jocular lord a narrow look.

Mr. Montgomery clucked his tongue. "Lord Crewe enjoys teasing people, Miss Burton."

"My cousin is correct about the teasing—and I enjoy teasing some more than others," he added with a smirk. "But the truth is, that to many people who live in the North, the divisions *do* exist and are quite deep." The earl swirled the small amount of liquid in his glass and regarded her with a hooded gaze. "But that is a boring subject. Let us talk more about you, Miss Burton."

"I'm afraid my life is even more boring, my lord."

He merely smiled.

Aurelia felt like a fool as the silence stretched and he did not dispute her claim. She decided she could add *most frustrating man alive* to her earlier assessment of *most fascinating.*

"Do you have plans for another expedition once all your paintings have been delivered to the engraver?" she asked.

The earl's eye widened, as if he could not believe that a subject could be changed without his approval. "I will go to the Cape Colony," he said after a long moment.

"I understand that is a very long journey?"

"Yes, almost three months at sea."

"Will you accompany his lordship?" Aurelia asked Mr. Montgomery.

"One expedition was enough to last me a lifetime," he said, smiling while his gaze slid nervously to the door.

Just what was going on? Why was he so—

The door to the room flew open hard enough to bang against the wall and a tall, dark-haired girl entered, the scowl on her face as she glared from Lord Crewe to Mr. Montgomery making it clear that she did not want to be there.

She flounced to the table, flung herself into a chair, and ignored the three of them.

Lord Crewe sighed and stood. "You can serve now," he told the butler, who was hovering on the threshold.

"This is my daughter, Lady Celsa," the earl said once they'd taken their seats. "Celsa, this is Miss Burton. Greet her correctly and apologize for making her wait for dinner."

Aurelia felt a stab of embarrassment, as if she were the one being chastised.

The younger woman glowered at her.

"Celsa," her father said, his voice quiet, but so sharply edged it could have cut stone.

"I am sorry I made you wait for dinner, Miss Burton," the girl all but spat.

Lord Crewe cleared his throat.

"It is a pleasure to meet you."

A less genuine greeting Aurelia had never heard, but she smiled at the girl, who looked to be fourteen or fifteen. "It is a pleasure to make your acquaintance, my lady."

Lady Celsa grunted.

Thankfully the arrival of the first course filled the awkward silence.

"Do you have siblings, Miss Burton," Lord Crewe asked.

"One brother and four sisters."

"You are the eldest?"

"Yes. How did you know?"

"You have a sort of quiet authority about you."

Yet again the words were not themselves taunting, but something in the way he said them was.

"How old are your siblings?" the earl asked.

"Three-and-twenty, one-and-twenty, twenty, seven-and-ten, and my brother is almost five-and-ten."

"I am an only child," the earl said, tearing off a chunk of steaming bread and dipping it into his soup. "Although Arthur came to live with us when I was three. He will tell you I was a spoiled little brat when he met me."

Mr. Montgomery smiled at Aurelia. "It is true; he was a monster."

Aurelia could well believe it.

"I admired Arthur greatly and he used his influence for good, thereby shaping me into the fine man I am today, isn't that right, Arthur?" the earl asked.

Mr. Montgomery laughed.

The earl looked amused. "Arthur is two years older—not a great difference now, but a vast one for children—and I looked up to him. Some people believe that children without any siblings are often over-indulged but still lonely, which causes them to misbehave in a constant bid for attention." His gaze slid to his daughter and stayed there.

Lady Celsa's face, already sullen, darkened under her father's stare.

"I have always believed it is a parent's fault rather than a child's when there are behavioral issues," Aurelia said.

Lord Crewe's single eye slid back to Aurelia and widened. Rather than look annoyed at her comment, he grinned. "Do you, indeed, Miss Burton? And with several younger siblings I daresay you fancy yourself something of an expert on the matter of child-rearing? I look forward to becoming the beneficiary of your expertise over the coming months."

"No, not an expert, my lord," Aurelia said coolly. "But I have had a certain amount of experience."

If Aurelia had hoped to earn any gratitude from Lady Celsa, the dirty look the girl shot her immediately set her to rights. Lady Celsa wanted her father's attention—good or bad—and she resented Aurelia getting in her way.

Aurelia ached for the poor girl. She, too, had tried to earn her father's approval—albeit by behaving exceptionally well rather than misbehaving—until she realized that short of turning into a boy, there was nothing she could do to please the Earl of Addiscombe.

"Are your siblings likewise gifted in the arts, Miss Burton?" Lord Crewe asked as he gestured for the footmen to remove their soup and bring the next course.

"They are each possessed of their own skills, but I am the only one who sketches and paints."

"Perhaps while you are here you might impart some of your skill to my daughter, whose watercolors could stand improvement."

"Perhaps her talents lie in another direction," she said, irked at the man's casual cruelty. "But I would be pleased to offer her any assistance she might desire."

Again, her kindness earned her a sardonic look from the master of the house and a glower from his daughter.

"Thank Miss Burton for her kind offer, Celsa."

Aurelia opened her mouth to say it was her pleasure, but Lady Celsa's voice stopped her.

"Thank you, Miss Burton."

Mr. Montgomery, whose presence Aurelia had almost forgotten even though there were but four of them at the table, cleared his throat. "Celsa is an excellent horsewoman," he said, smiling at the girl.

Lord Crewe ignored his cousin's comment and said to Aurelia, "Do you ride, Miss Burton?"

"Yes, although it has been a few years."

"You will find my stables have horses for any rider. Just tell my stablemaster, Silas, what you need and he will see that you are well mounted.

"You are generous, thank you."

"Not generous, but crafty and self-serving."

She gave a startled laugh. "How… diabolical that sounds."

"I want you to be contented while you are here. The happier you are, the more likely I will have my paintings done when I need them."

"I assure you that I will aspire to finish them regardless of your blandishments, my lord." Try as she might, Aurelia could not keep the sharpness from her tone.

Yet again, the earl looked pleased by her asperity. "Your work ethic is commendable, Miss Burton. Regardless, I do believe you will be happier and more productive if you feel at home on Crewe. To that end, tomorrow I will show you my island so you can get your bearings."

"May I come, Papa?"

Lord Crewe turned to his daughter, the air chilling as he did so. "You will benefit from a month away from the stables, my dear. Perhaps it will help you remember your manners."

"You cannot mean it!"

"Lower your voice, Celsa. I assure you that I mean what I say." His eye narrowed. "Until you learn how to behave like a young lady rather than a feral beast you will have no riding privileges."

"No," Lady Celsa said, the word more of a whisper.

Lord Crewe ignored her and turned to Aurelia. "I would also like you to learn to handle one of the skiffs we keep at—"

Lady Celsa flung down her cutlery with a clatter and jumped to her feet. "You cannot do this, Papa!"

"It seems you are finished with your meal," the earl said, sounding bored. "You may go to your room."

Lady Celsa flinched at the ice in his tone, her gaze pleading. "Papa?"

When her father refused to even look at her, she gave a pitiful little cry and ran from the room.

Aurelia wanted to crawl under the table.

Mr. Montgomery began to stand. "I should go and—"

"You should stay and finish your meal, Arthur," the earl said, and then gestured for the footmen to bring the next course. Aurelia couldn't help noticing that three of the plates on the table were still largely untouched, only Lord Crewe appeared to have any appetite.

"I apologize for my daughter's behavior," the earl said.

Aurelia had to bite her tongue to keep from telling him to apologize for his *own* while he was at it.

"You think I have been too cruel," he said, reading her mind in a way that unnerved her. "Tell me, Miss Burton, you mentioned a governess in your past?"

"Yes."

"Only one?"

"There were two."

"And did you or your sisters drive off the first one?"

"Of course not. She was of an age to retire." And the poor woman had also grown tired of earning chicken scratch wages from her father, who often couldn't even pay *those*.

"My daughter has had nine governesses in the past six years. Nine. Tell me, why do you think that is?"

"Miss Neville did not care for the castle or the island," Mr. Montgomery cut in before Aurelia could come up with an answer.

Lord Crewe gave his cousin an exasperated look. "I stand corrected. *One* of the nine women said she left because she was constantly cold and did not like living remote from the mainland. But why do you think the other eight left, Miss Burton?"

"Are you trying to tell me your daughter is a difficult pupil, my lord?"

"You tell me. Nine—eight—governesses in five years."

"It does seem excessive."

He laughed.

"But perhaps there are reasons." *Such as you being an uncaring, dismissive, obnoxious father?*

He eyed her with amusement. "Oh, there are reasons."

"She merely has high spirits," Mr. Montgomery said, his jaw firm as he regarded his cousin. "You likely have forgotten, Crewe, but there were a few years during your youth when your behavior was hardly commendable."

Lord Crewe turned to his cousin slowly. "I think we both know the circumstances were rather different for me, Arthur."

Mr. Montgomery flinched, even though the earl hadn't raised his voice. "Er, yes. Quite. I beg your par—"

"But my cousin does have a point," the earl said. "I am not claiming perfection, believe me. I *was* wild, selfish, and reckless, Miss Burton."

Aurelia somehow suspected a few of those behaviors still lingered.

He grinned, as if he'd once again heard her thoughts. "Do you know why I am so angry with my daughter?"

How had this uncomfortable conversation begun? Aurelia could not remember. She hesitated, considering her next words carefully. "It is really none of my affair, my lord."

The earl ignored her answer and said, "She locked her governess in the dungeon today. The woman was left in there for five or six hours before somebody thought to go searching for her."

The castle was cold and damp; Aurelia shuddered to imagine what the dungeons were like.

"The poor woman was beside herself, not to mention badly chilled. She might have taken ill and she certainly would have given her notice this very day if my cousin had not begged her to stay—at least until we can locate victim number ten." He was still smiling, his rapidly shrinking pupil the only sign of his displeasure.

His eye was hypnotic, the blue of his iris as mesmerizing as a flame.

Aurelia was alarmed to realize that she could have happily sat there staring at him all day long.

She resolved, then and there, to commence sketching him out of her system the moment she returned to the privacy of her room. Even if she could not manage to exorcise him, Aurelia knew she would enjoy trying.

Mr. Montgomery coughed lightly, breaking the spell. "Perhaps after dinner, I can show you some of the subjects you will be recreating over the next months, Miss Burton. That is, if you are not too tired?" He chuckled nervously, as his eyes—the color of the sky with no storms on the horizon—slid between his cousin and Aurelia.

"I would very much like to see your work, Mr. Montgomery," Aurelia said.

And you'd also like to run as far away from the Earl of Crewe as possible, a taunting voice in her head jeered.

Aurelia did not argue with the assessment. How in the world was she to spend close to a year on the Isle of Crewe in proximity to such a man without making a terrible fool of herself?

Chapter 5

The earl and his cousin did not indulge in the masculine custom of postprandial port, so directly after dinner, Mr. Montgomery escorted Aurelia from the dining room down into the bowels of the castle.

"I have set up my workshop in the armory." Mr. Montgomery gestured to her light wrap. "Will you be warm enough?" He smiled at her, sweetly tentative. Or perhaps he only seemed tentative when contrasted with his cousin's arrogance.

"Yes, I should think so." And if she wasn't that would give her an excuse to leave. Mr. Montgomery seemed nice enough, but an entire room full of stuffed animals sounded rather… grim.

"I hope his lordship did not make you too uncomfortable at dinner, Miss Burton."

"No, not at all," she lied.

"He is frustrated by his daughter's behavior and is quite short-tempered on the subject."

"I can imagine." And she *did* have some sympathy for the man, although she condemned his method of addressing the problem. "Do you live on the island year-round, or do you keep a home elsewhere?" she asked to change the subject.

"I live here all the time. It is really the only home I've ever known. My uncle took me in after my parents died. My father was his younger brother," he explained. "I love it here and wouldn't want to live anyplace else." He smiled. "Lord Crewe was not really a spoiled brat—I was only teasing him. Indeed, he was a quiet and thoughtful child, interested in the natural world even back then."

Aurelia found that hard to believe.

She also found it hard to believe that Mr. Montgomery was only a few years older than his cousin. She would have guessed he was at least a decade older than the earl. Crewe's face—the unscarred half—had obvious sun damage from too much time spent in tropical climes and he had more wrinkles around his eyes than the man beside her, but Montgomery had the papery skin of a much older person. He also had a slight palsy that was unusual in one so young. At first, she had thought it was nervousness brought on by his cousin's behavior, but he seemed to shake all the time.

Aurelia wondered if he might be ailing from something.

They reached one of the four principal turrets and he pulled aside one of the weighted drapes that she had seen covering the doorless entrances all over the castle.

"Hold on tight to the railing," he cautioned. "Some of the steps are quite worn. As you can imagine, the armory is not much in use any longer," he said as he led her into a section with such a low ceiling that his head almost skimmed it. "People were much smaller when this was constructed, but the ceiling would have been low even to the builders. It makes one aware of all that rock overhead, doesn't it?"

"Indeed." It *hadn't* made her think about that. But now she was.

He opened a rough-hewn wooden door and Aurelia paused on the threshold, staring.

"Rather dramatic, isn't it?" he asked, pride in his voice as she gaped at the menagerie of death. Dozens, if not hundreds, of taxidermized animals filled the vast room, some behind glass, but most of the larger ones exposed to the open air.

"This is… incredible," she finally managed.

"Thank you!" he looked as gleeful as a little boy as he used his candlestick to light a massive candelabra that sat on a long trestle table. "The lack of windows is the only drawback of being down here, but I tolerate it because the cold is so good for the pieces. Indeed, there is an ice room several chambers over. I keep untreated samples in there." He turned to her, the light from a dozen candles causing red and gold flames to dance over his pale skin and making him bear more than a passing resemblance to an inhabitant in a Bosch painting of Hell.

Aurelia shivered.

His glee melted away immediately, concern taking its place. "Oh dear! You *are* cold. Well, I shan't keep you long. I just wanted to give you an idea of what there is." He strode toward one of the walls, which was covered with birds forever in flight. "Anything small you can just carry up to either the library or whatever workroom Crewe has set up for you. If you need something large one of the servants can carry it up for you. For example, you will get to paint that—" he turned to point at the far corner of the room.

Aurelia gasped at the huge panther, which was frozen in mid-leap. "My goodness! It is so lifelike."

Mr. Montgomery chuckled. "Yes, that is one of my most impressive pieces." His mouth turned down at the corners. "Although there are some flaws on the other side where the exit wound is. It is most unfortunate."

Aurelia forced herself to approach the giant beast. "How big is it?"

"Seven-feet-one-inch from his nose to the tip of his tail. He was the biggest of his kind that we saw during the expedition." He lowered his voice. "This is the very same animal who killed her ladyship and injured Crewe."

The creature's paws were massive. Now she understood the destruction on his lordship's face. "I am surprised this is the same animal, I would have thought—"

"That the earl would not want such a reminder?" Mr. Montgomery guessed.

"Well… yes."

His mouth shifted into a cynical smile that looked odd on his angelic features. "Crewe does not have delicate sensibilities, Miss Burton. He is a scientist through and through. Even that night—when he was in danger of bleeding to death—he made it clear that the animal needed to be preserved."

"The eyes are amazing," she said, barely having to bend to be face-to-face with the savage creature. "So lifelike."

"I get them from a glass artist in Venice. The same place that—" he broke off. "Murano, it is called."

For some reason, she didn't think that was what he'd been going to say.

Aurelia turned away from the disquieting panther and inspected the dozens of birds. "You are an artist, Mr. Montgomery." She was astounded by the gleam of feathers on the neck of a small bird, the posture of the animal so lifelike it was almost… mocking.

"Thank you. And please, as we will be working closely together won't you call me Arthur?"

Aurelia turned around and was startled to find him so close they almost touched. She gave a nervous laugh and took a half-step away. "I would be honored. And you must call me Aurelia."

"Aurelia," he repeated, entranced. "How lovely"

Aurelia shivered. Whether at the chill or the dead animals or the odd man standing almost on her toes, she couldn't have said.

He shook himself. "But you are cold. I will escort you back to—"

"I can find my room—truly. Please. Don't bestir yourself."

"If you are sure?"

"I am sure."

"I was going to work a bit." He gave her an almost dreamy look. "I do a great deal of work during the night. My cousin likes to say I was an owl in a former life."

With his almost round eyes he certainly looked like one.

"Good night, Mr.—"

"*Tut, tut*—Arthur," he said, his smile puckish.

"Good night, Arthur."

She breathed a sigh of relief once she'd left behind the museum of the dead. Fortunately, she had paid attention on the way down to the bowels of the building so she took no wrong turns going back up.

As she made her way through the sprawling building, fatigue suddenly struck her and her feet felt like lead blocks as she climbed two sets of stairs and plodded down a half dozen corridors to reach her room. It wasn't terribly late, so it must have been the sea air that had sapped her of energy.

Or perhaps the strain of being in Lord Crewe's company for almost two hours tonight?

That was certainly a possibility. While his lordship hadn't been harsh or peremptory with her as he'd been with Sir Gideon, his daughter, and even his cousin on occasion, there was something about his knowing gaze that required a degree of vigilance she didn't recall needing in the past.

Aurelia smiled when she saw the doorway to her room just ahead, pleased she'd found her way back without a problem.

She opened the door and then gave an undignified squawk of surprise at the figure standing in the doorway between her bedchamber and dressing room.

It was Lady Celsa.

And she was wearing Aurelia's best hat.

"What are you doing?" Aurelia demanded, irked by her frightened squeaking.

The girl shrugged, her face still in shadow as she removed the hat. "It is my father's house; I am allowed anywhere inside it."

"It is rude to root through your guest's things."

"But you are not *my* guest."

Aurelia closed the distance between them until she could see Celsa's sneering expression. She took the hat. Or at least she tried to, but for one tension-filled moment, the girl held onto it. Whatever she saw in Aurelia's face—likely fury at having her privacy violated—made her release it.

"I didn't hurt it," Celsa said sulkily, giving a forced laugh as Aurelia inspected the delicate plum silk pleating on the underside of the brim. The hat was one of the few things she'd retained for herself from her year in London and it flattered her as no other item of clothing.

Satisfied it was unharmed she looked up. "It is obnoxious to handle a person's possessions without asking permission."

Rather than respond, the girl drifted away, idly examining the few items Aurelia had scattered about the room when she'd unpacked.

Aurelia returned the hat to its box in the dressing room and came back to her bedchamber to find Lady Celsa examining the small painting she had made of her sisters and brother only the year before.

"Is this your family?"

"Yes. You may pick it up if you like."

Celsa did so, staring at the faces with rapt fascination. "Who is this one?"

Aurelia knew who she meant before she even looked. "That is my sister Selina."

"She is beautiful." There was a wistful note in the girl's voice.

"She is. But that is not the best thing about her."

Celsa turned to her, her dark brown brows—which looked like wings—lifted. "What is?"

"She is kind, thoughtful, and loving."

Celsa rolled her eyes. "I suppose she is very *good* and never gets into scrapes, either."

"Rarely."

"She sounds boring."

"She is not nearly as boring as rude people."

The winged brows came down and the girl opened her mouth, probably to say something even ruder, but then seemed to think better of it. "What about this one?" she asked, pointing at Aurelia's tallest sister.

"That is Hyacinth."

"Hyacinth," Celsa repeated, trying out the name on her tongue. "She looks like a boy—I don't mean to be rude," she hastened to add.

Aurelia smiled. "Hy would be glad to hear that."

"Truly?"

"Oh, yes. She likes to dress in breeches and coats."

"And your father lets her?"

"My father is dead," Aurelia said, remembering to stick to the story at the last moment. "But he never cared what any of us did when he was alive."

Lady Celsa digested that. "Is your mother alive?"

"Yes, but she doesn't know about Hy's nocturnal adventures. If she did, she would not like it."

The girl leaned closer and closer to the painting until her nose almost touched the canvas. "Is that a—a squirrel looking out of the boy's coat?"

"Yes, it is my brother Dauntry's pet."

"How lucky he is! I have only seen them a few times as we don't have any here. I understand they are quite clever. He is adorable. What is his name?"

"Silas. And he is a little thief."

"That is the name of our stablemaster! Wait until I tell Silas that a squirrel shares his name." Celsa laughed, and the expression turned her from an awkward girl with too-big features into a handsome young woman. She would never be beautiful, but there was a good deal of character in her face and Aurelia would enjoy sketching it.

"What does he steal?" Celsa asked.

"Everything. Stockings, gloves, sweets if he should happen to find any."

"Where did he—"

A sharp rap on the door cut off her question and the door opened before Aurelia could call out permission to enter.

The woman who marched into the room was a stranger, but—based on her clothing and pinched expression—Aurelia decided this must be the unfortunate governess.

"I am Miss Hatchet," the woman said, confirming her suspicions. "You must be the artist—Miss Burton." Her eyes narrowed when she saw her charge. "I knew I would find you here, my lady. Your father said you were to come to the schoolroom immediately after dinner and work on memorizing your poem before bedtime."

Lady Celsa regarded her governess with seething dislike. "I will get it done."

"Your father said it should be done in a *timely* fashion." Her unspoken threat hung in the air: *I will tell him, and you will be punished.*

While Aurelia could see Lady Celsa was not the most tractable of pupils, she could not bring herself to like a woman who clearly enjoyed wielding her power over her student.

Celsa shoved the painting she was still holding at her governess and pushed past her, stomping from the room.

Miss Hatchet gave Aurelia a look that said, *You see what I must tolerate?* and then glanced down at the painting. "This is your work?"

"Yes."

"It is very good," she said, sounding more than a little grudging.

"Thank you."

The governess handed her the portrait while giving her a thorough once-over. "Did she come into your room and pry into your things? If she did, you must tell his lordship." Miss Hatchet's eyes glittered with malice. "I will tell him if you'd rather not."

"I invited her in," Aurelia lied, not wishing to throw any more fuel onto the fire that already raged between father and daughter.

Miss Hatchet grunted and glanced around Aurelia's bedchamber, her expression growing even more pinched. "This is a very nice room. Mine is near the schoolroom. And Lady Celsa's chambers," she added with a slight flaring of her nostrils that told Aurelia just how she felt about that.

Aurelia returned the portrait to the small wooden stand, debating how to get the other woman out of her room.

"You ate dinner with the family," the governess said, her tone accusatory.

"Yes."

"Will you do so every evening?"

"I don't know."

Miss Hatchet wandered around the room much like her recalcitrant charge had done a short time earlier. "It is unusual for a woman to accept such a commission in the house of an unmarried man."

"You work in his lordship's house."

Miss Hatchet blinked. "I am a governess."

"Does it really matter what occupation a person engages in? We are both of us unmarried women earning our own way."

Miss Hatchet made a dismissive sniffing sound, her long, pointy nose quivering. "You are very young."

Aurelia had no intention of sharing her personal information with this woman.

"This is the third house I have worked in," Miss Hatchet said when Aurelia did not respond, still prowling the room. "My other positions lasted four and six years respectively. I doubt I will complete six months here."

Aurelia merely smiled.

"I'm sure you heard what Lady Celsa did today. I daresay she boasted to you."

"She did not mention anything."

"Indeed? The monster locked me in the dungeon. I was there for almost eight hours before somebody thought to look for me."

It seemed her time in the dungeon grew with the telling. Still, the experience must have been miserable, no matter how long she languished.

"That must have been dreadful."

Miss Hatchet shivered. "It was dark and cold and the stone was covered with that dreadful black lichen the islanders regard so highly. It may look dry, but it has an unpleasantly slimy texture. It was awful."

"I can imagine."

The governess examined Aurelia's silver-backed brush and ivory comb set, which had been a gift from her paternal grandmother. She ran a long, spidery finger down the back of the brush, as if she were petting a cat. "Pretty," she murmured, and then swung abruptly back to Aurelia. "I have agreed to stay another month—if her ladyship behaves." She gave a brittle laugh. "I daresay I shall be looking for a new situation before the week is over."

Aurelia thought she was probably right.

"I lock my door at night."

"Er, because of Lady Celsa?"

Miss Hatchet gave another high-pitched laugh. "Oh, dear me, no!" She sidled closer to Aurelia and lowered her voice. "Mr. Montgomery is a perfect gentleman, but his lordship is… restless."

"Restless?"

Miss Hatchet nodded vigorously, her bow-shaped lips puckering like a drawstring had pulled them tight. She jerked her chin toward the window. "I just saw him out there. Go ahead—look."

Aurelia sighed but did as the woman bade her. There was indeed a man on a massive dark horse, his tall, commanding figure immediately recognizable as his lordship.

"He is going for a ride. The moon is out, there is nothing unusual in that," Aurelia said.

"Oh, my dear naïve Miss Burton! The earl leaves the castle most nights—moon or no."

"Surely that is not so—"

Miss Hatchet leaned closer, until Aurelia felt her hot breath on her face. "He visits his lover—one of them—in the village. Mary Neel is the widowed owner of the pub, a brazen, blowsy woman no better than a prostitute. The man has no shame. He is like a feudal lord, exercising his *droit du seigneur.*"

"I believe that alleged right applied to virgins on their wedding night, not willing widows."

The governess's jaw dropped and she regarded Aurelia as if she was a serpent that had slithered into her midst.

Aurelia opened her mouth to say she was tired. But Miss Hatchet wasn't finished.

"He has a son, you know?"

"I was under the impression Lady Celsa was his only child."

"His only *legitimate* one. He has children all over the island and on the mainland, too. But there is one—*Guustin Walker* he calls himself—who even stays in the castle like an honored guest. He dresses in fine clothing and struts about as if he were one of the family. Indeed, his lordship openly acknowledges him as his son."

Fathering children outside of marriage was irresponsible and selfish, but Aurelia thought the earl's acceptance of his illegitimate child showed at least a modicum of decency. Most men disavowed their by-blows. Still, it couldn't have been easy for Lord Crewe's wife to put up with his behavior. Not that such a man would care.

"You will meet him, I am sure. He is a captain and visits whenever his ship is in port."

"A captain? He must be quite old," Aurelia said, and then wished she kept her mouth shut so the woman would leave.

No, you don't. You love gossiping about your new employer.

"I daresay he is in his middle twenties. His mother lives on the island too. She is no better than she should be, but behaves like a grand lady—one of the island luminaries. Ha! And where is her husband? *Mister* Walker? Conveniently dead and out of the picture. Not that a person would believe her son belonged to anyone but the earl. He is a great swaggering lout who is the very image of Lord Crewe. When the two of them are in this house…" She shivered. "Well, I do not sleep easily, I tell you. It is no surprise that his daughter is an ill-behaved little savage given the example he sets for her. You would be well advised to lock your door, too, Miss Burton."

"If his lordship has a mistress in the village then you and I are likely safe from his predation, Miss Hatchet." Aurelia was amused at the thought of Lord Crewe pursuing the woman in front of her. Or herself, for that matter. She might be ignorant, but even she could see that the earl did not look like the sort of man who was much interested in virginal spinsters. He would demand sensual, experienced lovers who knew how to pleasure a man.

A shiver wracked her at the images that flooded her mind's eye—chiefly those featuring his lordship's long, lean body and wicked, laughing expression.

"His sort can never have enough women, Miss Burton. They cannot stop themselves—like dogs in rut. You would be wise to trust to my greater experience in such matters." She cut Aurelia a look that was irritatingly superior.

"Thank you, Miss Hatchet, I certainly appreciate your suggestion. Now, if you don't mind, it has been a long day and—"

"Sir Gideon brought you over to the island today, I hear."

"Yes, he—"

"Now *there* is a gentleman." Miss Hatchet's rather stark features took on a dreamy, romantic cast. "He rescued me when I sprained my ankle in the small wood outside the village. Nothing would do except that he escorted me back to the Laughing Hen." Her stern face became quite pretty as she recounted the experience.

"Yes, he is very kind," Aurelia agreed. "Now, if—"

Miss Hatchet heaved a sigh. "I daresay you are tired and wishing to go to bed." Her face creased into a spiteful smile. "And I must go and see that Lady Celsa is obeying her father's order." On that note, she turned and left.

Aurelia closed and locked the door behind her, not out of fear that Lord Crewe would pester her, but against any further invasions from Lady Celsa or her nosy keeper.

Rather than ready herself for bed, Aurelia drifted back to the window, her thoughts on the earl rather than the annoying governess.

Was it true that he had ridden off to see his lover? Why did the thought make her belly churn so uncomfortably?

Aurelia frowned at her own foolishness and yanked the drapes closed. It was just as well the earl had a mistress to occupy him. She would do well to keep that information at the front of her mind, should she be in any danger of succumbing to his wicked charm.

Chapter 6

T he following morning after breakfast Aurelia was in the library, jotting notes for herself in her journal when Lord Crewe entered the rather cavernous room.

"Ah, hard at work, already," the earl said, his wind-ruffled hair and riding leathers indicating he must have just come in from outside. He smiled down at her, tapping his calf with his crop. "I have come to show you around the island."

Aurelia hesitated and glanced at her journal.

"I know you've just begun work, but we must embrace lovely weather when it comes to us. Trust me when I say there will be many rainy days that will keep you inside with your paints and brushes. Now, run along and change into your habit and I shall meet you in the stables." He turned on his heel and strode away before she could reply, not that there was anything to say except *yes, my lord* when one's employer required one to skip work and go play.

Twenty minutes later she was garbed in her riding habit—a rich coffee brown garment with dusty rose piping that brought out the gold flecks in her eyes and made her abundant hair look more chestnut than mousy brown—and on her way to the stables, excited about riding for the first time in almost four years.

Lord Crewe stood beside a magnificent smoke-gray stallion, his glossy boots, black leathers, and exquisitely fitted black clawhammer making his lean frame appear even taller.

The lines of his body were long and elegant and Aurelia's fingers twitched to sketch him.

She had honed her artistic skills on naked male bodies beyond counting—most of them, unfortunately, deceased—but she knew enough about the masculine form that she could easily visualize how the earl would look stretched out in front of her.

His scarred face shifted into a saturnine smirk as he stared down at her, as if he knew she had just been imagining him naked.

Aurelia swallowed. "Thank you for taking the time to show me the island. I hope it is no bother."

"Why would it be? It is my island and I enjoy showing it to my guests," he said, his well-marked, dark gold eyebrow lifting along with the tattered tufts over his left eye.

He turned to the hovering groom. "Saddle Black Prince for Miss Burton, Jemmy."

"Aye, master," the groom said, and then disappeared into the stable, leaving the two of them alone.

Aurelia jerked her gaze from the scars that marred the left side of his face. His remaining eye glinted with amusement; he knew exactly what she had been looking at.

What was wrong with her? First imagining him nude and now ogling his scars. It was gauche to get caught staring and she was ashamed of her behavior. But there was something about his face—both sides—that made it difficult to look at anything else when he was in the vicinity.

"You have already been riding?" she asked.

"I have, but that was work. This will be for pleasure."

Aurelia squirmed at the way he said *pleasure*, and it was a struggle not to fidget under his sardonic gaze. She *never* fidgeted! Why on earth did the man disconcert her, so?

Because you are accustomed to overseeing your siblings, a small household, and the local gentry. You are far away from Queen's Bower and Little Sissingdon now…

The earl gestured to her satchel. "You are going to sketch?"

"I always bring it along, just in case."

He reached into the pocket of his coat and extracted a small leatherbound notepad with a pencil tucked in a holder. "As do I, even though it drives my valet to distraction that I ruin the lines of my garments."

Aurelia could see no evidence of such ruination, and it was certainly not for a lack of looking.

He flipped open the book and she studied the drawing. It was a cottage, with more detail and attention expended on the roof.

"You are a fine draughtsman," she said, and then wished she had held her tongue. "I hope you do not find that term offensive."

"I am flattered by your assessment given how I struggle with this"—he raised his slightly shaking left hand— "even making rude sketches is a challenge."

"You cannot paint at all?" she couldn't help asking.

"Nothing worth the effort." He smiled at whatever he saw on her face—likely horror at the thought of not being able to paint. "Do not pity me too much, Miss Burton. I have other interests to keep me entertained."

Aurelia's dratted face heated at his words and Lord Crewe's lips pulled up at the corners.

Just what did his other eye look like beneath that patch? The thought came out of nowhere and she hastily shoved it aside.

The groom emerged from the stable leading a glossy black gelding.

"He is lovely." Aurelia extended her hand for the horse's inspection.

"He is spirited, so you will need to keep your wits about you," the earl said.

Aurelia looked into Black Prince's intelligent eyes. "He will do nicely, I think." She paused and then added on impulse, "We rode quite a bit when I was younger. It is only these past few years I have rarely had the opportunity."

"We?" he asked, his hand stroking Black Prince's neck, making her realize that he'd come closer.

She swore she felt the heat of him all along her side even though he wasn't near enough for that to be possible. "My siblings and I."

"Ah, yes—you mentioned that you are the eldest of six. I recall thinking that you are accustomed to being in charge."

"In charge of my siblings, perhaps, but little else, I assure you."

"I find that difficult to believe."

Aurelia saw the groom was patiently waiting, his ears practically on stalks as he listened to her employer tease out her personal details.

"Here, let me help you," the earl said. His large hands closed around her waist and Aurelia found herself being lifted into the saddle before she could protest.

"Thank you, my lord," she said in a stupidly breathy voice.

"This was my wife's saddle," he said, his hands on the stirrup. "Your legs are longer than hers, so I will adjust this for you."

Aurelia's face scalded at the familiar way he manipulated her booted leg, changing the length of the stirrup twice before he was satisfied. The groom, Jemmy, stared respectfully at his feet, but Aurelia swore there was a smile tugging at his lips as his master manhandled the *lady artist*.

"There," he said, his hand lingering on her ankle as he looked up and met her mortified gaze. He gave the supple leather an almost imperceptible squeeze before stepping over to where his own mount waited.

***

Roland had no idea why he enjoyed disconcerting the prim, frosty Miss Burton so much. Perhaps because she *was* so frosty and acted far too old for her age. The way her full mouth pinched whenever she looked his way told him that she heartily disapproved of him.

Last night at the dinner table, when he had, lamentably, given in to his anger and frustration and behaved badly toward Celsa, Miss Burton's hazel eyes had become fierce with a protective instinct, her pale cheeks sporting flags as if she were ready to cruise into battle.

Roland usually did not have either the patience or inclination to enjoy baiting virginal young misses, but Miss Burton brought the devil out in him by snapping at his teasing lures like a starving fish, regardless of the bait.

He must be bored, that was the only explanation for it.

You are not bored; you want to fuck her.

Well, that was true. But then what man wouldn't? She was bloody gorgeous and her tightly repressed façade only added to her attraction. Roland could very easily imagine how much pleasure he would derive from peeling away her reservations layer by layer, until nothing but a sensual, responsive woman remained.

63

Unfortunately for his excitable cock, he would *not* be doing any peeling. The last thing he needed was to alienate his new artist. Certainly not before she had finished the work he was paying her to do.

After that, however…

There would be no *after that*. Roland would pay her, deliver the paintings, and then plan his next expedition. There was no part in his agenda for deflowering virgins. Especially not if he wanted to use her for any future work.

However, if he was going to be this physically *stimulated* while the woman was living in his house, he needed to do something to sate those urges.

Unfortunately, his visit to Mary Neel last night had been less than satisfying. Rather than come away relaxed from a vigorous bout of sex, Roland had felt as if he'd just spent an hour being hectored by Arthur.

Mary was a skilled, confident lover, but she was always conniving for *something* when Roland was with her. Last night, both before and after they had slaked their appetites on each other's bodies, the wily innkeeper had nagged Roland to give her useless, feckless son Mick one of the worker cottages, even though Mick was not one of Roland's workers. Nor did the boy know *how* to work, as far as Roland could tell.

It was not the sort of behavior that made him eager to visit her bed again.

Roland had also been more than a little ashamed that he had thought about Miss Burton the entire time he'd been balls-deep inside Mary.

Yes, it was time for Roland to move on when he could not give a lover the attention she deserved.

"What is the population of the island?" Miss Burton asked, reminding Roland that he had promised the woman a tour of the island, not a brooding would-be ravisher for a companion.

"It is two-hundred-and-three—soon to be four."

"That is very precise."

"We take a census at the end of each year and there have been three births thus far, another should occur within the next few days." He gestured to the narrow but hardpacked path they rode on. "You will use this road most often as it encircles the island. There are several others that cross it and of course, a few roads leading to individual houses, but we will stay on this so you can familiarize yourself with the village of Crewe."

"Is that another island?" she asked, pointing toward the south.

"Yes, although the term *island* is rather grand to describe it. It has been built over the centuries by the Lairds of Crewe. We still haul rocks on barges from the mainland, although not to increase the size of it anymore, but to add to the protective barrier around it. It hosts one of the smallest lighthouses in Britain, which is operated by Old Walter. The island is called Nesta's Perch after an eccentric ancestress of mine who went to live there after her husband died. She is believed to have died there, although nobody ever found her body."

Miss Burton's lips curved into a charming smile. "Does she haunt it?"

"Of course."

"And Old Walter does not mind?"

"His wife ran off with a lover ages ago and he is fond of saying that Nesta's shade is the only woman who could abide him."

As they rode up over the ridge Roland gestured to a tiny bay down below. "Down there, hidden in a system of caves, is the home of the Thorsson family, the only inhabitants of the island who can claim a more ancient lineage than my own. Thorsson claims his ancestors came with the original jarl who settled the place hundreds of years before the Conquest."

Miss Burton gazed around her with obvious admiration. "The island must have been desolate, but also wild and beautiful without a human presence."

Roland gave her a look of surprise.

She flushed slightly. "You are thinking that is a rather naïve and romantic view."

"Not at all. I am pleased that you appreciate the stark and unusual beauty of Crewe."

They rode for a while in silence as they gradually descended to the water's edge.

Roland gestured to the right. "This is the largest pier and most protected of our bays. When you decide to practice your rowing, you should do so here, where you can experiment in relative safety. There is usually somebody nearby if you should get into any trouble. Have you rowed before?"

"Only on a little pond near home. I imagine it could be quite dangerous here?"

"It can be if you are not paying attention. A smooth glassy sea can turn violent in the blink of an eye, so you must always be aware of your surroundings." He paused, and then said, "I will have Celsa take you out tomorrow if conditions are favorable. She is very comfortable in a skiff and has been rowing since she was a child. Do you swim?"

"Yes, but—again—only in a stream or a pond, never the ocean."

Roland was assaulted by an image of her with a wet, transparent chemise plastered over her lithe body, full, high creamy breasts floating on—

"I daresay the water is extremely cold?" she asked.

Like a rock thrown into a pond, her question shattered the arousing image. Which was just as well as it was bloody uncomfortable to ride with his cock at full mast.

"Most of the time the water is frigid," he agreed. "But we also get tropical currents at certain times of the year."

Miss Burton reined in and pointed to something near the water line. "What is that?"

Roland followed her gaze. "It is a ducking stool. Or *cucking stool,* as some of the older people call it."

"Ducking stool?" she repeated, her tone less certain than any he'd heard out of her yet.

"Yes, for punishment."

"You can't mean—" she bit her plush lower lip, halting the flow of words, her hazel eyes growing rounder by the second.

Roland waited for her to finish, amused when she couldn't muster the words to finish her thought. "It is where men bring willful wives to discipline them," he said.

Her full, coral pink lips parted, the sight evoking such carnal thoughts that Roland had to shift in his saddle. Christ but she was lovely when she shed some of her prim, stern façade.

"Discipline?"

Roland had to bite the inside of his cheek not to burst out laughing. He could almost hear Arthur scolding him. As usual, he ignored it.

"Yes, discipline," he said, somehow managing to keep a straight face. "Scolds, harpies, those women who don't obey their lord and master. A few hours on the ducking stool usually sets them to rights."

She sputtered. "But—that can't…. You are jesting."

"No, I am not. It is an excellent way to ensure one's woman remains obedient."

"But…"

"But?" he prodded, enchanted by the emotions flickering across her face.

"Surely that cannot be legal?"

"We are a law unto ourselves here on the island. The Lords of Crewe have special authority similar to a palatinate. King David I granted the first Crewe—then spelled Cruwys—dominion over the island in exchange for his assistance subduing the unruly Scots. My ancestor was essentially a king of his domain, his power unchallenged so long as he remained feal to David. Much later, our special status was again upheld when we helped suppress the Jacobite Rebellion. While others lost control over their fiefdoms—not to mention their lives—we expanded our reach thanks to a special land grant from a very grateful monarch."

She was still staring at the old stool, her mouth open. Roland doubted she had heard a word he just said.

"So you permit men to—to strap their wives into that contraption and—and—"

"The tide comes in and the scold is then submerged. It usually does not take too long—perhaps five or six good duckings—before she learns the error of her ways and becomes a more submissive wife."

"But—I don't—"

"You seem outraged by the notion, Miss Burton." And it was extremely entertaining. Not to mention bloody attractive. Gone was the cool ice queen and in her place was a fiery flesh-and-blood woman.

"Of course I'm outraged!" she all but shouted, her nostrils flaring.

"How else is a man to ensure his wife's obedience?" he asked, giving her a puzzled look.

"How else?" she repeated. "*How else?*" And then her face hardened, putting Roland in mind of a fierce warrior queen preparing to engage in battle. She looked bloody glorious! "I cannot believe—" She stopped, her eyes narrowing as they flickered over his face, lingering on his jaw which was painfully tight to keep his laughter contained. "You are teasing me."

Roland threw his head back and laughed—and then laughed even harder at the scowl she gave him.

"I cannot believe I swallowed that."

"Like a hungry fish swallowing a hook," he agreed once he'd regained control of himself. "I know I should apologize," Roland said, "but I find that I cannot. You are so serious for such a young woman and—"

"I am five-and-twenty. That is hardly a child!" she snapped, yet again taking his bait.

"No, of course not," he soothed.

"How old are you, my lord?" she retorted. But her anger all too quickly gave way to chagrin. "I'm sorry. That was—"

"Never apologize for giving as good as you get, Miss Burton," he said, smiling. "I am almost one-and-forty."

When she merely nodded, Roland laughed. "You have just delivered a killing blow to my fragile *amour propre*, Miss Burton. You were supposed to say, *one and forty! Why, you do not look a day over thirty, my lord.*"

"I suspect your self-esteem is healthy enough to survive it."

He laughed again, beyond delighted.

They rode in silence, Miss Burton studiously looking anywhere but at Roland, giving him an opportunity to admire her lovely profile. And it *was* lovely.

And young. Somewhere along the way Miss Burton had convinced herself she was a matron—or perhaps someone else had convinced her—and her self-possession and stern mien was that of a much older woman. It was also obvious that she was not accustomed to being teased.

Roland was a bastard for how much he enjoyed disconcerting her and bringing out that adorable blush and chiding tone.

And he had no intention of mending his teasing ways any time soon, either.

***

Aurelia was furious at herself for snapping at the earl's lure and tugging so hard, over and over and over again. The wretched man had reeled her in with the skill of a seasoned angler.

"Do not be angry about the ducking stool, Miss Burton," Lord Crewe said, his voice cajoling.

"I am not angry," she said. And then was annoyed by her clearly angry tone.

He laughed again and the sound was so rich, vibrant, and masculine that she felt her lips pulling up into a tiny smile.

"There, that is better," he said. "If we cannot laugh at ourselves, then who can we laugh at?"

"You seem to be doing fine laughing at *me*."

He grinned. "You are absolutely right. And I promise not to do so again—"

Aurelia gave him a look of disbelief.

"—for the rest of our ride," he finished.

Yet again she felt herself beginning to smile and quashed the urge.

Lord Crewe pointed toward a ruin not far from the castle. "There is the abbey my ancestor built to curry favor with King David I."

"There doesn't appear to be much remaining."

"No, it was pillaged for stone by yet another ancestor of mine. Yet again to curry favor, this time to a Tudor monarch when he built an addition to the castle to lure the king for a visit."

"I think you are proud of your opportunistic ancestors and how willingly they changed sides to suit their needs."

He grinned. "Again, guilty as charged."

Aurelia lowered her gaze, unable to meet his bold eye. How much more disconcerting must he have been when he'd had a perfect face and the use of both eyes?

She stole glances at him from beneath her lashes as they rode. Not surprisingly, his seat was excellent, his posture kingly. Well, he *was* a sort of king on this island, wasn't he?

Aurelia suddenly noticed that his left hand rested on his thigh, the gloved fingers flexing into a fist and then relaxing. Flexing and relaxing.

She glanced up and found him looking at her. "My physician in Edinburgh says I must exercise my arm to regain dexterity," he explained.

It was unfair how easily he was able to read her thoughts, especially when the only emotion she had been able to recognize on his face had been amusement, usually at something she had said or done.

He pointed to a long, low building on a pier where a half dozen larger boats were docked. "That is part of our guano operation."

"Guano?"

"It is a South American term—from Peru, I am told—for animal droppings, usually those of bats or birds."

"To make gunpowder?"

His eyebrow lifted. "You have heard of it?"

"I read about the Spanish harvesting it somewhere—an island, I believe."

"Yes, they have several mines in South America. It is indeed used for gunpowder if the chemical composition is correct, but this will be used for farming."

They started up a slight incline and as they crested the rise the village of Crewe spread out before them.

The small town was essentially one main street, and as they approached people called out greetings, doffed caps, or curtsied. Lord Crewe responded with names and a special comment or question for everyone they encountered. It was clear he knew all his subjects well enough to be on a first-name basis.

A surprising number of businesses lined the main street, including a tiny mercantile, a smithy, and a bakery and tea shop.

They were just approaching the public house—The Sea Hag—when a woman stepped out and Lord Crewe brought his mount to a halt.

"Good day, Mary."

"My lord." She curtsied and gave the earl a smile that seemed extremely friendly and glanced curiously at Aurelia. "I was just about to send a messenger up to the castle, my lord. Lizzy Levitt gave birth not even an hour ago—another fine boy—and Des is inside celebratin'."

Lord Crewe turned to Aurelia. "Let us go inside and drink to the child's health." He dismounted and Aurelia followed suit, sliding down clumsily before he could come around and lift her down. A lad seemed to spring up from nowhere to take their reins.

The taproom was crowded with celebrants of both genders and there was a murmur of welcome for the earl and more than a few inquisitive looks in Aurelia's direction.

Lord Crewe strode toward a young man and clapped him on the shoulder. "Congratulations, Desmond. A fine son, I hear."

"Aye. Thank ye, me lord." The young man grinned dazedly up at the earl, making Aurelia suspect the glass in his hand wasn't the first.

"And how are Lizzy and the babe?"

"Fit as a fiddle, sir. The wee'un, as well."

Lord Crewe turned to the man behind the bar. "Two gins, Marcus. And another round for everyone."

He handed one of the glasses to Aurelia and said in a quiet voice, "It is extremely potent, so have a care." He lifted his own glass and said in a loud voice, "To Des, Lizzy, and—" he turned to the proud father and raised an eyebrow. "What is the lad's name?"

"Er, we've named him Daniel, my lord."

"—and Daniel!" The earl took a drink and so did all the others.

Aurelia had tasted gin on occasion and didn't really care for it. But she knew it would be rude not to have any, so she took a small sip.

"How do you like it?" his lordship asked.

"It is… interesting."

"A few sips only or I will have to carry you back on my horse with me, Miss Burton."

Aurelia compressed her lips, as if that would stop the foolish leaping in her belly at his ridiculous threat. "I have had spirits before, my lord."

"*Pah!* Southern spirits—mild like your fair clime," he said, his eye sparkling. "This is proper island gin, distilled from sweet kelp."

"Kelp? Is this another tall tale like the ducking stool, my lord?"

He laughed. "No. I promised no more teasing today, remember? Kelp gin is a specialty of the islands and there are as many recipes—slavishly guarded—as there are people who brew it."

The woman who'd greeted them outside drifted up to their table.

"Mary, this is Miss Burton, my new artist. Miss Burton, this is Mrs. Mary Neel, the proprietress of the Sea Hag."

Aurelia started at the name *Neel.* So, this was the earl's lover.

"It is a pleasure to meet you, Mrs. Neel," Aurelia said.

"How do ye like the homebrew, Miss Burton?" The older woman's eyes crawled over Aurelia with more curiosity than politeness.

"It is delicious," Aurelia lied, lifting the glass again and taking another tiny sip.

Mary Neel turned to his lordship, "I was wonderin' if you'd given some thought to Mick and the cottage, my lord?"

"I will see him along with everyone else on my public day."

"But, sir—"

"Not today, Mary."

His voice, if anything, had become quieter.

Mrs. Neel's face reddened, but she nodded. "Aye, 'course, me lord. Would ye care for another?" she asked, glancing at the earl's almost empty glass.

"No, we must be off." His lordship stood and tossed some coins onto the table. "The celebration is on me today, Mary."

She dropped a curtsey. "Thank you, me lord." She cut Aurelia a faintly condescending look and then sauntered back to the bar, her full hips swaying in a way that Aurelia would never be able to imitate, at least not without resembling a cart with one wheel missing.

Outside, Aurelia took advantage of the mounting block before his lordship could pick her up again.

They rode without speaking through the rest of the town. Aurelia was aware of eyes on them—far more than were visible out on the street—and could imagine the sort of speculation that was currently running through the village. A single woman living with a widowed rake. It didn't matter that he already had *one* single woman—Miss Hatchet—at the castle. In people's minds there was something scandalous about a female artist.

Once they reached the outskirts of the town they came to a fork in the road and he turned left onto the smaller of the two roads.

"So, tell me, Miss Burton, how did you spend your time in—Little Sissingdon, was it?"

"Yes, that is the name of the village. I spent my time working on my various commissions and also helped teach my two youngest siblings."

"Surely there must have been assemblies or country dances?"

"We did not attend such functions."

"No dinner or house parties?" he persisted.

"No, none of those."

"Is that because you were in mourning?"

"Mourning?"

"For your father," he reminded her.

"No, my mother didn't like—" she broke off, realizing she was about to say her mother hadn't liked entertaining after they'd been forced to move out of Wych House.

"What didn't she like?"

"She didn't feel it was right for us to accept invitations when we could not reciprocate given her illness." That was at least partly true.

"Five young women and no entertainment. It seems like a waste."

It *had* been a waste and they had all of them—except Hy and Doddy—very much lamented the lack of socializing. Now that they were all scattered around the country Aurelia realized not having dances or parties was not the worst that could happen. After all, at least they had been together.

"Have I made you homesick?" the earl asked, giving her a surprisingly kindly look.

"Perhaps a little."

"I am not a stern taskmaster, Miss Burton, you will have ample time to enjoy yourself," the earl said, thankfully leaving behind the subject of homesickness. "You will find plenty to do and lots to explore on the island."

"I am looking forward to it," Aurelia said, and that was the truth. This was an adventure and she planned to take advantage of her new freedom.

The path suddenly narrowed, necessitating riding single file, which curtailed any further conversation. A few moments later they came up level with the castle, approaching it from behind the stables.

Lord Crewe turned to her and smiled when they rode into the courtyard. "So, there you have it—a brief tour. Now you will know enough to venture out on your own."

"Thank you for taking the time to orient me, my lord."

The glint of amusement was back in his eye. "It was my pleasure, Miss Burton. I want you to be very happy here so you will stay a long, long time."

Aurelia did not think that she imagined the weight of his gaze on her back as she walked back to the castle.

Chapter 7

Aurelia's second evening at Castle Crewe was far less eventful than the first, but still a tense affair with his lordship doing most of the talking during dinner. Arthur seemed preoccupied with something and Lady Celsa spent most of the meal glaring at Aurelia every time Lord Crewe directed a question or comment at her. Which was most of the time.

Not until they were almost finished eating did the earl directly address his daughter. "You must show Miss Burton your boat tomorrow if the weather is nice and give her a rowing lesson, Celsa."

The girl looked as if she'd just been condemned to a few hours on the ducking stool.

"Of course, father." She cut a surly glance at Aurelia. "Mornings are best as the wind often picks up in the afternoon. My lessons start at nine, so it will have to be early. Very early," she added, as if that might rule out Aurelia's acceptance.

"I will be ready."

Celsa grunted at that and then turned to her father. "May we take horses to the cove, Papa?" she asked, a wheedle in her tone.

Lord Crewe fixed his daughter with a long, brooding stare and the girl's cheeks darkened. "Yes, you may. But for the rowing lessons with Miss Burton, only."

The girl's transformation was startling. "Thank you, Papa!" She cut Aurelia a far friendlier look and said, "Seven o'clock in the stables."

"I will be there."

***

"I'm glad you are on time," Lady Celsa all but snarled the following morning when Aurelia showed up at the stables. "Silas said you rode Black Prince before, so they are saddling him for you again."

"Thank you," Aurelia murmured.

That was the last conversation they had until they were both in the saddle.

"I am only doing this so I can ride," Lady Celsa said after five minutes of silence.

"I'd assumed as much," Aurelia said dryly.

Celsa cut her a startled look, as if she'd expected Aurelia to be hurt.

A few moments later, she said, "I daresay you don't know anything at all about boats."

"Not much," Aurelia agreed cheerfully.

"Hmmph." Celsa led her south, toward the small island she'd seen yesterday—Nesta's Perch.

Their horses picked their way slowly but confidently down a steep path that ran along the cliff. Not until they were almost at the bottom did Aurelia see there was a tiny cove. High up on the beach was a rowboat with the name *Island Sylph* painted on the side.

They dismounted and loosened the girths on their horses' saddles before leaving them free to wander. There wasn't more than a spot of land with sand and rocks, a bit of sea grass, and a rill running down the cliff that flowed into a rock pool. The horses, obviously familiar with the place, sauntered to the pool and drank.

"First off, you always check your skiff before you go out," Lady Celsa said, using a tone of voice more suited to army sergeants drilling their troops. "Obviously, you want to make sure there are two oars and an anchor." There were three bench seats and Celsa lifted the top of one, which was hinged for storage. Beneath it was a small anchor and coil of rope.

Aurelia nodded.

"Help me push this into the water," Lady Celsa ordered. The boat moved easily over the sand and when it reached the water the girl said, "You hop in now."

Aurelia did so and Celsa hiked up her skirt exposing tarred boots like the kind fishermen wore. She pushed the boat out a bit further and then deftly pulled herself into the boat.

"You sit in the middle and show me what you know," Celsa ordered as the current caught the skiff and began to pull it back to shore.

The next ten minutes were comprised of Aurelia rowing and Celsa alternately barking orders and criticizing Aurelia's efforts.

"Here, you do it and I will watch," Aurelia said when it was clear the girl was getting far too much enjoyment from upbraiding an adult.

Celsa looked like she wanted to argue but was clearly too eager to show off her superior skills. She quickly scrambled to the middle seat and took up the oars. "Watch how smoothly I pull—not choppy and jerky as you were doing."

"You row very well," Aurelia said, pleased to sit back and let the girl do all the work.

"I suppose you are hoping that my father will fall madly in love with you and marry you," Celsa said after a few moments of silence.

"What a remarkable thing to say," Aurelia said, deliberately keeping her tone cool even though she would have liked to box the obnoxious brat's ears.

"Not really. It is what the Hatchet hopes for. She has some books in her room from the Minerva Press and at least two of them are about governesses who marry their master and live happily ever after." Celsa gave a spiteful laugh. "Although I daresay her hopes are dashed now that you are here." She swept Aurelia with a scornful look. "You are much prettier than she is, but it still won't be enough to tempt my father." Her expression turned sly and unpleasant. "At least not to marry you, although he does keep several mistresses so perhaps you might suit that position."

"What a pity you have such a low opinion of his lordship."

Celsa's arms stilled their rhythmic pulling. "What do you mean?"

"If you think he is the sort of master to impose on his servants, you can't think too highly of him."

The girl's forehead furrowed and it was clear that she'd not considered her father's raking in that light. She shrugged the thought aside and resumed her rowing.

Aurelia closed her eyes, tilted her head back, and allowed the sun to warm her face. It was a beautiful morning and warm even though it was still early.

"What is in the satchel?" Lady Celsa asked a few minutes later.

"My sketchpad."

"What do you want to sketch?"

Aurelia opened her eyes and faced the girl rather than be rude. "Whatever catches my interest."

"You had better not try drawing me."

"Why not?"

"I don't like seeing pictures of myself."

"Perhaps you just haven't seen the right one yet."

The girl laughed, but there was little amusement in it. "I might like it if you make me look pretty."

"You are pretty when you smile." It was true; she looked like a different girl entirely when she forgot to be surly and obnoxious.

"Ha!"

But Aurelia could see the compliment had pleased her.

"I'm going to take you over to the pier," Celsa said after a moment. "It is more of a dock, really, just big enough for boats to come with provisions for Old Walter."

"Will he mind that we are visiting his island uninvited?"

"It is not *his* island," Celsa scoffed. "It belongs to my father, just like everything else."

"But Old Walter—" Aurelia made an exasperated noise. "What is his surname?" she asked, not wishing to call a stranger by his Christian name, especially not with *old* preceding it.

"I don't know." She laughed. "He probably doesn't remember it, either."

"We are calling uninvited and he lives here," Aurelia pointed out.

"He likes it when I visit," Celsa said with the confidence of youth.

The pier—or dock—in question was protected by two tiny jetties. A boat a little larger than Celsa's sat atop the dock, both ends tied down.

"That is Walter's skiff, so he is home," Celsa said and then leapt nimbly from the boat and tied both ends before pausing and grudgingly offering Aurelia a hand.

"Thank you," Aurelia said.

"You will want to sketch birds and such, I am sure," Celsa said, not waiting for an answer before charging toward the shore. "There are a great many that nest on the other side of the lighthouse where there is a marshy area. Hurry up and I will take you there," she called over her shoulder.

Aurelia followed at a much slower pace.

They walked along the shoreline which was not an easy task given how rocky it was, and Aurelia was soon perspiring profusely.

"It's just over here," Celsa called from a slight rise that was tufted with seagrass.

Aurelia was breathing hard when she came up beside the girl. "Oh, it's delightful." The marsh, like everything else on the island, was in miniature. There were mergansers and several varieties of ducks lazily paddling about.

"You can have a half hour or so before we need to go back," Lady Celsa said.

"Are you sure? What will you do while I'm sketching?"

"I will go see Old Walter."

"Should I come along and introduce myself?"

"You needn't bother. I doubt he wants to meet you."

Aurelia snorted at the characteristically rude comment and watched for a moment as Celsa began clambering up the slope, as nimble as a monkey, toward the lighthouse.

She found a large piece of driftwood that had obviously been dragged beside the slough so that somebody—Walter-of-the-no-surname perhaps—could enjoy the birdlife.

As usually happened when Aurelia drew, time passed without her realizing it. Only after she'd filled several pages did she realize that she must have been sketching for quite some time. She set aside her sketchpad and stood, stretching her muscles before checking her watch. It was nine-thirty! She had been sitting on the log for more than an hour. Celsa needed to be back for her lessons and now she would be late—thanks to Aurelia.

Aurelia hastily packed up her things and hurried back to the boat.

Before she'd even made it to the dock, she saw there was only one boat, and it wasn't Celsa's.

She shaded her eyes with one hand and looked toward the cove where they'd left the horses. From this angle it was difficult to say, but it looked like the horses were no longer loitering on the beach.

Had the girl just left her there? Or had she rowed around the island and put up somewhere else? Aurelia took a deep breath and considered her options. Other than swimming back, she had no choice but to find Celsa, who might still be at the lighthouse—perhaps Old Walter had taken her boat for some inexplicable reason?

Aurelia sighed, slung her satchel crosswise over her body, and scrambled up the boulders and scree. By the time she reached the top she was sweating in earnest and feeling more than a little out of charity with Lady Celsa, mentally composing the raking she'd deliver when she saw the monster.

"Hello!"

Her head whipped around and she saw an old man—no, an ancient man— walking slowly toward her, his back so bent he was almost doubled over.

She strode toward him. "Hello. I am Miss Burton. I came over with Lady Celsa."

The old man chuckled. "Aye, I know who ye be. Lookin' for the wee lass, eh?"

"Yes, I am."

"She be gone this past hour." He clucked his tongue. "Playin' 'er tricks she is."

"You mean she rowed back to Crewe?"

"Aye, aye. Did it to the last governess—a pretty thing like you. But I was off at me daughter's house. Poor lass were here most o' the night 'til master rowed over for 'er."

Honestly, what a little witch! Aurelia was beginning to understand Lord Crewe's frustration with his daughter.

The old man chuckled at whatever he saw on her face and patted her shoulder with a gnarled hand. "Ye needn't worry. I'll row ye back over."

"I'm terribly sorry to put you out."

"I've a need for more of Mary Neel's gin. Jest let me fetch me jug." He cocked his head at her, reminding her of a bird. "Would ye like to come up and see the view?"

"I would love to, if you don't mind."

"It's nae bother. And a finer sight ye'll never see."

She walked alongside Walter, which meant they moved at a snaillike pace toward the lighthouse.

The cottage at the base of the tower was charming, and the old man led her through his domain, which was composed of five chambers, making for a generously sized house for a bachelor. But then she recalled what Lord Crewe had said, that his wife had run off, and felt a pang of sympathy for the sweet old man.

"It be sixty-one feet," he said as he led her up the spiral stairs to the light. "Built in 1787 by Thomas Smith and 'is stepson, Stevenson," Old Walter said, not breathing heavily at all—unlike Aurelia, who sounded like an old draught horse by the time they reached the top.

"It is an amazing view," Aurelia said, slowly walking around the glass-enclosed circle.

"It be higher than the turret towers on the castle," Old Walter said, sounding as proud as if he'd laid all the stones himself. "This 'ere be a dioptic lens." Those were the last comprehensible words she heard while he enthused about the big light with its thick magnifying glass and complicated mechanism for spinning and tilting and raising and lowering the light for cleaning and maintenance.

He broke off, laughing. "Listen to me, rabbitin' on, aye?"

"It is all very interesting."

"Yer a kind lass." His eyes, cloudy with cataracts, slid over the view out the window. "Ah, the white horses be comin'. We best get ye back, miss."

Aurelia had not noticed the whitecaps until he'd mentioned them. "Is there time?"

He chuckled. "Aye, Old Walter will get ye back safe and sound."

***

"Your cheeks are rosy. You got a bit of sun today, Miss Burton," Lord Crewe said that evening at dinner as the footmen set out the second course. "You need to be careful here, it can be deceptively cool thanks to the ocean breezes, but the sun is harsh."

Aurelia touched her cheek, which still felt hot from her long morning outside. "I will heed your advice in the future."

"Did you enjoy your first rowing lesson?" he asked, his gaze sliding from Aurelia to his daughter.

"Yes, it was very instructive." She turned to Celsa. "Thank you for the lesson, Lady Celsa."

The girl had the grace to blush. Aurelia had not seen her since returning to the castle after Walter rowed her over to the pier, where she'd been fortunate enough to get a ride with a wagon headed to the castle with supplies.

"It was kind of Walter to row you back to the island," the earl said. "I apologize for my daughter's ill-mannered behavior in leaving you at his mercy. And no, Celsa," he added, turning his cold gaze on his daughter, "you needn't glare at Miss Burton. She did not tell me about your childish behavior, it was your governess who informed me that you came back to the house alone but with two horses. Apologize," he said, the word low and menacing.

"I'm sorry, Papa."

"Not to *me*."

Celsa turned to Aurelia, the very image of misery. "I'm sorry, Miss Burton."

Aurelia did not know what to say, but Lord Crewe did not give her the opportunity as he said to his daughter, "I will see you in the library after dinner, Celsa."

"Yes, Papa."

He turned away from her, his expression softening when it landed on Aurelia. She squirmed, hoping Lady Celsa did not notice how her father looked more happily on just about anything and anyone other than his daughter. Unfortunately, a quick glance at the girl told her she hoped in vain.

"Did Walter give you a tour of the lighthouse before he brought you back?"

"Yes, he did and it was fascinating."

Lord Crewe spoke about the process of building the lighthouse, which had been done during his father's tenure as Laird of Crewe.

Mr. Montgomery chimed in with details his cousin had forgotten and the remainder of the meal passed quite pleasurably—at least for the adults. It was clear from Celsa's expression of dread that she could think of nothing but the impending meeting with her father.

When dinner was over, Aurelia hung back. "May I have a moment of your time, my lord?"

She was once again reminded of his height as he gazed down at her, the frosty blue of his eye warm. "You may have as many of my minutes as you wish, Miss Burton. Would you like to accompany me to the library?"

"This should not take long. I just wanted to tell you that I suffered no harm this morning. I was only on Nesta's Perch for a few hours."

"It is kind of you to try and excuse my daughter's behavior, Miss Burton. But this is not the first—or even the fifth—time that something like this has happened. While you were fortunate to return unscathed, that is not always going to be the case. My daughter needs to learn there are repercussions for *her* when she does such irresponsible things."

"I understand. But—" she broke off and bit her lip.

"But?" he urged with a gentleness that sat strangely on his sharp features.

"Perhaps she would not do such things if—" she stopped again.

He cocked his head, his expression one of intense curiosity, although she saw something else just below the surface—annoyance? Amusement? "Please do not curb your opinions, Miss Burton. If you believe there is a way to stop my daughter from behaving callously and dangerously, please do share. I am all agog."

Yes, there was definite mockery there.

"Walter told me about the governess who was stranded at the lighthouse, so I understand your concern. But today I was not discommoded beyond a few minutes spent looking at the lighthouse."

"I am relieved that *you* did not have a miserable or dangerous experience, Miss Burton."

She flushed at his slightly cutting tone.

"Did Walter tell you about the time my daughter left one of her governesses in a cove during an incoming tide? If he had not been watching and noticed that only one person returned in the skiff rather than two, the woman would likely have drowned when the tide came in."

Aurelia swallowed, suddenly sick to her stomach. What if Lady Celsa had done that to her?

"No, he did not tell me that story, my lord."

"Then there was the time she put a bur beneath my wife's saddle. Only the fact that the countess was an excellent rider saved her from a very nasty spill."

Aurelia was horrified. And desperately wished she had kept her mouth shut. "I didn't know about that, either."

"I thought not. And these are just a few of the *pranks* my daughter has pulled over the years. You may think I am unnecessarily cruel and harsh, but I break out in a cold sweat imagining the day when there *isn't* someone there to rescue one of her victims."

"I understand, my lord," she said stiffly, feeling like a fool for getting involved in something that wasn't her concern. She had come to Crewe to paint. Not offer parenting advice.

"Good, I am pleased to hear it," he said, yet another unreadable emotion glittering in his eye. "If that is all, I will bid you good evening, Miss Burton."

***

Aurelia was in her room looking over the sketches she'd done that morning when there was a rap on her door. It opened before she could say *come in* and Miss Hatchet bustled into the room, all but rubbing her hands in glee.

"Her ladyship has landed in the soup this time!"

Aurelia closed her book. "Er, what do you mean?"

"His lordship is sick to death with her tricks. It won't be a mere restriction from riding. Oh no, this time there will be *consequences*. We can all hope that Lady Celsa will not be sitting comfortable for a week."

"Good Lord! You are not saying that he will beat her?"

"Why do you look so horrified?" Miss Hatchet demanded. "If ever I met a child who required a proper whipping, it is Lady Celsa."

Aurelia found the other woman's enjoyment of the situation sickening. "Physical violence is never the answer."

Miss Hatchet's eyebrows shot up. "Why are you defending the little wretch? You are the one who was abandoned." Her mouth tightened. "You would not be so sanguine if you were left in a dungeon for an entire day."

"I thought it was only five hours," Aurelia retorted, immediately wishing she could snatch the words back.

Miss Hatchet inhaled deeply, filling her lungs for a glorious harangue.

Thankfully, a knock on the door interrupted whatever she was about to say, and the girl they'd just been discussing opened the door and hovered uncertainty on the threshold.

"Did you need something Lady Celsa?" Aurelia asked, feeling a bit like a toad to be caught gossiping about her with her governess.

"Could I speak to you for a moment, Miss Burton? Alone." She gave her governess a sullen look, her eyes swollen and reddened from crying.

He *had* beaten her. Aurelia felt nauseated at the knowledge the earl had laid a hand on his child in anger.

"Would you please excuse us, Miss Hatchet," Aurelia said, when the woman looked inclined to linger.

Miss Hatchet's pale cheeks flamed when she understood that *she* was being dismissed. She spun on her heel and stormed from the room in a flurry of skirts.

"What can I do for you?" Aurelia asked more sharply than she'd intended, but Celsa's smug enjoyment of the governess's embarrassment annoyed her. She might not like the tittle-tattling of Miss Hatchet, but neither did she care for the pulling-the-legs-off-flies enjoyment the girl was showing.

"I am sorry for leaving you on Nesta's Perch today."

"And I am sorry you were whipped."

Celsa's jaw dropped. "What?"

"Your father gave you a whipping, Miss Hatchet said."

The girl gave her a superior look. "You should not listen to gossip, Miss Burton. My father did not whip me. He never has."

Aurelia was flooded with relief. And then annoyance that she cared so much about the earl's behavior.

"Why did you do it?" she asked the girl.

Celsa shrugged.

"Are you saying that you don't know why you left me there?" she asked, allowing all the irritation and scorn she felt to show in her tone.

Celsa bristled. "I did it because I don't like you."

"You don't even know me."

"You are like all the others."

"What others?"

"The women who come here—all of them fawning over my father and trying to get his attention."

"I don't know about these *others*, but that is not what I'm trying to do," Aurelia snapped, more than a little aware that she wasn't being entirely honest.

"That is a lie! The only reason you spent any time with me today is to curry favor with him."

Aurelia stared, unsettled by the truth—albeit only a grain—in the girl's words.

"What? Why are you staring at me like that?" Celsa demanded, crossing her arms.

"Because I think it is sad that you consider your own company so lacking in appeal."

Celsa's eyebrows drew together over her nose and Aurelia could see the girl was trying to figure out if she had just been insulted.

"I would like to propose an agreement, my lady."

"What sort of agreement?" Lady Celsa asked, looking far too suspicious for one so young.

"I promise I won't spend time with you unless it is something that *I* want to do. You, in exchange, agree not to accept my offer of company if you have plans to abandon me, lock me away, or generally abuse my offer of friendship. What say you?"

"How do I know that you will be telling the truth?"

"Rely on your own judgment. If you don't trust me or my motives, then you should decline any offers."

"But my father will not allow me to ride my horse if I am not going somewhere with you."

Aurelia chuckled.

"What is so amusing?" Celsa snapped.

"You just accused *me* of only doing things with you to curry favor with the earl. And now you are admitting to the same behavior. How do you think that makes me feel?"

"I suppose that is true," Celsa grudgingly admitted after a moment.

"Come, my lady," Aurelia cajoled, smiling at the obviously miserable and lonely young woman. "What do you have to lose by accepting my offer?"

Lady Celsa regarded her through narrowed eyes for a moment, but then nodded. "Very well. I agree to your terms."

"Perhaps tomorrow we might meet up at the stable and you can take me for a ride around the island. I've only been on the one main road, really."

She brightened at that. "Yes, I could do that. What time? I am not finished with lessons until three."

"Three-thirty?"

Celsa nodded, a smile tugging at her lips.

"Goodnight, then," Aurelia said.

"Goodnight, Miss Burton."

The moment the door shut behind the girl Aurelia sagged onto the bed.

She hoped Lord Crewe found out about their bargain and understood that he didn't need to shame and punish his daughter to get results. Kindness was far more effective.

Aurelia imagined him eating his words and smiled.

She paused at the thought. Good Lord! Why was she even considering what the earl would think? Could Celsa be right that women only wanted to spend time with her because of the earl?

No, Aurelia decided after a long moment of introspection. Proving the earl wrong wasn't the main reason for doing things with the lonely girl. It was just a happy benefit.

Chapter 8

The days fell into a pleasurable rhythm and flew by and Aurelia's first month on the island passed before she had even realized it.

She worked from early in the morning until two or three o'clock. After putting away her paints and brushes she spent the hours before dinner either exploring the island on her own or, more often, riding or—weather permitting—rowing with Lady Celsa.

On her first four visits to the village, Aurelia had been cornered and interrogated by Mary Neel. Indeed, the innkeeper appeared to have developed some sort of mania for Aurelia and managed to apprehend her no matter whether she slipped into town on foot or on horseback.

"She has always been bothersome," Lady Celsa said after they had gone to the village tea shop one afternoon and had both been trapped by Mrs. Neel. "But she seems even worse lately."

The innkeeper made it so unpleasant to go to town that Aurelia took to avoiding the village entirely, only going there unless she needed something from one of the shops.

Although she had not seen Lord Crewe venturing out on one of his late-night visits to Mrs. Neel, she had no reason to believe that he had curtailed his nocturnal activities. Thinking about the voluptuous innkeeper, and what she did with the earl, was not something Aurelia liked to ponder.

Indeed, she tried not to think about the earl at all—although of course that was difficult to do when they had dinner together each night and often encountered each other during the day while working on the various samples.

Oddly, she did not see him as much as she had feared. In fact, sometimes she wondered if *he* was avoiding her every bit as sedulously as she was avoiding him.

But that was ridiculous.

It was far more likely that overseeing an entire island—as well as vast holdings on the mainland—absorbed a great deal of his time. His naturalist work, for all that it appeared to consume him, was only a small part of his responsibilities. In any case, Aurelia was relieved that she only had to deal with his disquieting person at the evening meals.

She would have been entirely content at her new job if she had only received some word from home. But thus far, Aurelia had written four letters to Queen's Bower and had received no answer from Phoebe, Katie, or Doddy, her three siblings who still lived with their parents.

Aurelia had begun to wonder if her mother was intercepting her letters and burning them.

And that was why she was sitting at her desk, already dressed for bed, staring at a blank sheet of paper and contemplating writing to the Countess of Addiscombe to see why her letters were going unanswered.

Every time she tried to start the letter her mother's final words rang in her ears.

After almost an hour with still nothing on the page other than, *Dear Mama,* Aurelia sighed and set down her quill. She would wait one more week. And then, if there was nothing, she would put aside her pride and pain and write to her mother.

Relieved to have pushed that decision off for another day, she turned to the sketch that was her current project. The subject was an indigo bunting and there was something about the angle of the bird's foot that was not quite right.

Aurelia turned to the copy of the specimen index she'd made—which showed every sample and its location—and flipped through until she found the indigo bunting.

It was in the library workroom, which meant she wouldn't need to go down to the armory, which gave her the shivers—and not just because it was cold.

Aurelia glanced at the clock on the mantle and saw it was half past eleven. There would be nobody about at this hour. She slipped on her heavy flannel dressing gown, slid a thick woolen shawl over her shoulders, and shoved her feet into the sheepskin slippers that had been a gift from her brother Doddy several years back. They were quite hideous, but Doddy had made them with his own hands and she simply could not bring herself to throw them away.

The only sound as she traveled through the empty corridors toward the library was the occasional shifting of ancient timbers. The castle was positively frigid even in the middle of summer, she hated to think of how cold it would be come December.

When she opened the door to the library, she was startled to see Lord Crewe seated at one of the trestle tables.

He glanced up at her, his vague gaze quickly sharpening as he removed his spectacles and stood. "Good evening, Miss Burton."

"I'm sorry to disturb you," Aurelia said, intensely aware of her less-than-attractive apparel. She hesitated on the threshold. "I can always return later when—"

"Nonsense. Come in. There is more than enough room for the two of us."

Aurelia stepped inside and closed the door behind her. Only then did she realize why he looked different: he was not wearing his eyepatch. And there was an eye in the socket. Why… it looked perfect—exactly like the other one!

The earl smiled, and Aurelia swallowed. Yet *again* she had been caught gawking.

"Have a seat." He gestured to the table across from him, the one closer to the fire. "There is a chill in here."

"Thank you," she murmured, setting down her sketch before turning toward the glass cases and speedily locating number sixty-one.

Aurelia spun the stool two turns until it was high enough and then sat. She peeked at the earl, but his face was tilted downward. He had donned his spectacles, with lenses for both left and right eye, she couldn't help noticing. She could not see the left eye, but the glimpse she'd caught of it had certainly *looked* real. But if that were so, then why did he wear a patch?

He shifted in his chair, cleared his throat, and began to look up.

Aurelia instantly lowered her gaze to her work.

Work. That is what you came down here to do. Not stare at your employer.

The tiny indigo bunting in the glass case had been expertly preserved— Arthur Montgomery was a master of his craft—the body mounted with wires that evoked flight so convincingly the creature looked alive.

Her gaze slid from the colorful body to the feet.

Ah, yes. She bent closer, studying the scaley appendages and referring to her drawing. She'd mistaken the angle slightly. Using gum elastic, she carefully rubbed away the light pencil lines, brushed off the detritus, and began to draw.

Within moments, Aurelia was lost in her art.

***

You should leave.

Yes, Roland knew he should. It was unwise to be alone in a room with Miss Burton at any time, but especially in the middle of the night, when the boundary between propriety and indiscretion was tissue thin.

Even though he knew what he *should* do, there he sat, suddenly wide awake and shockingly tumescent while Miss Burton appeared to be insultingly unaware of him and engaged in her work.

Roland was amused by his own frustrated desire. When had he last needed to curb his appetites? Long ago. Perhaps even as far back as his first London Season—a vapid, tedious waste of his time that he had agreed upon to please his father. The bargain had been simple: for each dreadful Season that Roland agreed to endure, his father would fund an expedition. Nothing so interesting as Africa or the Americas, but the earl had paid for Roland's nine-month stay in Greece and then an eight-month excursion to Ireland.

After Roland had accumulated enough information to compile his first book—which had sold more than eight hundred copies, enough to cover production and fund his next expedition—his time in the Great Marriage Mart had been over, much to his father's displeasure.

As long ago as it had been, Roland could still recall the *look-but-don't-touch* frustration he had felt at *ton* functions. At every ball and Venetian breakfast, there had been dozens of beautiful young women clothed in gowns designed to whet a man's appetite. And the most an admirer could hope for was the touch of a woman's hand with two pairs of gloves separating flesh.

Roland was feeling a similar frustration right now as he stared at Miss Burton's ridiculously ugly mobcap and the glimpses of rich brown hair that peeked out from beneath it. It was like seeing an Old Master painting that had been clouded by time and destroyed by milky bloom. Why in God's name did women wear such appalling garments?

Her gaze suddenly lifted to his. She was lost in thought but her rich hazel eyes rapidly sharpened when she caught him staring.

She stole a glance at his false orb and then quickly looked back.

"No, it is not real," he said, amused when her cheeks flared to life.

Her expression was one of mortification and Roland suspected that she was not accustomed to being discountenanced. It was unfortunate for her that he enjoyed how lively and full of passion she became when her rigid composure slipped.

"You needn't feel embarrassed for looking, Miss Burton. Nor for asking questions. Curiosity is a sign of a healthy mind."

"It also killed the cat."

He laughed. "Ah, but we are not talking about a pussy, are we?"

The slight notch that formed between her eyes told him that she did not understand the double entendre. Roland really was a bastard.

She set down her quill and pulled her ugly shawl tighter, as if girding herself. "It is very lifelike."

"Except for the fact that it does not move."

"Oh," she said, her brows knitting. "Of course that would be the case. Is it ceramic?"

"Glass. A man in Venice makes them for me. I have several, and they are made specifically for my eye socket."

"Why do you cover it with the patch?"

"I have discovered that people are even more discomposed by an unmoving eye than the black patch."

"Then why—" she broke off. "I'm sorry, I should not be asking these questions."

"Why not?"

"Well… it *is* a sensitive topic."

"Not to me. It is true," he said when her expression turned skeptical. "I deeply regret the loss of function, of course, but I don't worry about my scars. To answer your question, I wear the eye to protect the socket. Without support and structure, the bone would eventually sag and become distorted and that would cause other problems.”

“I hadn’t considered that.” She hesitated and then asked the question he expected her to ask. “Will you tell me how it happened—if you don’t mind?”

“I don’t mind. Unfortunately, I do not recall a great deal of what occurred that night.” He gestured to the left side of his face. “The first strike from the panther knocked me to the ground and I hit my head on a rock. I was unconscious when the beast clawed my arm, so I thankfully recall none of that. The last thing I *do* remember clearly before being attacked was lifting the flap to my wife’s tent and seeing the creature on top of her.” Roland omitted the part about the bare arse of the man who’d been fucking Jane at the time, his body between the big cat and Roland’s wife.

“I had grabbed my gun when I heard the screams coming from her tent. But when I pulled the trigger, it did not fire.” *That* fact more than almost anything else except Jane’s death, haunted him. Roland never left his gun unloaded on an expedition unless he was cleaning it. He’d gone over it and over it and still could not understand why that night he had forgotten to load it that night. He shook the thought from his head.

He saw she was waiting and continued, “The panther left off its attack of my wife when it noticed me. I took a swing at it with my gun, but it was far more dexterous with its paws. One of the bearers shot the animal while it was mauling me on the ground. The kill was messy and the animal was badly damaged, but then you’ve seen the creature. It was fortunate Arthur was there and did what he could to preserve the hide.”

She suddenly smiled and the expression made her so beautiful that Roland felt as if he’d just been kicked in the chest. “You are a naturalist even in the face of death.”

He smiled. “Yes, I suppose so.”

“You must have been very far from any doctor or surgeon?”

“We were hundreds of miles from any settlement.”

“How were you able to treat your wounds?”

“I was lucky that one of the bearers knew enough to save me.” He traced his fingers lightly along the four jagged black lines. “The man—Micco—is a Seminole. The Seminoles are a people who only recently settled in Las Floridas after the original inhabitants were all but eradicated by disease. In Micco’s tribe, battle wounds are considered a source of pride, not something to be ashamed of. The black in the wound is the result of the poultice he used. Rather than healing to leave no scars, the poultice enhanced it." He smiled. "Micco believed he was doing me an honor."

"The scars are not unattractive—" she broke off, distress flickering across her face as she struggled to find the words she wanted. "I just meant—"

"Thank you," he said. "I am pleased you think so. As I mentioned earlier, I do not find the scars a burden, but I wish my arm and eye still functioned properly. Still, I was far more fortunate than my wife." *Or her lover*, he added silently.

"I'm sorry to keep staring, but that eye is so remarkably lifelike."

"You may look at it closer if you like. Or I could pop it out and hand it to—"

"You needn't do that," she hastily assured him. "But I would like to look at it more closely."

Roland slid the blazing candelabra on the table closer to him. "Come here and sit on this chair." He nudged the empty chair beside him.

She was as hesitant as a fawn as she came around the table and then perched on the very edge of the seat.

Roland leaned closer to her, watching her face while her gaze was focused on the glass orb.

Her eyes slid to his real eye and her throat flexed. Her breathing hitched and her lips parted, her chest rising and falling faster as she held his gaze, her pupils telling him the truth of what she thought about him.

He smiled and her eyes lowered to his mouth before jumping back up.

It was the oddest moment, as if time had slowed. There was just Roland and the desirable—and forbidden—woman across from him. Out of the corner of his vision he saw her fingers twitch—as if she wanted to touch something. Him?

"You can feel the scars, if you like. You won't hurt me."

She jolted slightly and swallowed again, her delicate nostrils flaring. For a moment, he thought he'd broken the strange spell that charged the air between them and worried she might flee like the deer she so much resembled.

But then she reached for him.

***

The air felt thick and hot, and it was difficult for Aurelia to fill her lungs. She was close enough to the earl to feel his warm breath and the heat of his big body.

Suddenly, she was assaulted by a powerful and utterly mad urge to bury her face in his broad chest and just…

Well, Aurelia didn't know what she would *just* do. Die of mortification, most likely.

She stiffened her spine and swallowed, both to rid her mouth of the copious moisture flooding it and also to make sure she still *could* swallow, because her body didn't feel like it belonged to her any longer.

It had been reckless to come so close to him, but there had been no way to resist. The glass eye had only been an excuse to get near him. And now that she was beside him, she only wanted to get closer.

Foolish, reckless girl! A voice chided in her head.

She was, but she could not bring herself to regret her impulse.

She studied the glass orb, the intricate shards of blues and grays creating an iris that was a work of art.

Her gaze slid to the real eye and her breathing, already ragged, stuttered.

The Venetian artist's skill was amazing, but it could not compare to that of the Almighty. Not only were there a thousand subtle shades in his rapidly darkening eye, but it contained pulsating, intoxicating *life*.

Aurelia's audacious behavior—inching ever closer to Lord Crewe and boldly staring—didn't seem ill-mannered so much as intimate. He had invited her to do so, hadn't he?

She allowed her gaze to drift to the savage scars that truly did enhance rather than mar his bold features.

The distance between the four jagged lines was awe-inspiring. Aurelia had seen the beast, of course, but she had been captivated by its height and length, not its feet. She now realized the panther's paw must be the size of her hand, or even larger. Her fingers twitched to touch the raised black scars and test her assumption.

"You can feel the scars, if you like. You won't hurt me."

His voice was low and velvety and rumbled through her.

Touch him?

Aurelia looked from his faint smile to his eye to the entrancing left side of his face.

And then she reached for him.

Part of her could not believe she was behaving so daringly. Touching another person's bare skin—especially a male person—was not something she had ever done before. She embraced her sisters and brother, of course, but Lord Crewe was all but a stranger.

Her hand shook slightly, but she did not pull back. Instead, she spread her fingers enough that the four of them could rest on the black lines. The scars appeared harshly rigid but the skin was soft and warm.

His cheek rose slightly beneath her fingers and she saw that he was smiling.

She began to lift her fingers but his hand, quick as a snake, closed around her wrist and he held her there, gently, but firmly.

"The scars go further," he murmured, guiding her hand around to the side of his head. A lock of sun-kissed gold hair shifted and Aurelia saw that his ear lobe was missing and the slashes carried on into his hair.

Aurelia carded her fingers into the thick warm silk, the sensitive pads easily finding and tracking the scratches, which diminished from two to one and then none.

Her gaze moved to the black line on his chin and jaw. "If it had been a bit lower—"

"Then I would not be sitting here right now," he said, his other hand coming up to cup her cheek. "And I would have missed out on the pleasure of meeting you, Miss Burton." His fingers caressed her lightly.

"That would have… er, I'm sure there would have been… um, more important things you'd have missed," she babbled.

He leaned closer, his thumb caressing her lower lip. "I can't think of any right now." And then he angled his head and kissed her.

Aurelia had been kissed—twice—years before, but those had been, by necessity, quick and furtive, mere pecks stolen behind the shelter of a potted palm at a *ton* ball.

This kiss was… something completely different.

She was distantly aware that he'd released her wrist as he twisted in his chair to face her, his knee pushing between hers and parting her legs. He framed her face with his large, warm hands as his mouth explored hers. He didn't just press his lips against hers, he teased and toyed with her mouth, first the lower lip, which he gently sucked, and then the upper, which he lightly nipped. That clever, mobile mouth of his was every bit as sensual as it looked.

Aurelia inched closer and closer to him, opening her thighs wider around his leg. The little bit of caution that remained to her fled into the darkness of the sleeping castle when his hard knee bumped her swollen sex.

She whimpered at the arousing friction and the earl made a low, approving growl, his hands moving lightly over her throat and shoulders, and settling on her waist.

Aurelia slid her hands up over his chest, marveling at the hard, solid body beneath the fine clothing.

The earl tilted her head, kissing her more deeply. And then he pulled her closer, his knee brushing against the most sensitive part of her and sending a tantalizing ripple of pleasure through her body. This time, Aurelia rocked her hips to chase the thrilling sensation, her hands dropping to his hips, bliss building in her womb with each roll of her hips until—

The earl suddenly broke the kiss, pulling his head back to stare at her with a startled look on his face, breathing heavily through parted lips.

She leaned closer, all but riding his thigh, but he cupped her face and held her immobile. "No," he whispered, and then he gave her cheek one last caress and lowered his hand.

Aurelia wanted to grab him and yank him back—why was he stopping? But that's when she noticed that she was *already* grabbing him, both her hands fisting the skintight pantaloons that hugged his thighs.

She jerked her hands back as if he were on fire and scooted back on the chair.

The earl cleared his throat, sat back, and pulled the black leather patch down over his eye. A faint smile curved his lips, but it wasn't the usual devilish or sensual smirk. Instead, it was… wistful.

"It is late, Miss Burton. You should go to your bed before I do something we both regret."

Chapter 9

A urelia did not sleep a wink that night.

She desperately regretted not staying in her room and writing the blasted letter to her mother rather than what she had ended up doing.

She had kissed Lord Crewe.

That's not all you did with him…

She winced at the memory of how she'd rubbed herself against him like a—like a bitch in heat, there was no denying that is how she had behaved. She'd seen female dogs behaving in such a way in the past and had looked away in embarrassment.

And now she had turned into one.

Aurelia groaned.

Everyone knew what decent society thought about women who went about kissing and rubbing against men. If Lord Crewe had not been a gentleman and sent her off when he had, who knew how much more might have happened?

You would have mounted his thigh, that is what.

"Oh, *do* shut up!" she snapped, burying her flaming face in a pillow.

Strangely, it wasn't the thought of that sensual rubbing that kept her up for the rest of the night, but what *might* have happened if Lord Crewe had not put a stop to it all.

As a result of all her tossing and turning, Aurelia rose later than usual and went down to the breakfast room with a heavy, muzzy head and was barely able to keep her eyes open as she gulped down a pot of tea and two pieces of toast before returning to her room and promptly dropping into a dreamless nap.

An hour later she awoke somewhat refreshed, until she recalled that she had kissed and groped her employer.

"*Urgh.*" She shook away the thought and tidied up her hair and clothing before marching determinedly down to the specimen room.

It was, thankfully, unoccupied and she managed to find her samples and scurry back up to her own workroom, where she put in a full day of work, despite her sluggish start.

She took a long, solitary walk before dinner, hoping to clear her head. Instead, the time alone only gave her more opportunity to ponder and fret and work herself into a lather before dinner.

What she should have done was go for a ride with Lady Celsa, instead. At least that way she would have spent the time fending off adolescent barbs rather than engaging in introspection.

For once, she wasn't the first to arrive for dinner. Indeed, she dragged her feet so long that she was even a few moments late.

"I apologize," she murmured when she slipped into the room.

"No harm done, Miss Burton," his lordship said easily.

Aurelia didn't know how she had expected him to behave—embarrassed? Amused? But he was no different from usual.

She blushed and stammered a bit for the first half-hour as he peppered her with questions the way he always did, but by the time the meal was over she was beginning to think that that she had imagined the entire episode.

Or maybe he was such a rake that something as innocent as a kiss— although there was nothing innocent about the way he kissed—was scarcely worth remembering for him.

Whatever the reason, the first and most awkward meeting was over.

Aurelia was still a bit concerned the following evening when she went down to dinner—not late, but not too early, either—that there might be some residual awkwardness but that meal, too, passed smoothly.

And so it went, day after day, until three weeks had passed and Aurelia was convinced that the kiss had been an especially vivid dream.

Even so, she made every effort to avoid being alone with his lordship. Not because she feared that he would ravish her, but because she couldn't seem to trust her normally prudent judgment whenever she was in proximity to him. The kiss might have been a dream, but there was no denying that she wanted it to happen again.

Badly…

Aurelia shook herself. She had been daydreaming. Again.

She wrenched her thoughts from her favorite obsession and stared at the painting on the easel, her brush suspended above it. She blinked her eyes and realized they were dry from staring. Instead of painting, she had been daydreaming.

Again.

She sighed and lowered her hand. A glance at the clock showed it was only half past eleven. Normally she would work for hours more, but she simply could not make herself continue. At least not without making a mess of her current painting.

She had been making excellent progress on the paintings and knew the earl had sent another batch of ten off to Edinburgh a few days ago. Things were going well. Why was she allowing a brief kiss weeks ago to consume her? It was time to put the matter completely out of her mind.

It was also time to take a day for herself. A few evenings ago, during dinner, she had mentioned her interest in the marine life of the area and both the earl and Arthur had given her directions to the best rock pools on the island. Today she would investigate at least one of their suggestions.

After she'd finished cleaning her brushes and putting away her paints, she changed from her morning gown into her habit and made her way down to the stables.

Normally she would have asked Celsa to ride with her, but it was only noon and the girl would still be at her lessons.

She was waiting for one of the stable lads to saddle Black Prince when Lord Crewe rode into the courtyard.

"Ah, Miss Burton. Fancy seeing you out and about," he said, smiling down at her from his perch on the imposing gray stallion. "Are you finished for the day?"

"My work was not satisfactory so I decided I need some time away," Aurelia said, wishing she didn't sound quite so defensive.

"You are an artist—not a drone tinting prints on an assembly line." He dismounted with the fluid grace of a man who'd spent a great deal of his life in the saddle. Even off his horse he towered over her, his glossy boots, black leathers, and exquisitely fitted coat making her feel gauche, although she knew her habit was still quite stylish.

"You are headed out to do some exploring?" he asked, chiseled features saturnine as he stared down at her, his lips curved into a slight smirk, as if he knew how diligently she had been avoiding him.

"That was my intention."

A slow smile spread across his face. "I shall join you."

"But… didn't you just return?"

"Yes."

She cleared her throat and gestured to her satchel. "I wasn't planning to ride so much as sketch. I was going to visit some of the rock pools you and Arth—er, Mr. Montgomery suggested. I believe the tide is right?"

"Yes, it is not quite low." He regarded her with an amused, overly familiar look that made Aurelia feel as if she was not wearing enough clothing. It also made her think about *his* clothing. And what was beneath it. Was he still going to see Mary Neel? Were they—

She scowled. What on earth was wrong with her to be thinking such things?

"Is something wrong, Miss Burton?" he asked her. "You look… flushed."

Aurelia blurted the first thing that came to mind. "Er, I wondered if it would be acceptable to ask one of the servants to row me over to the mainland?"

"Tomorrow?"

"Oh. Well, I am not sure when," she dithered. "Perhaps not tomorrow as I am not working today, so that would be *two* days of no work, but—"

"Your work has been exemplary, Miss Burton. Take off as much time as you like."

Aurelia flushed at his praise. "Thank you."

"Going to visit your friend?"

"My friend?"

"Sir Gideon."

"Oh. No, I had not planned to call on him."

Thankfully Jemmy led out Black Prince before his lordship could probe any further.

"Allow me," the earl said, and then lifted Aurelia into the saddle as swiftly and easily as he had done the last time they'd ridden together. Unlike the last time, however, the saddle had already been adjusted for her use, so he merely smiled up at her and then mounted his horse. "We should make haste so you have enough time to explore before the tide changes."

"It is very kind of you to take the time to escort me," she said as they cantered down the long driveway side-by-side.

"It is my pleasure."

Aurelia stole looks at him from beneath her lashes. Although the scenery around her was wild and beautiful Lord Crewe was the only thing she could look at when he was at hand.

Or think about.

Over and over her gaze slid sideways without her permission.

His pale blond hair glinted like gold beneath his high-crowned hat. His unscathed right profile was facing her and she marveled at how different he looked without the scars. Not for the first time did she think that he resembled a starker and more powerful version of his cousin. Lord Crewe and his cousin shared many of the same features, but the man beside her looked like a savage Viking invader rather than Arthur's gossamer angel.

His black riding boots were polished to a glossy shine, the leather closely molded to his calves. His breeches were far too supple to be buckskin—perhaps they were deer, or even doe. Aurelia had never seen black riding leathers before. Nor had she ever seen any that fit so… lovingly. Perhaps the current fad was for skintight black breeches? It had, after all, been eight years since Aurelia had last been to London and seen the fashions, so his clothing might well be all the mode.

Or, far more likely, this was a style of the earl's devising, something he wore just because he knew how well it suited him. Not that he wouldn't have looked striking even if he'd been garbed in sackcloth.

Aurelia stole a glance at the path to make sure she wasn't about to ride off a cliff, and then pulled her gaze back and continued her exploration. He held the reins in his right hand while his left rested on one well-formed thigh, gloved in black, just like the rest of his ensemble.

Her gaze lingered on his broad shoulders and then her eyes continued their journey upward.

And ran right into Lord Crewe's ice-blue eye and smiling lips.

Aurelia's head whipped around, her face on fire. She had blushed more in the last month than she'd done in the previous five years. Could a person die from blushing too much? If so, her life was definitely in peril.

Thankfully, he did not say anything until they reached the well-rutted road that led to the west side of the island.

"Have you published anything about the islands on this part of the coast?" she asked, captivated by the beauty around them as they crested the rise.

"I must show you some of the journals from my boyhood. I made it my goal to document every living creature on the island." He chuckled. "Well, except the human inhabitants."

From the gossip Aurelia had heard, the earl had been quite thorough when it came to the young, female population.

"But as for publishing anything, no. I suppose I am simply too familiar with the island at this point." He cut her a quick glance, his grin disarming. "And my greatest character defect is a propensity to get bored."

"I find it difficult to believe it is your *greatest* defect," she retorted, and then bit her lip.

He turned to her slowly, his eye wide.

"I'm sorry, my lord, that was—"

"Truthful. Brutally so." He laughed. "Indeed, I'll wager enough people on the island—and on the mainland—have been eager enough to inform you of my many defects. Talbot among them."

"That is the third time you've mentioned Sir Gideon in a sneering fashion."

"No? Is it really? How interesting that you are keeping a tally."

She ignored his taunt. "Sir Gideon helped me fend off the ruffians and then rowed me to the island. There is no deeper connection."

"He would like one."

"I find it difficult to believe that you discerned that much from a ten-minute conversation."

"Men recognize that sort of thing in one another. We are much like dogs—or wolves, if one wishes to elevate oneself to a more interesting level—who are constantly scenting one another and seeking to establish dominion. We humans are more sophisticated than other mammals, but when fear, anger, lust, or any of the more compelling emotions are in play, then our less civilized, more primitive self comes to the fore."

"And that primitive self is what allowed you to *smell* Sir Gideon's interest in me?"

He laughed. "Perhaps *smell* wasn't the best word. But I could see what he wanted." His gaze turned hot. "Because I want it, too."

Memories of *that* night and their kiss—which she had worked so hard and diligently to repress—suddenly flooded her. Aurelia opened her mouth, but then realized she had nothing to say, and closed it again.

She faced forward, staring at the beauty all around her, but only seeing the man at her side.

***

A short time later Aurelia was crouched on a rock, staring intently into a tide pool, and sketching like mad when something shockingly cold engulfed her ankle boots.

She yelped and lurched to her feet so abruptly that she slipped off the rock and promptly staggered backward, dropping her sketchpad into the water.

Hands closed around Aurelia's waist and she was suddenly moving through the air. "Wha—"

"The water is coming in fast," Lord Crewe said, his voice terse as he deftly swung her to the side of his body and hitched her on his hip as if she were an infant—an extremely big one—his large hand splayed beneath her buttocks and holding her tightly. "I should have been paying attention to the tide," he muttered, trudging through water that was deep enough to reach his calves and staring down at his feet, which were barely visible in the churning froth. "The way you were leaning over that rock pool I'm surprised you weren't swept right in."

Aurelia was too aware of his hand on her bottom and her spread sex pressed against his hard hip to generate a sensible response. He was carrying her along as if she weighed no more than her satchel.

Her satchel.

"Where is my satchel?" she cried, feeling her chest for the strap that was usually across her torso.

"You left it with the horses," he reminded her. "But I'm afraid your sketchbook was lost before I got to you." Lord Crewe suddenly staggered and Aurelia bit back a startled squeak as one of his legs sank into what must have been a pool.

"Damnation," he muttered, pushing himself out of the hole, his arm like an iron bar around her. He took a few steps and then shrugged her up higher on his hip and soldiered on.

Once again Aurelia had to bite her lip, but this time to hold back a gasp of pleasure as his hip rubbed against exactly the right spot.

Oh Lord, she silently prayed.

"Here we are," the earl said, his voice slightly breathless. But instead of putting her down, he turned to her, his eye squinting against the sun, only a slice of icy blue iris visible. "Well, hell," he muttered, his lips twisting into an odd smile.

And then he lowered his mouth over hers.

***

You bastard, Crewe!

The voice in his head sounded like his cousin's—if Arthur had ever used such vulgar language. Roland *was* a bastard for wanting Miss Burton. And an even bigger one for acting on his desire.

His arm ached from carrying her, but by God, she was a delicious armful— tall and slim and delicate with soft, gentle curves that fit against his body in a way that felt shockingly… right.

Her lips were as plush and soft as he remembered and, just like their all-too-brief kiss in the library, her response was adorably eager and innocent, once again driving home the fact that she knew next to nothing about kissing.

Because she was an innocent.

That realization had stopped him that night, but it didn't do a damned thing right now.

She tasted, smelled, and felt bloody intoxicating. And then she gave a soft moan and pressed her mouth against his, and Roland needed more.

He let her slide down off his hip, her soft body grinding against his far harder torso. Rather than release her when her feet touched the ground, he embraced her slim back with one arm and cupped her face with his free hand, tilting her until he could reach her better.

When her hands came up to rest on his hips he slid his tongue between her primly pursed lips. She gasped at the bold move, but then pressed herself closer rather than pulling away.

Encouraged, Roland invaded her with all the finesse and gusto of one of his ancestors ransacking a village, his self-control rapidly splintering as he explored her soft wet heat.

Her hands tightened on his hips, her fingers digging into his flesh and pulling him against her. It was his turn to moan when his erect cock pushed against her belly.

She stiffened and lifted her mouth from his, meeting his gaze with eyes so wide and shocked he might have laughed if he wasn't so bloody hungry for her.

Frustration and restraint warred within him.

Grab her and kiss her and take her! Frustration yelled.

Be thankful she ended this, Sober Restraint counseled.

Yes, it was a damned good thing that she, at least, possessed sense, because Roland didn't seem to have any. Debauching his virginal employee was not something he should be doing now. Or ever.

He forced a calm smile and met her chaotic gaze. "Are you—"

She grabbed his head, yanked it low, and claimed *his* mouth.

Roland's moment of good sense dissipated in a blink and he submitted joyously to her clumsy explorations, reveling in the sensation of her body against his. This time, rather than flinch away when she rubbed against his erection, she *ground* herself against him, the sinuous action the sensual caress of an experienced seductress.

He stroked over her soft curves with his hands, his caresses earning an encouraging moan. Perhaps his initial belief that she was innocent—based on her clumsy kissing—was wrong?

Perhaps she's only had lovers who do not care for kissing? a third voice—this one called Selfish Delusion—chimed in.

Roland had heard more than one man say he found kissing pointless—or even unpleasant. If that were true, then maybe she *wasn't* a virgin?

Emboldened by the thought, he pulled her closer, his hands revisiting the glory of her arse, which he'd probably clutched so hard earlier that there would be bruises.

If there were any marks, Roland wanted to see them. Lick them. Bite them.

Rather than rebuff him, his bold caresses appeared to incite her and she slid her own small hands down his waist to his buttocks, fingers squeezing lightly, then harder, the tips digging into him in a way that made him growl.

Obviously, he had been wrong about her lack of experience. Sorely mistaken…

He stroked back up her sides until he could cup her breasts, and then he grazed his thumbs over the fitted habit, wishing like hell she wasn't swathed neck to feet in wool. He stroked harder, until he could feel the tightly pebbled tips.

She jolted more violently than she'd done earlier.

Just like a virgin might do…

Blast and damn! What in the hell was he doing? This was his bloody employee—whose skill and artistry he needed far more than a quick fondle and fuck.

Roland cursed beneath his breath and stepped away, breaking all contact with her too-beguiling body.

Chapter 10

Lord Crewe dropped his hands from Aurelia abruptly and stepped away from her.

The sudden rejection was like a slap, bringing Aurelia back to herself. She'd been groping him. Mauling him, really. What had she been thinking?

Aurelia wanted to crawl under a rock and hide, but she forced herself to face him.

His eye, so dark and filled with desire only moments before—was icy blue and distant, making her wish that she had opted for the rock, after all.

And then—shockingly—he dropped his hand to his tight breeches and squeezed the thick ridge hard enough to make the veins and tendons stand out on the back of his hand.

Aurelia's jaw sagged. "What—what are you doing?"

He barked an unamused laugh. "What is necessary." When he lowered his hand, his erection had become less prominent, but hadn't disappeared entirely.

He took her chin in his fingers and tilted her, moving her gaze from his groin to his face. "If you look at my cock that way, I shan't be able to hang on to my good intentions."

Her face scalded at the word *cock*. "Wh-what way was I looking at… it?" As much as she wanted to, she could not make her mouth form the wicked word.

"You know what way."

Aurelia did know: yearningly, lustfully, *desperately*. All three were emotions she had known nothing about until meeting Lord Crewe. The powerful feelings were shocking and frightening, but they also made her feel more alive than anything she had ever experienced.

She didn't just want to kiss and embrace him again, she wanted to see his *cock*—and the rest of his body, too—and touch and squeeze and stroke the hard ridge, but not as cruelly as he had just done.

And of course she would have liked to sketch not just *it*, but all of him.

The earl gave another snort at whatever he saw on her face and turned away. "I will fetch the horses."

Aurelia flooded with shame. While she was fantasizing about his body, he was trying to get away from her.

She squeezed her eyes shut briefly, wishing she were anywhere else but on that beach.

He led Black Prince over without speaking and silently lifted her into the saddle, waiting until she'd shifted her soaking wet habit to the side and hooked her knee properly before mounting his own horse.

The longer they rode, the more mortified Aurelia felt. What was it about this man? She had lived to the age of five-and-twenty without behaving like such a trollop. Indeed, she had rebuffed an untold number of advances during her single London Season, and even in the tiny village of Little Sissingdon she'd had to repeatedly reject unwanted male attention.

Never in a hundred years would she have imagined that *she* could be an aggressor.

Never had she imagined that *her* advances would be rebuffed.

It was beyond humiliating.

"I am leaving in a few days."

The earl's words pulled her from her mortified misery.

"I must go to Edinburgh and then to London. I will be gone some weeks."

Aurelia had nothing to say.

"I am leaving all my journals at your disposal. Arthur is a good source of information as he saw a great many of the animals in their native environment and kept his own notes about colors, habits, et cetera, to help him with his recreations. He can help describe foliage, behavior, that sort of thing."

"Thank you." It was all she could manage and it earned a cursory glance from him.

Not until the stables were in sight did he speak again. "I do hope what happened back there does not sour you on working for me, Miss Burton. I promise I will not importune you like that again." He reined in his horse when she didn't answer. "Stop a moment," he ordered.

Aurelia sighed and did likewise.

"Miss Burton?" he said, forcing her to look at him. "Will what happened pose a problem for you?"

"There is no problem." She was going to leave it at that, but something spurred her to add, "And if you are going to apologize then I should too. You weren't the only one who did some *importuning*. Let us just forget that it ever occurred. I am happy with my work and have no wish to leave."

He nodded and those were the last words on the subject.

Indeed, that was the last conversation Aurelia had with the earl for the next two days. She did not even see him at dinner as he took his meals in his chambers while he prepared for his journey.

And three days later, without having seen him again, the Earl of Crewe was gone.

***

The day after Lord Crewe's departure Aurelia was seated at the breakfast table, pushing food around her plate and feeling decidedly out of sorts when Beekman entered.

"This just came for you, Miss Burton." He held out a salver with a single piece of mail on it.

"Thank you," she said as she examined the envelope. The handwriting wasn't familiar and there was no return direction.

Aurelia opened it and glanced down at the signature in surprise. It was from Larissa Clifford.

Dear Miss Burton,

No doubt this letter will take you by surprise, but I have repeatedly regretted my hasty and uncivil behavior toward you that day on the beach. You put your safety at risk to help me and I was… abrupt. I wanted to let you know that I deeply appreciate your actions and wish I had told you—and Sir Gideon—as much that day.

The woman I have been caring for is very ill. I have agreed with her daughter to remain in Balcrewe until I am no longer needed. I am not sure when that will be, but I suspect I shall be leaving to join my sisters in London sometime near the end of the year. I am free on Tuesdays every week, so if you find yourself on the mainland on any Tuesday, please do call on me.

With respect and gratitude,

Larissa Clifford

She folded the letter and looked up to find Arthur watching her. Sometimes the man was so quiet and self-effacing that she forgot he was even in the room.

"Good news?" he said.

"Hmm?"

He gestured to the letter. "You looked tired before reading that. Now you are smiling."

"I do feel better," she said, and then added, "I think I will go to the mainland today. Do you think Charles or one of the other footmen might row me over? I don't feel confident enough in my abilities to try it yet," she explained, feeling a bit guilty for pulling one of the footmen away from the castle just to row her across.

"I have a few errands myself. I can row you over if you like."

"That is very kind of you, thank you."

"It is my pleasure, Aurelia." The bright red spots that always seemed to mark his pale cheeks darkened and spread at her words. What a gentle soul he was—especially when compared to his cousin. They might share similar coloring and builds, but the two men honestly had nothing but a mutual interest in nature in common.

"Would an hour be too long to wait?" he asked. "I have a few things I need to see to."

"That sounds perfect."

He turned to his rather bland breakfast of boiled potatoes and sheep's milk. He ate the same breakfast every day and avoided most of the richer dishes at dinner.

Aurelia studied him in the bright light of the breakfast room. The color in his cheeks appeared feverish rather than healthy, making her think, yet again, that he must be ailing from something. Or perhaps his odd coloring was the result of his awful diet. She had read somewhere that Lord Byron ate similar food to slim himself. Surely Arthur could not be doing that as he was already too slender?

Whatever the reason for his diet, she doubted he would welcome any prying from her.

Instead, she said, "I don't suppose you know where a woman named Miss Clifford lives?"

His handsome face creased into a look of disapproval. "You must be talking about the women who have been staying with Judith Pomeroy just outside the village, but I'd heard they'd all left." He fixed her with a stern look. "They are the former Earl of Daventry's daughters. Were you aware of that?"

"I know who they are."

"What do you want with them?"

She recoiled at his hostile tone. "I wanted to visit Miss Larissa Clifford before she leaves to join her sisters."

"Why?"

Aurelia frowned.

Instantly, his expression lightened. "I am sorry if that sounded abrupt."

She wanted to tell him that her reasons for the visit were none of his affair, but it seemed churlish, so she settled for saying, "This letter is from her. She has asked me to call and I think she must have assumed I knew where she lived."

"I know you are an independent sort of young woman, Aurelia," he said, using a gently chiding tone more suitable for speaking to a puppy that has just made a mess on the carpet. "But while you are our guest, I feel that we are responsible for you. To that end, I should point out that it is unwise to associate with such women."

Aurelia's temper, which was slow to rouse, reared its head at his condescending tone. "I am honored by your concern," she lied. "But I'm afraid I fail to see the danger in visiting a single woman."

"Any association with those females can only damage your standing in our small community."

"You do know that they were not accused of treason. It was their father who was guilty."

"Such rottenness in a family is not dissimilar to sickness in a tree. Sometimes pruning the branches is not sufficient to stop the disease. Sometimes the tree itself must be destroyed. All the way down to the roots."

Aurelia stared. "What are you proposing? That somebody *execute* Miss Clifford and her sisters?"

The flames that had briefly flared in his bright blue eyes guttered at her obvious horror. "Of course I am not advocating such a thing. I am just saying that associating with that sort of person can leave a taint. You are a young woman whose future work will rely on maintaining an excellent reputation." He regarded her kindly, once again looking like the man she knew. Or at least the man she believed she knew. "You are free to do as you choose," he added. And then he smiled. "Indeed, your charitable impulses speak well of your kind heart. You will find Judith Pomeroy's house is just off the road that leads north out of the village. It is a gray cottage with lots of flowers out front."

Aurelia got to her feet. "Please, finish your breakfast," she said when he began to stand.

She was at the door when his voice stopped her. "Aurelia?"

She turned. "Yes?"

"I was only thinking of you and your reputation. I hope we are still friends?"

He looked so concerned—so much like the sweet, somewhat bumbling man she'd come to know—that she smiled and said, "Of course we are still friends."

He gave her a look of relief. "I am glad."

Before Aurelia could open the door, it opened and Beekman entered.

The butler gave Aurelia an apologetic look as he held out the salver which once again held a letter. "I'm terribly sorry, but this must have fallen out of the mailbag and one of the maids only found it a few moments ago."

Aurelia took the letter and gawked at the sender's name: Viscountess Needham?

"Thank you, Beekman," she said, unable to look away from the bold frank of Lord Needham.

Aurelia tore open the letter the minute she reached her room.

Dearest Aurelia,

You are no doubt frantic wondering what has become of us all. I only recently discovered that Mama has been throwing away all the letters I wrote to you over the past months. She did so to keep my marriage a secret—fearing that news of my betrothal to Needham would damage Selina's chances of marrying well while she was in London.

Aurelia gasped. "How could you, Mama!"

Just when I think Mama has done everything she can to surprise me—and not in a good way—she sinks one rung lower.

Which leads me to my news. Yes, Aurelia, I am a married lady. As I'm sure you noticed the frank on this letter, you will have guessed that I married Lord Needham. And before you chide me for sacrificing myself, please let me assure you that his lordship and I deal quite well together. It is true that his dying ex-mistress and illegitimate daughter live at Wych House with us, but I am slowly learning that not everything is exactly what it seems. But more on that later.

As for my husband, Needham is a very generous man—not just to me, but to all of us, Aurelia. He has paid off Papa's debts and set up both Mama and Papa in their own—separate—luxurious establishments. Doddy is off to school soon and Katie has been spending some time with Aunt Agnes in preparation for a Season.

Needham wants you to know that our home is your home and if you wish to return, he will send a post chaise for you immediately. Our days of worrying are over, darling Aurelia. You need only send word and we can have you home before the month is out.

We are leaving shortly for a journey to one of Needham's other properties, but I just wanted to drop you a quick word and assure you that we are all well here in Little Sissingdon and have not forgotten you.

As for London, that is another matter. I have written several times to Selina but received nothing from either her or Hy. I am beginning to wonder if our Aunt Fitzroy conspired with Mama to keep our two sisters ignorant of my marriage. I have written to our aunt and will keep you abreast of any developments on that matter.

I hope to hear from you soon.

Your loving sister,

Phoebe

Aurelia re-read the letter again and then a third time before lowering it.

"How remarkable," she murmured. Not just the marriage, but their mother's shameful behavior. Aurelia never would have believed the countess would sink to such a level as stealing their correspondence.

It was even more difficult to imagine her practical, common-sense sister married to Lord Paul Needham. Although Aurelia had only met the man once, he had seemed positively unpleasant. Oh, not to look at, but his behavior had been cold, callous, and beyond the pale.

Then there was the matter of his mistress and illegitimate child. In her letter, Phoebe seemed remarkably sanguine about her new husband's ex-lover living with them. Aurelia couldn't help thinking about Lord Crewe and *his* love children and wondering if she would be equally understanding in the same position.

But then she recalled Lord Crewe's hasty departure from the island—and his mad, desperate haste to get away from her—and knew she would never have to worry about how she would live with the earl's lovers and children. Because she would never have the chance.

Chapter 11

The sky was cloudless and clear when Arthur rowed her across to the mainland an hour later.

"If we stay until two-thirty will that be enough time for you?" Arthur asked as several men came down the pier to meet their skiff.

"That should be plenty of time. Should we meet back here?"

"That sounds perfect," Arthur said. "Enjoy your afternoon, my dear." If he were still harboring any judgment about whom Aurelia was going to visit, he showed no sign of it.

It took her less than a quarter of an hour to reach Miss Pomeroy's house, which looked well-maintained, although there was something about the tightly drawn drapes that made one think of sadness within.

Rather than knock, Aurelia paused when she reached the front door. It was not like her to hesitate when it came to social matters, but then she had never been in a situation quite like this one before.

Life as the Earl of Addiscombe's daughter meant she'd faced innumerable humiliations over the years—poverty and gossip, to name a few—but never had she been forced to endure the ire of an angry nation.

Larissa Clifford would have suffered agonies that Aurelia could not even imagine. What would Aurelia want if she were in the same situation?

A friend.

Yes, that was certainly true. And it made her decision easy; now more than ever the woman in this house needed friends.

Aurelia knocked and a few minutes later the door opened and Larissa Clifford's face registered a second of surprise before a warm smile creased her pretty face. "Miss Burton! How delighted I am to see you. I felt terrible about how abrupt I was to you that day."

"The situation was terribly upsetting—not to mention dangerous—so I certainly understood your desire to get away as quickly as possible," Aurelia assured her.

"You are generous as well as brave and kind. Please, come inside." She opened the door wider, exposing a small entry hall. "I was just about to have tea. Would you care to join me?"

"I would love to," Aurelia said.

Miss Clifford pulled a wry face. "I hope you don't mind, but we will need to enjoy it in the kitchen as that is where my only table and chairs are."

"I don't mind at all."

"I will lead the way," Miss Clifford said. "I thought selling everything would take a great deal more time than it did," she said over her shoulder. "But I sold the last of the furniture—excepting the bed, nightstand, and armoire in my room—yesterday and this morning a man came to haul it away. It is odd walking through the empty, echoing rooms, but it means I shan't have to bother with getting rid of it all when I am finally ready to leave" She opened the door to a sizeable kitchen and gestured to a battered table and two mismatched chairs. "Have a seat." She filled a kettle from a jug and then hung it on the tripod over the glowing coals.

"I was so glad to get your letter," Aurelia said. "I have thought about you often and considered calling, but time has simply sped by and this is my first visit to the mainland."

"What an adventure to live in that magnificent castle!" Miss Clifford said. "At least it looks magnificent from here, although I've not been fortunate enough to see the inside of it.

"It is a remarkable place and the island itself has a great deal to offer."

"Perhaps I will visit on one of my free days before I leave," Miss Clifford said.

"That would be lovely," Aurelia said. "If you do, there is a delightful little teashop in the village of Crewe where we could meet. You mentioned in your letter that you might be here until the end of the year?"

Miss Clifford took a tin from a cupboard. "The woman I am caring for is a kind old lady—one of the few in the area who did not make life miserable for me and my sisters—and has taken a liking to me, so I feel compelled to stay now that she has become deathly ill. And of course, the money is helpful." She gave a bitter laugh. "Money troubles. Something I never dreamed I'd sink so low to mention in polite company."

"I'm not sure I qualify as *polite company*. There are a good many people who believe my presence at Castle Crewe is exceedingly scandalous."

Miss Clifford laughed. "Yes, you have certainly nudged me off the gossip ladder. I must confess that my sisters and I had not considered how our arrival in such a small village would agitate the local populace. Although I suppose we should have guessed given how ugly things were in our *last* village. In our defense, we did not have a great many options other than Balcrewe."

"And now all your sisters are in London?"

"Yes. My oldest sister, Penelope, went there a few months ago to appeal for help from a cousin on our mother's side." Miss Clifford's mouth flexed into a grim smile. "Our mother was the daughter of a wealthy industrialist. For years her relatives were delighted to claim a connection to the Earl of Daventry. I am sure you can imagine how delighted they are now."

Aurelia was spared from having to answer when the other woman stood and removed the boiling kettle.

"It has been fairly awful here, but you are a bright spot, as is Sir Gideon," she said as she spooned tea into the pot. "And Lord Crewe has been very kind to us, as well."

Aurelia felt a stab of jealousy at the sound of his name. What right did she have to be jealous? Lord Crewe did not belong to her; he did not even want to be near her.

And yet she could not stop herself from asking, "How has Lord Crewe been helpful?"

"Some of the villagers, led by the vicar, wanted to eject us and our former governess, Miss Pomeroy, who leases this house—how do you like your tea, Miss Burton?" she broke off to ask.

"A little milk if you have it, otherwise black is fine."

Miss Clifford brought her the cup.

"Thank you," Aurelia said, and then took a sip of tea, silently willing the woman to continue her story.

Miss Clifford sat down, took a drink, and gave a happy sigh. "Now, where was—oh, yes, Lord Crewe put a stop to the vicar's nastiness by reminding them that he owned all the land everyone in the area lives on. Not just *this* house, but all of theirs, too." She laughed. "That put a stop to that particular persecution. But enough about me. Where do you call home, Miss Burton?"

Aurelia had debated long and hard whether to confess her identity and had decided that if she truly wanted to show solidarity, there was nothing like sharing her secret."

"I, too, have come here to escape an unfortunate family situation."

Miss Clifford's cup stopped midway to her mouth. "Really?" And then she laughed. "Listen to me! So quick to pry, even given my own situation."

"You are not prying. I want to tell you. Burton is not my real name. My father is the Earl of Addiscombe."

Miss Clifford's eyebrows shot comically high. "I thought you were exceedingly well-spoken and genteel, but I must admit I wasn't expecting *that*. And you have come here *incognita* as it were?"

"Yes. While my father is not as notorious as yours, he has managed to make mine and my siblings' lives quite unpleasant." Aurelia took a deep breath and commenced to share the sordid details of her father's gambling and their family's gradual fall from grace.

"And so," Aurelia said, about five minutes later, "when this position became available, and Lord Crewe did not care that I was a female, it seemed the perfect opportunity to strike out on my own."

Miss Clifford's eyes sparkled with admiration. "You decided to take your life into your own hands and earn a living—even though you've essentially been disowned. How brave you are!"

"My situation is not nearly so fraught as yours." Aurelia hesitated. "If you don't mind me asking, what are your plans when you reach London?"

Miss Clifford's shoulders slumped. "I am not sure what I will do. All but my youngest sister—who is only seventeen—are employed, if not exactly happily, then at least gainfully. Not surprisingly, our mother's cousins in London refused to publicly acknowledge us, but they offered my sister Penelope a position in one of their flower shops, which was generous as the only thing we were all raised to do was marry well. And now we cannot even do that to salvage our futures."

Aurelia knew that was the truth. No peer in Britain would want to align himself with the disgraced daughters of the Earl of Daventry. Even social aspirants of the merchant class would avoid the sisters.

"I would like to help you," Aurelia said.

"That is kind. But how can you?"

"I have a friend who owns a school for young ladies in London. If I had not been able to secure work as a painter, I was planning to join her as a teacher. She might have already filled the position, but I will write to her as soon as I am back on Crewe and recommend you to her if you like."

"What parent would want their child taught by me?"

"I think you might need to do something… dishonest."

"You think I should lie about who I am—even to my employer?" Miss Clifford's expression was disapproving.

Aurelia smiled. "Yes. Just as I have done."

Miss Clifford's face fell. "Oh, I am sorry! I did not mean—"

"Do not apologize. It is regrettable that we are forced to hide who we are. I am not ashamed of the lies I've told to secure this position. Women of our class have so few options, Miss Clifford. And the truth is that you cannot outrun your father's shame anywhere in Britain. You will have to falsify a past to have any future."

Miss Clifford took a deep breath and then exhaled slowly. "You are right, Miss Burton. Please do write to your friend on my behalf. I am very grateful for any help you can offer."

Aurelia only hoped it would be enough.

***

The following afternoon Aurelia had just put on her bonnet and pelisse and was headed out for a walk when Lady Celsa appeared at her door.

"Did you need something?" Aurelia asked, pulling on her gloves.

"Do you want to go for a ride?"

Aurelia had avoided asking the girl to go riding today because she wanted to ponder Miss Clifford's situation and see if she could come up with any other solutions for the woman and her sisters. She had sent off the letter to her friend in London just that morning, but there had to be more she could do—some other way to help, she just needed to put her mind to it.

"I would rather take a walk today, my lady," she said.

"I will join you."

Aurelia opened her mouth to say she'd rather walk alone, but then noticed the girl's hopeful smile and said, "Yes, I would like that."

"So," Lady Celsa said, falling into step beside her. "Where are we going?"

"Your Uncle Arthur told me there was a lovely pond tucked away near the—"

"—abbey ruins," Celsa finished for her. "I can take you there. It is almost hot enough today that we can go bathing."

"I have no intention of bathing, but I will relax on the shore if you wish to do so."

"It is not exceptionable, even my father goes," Celsa protested, and then suddenly scowled. "Although he takes Guustin with him and not me."

Aurelia knew that Guustin Walker was the earl's illegitimate son. Not only had Miss Hatchet mentioned him, but Lady Celsa brought his name up with some regularity even though she claimed that she could not abide the man.

"Does your Uncle Arthur go?" Aurelia asked, more to distract the girl from her brooding than because she was interested.

Celsa laughed. "Uncle Arthur go swimming? He never does anything that isn't proper."

"I thought you just said that bathing was unexceptionable?"

"Yes, for most people, but not for uncle."

"You seem very close to him," Aurelia said.

"He is the only family I have. Other than my father, of course." Her eyes dared Aurelia to mention her half-brother Guustin—or any of the earl's other illegitimate children.

When it became clear that Aurelia would not take the bait, Lady Celsa said, "Tell me more about your sisters and brother."

"*Please*," Aurelia said.

The girl rolled her eyes. "Tell me more about them *please*."

"What do you want to know?"

"I'll wager you are the boss of them all—using that governess tone you like to employ."

Aurelia lifted one eyebrow.

"What? Is that wrong? You do like to tell people how to behave and what is proper."

"I can't imagine why you'd want to walk with such an objectionable know-it-all."

"Now you are angry. I didn't mean to be rude. *Please* tell me about your sisters. Do you have a favorite?"

"No."

"Oh, Miss Burton, what a bouncer!"

"Why would you say that?"

"Because it is true. You are fibbing," she accused, skipping alongside Aurelia like a girl of ten rather than fifteen. "It is impossible to like everyone equally. Everyone chooses. Everyone has a favorite," she said, the last words grim.

"I love them all equally, but I suppose it is true that I spend more time with Phoebe."

"Why?"

"Phoebe is restful and kind and she is always taking care of everyone."

"Even more than you?"

"I don't take care of everyone."

"You try to. You get angry that my father doesn't like me—I have seen it on your face."

Aurelia was shocked—both that the girl had noticed and that Lady Celsa believed her own father did not like her.

"And if you chide me for speaking the truth, then I shall leave right now," Celsa threatened, evidently forgetting that she was the one who had begged to come along.

But Aurelia did not want to hurt the girl, so she considered her next words very carefully. "I think your father gets annoyed by your behavior and allows his irritation to influence his treatment of you."

Celsa stopped and set a hand on Aurelia's arm to stop her. "But beneath that—beneath his annoyance—he hates me. Doesn't he?" The pain in the girl's dark brown eyes made Aurelia's chest hurt.

"You are asking my opinion," Aurelia reminded her. Celsa nodded. "Then I'll tell you what I think: he does *not* hate you."

The relief that flashed in the girl's eyes was heartbreaking.

Unfortunately, it was also short-lived. "If he doesn't hate me then why doesn't he want to spend time with me like he does with Guustin? Or—or even *you*!" Fury flared in her eyes. "And don't try to look innocent and pretend you do not know what I mean. I have seen you riding with him. He likes you. He laughs and teases and—" She bit her lip, her stark, miserable profile facing Aurelia.

"My lady."

"What?" Celsa snapped.

"This is just a suggestion, but—"

"But what?"

"Could you try not to antagonize him so much?"

Celsa swallowed hard, her eyes shimmering with tears. "You mean stop doing things to the Hatchet?"

Aurelia bit back a smile. "Yes. You could start with something easy—like calling her *Miss* Hatchet."

Celsa gave her a watery smile. "That won't be easy at all."

"Perhaps not. But do try, my lady. Just… try."

Celsa met her gaze, her jaw set mulishly. After a long moment, she gave an abrupt nod. "Very well. I will try. When he returns."

"Try *now*, so that Miss Hatchet does not greet him at the pier with a list of infractions as long as her arm." Although Aurelia suspected the woman probably already had a list twice as long.

"If I promise to try and be better, will you ride with me every day? Because you know that is the only way I'm allowed to ride," she said, a wheedle in her voice. "I am much better behaved if I get to ride a few hours *every* day."

It seemed churlish not to promise such a small thing. "Fine. We will ride *every* day—at least if the weather permits it."

"Huzzah!" Celsa cried.

Aurelia's smile faded as Celsa skipped ahead of her, leaping and jumping like a happy girl-child. She hoped that she had done the right thing by encouraging her to earn more positive attention by curtailing her tendency to mischief. But what if good behavior made no difference to the earl? What if— perish the thought—Lord Crewe truly did not like his own daughter?

Chapter 12

Six Weeks Later…

Aurelia settled into her life and the days and weeks sped past in a blur.

Without the earl's presence, one day was much like another—not boring, necessarily, but without any… texture. She told herself that she was glad Lord Crewe was staying away.

She told herself that often.

Life in the castle was almost suspiciously calm and peaceful. Lady Celsa had stopped goading her governess, which—thankfully—meant that Miss Hatchet had ceased paying late-night visits to Aurelia's bedroom to complain about her charge.

At least four afternoons every week Aurelia went on rides with Celsa. To say they had become friends would have been an exaggeration, but they had settled into a truce and Aurelia learned a great deal about the island while Celsa got to enjoy time with Helios, her horse, and the one living thing in all of Christendom that she did not argue with.

Aurelia's work progressed apace and she had produced a truly impressive number of paintings. At least Arthur seemed impressed. She was hopeful that the earl—if he ever returned—would be pleased with her output, as well.

Between her work, the time she spent with Celsa, and her own artistic endeavors, her days were full. But just because she tried to stay busy did not mean she didn't spend plenty of time dreaming—at night and often during the day—about her employer.

She had pondered that last afternoon they'd spent together so often that the memory should have become threadbare. Instead, she had embellished it as the days and weeks passed, until Lord Crewe had not stopped with kissing. His hands, which had scarcely grazed her nipples, had gone further, stripping her bare right out in the open where all the world might see.

Why on earth the thought of such a public seduction would arouse her Aurelia did not know.

But it did.

In her imagination, he continued once he'd laid her bare. Aurelia knew a great deal about the fundamentals of intercourse and she had *felt* the way his body had responded when she'd kissed him. He had hardened and thickened and his breathing had become ragged and fast. He had *liked* it when she'd been the aggressor. That sort of initiative was probably what he wanted in a lover. He would want women who were capable of bestowing as much pleasure as he knew how to give.

All her life Aurelia had been a responsible, obedient *good girl* and had kept herself pure and untouched. As her mother's oldest daughter, the same message had been drummed into her since girlhood: her maidenhood was her most prized possession. Without it, she was irreparably damaged, like a once valuable vase that was now cracked.

It was her duty to guard her virtue with her life, because once it was gone, so was her chance of enticing the right man to marry her.

Looking back on her younger days, it was painful to recall just how religiously she had followed her mother's instructions, to the point that she had rejected or actively repelled almost all the young men who had admired her during her one Season, too restrained and inhibited to ever allow herself to enjoy even mild flirtation except for those two pitiful kisses. It would have been laughable if it were not so tragic. Taking advice about love and sex and men from a woman who had one of the unhappiest marriages in England; what a fool she had been.

And what had being a good girl yielded? Aurelia still had her virginity and—at five-and-twenty and banished from her family and any good society—she was unlikely to ever marry. Indeed, it was probable that she would die a virgin spinster.

And then Lord Crewe had come along…

To be honest, it had not taken kissing and touching him to become fascinated by him. There had been something irresistible about him from the first day she'd set eyes on him. While it was true that she never would have instigated anything if he'd not done so first, something had changed inside her now, some barrier had been breached—she was not unaware of the irony of her choice of metaphor—when he had touched her, setting fire to something that could not be extinguished.

It had been humiliating when he had rejected her. Not because he had not wanted her—Aurelia had felt proof of his desire in both his hot gaze and pressing against her belly—but because he was a gentleman, and gentlemen did not debauch their employees. It had been easy for him to stop as he had not been as besotted as she had been.

Besotted was too tame a word. She had been insane with desire for the man, throwing aside common sense and everything she had always lived by just to touch him.

It was mortifying, but what surprised her was that it wasn't *more* mortifying. Part of her was embarrassed, but a greater part of her was… proud that she had not only experienced such powerful desires but had—for the first time in her life—behaved impulsively, allowing her emotions free reign.

Aurelia knew, without knowing *how*, that if Crewe had believed she'd had lovers before, they would have consummated their passion that day. Quite possibly right then and there on that beach. Or even before then on that night in the library when he had first kissed her.

But they had not consummated anything. Instead, he had twice pulled himself up short and then left without a word.

By the time six weeks had passed, Aurelia was truly beginning to believe that the earl was not planning to return to Crewe until she had finished her job and departed.

But then—six weeks and one day after Lord Crewe had departed—Arthur made an announcement at breakfast.

"Crewe is coming home today. I just received his letter saying to expect him this afternoon," Arthur said.

Aurelia's coffee cup hovered halfway to her mouth, and she lowered it without drinking. "That seems sudden."

Arthur grunted. "He sent the letter from London several days ago, but it was torn and badly stained with mud, so I think something must have delayed it." He looked up at her, his gaze sharpening. "By the way, this came for you this morning. It was mixed in with my mail." He slid an envelope across the table, his expression curious.

Aurelia's heart leapt at the sight of her sister Hyacinth's spidery handwriting. She squinted at the frank that was scrawled across the corner of the envelope and understood Arthur's curiosity. It was signed by the Duke of Chatham.

Aurelia tore open the envelope.

Dear Lia,

You are wondering why I have not written in so long. Well… I guess there is nothing for it but to say it plainly: I have married the Duke of Chatham.

A choked laugh slipped out of her.

"What was that?" Arthur asked.

Aurelia's head whipped up. "Just a bit of pepper in my throat." She coughed delicately to illustrate.

He turned back to his letter and she hastily returned to hers.

You cannot be more surprised than I am, dear sister. I am sorry you were not there, but it was a small affair—necessarily hasty because of… well, that is a long story and right now I am in the process of leaving London and heading to Chatham's estate, so I do not have time to chronicle the last few months, which deserve the title of epic.

I will write more once I am settled, but I just wanted to let you know you have a home with us, should you need one. Unlike Selina, who thinks that you have sold yourself into wage slavery, I suspect you are as happy as a lark working at what you love best. If I am wrong, you must let me know immediately and Chatham and I will come fetch you.

Being a duchess is a bit of a bore, and it will likely get worse next year as I've been threatened with a Season—a real one, this time—and cannot avoid it by sneaking into the card rooms at balls.

Don't worry that I married Chatham against my will, Lia. I am happy with him— almost worryingly happy—and he is an excellent card player.

More soon, dearest sister.

Yours,

The Duchess of Chatham

P.S. I thought you would find my new, august, signature amusing.

Aurelia stared blankly at the single, mostly blank sheet of paper. Hy always had been a woman of few words. It seemed becoming a peeress had not changed her.

She was not sure she believed what she'd just read but knew it must be true. Hy was a duchess. Inconceivable.

The urge to laugh hysterically was strong.

Aurelia made haste to get up to her chambers. She desperately needed a few minutes alone to ponder the news she had just heard. Not just Hy's startling announcement, but also the more immediate fact that the earl was coming home today.

The mere thought left her breathless.

She scowled, annoyed with her body's reaction. The man hadn't even stepped foot on the island and already her pulse was pounding!

Aurelia had hoped that by the time he returned—*if* he returned—she would have exorcised Lord Crewe from her system. His behavior that day on the beach might have hurt her feelings, but stepping away had been the best thing he could have done. She should be thanking him for his responsible behavior and banishing her memories of those painfully erotic few minutes from her thoughts.

Instead, there was a distinct knot of anticipation in her belly at the thought of his return.

Rather than diminish, her excitement only became more pronounced as the day wore on. Indeed, she was so agitated that she'd decided to put aside her paints earlier than usual, worried she would ruin the painting she was working on because her entire body felt as if it were vibrating.

One positive effect of Lord Crewe's long absence had been his daughter's improved behavior while he was away. Celsa had not played cruel tricks or sneered and sniped at Aurelia for weeks.

Until today.

***

Aurelia slid a surreptitious gaze toward the girl who rode beside her. Celsa's face was twisted into a scowl and her mind was clearly elsewhere. Indeed, she'd been in a foul mood since they'd met at the stables. It was unusual for the younger woman not to enjoy every single minute riding and Aurelia did not think it was a coincidence that Celsa's mood had taken such a grim turn on the very day that his lordship was to return to Crewe.

As they rode through the village of Crewe, Aurelia silently prayed that Mary Neel did not come out to talk to them today.

They were almost past the inn, and Celsa was railing about something *the Hatchet* had said or done, when Mrs. Neel all but sprinted from the Sea Hag to greet them.

"Good afternoon, my lady, Miss Burton," she said, wearing the knowing smirk that she always seemed to sport. For all Aurelia knew, it was the woman's natural expression, but she didn't think so. She thought it was a little bit of mockery that she saved just for Aurelia. Or perhaps Celsa.

"Good morning, Mrs. Neel," Aurelia said when it was clear that Celsa had no intention of speaking to the woman.

"The master returns today, aye? Ye'll be happy to have him home, won't you?"

Aurelia wasn't sure who the question was for given that Mrs. Neel's eyes bounced between both Aurelia and Celsa.

"How nice of you to tell us about my father's return," Celsa retorted, giving the woman a look of such loathing that most people would have slunk away at that point.

But Mrs. Neel, who was made of sterner stuff, merely laughed.

Celsa spurred her horse into a canter.

"It was nice to see you, Mrs. Neel. I'd better be off," Aurelia said, before allowing Black Prince his head.

Not until they were a few minutes outside the village did Celsa slow her mount.

"Why are you in such a wretched mood today?" Aurelia asked.

"I'm not in a wretched mood," Celsa snarled.

Aurelia laughed. "Clearly."

Celsa opened her mouth—as if to argue—and then gave a slight, miserly laugh. "Very well, perhaps I am a bit out of sorts. But I *do* wish that Mrs. Neel would leave me be. She is always fluttering about and saying things about how *nice* I look when I know she is laughing at me."

"How do you know that?" Aurelia asked, although she, too, had frequently felt the voluptuous beauty enjoyed herself at Aurelia's expense whenever they encountered each other.

"I know because I *know*," Celsa said, exasperated.

"Oh, I see. Because you *know*," she said, hoping to tease the younger woman out of her vile mood.

Instead, Celsa's head whipped around and she skewered Aurelia with furious eyes. "I know because she is my father's mistress—or one of them—and wishes to curry favor with me for some reason, and so she flatters me. As if I have influence with him and can convince him to abandon all his principles and sense and wed a common barmaid."

Aurelia knew Celsa expected a shocked, chiding response, but she refused to provide it.

"Well?" Celsa taunted. "Are you going to pretend that you don't know about his evening visits to her? That *everyone* doesn't know that?"

"Gossiping is a pernicious habit."

Celsa gave a derisive laugh, which Aurelia had to admit she deserved. "Oh, Miss Burton! I have seen your eyes glisten when you've heard a particularly interesting tidbit of information, but you adopt your governess veneer when it suits you. I must say it is a relief to know you are not nearly as virtuous as you pretend."

Aurelia changed the subject. "Do you know what time your father's boat is meant to arrive?"

"Why do you care when he's returning? Are you planning to be there to welcome him home?"

Aurelia gave an exasperated huff. "If you are going to be unpleasant then we should—"

"Oh, I know! If I don't agree with everything you say then I should just go back. Well, I don't see why my pleasure should be truncated because I don't agree with you." She wheeled Helios around and thundered back the way they'd just come.

Aurelia paused, considering whether she should go after her. After all, Celsa was not supposed to be riding unless they were together. While Aurelia wouldn't say anything to the earl, she knew Miss Hatchet lived to tattle.

Aurelia decided that the irritation of seeing Mary Neel again wasn't worth saving Celsa's ungrateful hide.

Instead, she continued on her way, putting the girl and her tantrums out of her mind.

Aurelia crested the rise that looked over the tiny bay and immediately spotted a far larger boat than the usual skiffs pulled alongside the pier.

And standing on the dock directing the unloading—tall and elegant and clad all in black—was none other than the Laird of Crewe.

Chapter 13

B loody hell but Roland was glad to be back home! If there was one thing he loathed, it was gadding about England with his hat in his hand begging Englishmen for money.

While he could finance the trips out of his own pocket, it was foolish to do so when many peers and rich industrialists wanted to be part of new discoveries and would—after the correct amount of arse-kissing—be convinced to loosen their purse strings.

His first few weeks in Edinburgh had yielded enough to pay for part of his journey to the Cape, but it had been the longer trip to London that had truly filled his coffers. The price of the travel had been steep—not in terms of money, but the emotional cost of consorting with his English peers was always a trial.

But the journey had been a very good decision as he'd been introduced to several industrials who—in their eagerness to thrust their way into the company of aristocrats—had committed generously.

The only unpleasantness had been having the various daughters of ironmongers and dry goods barons flung at his head. Roland had been bloody fortunate to escape the city with his hide intact.

"If you want to go up to the castle, I will see to the rest of the unloading, my lord," Guustin said.

Roland turned to his son. "I believe I will take you up on that offer. You will join us for dinner tonight. Shall I have Beekman ready your rooms?"

Guustin smiled, looking so much like Roland—but with an unscarred face and two eyes—that it always startled him. "I will be pleased to join you for dinner, sir. But I will stay at Mama's house tonight." Guustin's green eyes, the only physical feature he'd inherited from his mother, slid toward the shore. "Now, who might that be?"

Roland knew who it was before he even turned.

And there she was, the woman he'd run from all those weeks ago. "That is my new artist," he said. Even from this distance, she looked damned enticing. Roland had seen her far too often in his mind's eye, especially the way she'd looked on that beach that day: eager, aroused, and utterly fuckable.

His cock stirred. Well, damn and blast. He had hoped that almost two months away would have subdued his baser urges and cured him of his infatuation. Evidently not.

"*That* is Miss Burton?" Guustin asked.

Roland turned back to find Guustin eyeing him in a far too knowing way.

"What?" Roland demanded.

Guustin smirked. "For some reason, I was picturing a matron."

Roland grunted and they both turned back to the woman, who was chatting with his groom, Jemmy, who had arrived with a wagon, Frost trotting behind it.

"Your arrogant beast won't like being lashed to a cart one bit," Guustin said, laughing at the stallion's outraged posture.

"No, indeed. I had best go and rescue him. I will see you tonight."

"I am looking forward to meeting your artist, my lord," Guustin said, his appraising gaze back on Miss Burton.

Roland felt an unexpected stab of irritation and opened his mouth to tell his son that Miss Burton was not a toy to be trifled with, but something about the amused glint in Guustin's green gaze made him shut his mouth.

"Why, Miss Burton!" he called out as he strode down the pier. "How very kind of you to welcome me home." Roland could see her blush even from ten feet away.

"I just happened to be passing by," she retorted. And then added after a slight hesitation, "But welcome back, Lord Crewe."

"Thank you. I am delighted to be home."

The moment they locked eyes Roland knew that staying away from her hadn't done a damned thing to make him want her less. If anything, he'd underestimated her appeal while he'd been gone.

Jemmy led Frost over. "He's been missing you something fierce, Master."

Roland stared into the haughty stallion's black gaze. "Have you missed me, Frost?"

The horse tossed his head and stomped one big foot as if to say, *don't be a fool.*

Roland hoisted himself into the saddle and then turned to look down at Miss Burton. "What about you, Miss Burton?"

Her eyebrows knitted. "My lord?"

"Did you miss me?"

She gaped up at him. "Er…"

Roland laughed, suddenly quite pleased with… everything.

"It is good to be home," he said, grinning at the flustered woman. Too damned good, he feared.

***

Aurelia had just clasped her pearls around her neck when the door to her chambers flew open hard enough to bounce off the wall and Celsa stormed in.

"Lady Celsa," she said flatly, giving the younger woman a level look.

"What?"

"How many times have I asked you to knock, first?"

Celsa glared and flung up her hands. "Ten? Twenty? I don't know. Why does it matter?"

"I might have been in a state of undress."

"I knew you would be ready for dinner." Her lip curled into a slight sneer. "You are always down early. When Papa is here."

Aurelia refused to be baited. Instead, she smoothed down the front of the antique gold silk gown, checking her reflection one last time before turning to the girl.

"That is a very nice gown," Celsa said. "Did you put it on especially for my father?"

"Thank you," she said, choosing to ignore her barb.

"I saw you arrive with him earlier," Celsa persisted.

"I happened to be passing the pier when he was coming ashore. You could have joined us if you'd not thundered off in a sulk."

"I suppose you told him that I was riding without you."

"Then you suppose wrong," Aurelia said, draping a gold-fringed wrap around her shoulders before leaving the room, not bothering to see if the surly girl followed.

She hadn't gone far when Celsa hurried up beside her. "I suppose I should thank you for not being a tattletale."

"Again, you suppose incorrectly. I don't want an apology if you don't mean it."

The girl had the decency to blush. "I *am* sorry. I should have known you would not tell."

That didn't mean Miss Hatchet hadn't, but it didn't seem worthwhile to remind Celsa of that.

"Guustin is coming to dinner tonight," the girl said after a moment.

"Oh?"

"That shocks you, doesn't it?"

"Why should it shock me? Everyone needs to eat."

"You are being purposely obtuse. You know what I mean—the fact that my father's bastard sits down at the same table as the rest of us."

"That is an unkind word."

"What word? *Table?*" Celsa taunted.

Aurelia laughed. "Touché."

Celsa lost some of her hostility. "If you don't like *bastard* then what would you call a child born outside holy wedlock?"

"*Illegitimate* is sufficient. Although why it bears mentioning at all, I am not sure."

"You really should have been a governess. You would make an excellent one."

"I am going to take that as a compliment."

"You won't wish to go riding with me now that *he* is here."

"I don't even know your brother."

Celsa stopped and stamped her foot. "You know I meant my father!"

Aurelia ignored her little tantrum and kept walking.

"Will you still ride with me even now that Papa is back?" Celsa asked, sounding so pitiful it plucked at Aurelia's heart.

"If you are civil, then I do not see why not."

"Thank you so very, very, very much, Miss Burton."

Aurelia lifted a skeptical brow at the girl's treacly tone.

Celsa laughed. "Was that a bit much?"

"Just a bit," Aurelia answered haughtily, but then spoiled it by laughing, too.

They were both chuckling when they entered the dining room.

Rather than being the first to arrive, all three men were already there.

They stood when Aurelia and Celsa entered, and—for a moment—Aurelia was rendered breathless by the display of male beauty. All three were blond, tall, and elegantly garbed. While Arthur and Guustin Walker were both more conventionally handsome than the earl, it was Lord Crewe who instantly drew a person's gaze.

Or at least he drew Aurelia's.

"Is that my daughter laughing and smiling?" the earl teased. "I almost didn't recognize her without a scowl."

The smiling, laughing girl disappeared in a heartbeat at her father's observation and Aurelia felt the distinct urge to kick the earl. Why could he not just appreciate Celsa's good mood rather than mock it?

"Good evening, Miss Burton," Lord Crewe said, smiling so warmly at her that she felt the tell-tale heat rising up her neck. "Allow me to introduce my son, Guustin Walker. Miss Burton is the extremely talented artist who is bringing my specimens to life, Guustin."

Guustin Walker took Aurelia's hand and bowed over it. "It is an honor to meet you, Miss Burton. I look forward to seeing your work."

"Thank you, Mr. Walker," Aurelia said. "Are you a naturalist as well?"

He chuckled. "I regret that I am not at all bookish."

The earl clapped a hand on his son's shoulder. "That is understating the matter, isn't it?" He grinned at Aurelia. "When he was only fifteen the headmaster sent him home with the request that I never send him back."

Both men chuckled and Aurelia couldn't help noticing the earl looked proud, rather than disappointed, that his son had been ejected from school. Yet again there was one standard for boys and another for girls.

Lady Celsa looked furious, and Aurelia could not blame her.

"Guustin is captain of his own ship, Miss Burton—the *Heart's Desire*, she is called." The earl gave the younger man a fond look. "While I am proud of him, it is unfortunate that his job keeps him away from Crewe so much of the time."

"I am here for the next few months, so you will all get sick of me." Captain Walker pointedly looked at Celsa as he said the last words.

"Come, let us eat." The earl led the way to the dinner table.

Guustin waved away the footman and seated his sister, while the earl pulled out Aurelia's chair.

While Celsa scowled at her half-brother just the way she did with everyone else, Aurelia could not help noticing the rosy blush that tinted her cheeks when she did so.

She fervently hoped the girl wasn't infatuated with Captain Walker. While it would be understandable—he was exceedingly handsome and charming—it would be unfortunate given their familial relationship.

"Guustin brought back several crates of specimens from America," Arthur said, reminding Aurelia that there was a third male at the table. "You should come and look at the new botany samples as many are much better preserved than the ones you've had to work with."

"There are also several more taxidermied samples—although they are not as good as Arthur's," his lordship added loyally, earning a smile from the man in question.

"I have something for you as well, Celsa," Captain Walker said, smiling at his prickly sister.

"I have no interest in dead animals or wilted plants," Celsa retorted.

Captain Walker laughed. "It is neither of those things. You will have to see for yourself. It—or she, rather—is in one of the stalls out in the stables."

Celsa dropped her spoon with a clang, no longer surly or hostile. "You brought a *horse* all the way from America?"

Lord Crewe and his son laughed.

"Not a horse, Little One," her brother said.

"Oh."

"Such becoming gratitude," the earl said, giving his daughter a look of exasperated amusement. "Perhaps you should give your gift to somebody more appreciative, Guustin?"

"No! I want it," Celsa said hastily. "Thank you, Guustin," she added when her father cut her a severe look.

"Do you want to come with me and see what Guustin brought?" Celsa asked, her smiling face and sparkling eyes making her look exceptionally pretty.

Aurelia was touched by the friendly gesture. "Of course," she said, even though she had planned to look at the new samples.

For a change, the three men stayed after the meal to have port and cigars when Aurelia and Celsa left the dining room.

"Shall we go upstairs and fetch our—"

"We don't need cloaks; it is warm out." Celsa grabbed Aurelia's hand and dragged her. "Come along! Don't be a slow poke."

Aurelia laughed, picked up her skirt with her free hand, and tried to keep up with the younger woman, marveling yet again how Celsa could be a surly adolescent one moment and a spirited child the next.

"Silas!" Celsa shouted the moment they entered the ancient, rambling stone structure. "Silas!"

The stablemaster came shuffling down a narrow corridor which Aurelia knew led to his quarters. "Ye'll wake the deid, me lady," he groused. "What de ye want?"

"Guustin said you had something for me."

"Did he then? Hmm. Nae, I canny think what—"

"*Silas.*"

He chortled. "Aye, this way, afore you make me deaf in t'other ear." He led them toward a stall meant for pregnant mares. "There she be, Lady Celsa."

She was a fluffy brown dog just on the cusp between puppyhood and adulthood.

Celsa gave a yelp of joy. "Why, she looks like a poodle crossed with a sheep!" She dropped to her knees in the straw, heedless of her finery. "Come here, you precious darling."

The dog gave an excited yip and shot into Celsa's arms. A frenzy of face-licking and delighted laughter ensued.

"Seems like a little girl at times like this," Silas said, his gaze fond. "The next minute she be all high-and-mighty lady o' the castle."

It was true. The girl rolling around in the straw and ruining her gown did not seem fifteen. It was a joy to watch her with her new pet.

Aurelia couldn't help laughing when Silas, whom she suspected was just as mad about the new hound as Celsa, entered the big stall and the two humans engaged in a game of keep-away with a knotted piece of rope.

Yet again Aurelia wondered why the earl didn't send Celsa off to school to be with other girls her age. Who did she have to play with at the castle other than adults? Who would—

"I see it is love at first sight."

Aurelia turned to find Captain Walker beside her. "Indeed, it is."

"I love her, Guustin!" Celsa shouted, and then collapsed laughing when her new pet leapt up and licked her chin.

"I think you are going to be very popular from now on, Captain."

"At least until I say something to vex her." He lowered his voice. "You are an excellent influence on her, Miss Burton," he said, his affectionate gaze on Celsa. "I have not seen her laugh and smile in ages until you two came in to dinner tonight."

"That is kind of you to say."

"It is the truth. She is lonely here. The earl does not understand how hard it is for a child to grow up in the castle."

"You sound as if you speak from experience?"

"I might be illegitimate, but my father never made any bones about whose child I was. I spent as much time at the castle as I did with my mother." He smiled at her. "You must come and meet her. She loves visitors and does not get out much these days."

Aurelia was startled at the invitation and tried to cover her surprise by asking, "I am sorry to hear she is housebound. Is she ill?" She had heard rumors about Mrs. Walker—how the woman was too proud to mix with islanders—but she'd not known how much credence to give the gossip.

"She has a disease of the joints which makes it difficult for her to move about." A look of intense sorrow flickered across his handsome face. "She is still a young woman, but she suffers so much pain that it is aging her before her time."

"I am so sorry," Aurelia murmured.

"My father says your own mother is ill?" the captain asked, making Aurelia feel like a toad for making up such a thing.

"What sort of dog is she?" Celsa called out, saving Aurelia from having to add more lies to the ones she had already told.

"The man I bought her from calls them Irish Water Spaniels, a cross that does well in wet, cold climates."

"She is lovely, Guustin. Thank you," she added, looking shy and very young.

"You are welcome, Little One. You will need to stay abreast of her grooming. The man said they are like poodles in that regard. Silas will know what she requires."

Celsa immediately turned to Silas and the two set about making a close inspection of the leaping, squirming puppy.

"How are you enjoying your time here?" Captain Walker asked Aurelia.

"The island is fascinating and I discover something new and interesting every day. It is quite… magical."

"Do you not yearn for the mainland?"

"No. Although I have gone over once since coming here."

"Only one trip?" Captain Walker teased. "You *are* an islander in the making. Most people who were not born here cannot wait for a chance to leave. You do not feel isolated?"

"No, but I suppose that might change if the weather made crossing impossible."

"That doesn't happen often," he assured her.

Aurelia shivered and rubbed her bare arms.

"You have goose pimples, Miss Burton." Captain Walker gestured to Celsa, who now had a horse comb and was grooming her dog under Silas's supervision. "I believe she will be busy for a while. May I walk you back to the house?"

"Yes, thank you."

"I am taking Miss Burton back inside, Little One," he called out.

Celsa nodded absently, not pulling her gaze away from her new pet.

"Do you always return home in between your journeys?" she asked as they strolled toward the castle.

"I try to. I am my mother's only child and she likes to see me and assure herself that I am well."

"How long have you been a sea captain?"

"Only two years, and four-and-twenty is still extremely young for that. I am fortunate that my father supported my interests from the beginning. Rather than insist I remain in school, he found me a position when I was fifteen. I think he believed the harsh requirements of such a life would have me running home within a year, but instead I took to the sea just like a fish."

"And you have worked your way up to captain."

"Aye, with my father's help in that, too," he admitted with a rueful smile. "I could not have afforded my own ship for many years, if ever, on my wages. The earl funded the purchase of my vessel. In exchange, I engage in work for him when he needs me." He opened the massive door to the foyer. "What about you, Miss Burton? Have you always known you wanted to paint and draw?" he asked as they ascended the main staircase.

"I've always liked art, but I didn't realize I could earn my living from it until a man who was collecting butterflies came to spend some time in our village. He saw me sketching and was impressed by my work. It was he who told me that a person might make money if they were good enough."

They paused on the landing and Aurelia turned to him and smiled. "Thank you for walking me back. I am going to fetch a wrap and then go look at the items you brought his lordship."

"I will accompany you, if you do not mind?"

"Not at all."

"I will wait here while you fetch a wrap. Perhaps you could show me some of the work that you've done for my father, if you have time?"

"I would be happy to," she said, more than a little flattered by his attention. He was exceptionally handsome and charming, his demeanor that of a well-bred gentleman. At twenty-four he was only a year younger than Aurelia.

And his eyes shone with regard for her, which he did nothing to hide.

It occurred to her that this was precisely the sort of man she would have liked to marry.

If she hadn't already been infatuated with his father.

Chapter 14

R oland heard masculine and feminine laughter even before he opened the door to the workroom. Guustin and Miss Burton—the source of the laughter—were so involved with each other that they did not notice his entrance.

The stab of irritation he experienced felt suspiciously like jealousy as he looked at his son's golden head bent near Miss Burton's tawny brown one.

The emotion was so foreign that he paused to examine it. It had been a long time since he'd felt such possessive intent toward anyone. In fact, had he *ever* truly felt that way?

Frustration, jealousy, and pique swirled inside him and he struggled with the impulse to grab Guustin by the scruff of the neck and drag him not only from the room, but from the castle. Perhaps even the island.

Wisely, he did no such thing. Not only because he loved his son and enjoyed a fulfilling relationship with him, but because the lad—at almost twenty-five—was nearly as big as Roland and it was doubtful he would be the victor in such a scuffle. At least not without some effort.

Instead of behaving like a fool, Roland noisily cleared his throat.

Both their heads whipped up in a comically identical fashion. But while the actions were the same, the expressions on the faces were not. His son, not unsurprisingly, looked wryly amused at being interrupted during his flirtation.

Miss Burton looked guilty and flushed, the color on her pale cheeks making her hazel eyes appear greener than brown in the brightly illuminated room.

"Something among the samples is enough to provoke laughter?" he asked, pleased that his irritation didn't come across in the question.

Miss Burton cleared her throat. "Er, not as such, my lord. It's just—"

"I told Miss Burton that this reptile bore a surprising resemblance to Mr. Bucket—you remember him, don't you, father?"

Roland smirked at his son's use of the word *father*, which he usually only used when they were alone. He wondered if Guustin was trying to remind Miss Burton, or Roland, of the great age difference between them.

"The housemaster at your school?" Roland asked, strolling toward the two. "The one you drove half mad?" he added, unable to suppress his smile at the memory of the man in question. "Let me see," he said, deliberately placing himself between them. "Which one did you mea—" He laughed when he saw the bulging-eyed, thick-lipped reptile in question, which was floating in a stoppered jar filled with clear preservative. "The resemblance is… uncanny."

"Perhaps you might name the creature after him—if it is a new discovery?"

"*Deforme magnum senes ingratum dispositio*," Roland suggested and then lifted his eyebrow at Miss Burton. "Can you translate?"

"Er… hideous big-headed monster with an unpleasant disposition?"

Roland and Guustin laughed. "I think she has a better grasp of Latin than I have," Guustin said.

"That would not be difficult," Roland said dryly. He turned to Miss Burton. "Arthur just showed me all the work you completed while I've been gone."

There was a subtle tightening of the muscles in her face, making Roland believe that Miss Burton was more accustomed to criticism than praise. For some reason, that made him think about Celsa. Roland shoved down the odd twinge of guilt that accompanied the thought and smiled at the woman in front of him. "Your work is excellent and the speed with which you've produced it surpasses my expectations."

"Oh, that is—that is a relief," she said, her normally serious features breaking into a smile.

"I received word from the publisher and he is delighted with what I've sent to him. When he finishes the first prints from the plates he is having made I shall make sure to show them to you."

"I would like that, my lord." Her lips parted slightly as she stared up at him, her eyes warm and… soft. And then she stiffened and her gaze shuttered as she took a step back, and Roland knew she was remembering the last time they had been together—that day on the beach.

"I just came down to have a quick look at the new specimens. I will say good night to you both. My lord, Captain Walker." She bowed her head and turned to leave.

Roland strode toward the door to open it for her. "Goodnight, Miss Burton," he murmured, amused when she scurried away without looking up at him. He closed the door and turned to find his son waiting for him, smiling faintly.

"You find something entertaining, Guustin?"

"Nothing. Father."

But it wasn't *nothing*, and Roland could see it by the familiar look in Guustin's eyes—not familiar because he had seen it on his son's face in the past, but because it was a look he had seen on his own face a long, long time ago. It was the look of a young man who was already more than halfway smitten. And Guustin had only known the woman half a day.

Viewed in a prudential light, a match between Miss Burton—an artist with no family to protect or support her—and Guustin Walker, a ship's captain and favored, if baseborn, son of an earl, was an excellent match for her.

But then Guustin didn't know what Roland had discovered about the prim and proper Miss Burton when he had been in London for almost a month.

Roland smiled at his son. "Have you time for a game of chess before you go to your mother's house?"

Guustin's green eyes glittered. "I always have time to thrash you."

Roland laughed and the tension that had invisibly gathered between them dissipated. He was glad; he loved his son and did not want anything to come between them. It did not surprise him that Guustin was immediately attracted to Miss Burton.

Sooner, rather than later, Roland would have to inform Guustin of exactly how matters stood between Miss Burton and himself.

Roland smiled. He would tell Guustin the truth right after he told the woman herself.

***

Aurelia was delighted when she received a message from Miss Clifford the following morning asking if she wanted to meet that afternoon at the tiny teashop in the village of Crewe.

Over the past six weeks they had visited each other three times, today would be the fourth. Aurelia had not realized just how much she missed her sisters until befriending Miss Clifford, or Larissa as she now called her.

149

In any event, Aurelia was too keyed up to do any decent work that morning so she was glad to have a reason to leave the castle for a few hours.

"I heard his lordship returned just yesterday. He was away a long time, wasn't he?" Larissa asked after they'd settled in the shop's tiny bay window and had given their order to the waitress.

"Six weeks." *And one day.*

Larissa thrust out her lower lip and eyed Aurelia thoughtfully.

"What?" Aurelia asked. "Why are you looking at me that way?"

"I have deliberated whether or not I should tell you—"

"Tell me."

Larissa lowered her voice and said, "Mary Neel and another widow from Balcrewe—Edna Green—have been complaining about the earl's absence in their beds not just these past six weeks, but for some time before that. Indeed, they have both traced his sudden lack of interest in their… charms to the arrival of a certain young lady artist."

Aurelia groaned. "This is just what I feared would happen."

"No, no—do not despair!"

"How can I *not* despair?"

"Because several Castle Crewe servants have vouchsafed that nothing untoward has occurred between you and his lordship. Indeed, the entire populace is agog at the earl's restraint."

"Perhaps the restraint is on my side," Aurelia retorted. And then sighed and said, "I'm sorry. I should not snap at you for the inevitable gossip. Indeed, I am grateful you have told me what is being said.

"You are in a most interesting position—"

Aurelia laughed.

It was Larissa's turn to blush. "I just mean that you have beguiled a man whom women fling themselves at incessantly. Every unmarried woman—and good many who are—view the earl as some sort of exotic animal they are determined to bag, stuff, and display in a trophy case."

Aurelia gave a decidedly unladylike guffaw. "I'm sorry," she said. "But that is a rather amusing image."

Larissa chuckled. "It is, but that does not make it any less true. What I was trying to say—rather clumsily, I'm afraid—is that you are proof that women can earn their way without doing anything *dire.*"

"My mother would say—and Society would agree—that I have behaved in a *dire* fashion just by coming here."

Larissa pulled a face. "Our mothers—and from what you have told me ours have more than a little in common—believed they had only one choice, which was to marry our fathers. You are living evidence that we do not need a husband to survive and even prosper. And you are—"

The waitress arrived with their tea and scones just then, thankfully putting a stop to the mortifying conversation.

Once they were again alone, Aurelia poured their tea while Larissa again leaned across the table, her eyes shining with excitement. "I have excellent news. Miss. Lindon wrote and offered me the teaching position, Aurelia!"

Aurelia wanted to shout *huzzah* as Celsa did when she was happy, but wisely settled for a big grin. "That is *wonderful,* Larissa!"

"It *is* wonderful and I must tell you that I already like Jenny Lindon a great deal—and she had lovely things to say about you, dear Aurelia."

Jenny had been Aurelia's closest friend during her one year away at finishing school, and the main reason Aurelia had been so sad that there had been no money for a second year.

"I decided to tell her who I really am," Larissa said, and then licked a dab of cream from her finger and added three teaspoons of sugar to her tea.

"And she hired you regardless."

Larissa nodded. "Yes. But I insisted that if anyone were to find out the truth that Miss Lindon would promise to say she was unaware of my identity. I have no desire to ruin her school."

"I am relieved that Jenny knows the truth. It is a difficult façade to maintain and it also made me feel lonely." Aurelia smiled. "Until I met you, Larissa. Our friendship has—"

"Hello Miss Burton, Miss Clifford! What a delight to see you two here."

Aurelia looked up to find Sir Gideon smiling down at them.

He looked from her to Larissa. "If I had known you were coming over, I could have brought you, Miss Clifford. I do hope you will allow me to take you back—if it is convenient for you, that is?"

Larissa blushed under his open, friendly regard. "That is very kind of you, Sir Gideon, and I would be delighted to accept your offer. Er, have you come to have tea?"

"I thought I might, but"—he turned to look around and then gave them a rueful look. "It appears there is nowhere to sit."

"We have two unoccupied seats," Aurelia said. "Why not join us?"

"Are you sure? I wouldn't want to—"

"Please do," Larissa seconded.

Once Sir Gideon had taken a seat and ordered tea and a scone from the waitress he turned to Aurelia. "Oh, by the by, Miss Burton. I have had your sketch framed. I do hope you will visit me the next time you are in Balcrewe so you can see it."

"Sketch?" Larissa asked.

"Miss Burton made a most excellent sketch of Balcrewe and it just so happens to have me in it."

Aurelia laughed. "It was a sketch of *you*, Sir Gideon, and the background sneaked in."

He grinned, well pleased.

"I would love to see your work," Larissa said. "I cannot believe I have not asked before!"

"We usually enjoy ourselves too much chatting to look at paintings," Aurelia said.

"You can show her now," Sir Gideon said, glancing significantly at her satchel, which hung from the chairback. "And me, too," he added with a hopeful look.

Aurelia chuckled. "I *might* have a few sketches to share."

She pulled out the book and flipped through until she came to her most recent drawings and then moved aside her cup and plate to make a space on the table.

Larissa gasped at the drawing. "What in the world is that?"

Aurelia smiled at their shocked faces. "It is called an *alligator*. The specimen I used for this sketch is actually quite small at a little over three feet. Mr. Montgomery said they saw animals as long as fifteen feet."

"Fifteen feet!" Larissa murmured. "It looks like something out of a nightmare."

"Are they aquatic?" Sir Gideon asked.

"That is their preferred environment, but they can also live on land."

Several people who'd come in to buy pastries or bread to take home were lured over to their table by all the *oohing* and *ahhing*.

"Look at those teeth!" one of the men exclaimed, a farmer by the look of his clothing. "How big are they?"

Aurelia opened her mouth.

"Some of the longest teeth are as big as three inches."

All heads swiveled around at the sound of the Earl of Crewe's voice.

He smiled at the small assemblage and pulled out his watch and held it up. One of the fobs was a yellowish fang which he removed from the chain and gave to the farmer to inspect. "This one came from a large male one of our hunters brought back for dinner one evening."

The shop erupted at that information, and the reactions were quite comical.

The young waitress—Betsy, who could not have been more than fourteen—made a gagging sound. "You *et* it, me lord?"

The earl laughed. "Indeed we did, and we were grateful to have it."

"What did it taste like?" The farmer who was inspecting the tooth asked.

"A great deal like fish, but the texture is a bit chewier." He met Aurelia's gaze, his own unreadable. "Perhaps we should have an exhibit here on the island once I've received the first prints back from the publisher."

There was a murmur of excitement at that news.

"That is an excellent notion, Crewe. You could have one in Balcrewe, as well," Sir Gideon said.

Lord Crewe looked from Aurelia to Sir Gideon and then at the vacant chair. "Do you have any objection to me joining you?"

"Please do," Aurelia murmured, her pulse already pounding.

"More tea, Betsy," the earl said, gesturing to their empty cups. "And I'll have one of those cream cakes. The biggest one," he added with a grin. "Anyone else?" he asked, looking around at them.

The three of them politely declined.

Once the waitress had left the earl turned to Larissa. "I have not had the pleasure, but I think you must be one of the Misses Cliffords as you resemble your sister, whom I believe was the eldest."

Larissa blushed under Lord Crewe's piercing gaze just as every other woman Aurelia had met.

"I am Larissa Clifford. It was indeed Penelope whom you met. We were all most grateful for your intervention when the vicar wanted to—"

"Ah, yes—that foolishness. I'm sorry you had to endure that. And then Talbot here tells me you were attacked the day Miss Burton arrived. Have you had any issues with those boys—or any others—since then?"

"I am pleased to say I have not. I have you to thank for—"

The earl gave a dismissive flick of his hand. "Nonsense. You needn't thank me for doing my job, part of which is to ensure that people living on my land are safe and unmolested." He turned to Aurelia. "I went looking for you this morning. I thought perhaps you had ventured out on another rock pool adventure," he said, his eye hooded as he smiled at her.

Thankfully Betsy arrived just then with a large teapot and an unusually huge cream cake.

"Ah, thank you my dear," he said. "Will you do the honors and pour, Miss Burton?"

"Of course," Aurelia murmured, grateful to have something to do other than blush and stare.

"You have been gone quite some time," Sir Gideon said as the earl attacked his cream cake with gusto.

Her mouth flooded with moisture at the sight of the earl's defined jaw flexing as he chewed, a smear of cream on his lower lip, which was twice as full as the upper one.

Aurelia had the most shocking urge to lean forward and lick it off.

Thankfully, she did no such thing. Instead, she wrenched her eyes away. And ran smack into Larissa's knowing gaze.

"Yes. I've been gone more than six weeks," the earl said after a moment. "I've been traveling about the country with my tin cup begging for alms." He took another wolfish bite, his gaze sliding to Aurelia.

"Alms?" Larissa asked, a notch of confusion between her eyes.

"Funding for his next expedition," Aurelia explained as the earl's cheeks were currently bulging with cream cake.

"Did you go to London?" Sir Gideon asked.

The earl swallowed and said, "Almost a month there and ten days in Edinburgh. It made me miss home." He gave Aurelia a brooding look before turning back to Sir Gideon. "What brings you out to Crewe, Talbot? Tea cakes?" He smirked.

"I came to see John Nicholson." A look of uncharacteristic irritation crossed the handsome baronet's face. "He is housebound with gout and no longer makes even brief journeys to the mainland. And so I bring my problems *to him* these days."

The earl grunted, making no effort to hide his utter disinterest in Sir Gideon's staffing difficulties. Instead, he turned to Larissa. "How is Miss Pomeroy faring? I know she went to be with her sister some time back."

"She is fading quickly, my lord. I had a letter from her sister only last week."

"That is unfortunate. She is a fine woman. At one point I had thought to bring her here for Celsa."

"She was a lovely, gentle governess and we all adored her," Larissa said. "I daresay your daughter would have loved her, too."

"Gentle?" the earl repeated, and then snorted. "Perhaps it would not have been such a good idea after all. Celsa requires somebody with the disposition of a lion tamer."

Larissa and Sir Gideon laughed as if his lordship was joking. Aurelia was not so sure.

Sir Gideon glanced out the window. "The wind is beginning to pick up." He turned to Larissa. "I will be happy to row you back, if you like."

"I do, indeed," Larissa said, and then turned to Aurelia. "Next week at the same time?"

Aurelia opened her mouth to say she would come to Balcrewe next time, but the earl spoke first.

"Next week I will send a servant to bring you over, Miss Clifford, and you will have tea at the castle." He smiled at Aurelia. "I'm sure Miss Burton would be happy to give you a tour."

Larissa looked at Aurelia and raised her eyebrows.

Aurelia could see her friend found the idea exciting. "Do come, Larissa. I can show you my workroom while you are there."

"I would love to," Larissa said, and then opened her reticule, reminding Aurelia they had not paid for their tea.

"Allow me." Sir Gideon reached into his coat.

The earl set a hand over Aurelia's when she opened her reticule, his naked fingers scorchingly hot on the bare skin of her hand.

"It is my treat," he said, smiling from Aurelia to Miss Clifford, ignoring Sir Gideon's protests and tossing at least twice as much money as was needed on the table. "It is the least I can do after crashing your tête-à-tête."

After Aurelia said goodbye to Larissa and Sir Gideon, she found herself standing alone with Lord Crewe, whose rather intimidating stallion—Frost—was irritably pawing the ground, as if waiting outside of teashops was beneath his dignity.

She forced herself to look at the earl. "Well, I see you are mounted so—"

"Frost can take both of us," he said, pulling on his gloves.

Aurelia gawked. "What? No, I can't—"

"Of course you can," he said, swinging into the saddle with a fluid grace that was impressive for such a tall man. He held out a hand. "Give me your left hand."

"But I don't—"

"Miss Burton," he said, his tone of quiet command not something she could have resisted if she'd wanted to. And Aurelia knew, not too deep down, that riding pressed up against Lord Crewe's body was something she would have given her eye-teeth to experience.

And so she held out her left arm.

His hand closed around hers.

"Put your foot on my boot."

Aurelia complied and he lifted her as if she weighed no more than a corn dolly. His arm snaked around her middle and he pulled her snugly against him, the side of her hip resting against his groin.

"There, you see? Plenty of room," he said, the words rumbling from his body to hers.

Aurelia bit her lip in time to catch the mortifying groan that wanted to slip out. She clutched the pommel even though there was no danger of falling off, more as a precaution against the shudder of desire that went through her as his big hand splayed over her belly.

"Comfortable?" he murmured as the stallion began to move.

The urge to laugh hysterically was almost overwhelming. "Yes, thank you," she croaked.

Frost's gait was so smooth it was like riding on the deck of a ship.

"How convenient that Sir Gideon managed to be in town just at the right time to join you for tea," the earl said, his sarcasm so thick she could have cut it with a knife.

"How convenient that you were there, as well, my lord," Aurelia retorted, so distracted by his delicious scent and the press of his ridiculously masculine torso that she could hardly force out the words.

He laughed. "When I did not find you in your turret lair, I asked Charles if he knew your whereabouts and he told me you often met with Miss Clifford on a Tuesday. I admit that I went in the hope of foisting my company on you—at least to escort you back to my castle. Was that so bad of me?"

Aurelia sighed.

"Why do you make such a pained noise?"

"I do not possess anywhere near your skills when it comes to flirtation, my lord."

He chuckled and the warm, velvety sound made her stomach clench. How she had missed his easy laughter, craving it the way a starving man fantasized about food. And now that he was back Aurelia wanted to gorge like any glutton.

"You have something far better than flirtation, my dear Miss Burton."

She bit her tongue to keep from asking what he meant.

"You are interesting—no," he amended, "captivating is a more accurate word. It is not only your beautiful face and desirable body"—he laughed at the way said body stiffened at his scandalous observation—"but the unique essence that makes you *you*. You are fierce, dignified, dedicated, clever, empathic, and a dozen other qualities I could list."

Name them! Name them! the needy, love-starved voice inside her—which Aurelia had always ruthlessly suppressed—begged.

Why is he saying this? the voice of reason demanded, loudly enough to all but smother that other, more hopeful, voice.

He rejected you, left without a word, and stayed away for weeks. And now he has come back and is bored, so he is dallying with you, said a voice that sounded remarkably like her mother.

His arm loosened and his gloved fingers took her chin and shifted her until their eyes met.

They were so close Aurelia could see the lines that fanned out from his eye, the deep grooves that bracketed his smiling lips, and the cruel details of the ragged scars that scored his cheek, chin, and left side of his mouth.

In short, she could see every single flaw on his battered face.

And never had he looked so appealing and so irresistible.

"Your lips are pursed and you are giving me a very severe look, Miss Burton." His gaze lowered briefly to her mouth, his own lips twitching before his eye slid back to meet hers. "I sense you are struggling to hold back a thundering scold," he said after a moment, his face wearing the same half-amused look it so often did. "Should I not have told you that I admire you?"

"To what purpose?" she demanded, far more sharply than she'd intended.

His eye widened and he looked considerably less amused. Not angry but perplexed.

Almost… hurt.

Could he really be so obtuse? Did he truly believe that she could engage in lighthearted banter and then simply go on with her day? Was he so thoroughly jaded that nothing disturbed his equilibrium?

Did she really mean so little to him that holding her close had no effect on him at all?

Aurelia gave an exasperated huff and deliberately turned away from him and faced forward. She refused to be toyed with. Not again. Not after girding her heart for weeks on end.

Lord Crewe's chest expanded, as if he were drawing air to speak, but after a moment he exhaled.

The rest of the brief journey took place in silence, which is exactly what she had hoped to achieve by snubbing him.

And yet, for the life of her, Aurelia could not understand why she felt the urge to cry.

Chapter 15

A urelia had finished work for the day and was cleaning her brushes when she heard the door to the workroom open behind her.

She heaved a sigh. "What have I said about knocking, my lady?" she asked as she turned. It wasn't Celsa at all, but Guustin Walker. "Oh! Captain Walker."

"I am terribly sorry to barge in on you like this. I was not sure which room you were in and have just been opening doors." He gave her an abashed look. "I can go out and knock?"

She laughed. "I will forgive you this time."

"You are wondering what I am doing invading your domain and interrupting your work."

"You are not invading and I am finished work for the day."

"My first night back you said you would show me your paintings, but we were… interrupted."

Aurelia recalled the evening well. Lord Crewe had come in and found them laughing and had looked almost frosty. No doubt he believed an impoverished artist was an inappropriate match for his son.

"I would be glad to show you some paintings."

Captain Walker grinned, the expression so like his father's that she felt an odd little flutter in her belly.

"I have another favor to ask, too."

"Yes?" she asked, taking three loosely wrapped paintings from the rack where she kept them.

"I wondered if you would come with me to visit my mother. She is very curious about you and I've promised to do my best to lure you to her cottage."

"Of course, I will come," she said, ashamed by how very, very curious she was to meet the woman not just because she was Guustin's mother, but because she was the earl's former lover. Or at least she thought they were no longer lovers. But who knew?

"Are you free this afternoon?" he asked.

"I can come today," she said. Celsa would be disappointed, but Aurelia would explain it was an unusual circumstance.

Aurelia gestured to the paintings she'd laid out. "The originals of these have already gone to Edinburgh, but I make copies of my favorite ones for myself. In my spare time," she felt compelled to add.

"What an astounding shade of pink!" he exclaimed when she removed the paper from the first painting. "And that is also an unusual bill—beak?" he asked, giving her a questioning look.

"It is called a *bill*. This is a roseate spoonbill."

"It certainly is striking. And very lifelike, although it is difficult to imagine such a flamboyantly colored creature surviving in the wild."

"Arthur said he saw great flocks of them. It must take one's breath away to see the sky turn pink," Aurelia said. She uncovered the next painting. "This one is called a red velvet ant."

He laughed. "It is shockingly red and velvety."

"Yes, it is. It is not an ant, but a wasp. And the earl says it has one of the most painful stings of anything he's experienced."

"Isn't there a saying about beauty often concealing danger?"

"I seem to recall having heard that," she said, amused. And then she uncovered the last one.

Captain Walker sucked in his breath and looked up from the painting, his expression one of surprise. "Is this—"

"Yes, it is the panther that attacked his lordship and killed Lady Crewe."

"You mean it is the same kind of animal."

"No, it is the exact same one. One of the bearers shot the panther and Arthur managed to salvage a great deal of the animal through some skillful taxidermy." She cocked her head at him, surprised. "Have you not seen Arthur's menagerie in the armory?"

He smiled, the action crinkling the skin at the corner of his eyes the same way it did his father's. "I'll be honest with you, Miss Burton—but don't tell my father or my cousin—but those stuffed animals give me the woolies so I've not actually gone down there."

Aurelia laughed as she returned the paintings to their proper places.

Just then the door opened and the earl entered. Aurelia could not help thinking this was exactly the way the three of them had encountered each other the last time.

"Beekman told me that you were looking for me this morning while I was out?" he said to Aurelia, his habitual smile nowhere in sight and his gaze reserved, which is how he had looked at her ever since giving her a ride back from the tea shop a week ago.

Aurelia told herself she was relieved he no longer teased her at dinner or sought her out to go riding or rock pooling or anything else. And the few times she had inadvertently encountered him—twice in the library and once down in the specimen room—they'd both hastily excused themselves.

She repeatedly reminded herself that a more businesslike relationship was what she had wanted all along. If she said it often enough, and for long enough, she might even begin to believe it.

"Did you need something, Miss Burton?" the earl repeated, making her realize that she'd been staring up at him like a slack-jawed dunce.

"Er, I had some questions about three of the new samples but Arthur answered them." She had told herself to be grateful for that, too.

"I am glad he could help."

"And I also wanted to thank you for sending Charles to pick up Miss Clifford yesterday, that was most kind of you. She greatly enjoyed her tour of the castle."

"You are welcome," he said, turning his cool gaze toward his son and lifting an eyebrow. "Fancy seeing you here, Guustin. Are you developing an interest in art? Or perhaps you are considering a hobby as a naturalist?"

Guustin's lips twitched at his father's arch tone. "I regret to say that I have no talent in either direction, my lord. I came to see Miss Burton's work and invite her to visit my mother this afternoon."

If the offer surprised the earl, he did not show it. Instead, he said, "And what paintings did you see?"

"A pink bird, a red ant that is not an ant, and—er…"

"A panther?" the earl guessed with a sardonic look.

"Yes. Quite an impressive animal."

"Indeed." His pale blue eye rested broodingly on Aurelia, making her squirm.

And then he turned to his son and said, "Could you come to the library? I just received a letter from the shipyard in Glasgow and wanted to ask you a few questions." It might have been phrased as a question, but Aurelia could tell Captain Walker knew it for the command it was.

"Yes, of course. I can come right now."

The earl glanced at Aurelia. "Don't worry, I shan't keep him long, Miss Burton."

Something about the faint curl of his lips made her feel… guilty. Was she doing something wrong talking to Captain Walker? Was he displeased about this visit to his son's mother?

Aurelia realized the two men were waiting on a response from her and hastily said to Captain Walker, "I need to change into my habit and then I will meet you at the stables."

"Of course. Shall we say a half hour?"

Aurelia nodded and Captain Walker followed his father from the room.

Twenty-five minutes later Aurelia had finished dressing and was pinning on her hat when the door to her room flew open and Lady Celsa skidded to a halt.

"I'm sorry!" she blurted, and then knocked on the door, giving Aurelia a sheepish grin. "You were late, so I thought we were not going today." Her eyes flickered over Aurelia's clothing. "But now I see—"

"I cannot go with you today, my lady," Aurelia said, picking up her gloves and whip.

"Why not?" Celsa demanded.

"Because your brother invited me to meet his mother and—"

"He's not my brother!"

"There is no need to raise your voice as I am standing right in front of you," Aurelia said calmly. "I am sorry for being imprecise. Your *half*-brother invited me to—"

"He's not that, either."

Aurelia opened her mouth to ask her what she meant, but then decided—based on the girl's scowl—that right now wasn't a good time to engage in a conversation.

Instead, she said, "I will ride with you tomorrow." She strode toward the door and looked pointedly at Celsa when the girl continued to block it.

Instead of moving, Celsa crossed her arms and took up even more space. "Don't act like you don't know the truth."

"What truth?"

"Guustin isn't my brother because we don't share the same mother *or* the same father."

"What do you mean?"

"If you weren't too high and mighty to listen to *pernicious* gossip you might have heard about it already. Although I'm surprised the Hatchet didn't tell you the very first night."

"Tell me *what*, pray?"

"The earl is not my real father, Miss Burton."

Aurelia had no response. As much as she would have liked to know what in the world Celsa meant—and who had told her such a thing—this was not the sort of conversation she wanted to have on her way out the door. Or at any time, really.

"Aren't you going to deny it, Miss Burton? Aren't you going to say something prim and irritating about how good girls don't say such things?"

"I am not going to say anything of the sort. But I do hope that you—"

"I don't care what you hope!" Celsa spun on her heel and stormed from the room throwing her parting words over her shoulder. "Just go with Guustin. Go with him every day, for all I care. I didn't want to ride with you, anyhow!"

Aurelia began to go after her, but then stopped. What could she say to calm her? She knew nothing about the claim the girl had made.

Could it really be true? Was Celsa not the earl's child?

***

"You have an excellent seat, Miss Burton," Captain Walker said as they left the stables a short time later.

"Thank you. I used to ride a great deal as a child, but it has been some years."

"Why did you stop?"

"Our family was forced to retrench several years ago and horses—at least hacks for me and my sisters—were among the first luxuries to go."

"That is unfortunate." He hesitated and then asked, "Is your family's financial situation the reason why you've taken this post?"

"In part. But I have been illustrating for several years, so this isn't my first position, just the first time I have worked away from home."

"And your mother and father are… sanguine about your decision."

"My father is gone, but, no, my mother was most unhappy."

"I'm sorry about your father. You have other siblings?"

"I have four sisters and one brother."

Guustin Walker was an attentive conversationist and kept Aurelia so busy answering his questions that she was startled when he stopped his mount not far from a lovely manor house. "We are here," he said, smiling at her look of surprise.

"I have done nothing but talk about myself the entire ride, Captain Walker!"

"Ah, but that was my plan. I already know all about myself, you see." He dismounted and then came around to help her down and handed the reins over to a young boy who trotted out from behind the house.

"You must tell me about *you* on the ride back," Aurelia said.

"I will—but I would ask one thing first. I know it is forward of me, but I will be here for several months and we will likely be thrown together often, so won't you call me Guustin?"

It *was* forward, but then how could she say *no* when Arthur used her Christian name. "Of course. Please call me Aurelia."

"The name is lovely and suits you."

"Guustin!" a voice called out before Aurelia could respond. A tall, beautiful blonde woman stood in the doorway. "I am so glad you are here."

"You should not be standing, Mama," Guustin chided.

Only then did Aurelia notice the woman was leaning on a cane.

"Oh, tosh. I wanted to greet my guest on my feet." She turned a charming smile on Aurelia. "I am delighted you've come to see me, Miss Burton."

"Thank you for inviting me," Aurelia said, startled by the warmth in the other woman's gaze. She was truly lovely and hardly looked any older than her son—except for her hands, which were terribly gnarled and twisted. Aurelia could not imagine how painful that must be.

Mrs. Walker looked lovingly up at her son and then heaved a sigh. "But you are right, darling. I should not be standing."

Guustin clucked his tongue and took the cane from her. "Will you carry this for my disobedient mother, Aurelia?"

"Of course."

He lifted up Mrs. Walker, holding her cradled in his arms. "Right this way, Aurelia."

The house was charming, elegant, and spacious and not at all what she had expected from a former mistress, although why she believed the earl would stint the mother of his son she didn't know.

"This is my gilded cage," Mrs. Walker said as her son carried her into a room decorated in sage green and dusty rose. Once Guustin had set her down on a chaise lounge, she said, "Will you tell Una to bring tea in perhaps a quarter of an hour, Guustin? Also, two letters came for you and I put them on your desk."

Guustin nodded and then turned to Aurelia. "I will leave you in my mother's capable hands for a few moments, if you do not mind?"

"Not at all," Aurelia said.

"Guustin is such a comfort to me," Mrs. Walker said once the door closed behind her son.

"You must miss him when he is away."

"I do. Intensely. But I am proud that he is making his way in the world. He works hard and is clever. One day he will be a wealthy, powerful man like his father."

"I'm sure he will," Aurelia said, distressingly aware that her face had heated at the other woman's casual reference to her former lover.

Mrs. Walker smiled, her green eyes—so like her son's—gently amused. "I daresay you are rather shocked at how freely I talk of my illegitimate child and his father."

"I think it speaks well of you that you are not ashamed of his birth," Aurelia said. "Too often mothers are shamed and ostracized while the fathers live without retribution. Or, more frequently, they take pride exhibiting proof of their virility."

Mrs. Walker chuckled. "I had heard from both Guustin and Celsa that you were a very forthright young lady. And I must say I heartily approve."

"Lady Celsa visits you?" Aurelia asked, surprised.

"She used to come almost every day but visits less often now that she has lost her riding privileges." Mrs. Walker clucked her tongue. "Poor Celsa is a troubled, unhappy girl. It is odd how the earl's illegitimate child is so much happier than his legitimate one. Roland despairs that she will ever grow out of her wildness and naughty tricks."

Roland. The name evoked epic adventures and Charlemagne's fierce, towering general, a man who had struck terror into his foes with his famed sword Durendal and his loyal steed Vigilance.

Yes, the name *Roland* suited the earl better than any other Aurelia could have chosen.

"I daresay you think he is too strict with Celsa," Mrs. Walker said.

"He is rather harsh," Aurelia admitted. "But then she does drive him to it.

"There was a time when Roland and Celsa got along well together, but something happened to cause a rift between them and I have never been able to find out what it was."

That was interesting because it had been Aurelia's impression that father and daughter had never been close. Had Celsa been the one to make her think that?

"When did that happen?" Aurelia asked.

Mrs. Walker pondered her question for a moment before saying, "It seems like Celsa must have been nine or perhaps ten."

Not so long ago. What had happened?

"I have remonstrated with Roland and begged him to be more… gentle with her. I've tried to explain what delicate, mercurial creatures adolescent girls can be." Mrs. Walker pulled a wry face. "Not that he listens to me, of course."

It was difficult to imagine anyone *remonstrating* with Lord Crewe.

"Was he the same with Captain Walker when he was young?"

"No, he was not. Perhaps because they were kept apart for those first few years so when they did finally meet, they were inseparable." She smiled fondly, looking into her past.

Why had Lord Crewe been kept from his child?

Before Aurelia could embarrass herself by prying, the door opened and the subject of their conversation entered the room. He looked from Aurelia to his mother and she fancied there was a hint of concern in his gaze, as if he worried about what Mrs. Walker might have said.

With Guustin's presence in the cozy room, the conversation turned to more traditional lines and there were no more fascinating tidbits about Lord Crewe.

By the time they had finished tea three-quarters of an hour later, Mrs. Walker was visibly flagging.

"Are you in pain, Mama? Shall I bring you some laudanum?" Guustin asked.

"No, no, I am not in any pain. Just a bit… fatigued."

"I know this is when you usually take your nap."

Mrs. Walker smiled wryly at Aurelia. "Only when one is old does one truly appreciate naps, Miss Burton."

"You are not old, Mama."

Aurelia thought it was a tragedy that her hands and, evidently, her knees, kept such a beautiful, youthful-looking woman housebound.

Guustin leaned low and kissed her cheek. "We will leave you, now. But I will come tomorrow, too."

Mrs. Walker wore a look of pure contentment and Aurelia was touched by the obvious affection between the two. Guustin might have been illegitimate, but—unlike poor Celsa—he was surrounded by love.

"You will come visit again, Miss Burton—please do not stand on ceremony. You needn't wait for Guustin to pay a call."

Mrs. Walker's meaning was clear: come alone and they could talk without restraint.

"I certainly will," Aurelia assured her, ashamed by how curious she was for any little bit of information about the man who already took up far too much of her thoughts.

Chapter 16

Aurelia's chance to visit Mrs. Walker again came a mere five days later when Lord Crewe, Guustin, and Celsa all made a trip to Balcrewe.

"Are you sure you do not wish to come?" Guustin asked Aurelia at breakfast.

One look at Celsa's scowl said that joining the group would be a terrible idea. The girl clearly relished the opportunity to spend the day with her father, even if she had to tolerate Guustin in the process.

"Thank you, but I've got too much work."

"You know what they say about all work and no play," the earl chided, teasing her for the first time in days—weeks, even.

Aurelia was so startled that she forgot herself. "Are you implying that I am dull, Lord Crewe?"

The earl laughed; his smile warmer than it had been since the tea shop. "You should keep going on exactly as you are, Miss Burton, because the results are truly delightful."

Aurelia snorted and then blushed when she met Guustin's amused look.

Aurelia had not lied—there were several things she had to catch up on—but when the clock struck two-thirty, she changed into her habit, made her way to the stables, and headed toward Mrs. Walker's house.

She had been a bit apprehensive about her welcome, but the moment the maid escorted Aurelia into her *gilded cage*, it was clear Mrs. Walker was thrilled to see her.

"I was hoping you might visit alone," she said, a slight flush accompanying her words. "I love to see my son, but sometimes women just need to have a comfortable chat without any men around."

Aurelia felt a flutter of excitement at the woman's words.

"Guustin said you are extremely talented," Mrs. Walker said as they waited for the maid to bring the tea tray. "He said you'd done some drawings of Celsa that were excellent."

"I have done quite a few sketches of her." Aurelia was also working on a small painting of the girl, but she had not yet decided when, or if, she would show it to her.

"I would like to commission you to do a portrait of Guustin, Miss Burton." She pointed to a large oil painting of a beautiful boy sitting with a spaniel at his feet. "That is the only one I have of him."

"That is a wonderful painting."

"Thank you. Roland commissioned it for me. But I would like to have a more recent picture of him to enjoy when he is not here."

"I'm afraid that anything I paint will not be up to the standard of the one you have."

Mrs. Walker clucked her tongue. "If Guustin said you are talented, I believe him."

"I have a few sketches of Guustin already," Aurelia admitted.

"I am surprised that he sat still long enough."

"I don't need subjects to sit for me. It makes it easier but it is not necessary." She gestured to her satchel. "I have my sketchpad with me. Would you like to see them?"

"I would love to! Come and sit beside me." She patted the settee.

Aurelia took out the sketchbook, flipped to the pages containing Guustin, and sat beside the other woman.

"Oh, that is wonderful!" Mrs. Walker said when Aurelia showed her the first one. She leaned closer to the drawing before asking, "Might I hold the pad closer? I promise I will be careful," she added, mistaking the reason for Aurelia's hesitation to let the sketchbook out of her hands.

But what else could Aurelia do?

"Of course," she said, handing the book over.

Mrs. Walker *oohed* and *ahhed* her way through the pages. "You are so very clever!" she gushed. "You've caught exactly that mischievous look he gets when he teases poor Celsa."

"Thank you."

"Oh! And here are some of Celsa. How pretty she looks when she smiles!"

"Yes, she does," Aurelia said, reaching for the book. "That is all there is of—"

Mrs. Walker flipped the page and froze. "Oh, my." She lifted the book closer, her lips parted, and then she turned another page.

Aurelia lifted her hands to her face, as if she could stop what was happening if she did not see it.

She sighed and forced them open, watching with mortification as Mrs. Walker turned the pages in silence, and then flipped through them again.

Once she had gone through them a third time, she looked up at Aurelia. "These are quite… powerful."

Aurelia wanted to melt between the floorboards. Instead of that happy occurrence, she merely sat there with her face aflame, slowly dying inside.

After an age, Mrs. Walker handed her the book. Aurelia busied herself replacing it in her satchel, the room so quiet she swore she could hear plants growing outside.

"I don't want to be intrusive," Mrs. Walker said, "but, the one of Roland in the Viking helm and, er, nothing else, is that—"

"The drawings are all from my imagination," Aurelia hastily assured her.

Mrs. Walker had bright pink slashes over her lovely high cheekbones. "What an imagination you must have!" She laughed and cupped her face with her hands. "Goodness. I don't recall the last time I blushed so."

"I'm glad I am not the only one," Aurelia muttered.

Mrs. Walker's face was both knowing, and a bit sad as she studied Aurelia. "You are very skilled," she said. But Aurelia suspected that was not what she was thinking about.

"Thank you."

"Would consider selling any of those drawings of Guustin?" Mrs. Walker asked.

"You may have them once I've finished the portrait," Aurelia said, grateful to leave the subject of her nude employer behind.

"That is very kind of you. I will treasure them." Mrs. Walker turned to look at her teacup, as if she were considering something. "Guustin is very taken with you. I had hoped—" she broke off and sighed, a faintly chagrined expression on her face. "I had hoped that you might feel the same way about him. I'm sorry, Miss Burton," she hastily added. "That was an extremely indelicate thing to say. Please forgive me. I hope you are not offended."

Aurelia took a moment to gather her thoughts and then said, "I appreciate your plain-speaking, Mrs. Walker. I much prefer that to pointless chatter. I am not offended." Stunned and embarrassed, but not offended.

"I am so glad to hear it. I talk to so few people now, and I find that I've taken an immediate liking to you. Won't you please call me Nora—I know you and Guustin have exchanged Christian names."

"Of course, and you must call me Aurelia. And—and I hope you always speak plainly with me." She felt a pang of guilt at her words because what she really wanted—more than anything but was too cowardly to say—was for Nora to speak plainly about *Roland*. Just thinking the name gave her flutters.

She was such an infatuated fool.

"Do you think you might come to love my son?" Nora asked, and then chuckled. "Is that *too* plain speaking?"

"No, it isn't," she said, only lying a little. "And no, I'm afraid my feelings for Guustin are platonic."

"Because you have stronger ones for his father?"

Aurelia didn't want to lie, but neither did she want to admit the truth— especially when she wasn't sure what it was. "As my sketches would indicate," she said, blushing fierily, "I am fascinated by the earl, but I suspect that a great many women are."

"That is certainly true." Nora hesitated, and then said, "I have not been Roland's mistress for many years—not since before Guustin was born."

The relief that surged through her at the other woman's admission made her dizzy.

"Because we share a son, we see each other and are friendly, although I would not go so far as to say we were *friends*, if you know what I mean?"

Again, Aurelia nodded, although she wasn't really sure.

"But just because Roland and I are not together does not mean—" she bit her lip, met Aurelia's gaze, and then said, "Roland has always had lovers, Aurelia, oftentimes more than one at any given time."

Aurelia's jaw sagged.

Nora's eyes went wide and she gave a bark of laughter. "Oh, dear! That did not come out the way I intended. I did not mean in the same bed at the same time. Although—" she broke off and gave Aurelia a strained smile.

Aurelia was so nauseated by the thought of the earl with another woman— *any* woman—that she could not even ponder the second part of what Nora had said. Or what she had *not* said, rather.

"I would like to be even more direct," Nora said, and then paused, giving Aurelia a questioning look.

Aurelia nodded, not trusting her voice.

"If what you are seeking is sensual pleasure and experience, then you could not find a more generous, skilled, and attentive lover than Roland. However—" she paused and chewed her lower lip. "If you are seeking a husband? Well…"

"I understand," Aurelia said, her voice barely a croak. And she *did* understand. More than Nora knew. Twice now she had flown too close to Lord Crewe's flame and had been scorched. Both times she had been spared a more painful burn when he had ended the flirtation.

She stared bleakly at her clenched hands. Nora hadn't said anything Aurelia hadn't already thought of herself, but it hurt to have her suspicions confirmed.

"Would you like to hear what Roland was like as a young man?" Nora asked, breaking the awkward silence that had begun to fill the room.

Aurelia snorted. "Bold, arrogant, and brilliant?"

"Would you believe shy, reserved, bookish, and—yes, also brilliant?"

"I'm sorry, but I find that very difficult to imagine. Er, all except the *brilliant* part."

"It is a bit of a long story, but do you want to know how Roland and I met and came to have a son?"

More than anything. "I would like to know, if you don't mind telling me."

"I don't mind. In fact, I would like to speak of it." She glanced down at her hands, which were gnarled and swollen and looked far older than her beautiful face. "I spend a great deal of my time alone" She gave a short, bitter laugh. "As you can imagine, I do not have many friends or even acquaintances here on Crewe. If I were just another of Roland's ex-lovers, I would not be such an outsider. After all, I *did* grow up on the island. But it is because of all this"—she waved to the elegant room around them—"that so many people envy and dislike me. Don't misunderstand me," she hastily added. "I am not lonely, but being solitary means I think about the past a great deal. About the decisions I made. That time of my life was so long ago that it matters to nobody but me anymore. So… I am glad to talk about it."

Aurelia realized that she had inched to the edge of her seat and forced herself to sit back.

Nora's gaze became vague. "I met my husband, Brian Walker, when he came to the island on a merchant vessel." She suddenly laughed. "Yes, there really was a Brian Walker, although many on the island will tell you I invented him to further my notorious trade."

Notorious trade? Aurelia wanted to ask her what she meant, but she did not want to interrupt the other woman.

"My grandmother died a few months before I met Brian. I had been her caretaker for years and was devastated. When Brian arrived in my life I felt as though I'd been rescued. We married and moved to Glasgow. We were very happy—very much in love, but we'd only been married six months when his ship sank. He did not leave much money and I had nobody to ask for help." Her words tumbled out faster. "I was desperate. I had no letters of reference or any skill to earn money." She swallowed. "So I did what a great many women do when they begin to starve. I sold myself." Nora met Aurelia's gaze. "For a gently bred young woman, you do not look especially shocked."

"I have lived a sheltered life, but I have made an effort to understand the ways of the world—especially as they apply to women." She paused, and then added, "I cannot imagine how frightened you must have been."

"You are wise, as well as kind," Nora said, her smile grateful, as if she had expected Aurelia's derision or disgust. "I worked at a brothel in Glasgow and it was… horrible. It did not take long for me to begin thinking that starvation would have been preferable. And then, one evening I had a customer I recognized from my old life. It was the Earl of Crewe—this earl's father."

Aurelia's eyes bulged. "Oh."

"Yes, *oh*, indeed. He recognized me from when I lived on Crewe, of course." She smiled wryly. "He was the kind of man who always noticed pretty girls and gave them plenty of his attention. He was stamped from a different mold than his son—an ancient mold—and believed it was his privilege and duty to scatter his seed widely." She cocked her head. "You are looking skeptical and thinking that Roland is like his father because of Guustin, aren't you?"

"I need to learn to guard my expressions better," Aurelia said, chagrined. "But you are right. That is what I was thinking."

"Guustin is Roland's *only* illegitimate child, Aurelia."

Aurelia frowned.

"I gather you've heard some gossip indicating otherwise?"

"Yes." Miss Hatchet had been delighted to tell Aurelia about at least three children and their mothers.

"Lies. All lies," Nora said, shaking her head. "Roland often accepts responsibility when women have no spouse. Especially if the real father is married. It is a way to keep the peace and take care of children who would otherwise go without."

"That seems a high price to pay—to have everyone believing the worst of you." Which is exactly what Aurelia had done.

"The price is not so high if you are the Laird of Crewe," Nora said. "The old earl was a dreadful rake, but at least he always compensated the women who bore his children and probably more than a few who were not his."

Aurelia thought about her own father whom she'd once caught in a compromising position with a parlor maid—back when they could afford such a thing—and suspected she probably had more than a few half-siblings in their neighborhood but knew that her father had never acknowledged or taken financial responsibility for any of them.

"The old earl took mercy on me when he met me in that brothel." Nora laughed bitterly. "I am not saying that he did not first avail himself of my services. He was nothing if not consistent in his behavior."

This time, Aurelia *was* shocked. Thankfully, Nora was too caught up in her story to notice.

"After the earl had taken his pleasure, he told me about his son. Of course, I recalled Roland from when I lived on the island. He was five years younger than me, so thirteen to my eighteen when I'd last lived on Crewe. I knew him to be a shy, bookish sort and often saw him combing the island for insects and plants and such. He was tall—almost as tall as he is now—but thin and lanky, yet to grow into his body. His lordship was worried that Roland was not masculine enough. It bothered him that his son had evinced no interest in women and he suspected Roland was still a virgin at sixteen."

Aurelia had a bad feeling about where this was going.

"The earl said that if I agreed to return to Crewe and instruct the young master in the erotic arts and turn him into a man that he would provide me with a cottage and an allowance and I could live without any worry, even after Roland eventually tired of me." Nora dropped her gaze to the floor, her pale cheeks tinting pink. When she looked up, Aurelia saw shame in her beautiful green eyes. "I am still deeply ashamed that I leapt at his offer so quickly. But the truth was that I probably would have done far worse to escape my wretched life. But my eagerness to accept his offer was not the worst of it. You see, Roland was not to know that his father had engaged me. The earl said that his son was too romantic and had a foolish, almost girlish, notion of saving himself until he fell in love."

Aurelia struggled—and failed—to recall any sign of that boy in the man she knew.

"I was told to pretend as if I'd just encountered Roland by accident. I was to evince an interest in birds, flowers, and whatnot. I was to become… smitten."

Aurelia felt slightly nauseated.

"To my shame, I played my part well."

"You mean you fell in love with him?"

Nora smiled sadly. "No, I'm afraid there has only ever been one man for me, Aurelia, and that was my husband." She sighed. "I only pretended to love Roland."

"When did you tell him the truth?" Aurelia's eyes bulged. "He *does* know, doesn't he?"

Nora laughed, but there was no amusement in it. "Yes, he knows. I did not tell him until we had been together ten months. Even then, my motives for telling the truth were less than pure. You see, I was pregnant. When Roland found out, he insisted that we marry. I was terrified the earl would throw me out of the cottage and stop the money." She inhaled deeply and then exhaled slowly. "The earl was furious about the child but even angrier that Roland wanted to marry me. He ordered me to tell Roland that I had been paid to pretend that I loved him. I was to confess the truth: that I felt nothing for him at all. And so I did exactly that."

Aurelia could only stare, horrified.

"Roland's reaction stunned both me and the earl. He was upset at the lies, but he said we must marry for the sake of our child. Even though I had lied to him, he claimed that he still loved me." She shook her head.

"You don't think he did?"

"How could he even know what love was? He was six-and-ten and I was his first lover," Nora said, as if that explained everything. "His father forbade Roland from seeing me—certainly there was no question of marriage—but, for the first time in his life, his mild-mannered son stood up to the earl. They fought and it was dreadful. Roland came to me and was furious at his father. He said he would disobey his father and we would have to leave the island. I was terrified! I knew how hard life could be. But Roland, for all that he was so smart, was only sixteen and naïve about the ways of the world.

"And so, when the earl approached me, I was willing to agree to whatever he proposed. I left the island in the middle of the night and was taken to a place where I could have my child. He would pay an allowance only so long as I never contacted Roland." A tear slid down her cheek. "By accepting his bargain, I ended any chance of love between father and son. Years later, after Roland found me and brought me back to Crewe, I saw firsthand the rift I'd created between them."

"It was hardly your fault. If anyone was to blame it would be the late earl," Aurelia said, irrationally irked at a dead man. "How like a man to believe his son isn't *masculine* enough unless he has engaged in the requisite amount of coitus. And once his son *did* behave like a man—a *gentle*man—and accepted responsibility for his actions then the old earl was disgusted."

"I could not have said it better myself, Aurelia." Nora gave a watery chuckle and dabbed at her eyes with a lace-edged handkerchief. "Roland began searching for me almost from the day I left, using his allowance to pay for an inquiry agent. When he turned one-and-twenty and came into his inheritance, then he had more money to spend on the search and he quickly found me. By that point, the old earl did not care that Roland brought Guustin and me back to the island. All he had ever wanted to do was to break the hold I'd had over his son. With that shattered, I was no longer a threat and the earl just ignored my existence."

Nora snorted. "The old rake got far more than he bargained for when he brought me into Roland's life. Before I came along, he had a reserved but obedient and malleable son. Afterward… well, Roland was his own man in every way. He still pursued his naturalist studies, but he was no longer innocent and shy. He was like a different man." She shook herself and tucked away her handkerchief. "So, there is my sad story—but with a happy ending because I have a fine son."

Aurelia suddenly recalled what Celsa had shouted at her the day she'd met Nora for the first time.

Nora cocked her head. "What is it? You look as if you want to ask me something."

"It is about something Celsa said."

"She told you that Roland is not her father, didn't she?"

"Yes," Aurelia said, startled that the woman had guessed so quickly.

"I would like to strangle whoever it was who told Celsa that."

"So, it is—"

"It is true," Nora said grimly.

Aurelia was about to ask Nora how she knew that when the door to the sitting room opened and Guustin entered, his eyes moving from his mother to Aurelia, confusion clear in his gaze.

"Aurelia. What a surprise."

"Guustin!" Nora held out her hands. "You are back early."

"We finished up sooner than expected." Guustin kissed his mother's cheek. "You are flushed. Have you been overexerting yourself, Mama?"

"No, no, not at all."

Aurelia glanced at the watch pinned to her habit. "I did not realize I'd been here so long," she said, getting to her feet.

"It has been such a delightful afternoon," Nora said, and then looked at her son. "The sky looks to be darkening. You should escort Aurelia back to the castle, Guustin."

Aurelia shook her head. "Oh, that's not nec—"

"It will be my pleasure," Guustin said.

The sky had indeed turned menacing as Aurelia and Guustin mounted and began the ride back to the castle.

"You have put new life into my mother with your visit," he said as they rode abreast.

"I hope I did not overtire her today."

"A nap and she will be as good as new." He hesitated a moment and then said, "She has become very fond of you quickly. I hope she did not… overstep?"

"Not at all." Aurelia wondered if Guustin was concerned about what his mother might have disclosed about him or his interest in her. But he did not pursue the matter and shortly afterward the sky opened up.

"Let us gallop," Guustin shouted over the rain.

The ride was exhilarating, even though Aurelia knew she looked like a drowned rat by the time they reached the castle gate.

"Ride up to the front door, Aurelia. I'll take your horse to the stables for you."

Thunder cracked just as they drew up in front of the huge front door.

Aurelia slid inelegantly off Black Prince and tossed Guustin the reins.

"I will see you at dinner," he said, and then cantered toward the stables.

Aurelia was shaking the rain off her cloak when Arthur entered the foyer.

"Oh dear! You are soaked through, Aurelia. You must go upstairs immediately and I will have hot water sent up. I also have a poultice that is good to fight chills."

"Thank you, that is kind. But I don't think—"

"It was irresponsible of Guustin to keep you out in such weather."

"He didn't. I was visiting his mother and he escorted me back."

"Oh." He looked strangely deflated. Aurelia had noticed that the older man didn't care for the earl's son and spoke to him sharply, if at all.

Arthur suddenly brightened. "I saw that you finished the painting of the *urocyon cinereoargenteus*. It is exceptional!"

"Thank you. I couldn't have done it nearly as well without your excellent specimen and the detailed descriptions in your journal."

"It is one of my better pieces. I used my newest formula and it seems to offer superior preservation with the mercury."

"I had heard there is some danger in working with mercury?"

"Not if you know how to use it correctly."

"Well, the fox is certainly so lifelike that I sometimes felt as if I were in danger of being bitten."

He chortled. "The highest praise for a taxidermist. But I shouldn't keep you chatting or you will take a chill. Upstairs with you and I will go and see about the hot water and poultice."

Aurelia obeyed him without arguing, amused and also touched by his concern. She wasn't in danger of taking a chill, but it was still nice to be fussed over on occasion.

Chapter 17

S everal evenings later the pleasant atmosphere that had reigned over the castle for months was shattered.

It was after dinner and Aurelia, Guustin, Arthur, and Lord Crewe were playing whist. The fact that she knew how to play had come up during the meal and all three men had begged her to play.

"Celsa despises cards and we never have a fourth," Arthur said.

They were all excellent players and Guustin and Aurelia had just won the first game and were about to begin another when the butler entered.

"What is it, Beekman?" the earl asked.

"I'm afraid there is a…er, well a problem."

"What?" Lord Crewe demanded when his old retainer hesitated.

"Miss Hatchet discovered a crab in her bed, my lord."

The earl froze for a moment and then flung his cards onto the table. "Damnation!"

"Crewe," Arthur chided.

"Er, I beg your pardon, Miss Burton," Lord Crewe said to Aurelia and then strode toward the door.

Once it had closed behind him, Arthur stood. "I suppose I should go along and see if I can help calm the situation." He clucked his tongue. "Poor Miss Hatchet."

"I was thinking *poor crab*, myself," Guustin muttered, earning a look of raw dislike from Arthur.

"You may find this amusing but I assure you that Celsa will suffer greatly," Arthur snapped.

"If she is the one who placed the crustacean in Miss Hatchet's bed then perhaps she *should* suffer," Guustin said.

Arthur glared at him with deep loathing and then turned to Aurelia. "Excuse me, please."

Aurelia nodded. "Of course."

Guustin gathered up the cards and commenced to shuffle once the other man had gone. "Shall we play a game of two-handed?"

Aurelia nodded absently, her thoughts on Celsa. "Why would she do it?"

Guustin snorted. "You *have* met Miss Hatchet, haven't you? If anyone could drive a person to do such a stupid thing it would be that woman. I don't know why my father allows Arthur to choose Celsa's governesses. All of them have been like this Hatchet creature: humorless, vindictive, and prudish."

"Miss Hatchet can be abrasive, but Celsa should know that she cannot go through life taking such actions against people she dislikes. Not to mention that the punishment will far outstrip whatever pleasure she gets."

"Sometimes a few moments of revenge are worth the cost," Guustin said, dealing out the cards.

Aurelia narrowed her eyes at him. "Is it my imagination, or does Arthur dislike you?"

He laughed. "That was rather to the point, Aurelia."

"I'm sorry, I—"

He dealt out the last card and laid a hand over hers. "No. Do not apologize. I like you the way you are."

He did not remove his hand immediately, but instead leaned closer. "Do you know what I am thinking?" he asked, his voice low and a little rough, his pupils swelling as she watched.

"I probably should not try guessing."

He clucked his tongue. "Ah, evasion from you, Aurelia?" He leaned toward her slowly enough that she could have backed away if she wanted to. But she didn't. It wasn't that she wanted Guustin, but she did want to know what it felt to be kissed by somebody who was *not* the earl.

His lips, warm and soft, brushed against hers and Aurelia closed her eyes and waited for the spiral of joy—the quickening of her pulse—to overwhelm her senses.

Guustin gave a soft moan of pleasure and cupped her cheek, deepening the kiss.

Aurelia waited and waited while his lips caressed her with undeniable skill.

Nothing.

As if she had spoken aloud, he pulled back, his expression one of amused resignation. "I'm sorry. I should not have done that."

Aurelia felt strange—as if she should apologize for *not* responding. His kiss had not generated so much as a spark of desire. The entire experience had felt like a scientific experiment: cool, detached, and interesting, but not absorbing.

When he saw that she wasn't going to respond, he collected the cards he'd thrown down and resumed organizing them.

After a moment, he said, "It is true that Arthur does not care for me. I think he believes that I usurped his place with my father. Before I came along it was just the two of them. I think he resents the attention the earl gives me. I daresay he would be just as jealous of Celsa if she and the earl were not so constantly at odds."

Aurelia thought his words had a ring of truth.

"It is nice that Lady Celsa has Arthur for a champion," she said, picking up her cards and ordering them in her hands. When he did not answer, she looked up. "You don't think Arthur is good for her?"

"I do not think his treatment does her any favors." He paused and looked up from his hand. "Perhaps I am doing him a disservice, but sometimes I think he feeds on her isolation and friction with my father because that way she will always be closer to *him*."

Aurelia certainly hoped that was not true. "What makes you think that?"

He shrugged. "Just something I overheard once."

Aurelia waited for more, but after a minute realized he wasn't going to share what it was that he'd heard. "What do you think will happen after this crab incident?"

"I don't know. But I doubt it will be pleasant for Celsa.

***

When Aurelia opened the door to her room a few hours later it was to find Celsa sitting on the bench in front of her dresser, trying on Aurelia's favorite pair of earrings.

"I'm sorry," Celsa said, immediately pulling them from her ears. "I didn't mean to snoop. I just got so bored waiting for you." Her habitual scowl settled over her face. "You were downstairs playing cards with Guustin, I take it?"

Celsa's jealousy of Guustin was far less unnerving now that Aurelia knew the two were not blood relatives. But she still felt sorry for the girl as it was clear that Guustin viewed her as a sister, not a romantic partner.

"Why did you put a crab in Miss Hatchet's bed?"

"She is so desperate for companionship, I thought she would enjoy some time with one of her own kind."

"Why now? Did she say or do something in particular?"

The girl's face darkened. "It doesn't matter, does it? My father is going to punish me regardless of my reasons." A sly, unpleasant smile took control of her face. "The Hatchet will be punished too because my father is sending her away."

Aurelia unfastened her pearls and set them in her small jewelry case. "It is unkind of you to take pleasure in her dismissal. The world is hard enough for women without other women making it *more* difficult."

Celsa rolled her eyes. "The world *should* be hard for a venomous snake like her."

Aurelia sighed.

"You sigh and look disapproving, but you did not like her either, did you?"

Aurelia unscrewed her earrings and ignored the girl's question.

"You are only asking about her. Don't you care what will happen to me?" Celsa demanded.

"Of course, I care. Are you banned from riding until you are old and gray?"

Celsa snorted. "I am to be sent away to school in the spring."

"Oh. Well, that's not so bad." Aurelia thought it was a very good idea, but she knew Celsa would not appreciate hearing that.

"Ha! What do you know about it? Were you forced to go to school?"

"I went for one year." And it had been one of the most enjoyable periods of her life, although she had missed her sisters and brother terribly.

"You probably enjoyed it because you were popular. Everyone will hate me and make fun of me because I am a yokel."

Aurelia laughed.

Celsa jumped to her feet. "I am pleased to amuse you."

"I am not laughing at you, you goose. I'm laughing at your assumption that being from an island means you are a *yokel*."

"Why wouldn't it?"

"It is exciting and exotic to live on an island that belongs to your family. I have never met another person who can say that."

Celsa looked arrested. "I have never thought of it that way."

"And if you treat people honestly and kindly—as you've been doing with me—*mostly*, then you will have plenty of friends."

Celsa stared, her eyes raw with hope, insecurity, and all the other torrid emotions of youth. "Did you make friends?"

"I did. And I still write to three of them to this very day."

"I will miss you," Lady Celsa suddenly said.

Aurelia could not have been more surprised. Or more pleased.

"Well, you are not gone yet," she said, and then—on impulse—reached out and embraced the prickly girl. "You will have the time of your life at school. I promise."

Rather than squirm away, Celsa hugged her back.

Chapter 18

After an evening filled with crabs in beds, a surprise kiss from Guustin, and an even more surprising embrace from Lady Celsa, Aurelia was simply too restless to close her eyes.

She glared up at the canopy over her head as if it were responsible for her current sleeplessness.

Finally, she groaned, rolled from the bed, and lit three candles on her desk before taking her sketchpad from her satchel and flipping to the sketch of Guustin that she liked best. She could get started on a canvas, but all the ones she had stretched were in the workroom section of the library.

Aurelia shoved her feet into her slippers, draped her heavy shawl over her shoulders, and picked up a candlestick.

Aurelia had already become accustomed to living in a building that was seven hundred years old, but tonight, she really felt the age of the structure as she made her way through the empty corridors. How many thousands of lives had been lived within these walls? Women like her, young and hopeful, now long dead and less than dust.

Aurelia shivered. "You idiot," she chastised. When she reached the library, she stopped and stared at the faint light seeping from beneath the warped old door.

Was somebody else inside? Arthur was a night owl and she had encountered him more than a few times in both the library and the armory.

Don't lie to yourself. You are hoping the earl is in there.

Aurelia's pulse sped at the thought of the last time she had been alone with him in the library.

She stared at the sliver of light. Before she could stop herself, she opened the door to the workroom and then stopped on the threshold and stared.

It was indeed Lord Crewe, and he had removed his coat and wore only his shirtsleeves and waistcoat, his blond hair disheveled and his chiseled jaw lightly dusted with gold glints.

His expression when he looked up from his work was preoccupied and it took him a moment to focus on her, and then he stood, blinked, and tossed his quill onto the table before pulling out his pocket watch. "I had no idea it had become so late" He dropped the watch back into his pocket, tipped back his head, and yawned, stretching out his long body in a truly mesmerizing display.

When he lowered his head, his gaze met hers and she watched, fascinated, as awareness came back to him slowly, like a beam of sunlight gradually penetrating a fog-shrouded day, until the knowing sparkle glinted in his ice-blue eye, which briefly flickered to her hair, his lips curving slightly. "Come in, Miss Burton."

"I did not think anyone else would be in here," she said, her face reddening at her brazen lie. She shut the door and then stood frozen.

"I could not sleep, so I thought I might as well be of use. What can I do for you this evening?" he asked.

"Er. I just wanted a canvas."

"Working at night, are you? What a slavedriver your employer must be."

"No. This is for something else—a personal project. I will reimburse you for the canvas, of course," she hastily added.

He smiled but didn't say anything.

"Please, you needn't stand while I look through the canvasses," Aurelia said, relieved when he finally sat.

She went to the wooden rack where a dozen or more canvasses were in the various slots. With shaking hands, she selected a medium-sized one and turned.

The earl was watching her. He was leaning back in his chair, his hands clasped behind his head, shoulder muscles and biceps rippling beneath the fine linen of his shirt.

Aurelia was vaguely aware that she was gawking at him, but… how could she not?

"What are you working on, Miss Burton?"

She blinked and tore her gaze from his body. "Er, I'm sorry?"

"I asked what you were working on?"

"Mrs. Walker has asked me to paint a portrait of Guustin."

His expression at the mention of his former lover and the mother of his child was… well, she didn't know what it was. Other than complex and inscrutable.

"That is very kind of you," he said after a long, pregnant pause. His chest rose and fell with slow, even breaths, the movement pulling her gaze down. He wore a shirt, cravat, and waistcoat. Logically, he was every bit as covered as if he had been wearing a coat.

But there was nothing logical about her body's reaction to him.

Aurelia knew she was standing and staring. Again. But she no longer cared if she were making a spectacle of herself. This man! Oh, this man and his ability to discompose her just by sitting in a chair.

"A portrait is an excellent idea."

Her head jerked up. "I'm sorry?"

"I was just thinking that I should engage you to paint both Guustin and Celsa, Miss Burton." He cocked his head. "Or may I call you Aurelia?"

Plenty of people had said her first name during her life, but there was something about hearing *Aurelia* without the *Lady* in front of it that seemed almost… naked.

She licked her unaccountably dry lips, briefly wondering how she could be all but drooling, and yet her lips were sticking to her teeth. "I am not sure that would be wise."

"Why not? Guustin and Arthur use your Christian name." His eyelid lowered. "Or don't you like me… Aurelia?"

"It has nothing to do with liking or not liking."

"Then what is the issue?"

"You are my employer."

"And employees and employers are forbidden by some royal edict from calling each other by their Christian names?"

"No, of course not. It is just—" she flailed. "Well, I don't know. It does not seem wise." She shut her mouth before any more idiotic babbling could pour out of it.

"Hmm."

Aurelia squirmed beneath his brooding gaze until she could bear it no longer. "I will leave so you can return to your work."

Naturally, the earl stood, because he was a gentleman.

"Why do I feel like you are always running away from me, Aurelia?" he asked, strolling across the room until he was right in front of her.

"I do not run," she said in a giddy, girlish voice that was most certainly not her own.

His gaze flickered to the mobcap that covered her hair and his lips flexed into a moue of distaste. "I don't care for this." He reached up, pulled it off, and then tossed it aside without looking to see where it landed. "There. That is much better."

"What—why did you do that?"

"Your hair is beautiful." He caught a strand between his fingers and stretched it out, his gaze assessing. "Brown is too simple a word for it. There is gold, red, and a rich dark shade like bitter chocolate." His eye met hers. "And your eyes are a constant source of interest."

"I-interest?"

"They are changeable. Not just green or brown or gray or blue—but all those colors."

Aurelia had no response for that.

"Why do you always leave a room when I enter it?"

He was so close that his low voice vibrated through her chest. "I don't do that." She paused and then asked, "Do I?"

"Yes."

"I—I'm not sure that is—" Her words broke off when his hand slid around her jaw. It was the same touch she'd experienced earlier with Guustin. But with Guustin she had felt nothing other than a mild, detached curiosity.

With the earl, her nerves and muscles were suddenly so jangly and… *needful* that it felt as if she would fly apart if she did not—

"When did you learn to be so self-contained? So in control?" he asked, each light stroke of his thumb causing her already irregular breathing to stutter and hitch. "Always taking care of everyone else, hmm?" He caressed the skin beneath her ear and she shivered. "Who takes care of Aurelia?" He slowly bent down, until their faces were almost level, and then lightly rubbed the sides of their noses together. The gesture was singular in her experience. It was also deliciously intimate. And arousing. "Why do you run away? Is it because of that day on the beach?" he asked as his slightly rough fingers stroked her jaw. "Is that it?"

Suddenly, Aurelia could not bear the weight of his gaze. It was safer to look at the blank black patch. "You made your opinion of me perfectly clear that day."

"You mean when I managed to restrain myself?"

"You—" she broke off and bit her lower lip, staring hard at the leather patch.

His hand moved from her cheek to her chin and he turned her, forcing her to meet his gaze. "Say what you are thinking."

"You could not get away from me fast enough that day. W-what has changed now?" she demanded, exasperated and angry the moment the pitiful words came out of her mouth.

"I had hoped that I would forget about you if I stayed away long enough," he said, and then smiled ruefully. "But leaving you only made me want you more."

Aurelia knew she was gaping up at him like an infatuated schoolgirl, but how could she *not* stare when he had just spoken the words she had not even allowed herself to imagine?

"Do you forgive me?" he asked.

"For what? Trying to be a gentleman? Or w-wanting me?"

He chuckled. "Both, I suppose."

Aurelia tried to think of something witty and sophisticated to say, but all she could manage was, "There is nothing to forgive."

"Good. Because I'm going to kiss you again. But this time I'm not going to stop kissing—nor do I want to stop with only kissing." He caressed her tightly clenched jaw. "This time I don't want to stop at *all*. Is that what you want Aurelia—to become lovers? If not, you should step away now." He released her but his hand hovered a tantalizing inch above her skin.

Aurelia wanted to kiss him more than she could remember ever wanting anything in her entire life. She wanted to wrap herself around his body and squeeze and touch and grab and explore every single inch of him—to know his thoughts as well as his body.

Where that terrifyingly intense impulse came from, Aurelia did not know, but she *hurt* with need for him.

She was tired of hurting and feeling empty.

And she was done waiting for what she wanted.

Aurelia deliberately slid her arms around his neck and pulled him down while straining upward to reach him, pushing up onto her toes.

The earl's big body stiffened for a fraction of a second, but then his arms closed around her torso and he pressed his soft, warm lips against hers.

How had Aurelia ever thought that a kiss from Guustin—or any other man—could compare with the inferno of desire raging inside her right now?

Aurelia licked at the seam of his lips, as he had done to her the last time they had kissed, and invaded him with her tongue the second he opened to her. She could not seem to stop shaking and he stroked her back, as if to soothe her.

Her kiss was a great deal less smooth and controlled than his had been, but she didn't care. For weeks and weeks and weeks she had told herself that she would never get the chance to touch him again.

Now that she had him, she would not—*could* not—let him go.

She explored every part of him she could reach, the hard, ridged palate of his mouth, the slick heat of his tongue, and the unspeakable softness of the inside of his lips.

He had no right to taste so delicious or smell so intoxicating. There were hints of port or whiskey and those little black cigars he smoked. But it was more than that, there was something aromatic and masculine and ineffably *Roland.*

Roland. A name she had never once spoken out loud.

Aurelia gave a whimper of frustration when he pulled away.

"*Shhh,* he murmured, tugging off the sash that held her robe closed and then pushing it off her shoulders.

The earl groaned as his hot gaze swept over her thin night rail. And then he suddenly slid an arm beneath her thighs and lifted her up just as easily as he'd done that day on the beach. He strode across the room and set her down on the table, roughly shoving aside his work. More than parchment hit the floor, and the sound of glass shattering was distantly audible, but it was all muted compared to the sensations his hands were unleashing inside her.

"Aurelia, you are like a fever in my blood," he whispered as warm, strong palms slid up her calves to her thighs, dragging her night rail higher, the naked pads of his fingers scorching her bare skin. He nudged her legs wider with his hips and took her face in both hands, positioning her the way he wanted before taking control of their kisses with deep, slow explorations that left her head spinning.

He pulled away, his breathing harsh. "Soon I will not be able to stop myself. If you want to end this—do so now."

"Do not stop," Aurelia whispered. Parts of her body she had never noticed before were suddenly throbbing. The underside of her jaw. The inside of her thighs...

One big hand slid down her body, grazing the side of her breast, skimming the curve of her waist, and then settling on her bare leg.

Aurelia shivered when he brushed the tender crease where her thigh met her sex.

"I want to see all of you, and touch all of you," he murmured, his hands working to undo the buttons of her nightgown. He began to lift the garment over her head, but once again he paused, his questioning gaze meeting hers.

Her mind reeled at what he wanted.

I will be naked, while he is fully clothed.

The thought of being so exposed to him caused her sex to clench and send intense ripples of arousal through her body, the sort of private thrill that usually only came from touching herself.

To bare herself to him would be crossing an invisible line, and there would be no retreating afterward.

I don't care if it is wicked or immoral. I want him to see me. All of me.

She swallowed, forced herself to meet his gaze, and nodded shakily.

He smiled and there was admiration in his eyes, as well as heat—as if he had seen the struggle inside her. "Good girl," he praised. "Never be ashamed of your own desires, Aurelia. Never be afraid to take what you want."

The words were so simple, but their effect on her was anything but.

It was as if a key had unlocked something deep inside of her and Aurelia saw the truth with blinding clarity. It was not infatuation that she felt for the earl; she loved him.

The fact that her epiphany did not surprise her told Aurelia that she had known, deep down, what her feelings were all along, but she had been too afraid to acknowledge them.

She was not so lost to passion at that moment that she didn't recognize the dangers facing her heart, but that was for the future.

Right now, Aurelia wanted him with all her being, and she would gladly pay the price for her desire.

"Lift your arms, sweetheart."

Aurelia complied and a second later her last layer of protection had been stripped away.

The earl's lips parted and he made a noise that was somewhere between a grunt and a groan, the sound so visceral she felt it in her core. He lifted his hands to cup her breasts and she hissed as his thumbs grazed her erect nipples. "So beautiful," he said, his fingers stroking. "So perfect."

He lowered his mouth and kissed the budded tips of her breasts lightly, his tongue flicking out to tease, his lips gently suckling as his hand caressed her thigh, his fingers drifting tantalizingly close to the source of her pleasure.

The need inside her coiled so quickly that Aurelia feared she could not contain it.

"Look at me, love."

Aurelia forced her eyes open and was stunned by the view. His normally pale eye had turned an inky black. Gone was the laughing, teasing lover, his expression now stern with tightly controlled need. The scars on the left side were savage and stark, the skin at the edges of the jagged black wounds white with tension.

"I want to give you pleasure without putting my cock inside you."

Aurelia's jaw sagged at the vulgar word.

Amusement briefly flickered in the earl's eye as he lightly stroked her breasts. "Do you know of what I speak?"

She nodded, her face flaming at acknowledging such a taboo activity.

His eyelid lowered as something hot and dangerous flared in his gaze. "Do you touch yourself, Aurelia?"

"How—how can you ask me such a thing?" she whispered in a choked voice.

His lips curved slowly, wickedly. "I will take that as a *yes*. I daresay thoughts of you touching yourself will torment me long into the night for years to come."

Aurelia squeezed her eyes shut.

He chuckled. "No, do not become shy. Look at me."

She forced her eyes open.

"Has nobody else touched you?"

She shook her head.

His nostrils flared and he made a pleased humming sound as he slowly slid his hands from her breasts over her belly.

It took every ounce of strength Aurelia possessed to put her hands over his wrists.

He stopped immediately, his gaze darting to hers.

"I have not changed my mind," she assured him. "I just want to say something before we go any further."

"Yes?"

"I am an adult woman—not a child."

A slow smile spread across his face. "I have noticed."

"I do not want you to apologize to me… after. You are not taking anything from me. I am aware of what I am doing and what I am *giving*."

The humorous look slid from his face. "You will get no apologies from me, Aurelia."

She nodded and released his wrists.

"Now, where were we? Oh yes, I believe we were *here*." He slid a hand down her thigh. "Smooth like silk," he murmured, his caress not stopping this time.

Aurelia bit her lower lip as he lightly stroked the springy curls that covered her sex.

He cupped her mound with the hot palm of his hand. "I have been dreaming of your sweet little pussy for weeks, Aurelia."

It did not take much imagination to understand what a *pussy* might be.

But before Aurelia could even blush, one of his fingers curled up and caressed the seam of her lower lips, wiping all other thoughts from her mind.

He claimed her mouth then, the kiss deeper and more demanding than any that had come before and his finger made a second, firmer pass, the damp tip caressing a part of her that only Aurelia had ever touched.

The earl moaned. "You are so wet for me," he said in a low, raspy voice, trailing kisses across her cheek. "So wet and hot and soft," he said, and then closed his mouth over a taut cord in her neck and flexed his jaws until sharp teeth grazed her tender skin.

She moaned, the combination of pain and pleasure startlingly arousing.

He kissed the spot he had just bitten. "Touch me, Aurelia."

Aurelia carded her fingers into his thick, silky hair, the fingers of her left hand finding the hidden scars.

"Yes," he hissed, biting her neck again, harder this time, stroking her sex and lightly grazing the swollen bundle of nerves, sending raw, jagged bolts of pleasure throughout her body.

Aurelia's cry split the air and she caught her lower lip with her teeth.

"No. Do not hold your passion back. I want to hear every whimper, moan, and gasp, Aurelia." He circled her clitoris, the touch frustratingly fleeting. "Understood?"

Yes," she moaned.

His finger fluttered in a spot that was both too much and not enough. Aurelia raised her hips, chasing the elusive sensation. "Please, my lord, I need—"

"Say my name."

Aurelia stared into his swollen pupil. "Please… Roland," she whispered.

He growled. "I like that."

And then he began to circle and caress the tiny bundle of nerves, giving her exactly what she needed, driving her toward the edge with shocking ease and then ruthlessly shoving her over.

Aurelia cried out, her back arching as the most intense climax she had ever experienced seized her.

He wrapped an arm around her waist and held her. "Yes—just like that, Aurelia," he praised, avoiding her too-sensitive bud and instead breaching her entrance, his finger pushing deeply into her body.

Aurelia's convulsing muscles clenched around him and the sensation intensified the ripples of bliss that washed over her.

"Beautiful," he murmured, his hand gently thrusting while his hot mouth closed over her breast and he sucked hard, his teeth closing on the taut nipple and tugging.

Aurelia shuddered at the sharp arrows of delight that shot from her breasts to her womb, scarcely noticing when his mouth moved down her belly, his breath hot over her quivering skin.

She was vaguely aware of hair tickling her thighs, gentle fingers parting her swollen folds, and then something unspeakably wet and soft engulfed the source of her pleasure.

Aurelia made a mortifying noise when his hot tongue resumed what his finger had been doing moments before. It was a feeling unlike anything she had ever experienced. She wanted it every day. All day.

She lifted her head, which felt as if it weighed ten stone, and looked down the length of her body, needing to see him.

He was waiting for her, his gaze searing her, a second finger joining the one moving inside her, his thrusts harder now. His eyelid fluttered and a look of pure bliss settled on his stark features, like a man enthralled with a feast—

The thought struck her at the same moment that a second climax rolled over her.

Aurelia closed her eyes and gave herself up to pure sensation.

Chapter 19

R oland stared down at her sprawled, exquisite body and contemplated making her come again. And again. Not just with his hands and mouth, but with his cock, which was leaking like a tap and leaving a big stain on the front of his pantaloons that would likely make his valet snicker.

God, she was so bloody beautiful! And so eager and sensual that it drove him half-mad with desire.

But she was also asleep, so instead of slaking his lust on her unconscious body, he lifted her in his arms and went to sit on the settee closest to the fire. She melted against his chest, limp and entirely relaxed for the first time since Roland had met her.

He took advantage of her momentary lapse of vigilance to study her. It was true that she was surpassingly lovely, but that was not all or even most of why Roland could not get her out of his head. Regardless of how brilliant she was as an artist or how gorgeous she was as a woman, there was something about her— something achingly vulnerable—that cried out for love, or at least for affection. Roland suspected that her role as the oldest sister had always been to nurture the younger ones because her parents had not wanted the job.

But nobody had ever nurtured *her*.

And it just about broke Roland's heart.

It had stunned him to realize—less than a week into this last trip away from Crewe—that he wanted to be the one to give her what she needed.

True, he also wanted her body, and the thought of being her first—her only—lover made his already hard cock throb even more. He had never been interested in virgins in the past. From his first bed partner, Nora, to the last woman he'd been with—Mary Neel several weeks before he'd left Crewe—he'd always had experienced lovers.

After his unpleasant experience with Nora when he'd been sixteen all he'd looked for in the arms of every woman was physical satisfaction. He hadn't wanted to explore rock pools with them, discuss books with them, play cards with them—all things he desperately wanted to do with Aurelia.

For the first time since he'd been a green, romantic boy he wanted to give more than he took.

Roland had been stunned tonight to discover that Aurelia wanted him. Stunned and honored. He suspected she was not the sort of woman who opened her heart to many people—especially not men.

Unfortunately, Roland also suspected that she would regret her moment of impulsivity when she came back to herself. He desperately hoped he was wrong and would do everything to make her glad of her choice.

Ironically, it had been Aurelia he'd been thinking about when the woman herself had opened the door to the library at two o'clock in the morning. He'd been so lost in his thoughts that for a moment he had thought that he had imagined her.

Roland had been pondering the same thing he always did where Aurelia was concerned: should he take what he wanted, even though he was a scarred, jaded, and bitter man almost twice her age? It had been so many years since he'd put anyone else's needs above his own that he wasn't sure he knew how to do so anymore.

If he truly valued her, wouldn't he step away and let her find somebody more suitable? But then, was it Roland's place to decide who was right for her? After all, what she'd said earlier—that she was an adult—was true. If Roland made choices for both of them, wasn't he treating her as a child?

Sometimes it was hard to see the line between chivalry and paternalism.

Or at least it was difficult for him.

Aurelia shifted in his arms, her eyelids lifting slowly.

Roland smiled. "Welcome back."

Her lips curved and the affection in her unguarded eyes knocked the air from his lungs.

But a scant second later the shutters slammed shut and she shifted, trying to sit up.

Which is when she noticed her nudity.

Roland was loathe to release her, but he lifted her from his lap and set her on the settee beside him. "I will fetch your night rail and dressing gown," he told her.

He stood and located both garments, shaking them out before bringing them to her.

"Thank you," she mumbled, snatching the clothes from his hand without meeting his gaze.

Roland gave a soundless sigh at her obvious shame and resumed his seat beside her. He draped his arm along the back of the sofa and watched with interest while she went about the business of collecting herself.

In less than a minute the wild, abandoned nymph had disappeared and in her place was a self-possessed, if not exactly tidy, ice queen.

"I hope you do not regret what we have done," he said, even though it was plain that she did.

"No, of course not," she said briskly, glancing around the room.

"Do you need something?"

"My sleeping cap?"

"I threw it into the fire."

Her jaw sagged.

Roland laughed and pushed to his feet. "I am jesting." He fetched the hideous cap from the floor where he had thrown it and brought it back to her, watching with resignation as she quickly tucked away her crowning glory and then stood.

Composed but flushed, she looked everywhere but at Roland. "Well, it is late."

"Very," he agreed.

Her throat worked, but she seemed unable to dredge up any other vapid pleasantries. After a moment she gave an abrupt nod and said, "I bid you goodnight, then."

"What about your canvas? Don't you want it?"

"Oh." She hurried across the room and snatched up her canvas. "Thank you, my lord."

Roland needed to walk fast to beat her to the door. He stood with his fingers resting on the handle until she looked up. "It was my pleasure, Aurelia."

They both knew he did not mean the canvas.

The moment he opened the door she shot out of the room as if she'd been fired from a pistol.

Roland leaned against the doorframe and watched as she hurried down the long corridor, until she disappeared around the corner. He was about to shut the door when he heard what sounded like footsteps coming from the stairwell.

He crossed the short distance to the arched doorway. "Who is there?" he called, his voice ricocheting eerily off the stone walls of the stairwell, which led all the way down to the armory.

When nobody answered he shrugged and turned back toward the library, which is when he noticed a piece of paper partly hidden by the rather moth-eaten carpet runner.

He bent and picked it up, turning it over in his hands for some sign of where it had come from. But there was only his name on the front, the handwriting unfamiliar to him. One of the servants must have dropped it when they'd brought up the mail. Who knew how long it had been lying there?

He sighed and entered the library, momentarily distracted from the letter by the sight of the mess he had made. Crumpled sheets of parchment, a shattered whisky glass, and an assortment of quills lay scattered all over the floor.

As his gaze settled on the empty surface of the table his thoughts turned to the woman who'd so recently been sprawled across it.

Aurelia had claimed their erotic encounter wouldn't change things between them, but—based on her awkwardness—it already had.

Had it been ill-advised to give in to his desire for her? Probably. But Roland could not bring himself to regret it. He was tired of dancing around his feelings for her. It was true that he'd had two terrible marriages, but then neither woman had been his choice, had they?

For the first time since he had been a boy, he *felt* something. And it was bloody inconvenient, that was true. But it also brought him back to life when he'd not even realized that part of him had been lying dormant.

Judging by the way Aurelia had stormed out of here, she believed that all he wanted was a quick fondle and was treating her the way he had treated every other woman for the past two decades.

That would not do. Not at all.

Roland might not have any experience wooing a woman, but it was about damned time he learned.

What he needed, he decided, was a plan. A wooing plan.

He smiled at the thought. Who would have believed that Roland Montgomery would be going courting for the first time in his life at almost one-and-forty?

He laughed aloud and then bent to pick up the scattered papers, only to see the letter he still clutched in his hand. He sighed and tore it open, unfolding a single sheet with only a few lines of writing. A quick glance at the bottom showed no signature.

Roland strode across the room and fetched his spectacles.

When he turned back to the letter the first sentence leapt off the page like a springing panther:

Lady Rebecca Crewe, and your son, are alive.

Roland's jaw hit the floor. "What the bloody hell?" he demanded of the silent room.

I saw her and the boy—blond, tall, and bearing an unmistakable resemblance to you— at the Rusty Scupper Inn in Aberdeen, where she has rented rooms for herself and the boy. She was living with a man named Thomas Carver—in much diminished circumstances—until his death four months ago.

Do what you will with this information, I will tell nobody of her existence. Or the boy's.

Roland read the letter again. And then again. And then one more time, but he still could not believe the contents.

Rebecca was alive? And with a *son?*

His son?

His heart thudded so loudly it seemed to echo in the cavernous room.

Roland shook his head. How could this be?

He turned back to the letter and stared. Whoever had written it was obviously educated. Who the hell was it? And how long had the letter been under the carpet?

Roland thrust a shaking hand through his hair and shook his head. "Bloody. Fucking. Hell."

Chapter 20

Aurelia tossed and turned for two hours after leaving Lord Crewe, feeling like a fool for the way she'd fled from the library as if the devil himself had been on her heels.

Her intention hadn't been to behave as if nothing had happened—that would have been impossible—but she *had* wanted to be sophisticated and act as if what they had done, or what *he'd* done, rather, had not changed anything between them.

Instead, she had behaved like a naïve fool, rebuffing every overture the earl had made to talk to her and behaving as if he had done something wrong to her.

She would set him straight on that score immediately.

Indeed, she would pull him aside after breakfast and ask for a few moments of privacy.

Exhausted by her fretting but relieved to have finally made a decision, she drifted into an uneasy sleep, waking perhaps an hour after dawn.

Lord Crewe usually ate after he had taken his morning ride, so she should be in good time to catch him.

But when she arrived in the breakfast room there was only Arthur.

"Are we the first?"

"Guustin is at his mother's, Celsa is still abed, and Crewe left this morning at first light," Arthur said, and then coughed in his napkin.

Aurelia wanted to ask where the earl had gone but was distracted by the horrific coughing bout. When it had passed, Arthur was pale and perspiring.

"Are you not feeling well?" she asked rather stupidly as he raised his badly trembling cup of tea to his mouth.

He swallowed several times and forced a sickly smile. "I seem to have contracted a rather nasty cold."

"Can I do anything for you?" she asked, alarmed by his condition.

"You are very kind, but I believe all I need is rest." He smiled, looking a little bit less peaked. "I'll be right as rain after a few days in bed. Indeed, I believe I will head that way now." He pushed up from his chair and tottered out of the room.

The door had scarcely closed behind him when it opened again and Aurelia looked up from her coffee cup, assuming Arthur had forgotten something.

But it was the footman, Charles. He glanced around, as if to see if anyone else was in the room, and then said, "I was to give this to you when you were alone, miss." He handed her a folded piece of parchment sealed with the earl's distinctive oxblood wax.

"Thank you, Charles," she said, her face heating at the implications of a letter delivered in such secrecy.

Aurelia's hands shook as she unfolded the parchment and stared down at the bold handwriting.

My darling Aurelia,

Unfortunately, an unexpected matter has summoned me away. I wish I could say how long I will be gone, but quite frankly, I have no idea just now. It is too important to ignore, or I would have waited to bid you goodbye.

I very much wanted to speak to you today so I could reassure you after last night. Oh, my sweet darling—how much I have to say to you. Please do not do anything rash or impulsive. I have so much I want to say to you.

But a letter is not the place for the thoughts I wish to share.

I am going to ask you to be patient for just a little longer. Wait for me, sweetheart, and know that I am counting the hours until I can see your face again.

Yours,

Roland

She re-read the brief message four times, puzzling repeatedly over the *rash or impulsive* part of it. What in the world did he mean? She never behaved impulsively—well, except with Lord Crewe. With *Roland.*

Aurelia smiled at the name, which she had been so careful to only speak inside her mind until last night.

Her gaze rested on the words *sweetheart* and *darling* and *yours*. Was he really hers?

Don't be a fool. That is only a figure of speech.

For once, Aurelia refused to allow the chiding voice to gain a foothold in her thoughts.

Aurelia was still smiling like a fool ten minutes later when Beekman entered the breakfast room. "Sir Gideon is here, Miss Burton. I have put him in the drawing room."

"I'm afraid his lordship is gone and Mr. Montgomery does not feel well."

"He is here to see you, Miss Burton."

"Me?" she repeated stupidly.

Beekman gave her a patient look and nodded.

"Thank you, Beekman. Tell him I'll be down in a quarter of an hour."

"Very good, miss."

Aurelia quickly took her letter up to her room. Recalling how much Celsa enjoyed snooping, she tucked the precious missive into the toe of her riding boot.

After briefly checking her appearance in the mirror she made her way to the drawing room.

Sir Gideon was studying one of the paintings when she entered.

He immediately strode toward her, smiling. "Ah, Miss Burton. Thank you so much for seeing me on such short notice." He took her hand and bowed low over it.

"Of course. What can I do for you?" Aurelia asked after she had taken a seat on one of the settees in the room, more than a little surprised when Sir Gideon sat down beside her.

"I know it is a barbaric time of the day to call on you, but I worried the weather would worsen later and prevent me from coming to the island today."

Aurelia nodded uncertainly. "I am delighted you called.

"I am sure you can guess why I am here."

"I am sorry, but I'm afraid that I cannot."

His cheeks flushed slightly. "I have come to ask you to do me the honor of becoming my wife."

Aurelia's mouth fell open.

He laughed. "You were not jesting when you said you did not know why I'd come."

"No, I wasn't."

"Clearly the notion has never entered your mind," he said. "Have I really concealed my interest in you so well?"

Aurelia laughed nervously. "I don't think it is that so much as the fact that we have spent so little time together—only twice, in fact."

"I only needed the first time, Miss Burton." He took her hand, his own warm and bare.

Aurelia's mind whirled. "I am extremely flattered by your proposal." Her first marriage proposal ever. "But, er, I—I'm afraid my answer is no, Sir Gideon."

He nodded. "I appreciate your honesty. Will you tell me—do I have cause to hope?"

She forced herself to say, "I am afraid not."

"Ah." He nodded and gave her hand a gentle squeeze before releasing it. "I must admit that I am disappointed—deeply."

"I am sorry," Aurelia said, feeling wretched.

He shook himself. "The heart wants what it wants, Miss Burton, and it cannot be coerced or forced. I will not raise the matter again," he promised. "But tell me, is friendship also out of the question? I do so enjoy your company. And, if I may be so bold, you are a woman on her own without family or connections in a new place—perhaps you could use a friend?"

The words from Lord Crewe's letter came back to her: *don't do anything impulsive or rash.*

Befriending Sir Gideon didn't qualify as rash. Did it?

Will you really turn away the offer of friendship out of concern for what the earl might think?

No. That would be foolish. And weak.

Aurelia smiled at the patiently waiting man. "I would very much like your friendship, Sir Gideon."

"I am delighted to hear it. I will be coming over to Crewe every Thursday for the next few months to meet with my steward who is housebound with terrible gout. May I call on you?" He smiled. "At a more reasonable hour, naturally."

"I would like that."

Sir Gideon gave her another of his glowing smiles. "Excellent. I expect to be—"

The door to the sitting room flew open and Celsa stormed into the room, making Aurelia realize the girl never just *walked* anywhere.

Celsa opened her eyes wide—the look too innocent to be believable—and said, "Oh, dear. I didn't realize you had company, Miss Burton."

"What a pleasant surprise, my lady," Aurelia said, not without irony.

Celsa had the grace to blush.

Sir Gideon went to greet her, bowing over her hand in his charming, courtly fashion. "Lady Celsa. How delightful to see you. It has been quite a while. You were a girl the last time I saw you and now you are a lovely young woman."

Celsa preened, clearly pleased by the comment.

"Come join us," Aurelia said, patting the seat that Sir Gideon had just abandoned.

The baronet sat in the chair across from them. "What have you been up to, my lady? I have not seen you in the environs of Balcrewe in quite some time."

"I am going off to school in the New Year,"

"Is that so? And where are you going?"

"The school is in Edinburgh."

"You will have a marvelous time—and still be close enough to come home on the holidays. I still recall when I went to Eton," Sir Gideon said, and then went on to describe several humorous incidents that made Celsa laugh. Aurelia had heard plenty about how brutal such schools could be and suspected he carefully culled any unpleasantness from his stories.

Aurelia was content to listen to the two chatter about school, her mind still spinning from his proposal.

If you had any sense at all, you would have leapt with joy at his offer. You will live to regret it.

She worried the voice might be right this time. Aurelia might not love him, but Sir Gideon was the sort of man who would make any woman an excellent husband.

But it would be cruel and unfair to marry when her heart already belonged to another. Especially when that *other* lived just a boat ride away from Sir Gideon. If she married the baronet, she would likely see Lord Crewe often. It would be… devastating.

Only when Sir Gideon stood to take his leave did Aurelia realize how rudely she'd neglected her guest while gathering wool.

"I shall come a bit later on Thursday," he said, once again bowing over her hand and then taking his leave.

Celsa barely waited for the door to shut behind him before grinning and saying, "He wants to court you. He is in *love* with you!"

"You do like to imagine things," Aurelia said coolly, leaving the room.

Celsa trotted after her. "Do you like him?"

"Of course I like him. He is a very nice man."

"But do you *like* him?"

Aurelia ignored the question. "Was there something you needed? Or did you just barge into the drawing room so you could practice your flirtation skills on Sir Gideon?"

"I did not!" Celsa denied, far too hotly for there not to be a grain of truth in Aurelia's accusation.

"Do you want to come up to my workroom and practice your watercolors while I work?" Aurelia asked.

"The day is too lovely." A grin spread across her face and she all but skipped down the corridor. "And guess what?" she asked, but then said before Aurelia could answer, "Papa left me a message before going—he said I am no longer restricted from riding!"

"Congratulations. You will not need me any longer, will you?"

Celsa laughed. "No, I don't. But I will still be waiting for you at two-thirty—unless you can be persuaded to leave earlier?"

"Three," Aurelia said. "I am getting a late start."

Aurelia suspected that she would be less than productive after the earl's mysterious letter and Sir Gideon's stunning proposal.

It wasn't even noon and the day was already one of the most memorable in her adult life.

Chapter 21

The first two weeks after the earl's departure were some of the worst weather Aurelia had experienced on Crewe.

And it perfectly suited her mood.

"Never fear, my dear Aurelia, it will not rain forever," Arthur teased at dinner one night. "September is temperamental, but October can often be one of the most beautiful months of the year." He smiled. "It is almost as if God keeps a special bit of the summer for us every year."

Across the table, Celsa rolled her eyes.

Aurelia ignored her bad behavior.

Arthur had been bedbound for eight of the last fourteen days and this was his first appearance at dinner. Even now, he looked less than robust, his skin patchy and red and his hands shakier than ever.

Celsa heaved a loud sigh and toyed with her food in a way that would earn sharp looks from her father if he were there. "I despise this time of year. Nothing of any interest will happen until Christmas."

"That is barely two months away," Guustin pointed out. And then grinned teasingly. "And this year you will have an extra gift because I will be here."

"I thought your ship would have been ready well before then," Arthur said, all semblance of his good humor gone at the news.

Guustin sighed. "Unfortunately not. I will have to go to Glasgow again at the end of the week."

Arthur grunted at that and turned back to his plate, vigorously attacking his dreary potatoes in vinegar as if it were Guustin's head on his plate.

Guustin cut Aurelia a wryly amused look. "While the delay is lamentable, I am delighted that I will be here on your first Christmas on the island, Aurelia."

Celsa's smile instantly turned into a scowl. "First? She will be done with her work next spring. This will be her *only* Christmas here. Unless you will be going home to be with your family this year?" Her hopeful smile told Aurelia where the girl stood on that issue.

Honestly. One minute Celsa was embracing her and telling her how much she would miss her, the next, she was all but shoving Aurelia out the door. It was enough to make a person's head swim.

Aurelia smiled sweetly at the younger woman. "I won't be going home, my lady. I'm afraid I will be here, plaguing *you* at Christmas."

Celsa had the decency to blush.

***

Several afternoons later—on the first sunny day in what felt like ages—Aurelia was finishing up her work when Charles knocked on her workroom door.

"Sir Gideon is downstairs to see you, miss."

"Thank you, Charles." She waited until the footman left before removing her apron and checking her appearance in the small mirror that hung beside the door. Once she'd assured herself there were no paint smudges on her nose she began the long trek to the drawing room.

Aurelia had not seen the baronet since the day he had proposed to her. Either bad weather or his other commitments had kept him away until now.

When she opened the door she found not only Sir Gideon, but also Arthur.

"Look who has come to visit!" Arthur said, looking so delighted that Aurelia would have thought that Sir Gideon had come to see *him*.

Once they had exchanged greetings and lamented the recent weather, Arthur stood. "I will instruct Beekman to have tea sent up. I would love to join you, but I have an engagement I cannot break." Arthur winked at Aurelia when he thought Sir Gideon wasn't looking.

Aurelia's face flared when she saw that Sir Gideon had indeed noticed the wink.

While they waited for the tea to arrive Sir Gideon chatted about growing up on the mainland and his visits to Crewe.

"So, you came to the island often?" she asked.

"More and more as I grew older. Because I am so much younger than his lordship, we never saw much of each other." Sir Gideon gave a rueful laugh. "Although I doubt Crewe would have had much to say to me even if we had been closer in age."

Aurelia wanted to demur, but she suspected that was true.

"Arthur, on the other hand, always made time for me, even though I was likely a pest when it came to his taxidermy."

"Oh?" Aurelia asked.

"Yes, I am a bit of an amateur taxidermist myself. The animals I preserve cannot compare to Arthur's work, of course, but my mother became very upset when I used arsenic, and her arguments against it were sound. There are those who say mercury is an even more dangerous curative, so I have had to rely on older herbal methods, with less satisfying results."

Could arsenic or mercury be a reason for Arthur's prolonged sickness? He seemed to be getting worse, rather than better. While Aurelia wanted Roland to return for selfish reasons, she really hoped he came back soon because he needed to do something about Arthur's deteriorating health.

"—and the earl was often quite cruel to him."

Aurelia's ears perked up at the word *earl*. "I have never seen his lordship be unkind to Arthur," she said with a little too much heat.

Gideon chuckled. "Not this earl—the last one."

"Oh." Aurelia felt a bit foolish for flying to Roland's defense.

"Crewe and Arthur were inseparable from the moment Arthur came to live here. Indeed, Arthur has only ever had good things to say about *this* earl. But the last Laird of Crewe could be a, er, difficult character."

"Why would he be unkind to his own nephew?"

Gideon's cheeks darkened slightly and he glanced at the door. "I thought you knew that Arthur was illegitimate."

"He is not his lordship's heir?"

"No. Arthur uses the Montgomery surname, but he is not in the line of succession. Celsa is the heir. Females are allowed to inherit under the Crewe patent. In any event," he said, clearly wanting to leave the distasteful subject behind, "you really must come and see my animals when you next visit the mainland."

"I would enjoy that," Aurelia lied. Why in the world would anyone pursue taxidermy as a hobby if not for its scientific use?

Soon afterward they had their tea and then bundled up and took their walk.

As Aurelia waved goodbye to Sir Gideon an hour later, she thought, yet again, what a nice man he was.

And yet again, she couldn't help wishing—just a little—that she had not already given her heart to a man who would likely break it.

***

Aurelia daily hoped for word of Lord Crewe. She knew that he could not send her a letter without raising eyebrows, but he had sent two letters to his cousin the first two weeks and Arthur had shared information about the earl's whereabouts during breakfast.

But Arthur had not said a word for the last three weeks and Aurelia was becoming desperate to know what had taken Roland away so abruptly and when he might return.

While she had heard nothing from Roland, the letters from her siblings had finally begun to pour in after months of nothing.

A week ago, Aurelia had received an especially startling letter from Selina.

Her sweet, biddable sister had surprised all of them when she had thrown off their mother's oppressive yoke and ran away, taking a position as a housekeeper to the reclusive Marquess of Shaftsbury.

Selina hadn't written often, but the letters she had sent had been happy and it was clear that her new position suited her. And her most recent missive explained at least part of her happiness. Selina was betrothed to Lord Shaftsbury and the two would probably already be married by the time Aurelia received her sister's letter.

The changes that had occurred over the past year were astonishing. Three of her sisters married; Doddy away at Eton; Katie preparing for her first Season; and her parents living in luxury, and all thanks to her sisters' husbands.

It was hard to believe.

It was also an unspeakable relief. When Aurelia had first accepted this position on Crewe, she had assumed that she would need to earn enough money to take care of her siblings after they were evicted from Queen's Bower.

And now it appeared they had all fared just fine without any help from her.

Part of her was sad that she was no longer the responsible big sister who solved everyone's problems. But another, larger, part was proud that her sisters had taken care of themselves.

Aurelia felt... liberated.

She also missed Roland so much it was hard to think straight.

And, as if Roland's absence wasn't bad enough, Guustin had left ten days ago to check on the repairs to his ship.

Not until the younger man had gone did Aurelia realize just how much she had come to enjoy Guustin's cheerful presence and friendly companionship. After that one kiss on the Night of the Crab—as Guustin amusingly called it— he had not touched her again.

Unlike Sir Gideon, whom Aurelia genuinely believed was in love with her, Guustin had quite happily settled into the position of friend.

Aurelia kept busy with work and spent part of every day with Celsa. They rode when the weather permitted and paid frequent visits to Nora, whose health suffered more in the cold weather, although Aurelia suspected it was really Guustin's absence that had left her so listless.

For some time, Larissa had been too busy with the woman she cared for to have a Tuesday free, but Sir Gideon came to the island almost weekly.

Sir Gideon's visits eased some of her restlessness, but—if anything—his company only made her miss Roland more. If she had ever believed she might marry him, Aurelia now knew for a certainty that would never be possible.

***

Almost six weeks after Roland's departure, Aurelia woke up to a bright, sunny day that might have been stolen from July and smuggled into October.

"This happens almost every year," Arthur said at breakfast when Aurelia commented on the balmy weather. "And the water, also, will be warmer if I am correct in my guess." He smiled at her, looking almost his normal self. Suddenly, his expression became conspiratorial. "I daresay Sir Gideon will come over today."

"Er, it's not a Thursday," she said, not sure what he was getting at.

Arthur just smiled—no, he smirked. "Sir Gideon is a fine man. I have known him all his life and never have I seen him so—if you'll pardon my indelicacy—enthralled with a woman as he is with you, Aurelia."

Aurelia stared, speechless.

Arthur continued, evidently mistaking her mortification for encouragement. "I would so like to see you happy. I have said in the past that I have paternal feelings toward you, so I believe—" he hesitated, as if torn, but then seemed to come to a decision. "I know my cousin has a magnetic appeal for women, but I should hate to see you hurt, my dear. You really should understand that Crewe is not the sort to marry."

"I do not like what you are insinuating," she retorted.

"Do not be angry, my dear," he hastily said. "It is only that I have watched so many women fall to Crewe's not inconsiderable charm. But—but you have so much talent and are so… vibrant that I would hate to see you hurt when he tires of you and casts you aside. And I am afraid that is exactly what he will do."

Aurelia clamped her jaws tight, not trusting herself to respond.

"Sir Gideon is the sort of man who will be a caring, faithful husband and a kind, thoughtful father. I would not see you throw away his regard because Crewe might have… dallied with you and gave you false hope."

Aurelia recoiled at his cruel words.

"I can see you are hurt, my dear." Arthur's face fell and he suddenly looked ill again. "I am very sorry—I didn't mean—" he broke off and pushed to his feet, muttering to himself as he shuffled from the room, his stooped form plucking at her sympathy even though she was furious at his words.

You are furious because you believe what he said. Lord Crewe has had you, and now he has disappeared.

As angry and hurt as Aurelia was, she greatly feared that the voice of reason might very well be right. It was becoming harder and harder to hold onto her hope with every day and week that passed.

It was time for Aurelia to consider the possibility that she might be a gullible fool just like every other woman who had lost her heart to the Earl of Crewe over the years.

***

"We shall have to dress quickly for dinner," Aurelia said as she and Lady Celsa cantered home from the west side of the island.

They had been taking advantage of the fine weather and exploring a secluded cove that had excellent rock pools but Aurelia had allowed the time to get away from her and now they would be late.

"I don't know why we bother changing our clothing for dinner. With only the two of us, we should just go as we are," Celsa groused, and then turned to Aurelia, a notch of concern between her eyes. "Do you think Uncle Arthur is sicker than he says he is?"

"I don't know," Aurelia admitted, not wanting to lie about such an important matter. Nor did she want to admit that she would be glad if Arthur did not come to dinner that night. She was still furious after their last conversation. "Hopefully your father will be able to convince him to see a doctor when he returns."

"*If* he ever returns," Celsa muttered. "I feel like he has been away forever."

Aurelia silently concurred.

The stables were a hive of industry when Aurelia and Celsa crested the hill that led to the main road to the castle.

Not only was there a wagon with all sorts of barrels and crates and trunks, but Silas held Frost's bridle and was leading the mud-spattered stallion back into the stables.

The Laird of Crewe had returned.

Chapter 22

Aurelia took a ridiculous amount of care with her appearance that night. Even so, she managed to arrive at the dining room a good five minutes before dinner, which had been set back an hour due to the earl's unexpected arrival.

Her heart, which had been behaving erratically since she had seen Lord Crewe's horse in the courtyard, thumped uncomfortably hard as she opened the dining room door.

There he was, standing in front of the huge fireplace, a glass in his hand, and his wicked lips already curving into a welcoming smile.

"I was hoping you would be the first to arrive Aurelia." He set down his glass, strode toward her, and seized her hands and held them in his, his gaze hot as he stared down at her. "You look even more ravishing than I remembered," he murmured, leaning low to kiss her.

His lips were warm and soft and the smell of him intoxicated her so quickly and completely that she wanted to grab him and yank him back to her when he pulled away.

"Ah." The smug smile on his lips told her that she was shamelessly broadcasting her desire for him.

Fortunately, his smirk brought her to her senses and she stepped away from him, putting several feet between them as she brutally shoved down all the joy she had felt at seeing him and quickly donned her mask of reserve. How dare he kiss her as if he had not just disappeared for almost two months without a word?

"Aurelia?" His forehead furrowed. "What is it, darling? Why are you—"

The door opened and Arthur strode into the room. "It is good to see you, Crewe!" he said, his blue eyes appearing almost purple in his red face as he strode into the room.

Roland's eye bulged when he saw his cousin. "Good Lord, Arthur—you look terrible! What ails you? Should you be up and about?"

Arthur made a dismissive gesture with his hand. "I am on the mend. Tell me, how were your travels?"

For a moment Aurelia thought Roland would insist on discussing Arthur's health, but he must have decided to wait until they could be private.

"The trip was overlong and I found nothing at the end of it." Roland's expression was harsh as he strode back toward the fire.

"So, there was no news of, er—"

"No, there was nothing," Roland snapped. "And it is not a subject that gives me any pleasure, Arthur."

Arthur nodded cautiously. "Of course, Crewe."

"Beekman said Guustin has been gone for almost three weeks. Did he happen to say when he is returning?"

"Your son did not deign to inform me of his plans," Arthur said stiffly.

Roland scowled. "And I daresay you didn't bother to ask him, did you?" he shot back. "Your jealousy of him is childish and tedious, Arthur."

Arthur gasped. "I am most certainly not—"

"Lady Celsa and I visited Mrs. Walker just yesterday and she expects him back any day now, my lord," Aurelia said loudly, hoping to deescalate the uncharacteristic tension between the two men before they came to blows.

Before the earl could respond, Celsa came hurrying into the room. "Welcome back, Papa," she said, her voice breathy and adoring.

The earl gave his daughter an appraising look. "You are looking very well, Celsa," he said after a long moment, his gaze lingering on her hair, which she had begun to wear up just before Guustin left. "Your hair suits you."

Celsa blushed to the roots of her coiffure at her father's kind words. "Thank you, Papa."

The earl nodded at Beekman. "You may serve."

His lordship and Arthur discussed several issues that had come up at the guano mine while the earl had been away, but Aurelia could see Roland had no interest in talking business. His gaze, over and over, slid to meet hers while Arthur raised one topic after another, evidently searching for something to capture the other man's attention.

"—which is what Sir Gideon said when he was here visiting Aurelia last Thursday."

Roland turned to her, his pupil shrinking to the size of a pin. "Talbot was here?" he asked in a quiet, almost menacing, voice. Aurelia suddenly understood why Celsa always appeared terrified when her father eyed her so coldly.

Aurelia opened her mouth, but Arthur spoke first. "Yes, he has been calling on Aurelia almost weekly. Isn't that right, my dear?"

"Er—"

"And what business is it that brings him to Crewe so often?" the earl demanded, his imperious tone enough to shake Aurelia from her daze.

"He does not appraise me of his business pursuits, my lord," she retorted just as imperiously.

Roland smiled thinly.

Arthur, evidently unaware of the tiger he was taunting, chuckled and said, "His business is pleasure, Crewe. Indeed, Sir Gideon makes no secret of the fact that he is in love with Aurelia. The young ladies in the neighborhood—and their fond mamas—have all gone into mourning knowing he will soon be off the marriage market."

Aurelia pulled her attention from Roland just long enough to give Arthur a look of outraged disbelief. Just what in the world was he on about?

"Is that so?" Roland asked coolly, his gaze brooding and hooded.

Aurelia told herself that she did not enjoy the jealousy that flared in his icy blue gaze as he glared at her.

But that was a lie.

"You should speak to Talbot about Aurelia, Crewe." Arthur—evidently the least observant man in all of Scotland—blithely smiled at his cousin.

The earl turned not just his gaze, but his body, toward the other man. "I beg your pardon?" His tone was the frostiest she had ever heard.

Arthur sighed and gave his cousin a chiding look. "Without a father, brother, or other male relative to protect her, the duty falls to us, Crewe. Or, to you, rather."

The air in front of Aurelia filled with a red mist and she opened her mouth to tell Arthur in no uncertain terms what he could do with his *protection*.

"I painted a watercolor of the castle that Miss Burton says is very good," Celsa piped up.

If it had been anyone else who'd spoken just then, Aurelia would have believed they were attempting to move the conversation in a less volatile direction.

But it was Celsa, so Aurelia suspected the girl was just bored listening to her father and uncle talk about Aurelia.

Whatever the reason, Aurelia was profoundly grateful for the interruption.

"I should like to see your painting," the earl declared, his unreadable gaze on Aurelia rather than his daughter. "I am pleased to hear you have found the time to instruct my daughter. Especially given your obviously busy social calendar," he added, his nostrils pinched.

Did Aurelia say that she *liked* the earl's jealousy? That was a lie.

She loved it.

***

Aurelia was just finishing her breakfast the following morning when Charles entered the breakfast room.

"His lordship asks that you meet him in the stables—prepared for riding—in half an hour."

Aurelia blinked at the footman. "Me?" she asked rather stupidly as she was the only person in the room other than Charles himself.

Charles's lips twitched slightly. "Yes, Miss Burton."

"Thank you," she murmured.

Aurelia stared unseeingly at her almost empty plate after the door closed behind the servant. What could the earl want with her?

He had been cool and clipped with her last night after Arthur had yammered on about Sir Gideon. Indeed, he'd scarcely spoken another word to her during the remainder of dinner.

Why did he want to go riding with her? Was he going to bring up Sir Gideon and hector her on the inappropriateness of her afternoon meetings with the baronet?

Aurelia's eyes narrowed. If he *dared* to scold her, he would discover just how quickly she could pack her belongings and be gone.

She had half a mind to leave him standing in the stables, but then decided on a better plan and rang the servant bell.

A few moments later Charles appeared.

"I would like another pot of coffee, please."

His eyes slid toward the clock on the mantle and then slid back.

Aurelia raised her eyebrows.

He inclined his head. "Right away, Miss Burton."

Aurelia would obey Lord Crewe's summons. But it would be on *her* terms.

***

An hour and a half later Aurelia strolled into the empty courtyard outside the stables, her heart thudding at what she had done. How long had the earl waited? Had he been angry? Where had he gone? And why did she feel so horribly disappointed that he wasn't waiting for her?

"Ah, here you are."

Aurelia's head whipped around at the sound of the earl's voice. He was striding out of the stables, Celsa's new hound—Princess—bounding along beside him.

"I thought perhaps you had not received my message," he said, his smile more of a smirk.

"No, I received it," she assured him, not wanting to get Charles in trouble. "I just had a few things to do, first." *Like stare at my coffee cup and then take three times as long to change into my habit.*

Just then both Silas and Jemmy came out of the stables, each leading a horse.

"Take this beast back to the kennel before she gets kicked, Jemmy," the earl said as Princess frolicked dangerously close to Frost's hooves.

"Aye, me lord." The boy snapped his fingers and the pup darted toward him.

Roland swiftly moved to Aurelia's side. "Allow me," he murmured, his hands landing on her hips and then sliding slowly to her waist before he lifted her up into the saddle.

He smiled up at her, his hand tight around her booted ankle, as if daring her to say something.

Aurelia ignored him, looking straight ahead.

He laughed, released her, and then swung up onto Frost's back.

"Where are we going?" Aurelia asked as she followed him out of the courtyard, Black Prince needing to trot to keep up with the far larger horse.

"It is a surprise, Aurelia."

"I don't like surprises, *my lord*."

He smiled. "I think you will be surprised how much you like *my* surprise."

Aurelia clamped her jaws shut, refusing to rise to his bait, and they rode down toward the bay in silence.

Lord Crewe reined in Frost some distance away from the pier.

Aurelia stopped Black Prince beside him and looked up at the earl. "Why are we stopping here?"

He gestured toward the rocky shore. "I thought a few hours over there might put you into a more biddable mood."

Aurelia squinted at him and then looked to where he was pointing.

A laugh slipped out of her when she saw the notorious *ducking stool*. "You are very droll, my lord. But if either of us deserves to be disciplined for bad behavior surely it would be *you*."

The earl threw his head back and laughed, the sound of his amusement causing a warm feeling in her belly.

"Where are you *really* taking me?" she asked when they resumed their journey.

"I thought you might like to see some flame scallops."

"Flame scallops?" she repeated, irked when she didn't manage to keep the excitement from her voice. "But I thought those were only in deep water?"

"Is that what you thought?" he said, his voice playful.

Aurelia gave an exasperated huff. "Is it not possible for you to answer a question directly?"

"Now where would be the fun in that?"

Aurelia pursed her lips, refusing to encourage his teasing behavior.

When they reached the pier, Aurelia saw that his lordship's personal skiff was ready and waiting.

Not until the earl was rowing toward Nesta's Perch did he speak again. "Why do you look so serious?" he asked, lazily but steadily pulling the oars, the action emphasizing the breadth of his shoulders.

"Perhaps that is just my face, my lord."

"No, it is an even more serious expression than usual. But then you are an extremely serious woman." He cocked his head, his smile secretive. "Too serious, sometimes. It is a lovely day—the sun is shining on the North Atlantic!"

She glanced up at the sky, which was a dull slate gray.

"Oh, very well," he admitted with a laugh. "You cannot *see* it shining, but it is there—just behind those clouds."

"The wind seems a bit brisk."

"Don't worry. You are safe in my hands, my dear Aurelia. Look there—a pair of mergansers."

Aurelia turned and quickly pulled out her sketchbook.

"I won't drop anchor because I don't believe they are staying," he said. "Indeed, it looks as if they are heading back to the island. They have only been taking a romantic swim together."

Aurelia snorted as she sketched. "Romantic?"

"Yes, romantic. They mate for life you know. See how they are whispering sweet nothings to each other?"

The birds were indeed bill to bill. "Perhaps they are having a row," she retorted. "She is complaining that it is too cold here, that she wants to go further south. He is offering some pitiful excuse in defense of his laziness at not wanting to fly that far."

He laughed, shipped the oars, and gracefully slid onto her bench, sitting right behind her. "So cynical for one so young," he murmured, his chin hovering just over her shoulder to watch her sketch, his proximity rapidly turning her hand into a block of wood.

"You are truly an artist, Aurelia."

She stopped pretending to draw and turned to face him.

He smiled at her from only inches away. "What? You are looking so fierce, Aurelia."

"I do not recall ever giving you permission to use my Christian name, sir."

"I believe you gave me permission that night in the library when you allowed my mouth between your glorious thighs," he said, reaching up and tucking a stray lock of hair behind her ear.

She narrowed her eyes as her neck and face heated. "You enjoy shocking me, don't you?"

He laughed. "I *do* enjoy it. You are always beautiful, but with your flags flying you are even more lovely and desirable."

"Are there really any flame scallops to be seen? Or was that merely a ruse?"

"Are you implying this is all an elaborate attempt at seduction? Now that would be shocking indeed. But as to the flame scallops, I am a naturalist, my dear Miss Burton. I would never lie about something as important as a flame scallop." He deftly shifted back onto his bench and took up the oars, skillfully aiming the boat toward the far side of Nesta's Perch. "All this week we will have some of the lowest tides of the year. You will get to see your scallops, fear not. What other bivalves are still on your list?"

Aurelia took her notebook from her satchel, relieved to be on safer ground. She flipped to the right page and studied her list. "If I really *do* see flame scallops today then all that remains is a fan mussel."

"Ah, the elusive *atrina fragilis*."

"Have you seen one?"

"Yes, but only while diving. You will not see them in tidal pools."

"What is it like to dive?" she asked.

"Unlike anything else I've experienced. It is liberating, exhilarating, and terrifying all at the same time. *We* are the interlopers and one is constantly aware that one's surroundings are entirely hostile to humans. One false or careless action and a diver will speedily succumb to the sea's deadly grasp.

"How long were you able to stay below the surface?"

"I have been below for as long as an hour, but—"

"An hour! But I thought barrels could only provide air for a few minutes."

"I have a metal helmet and full leather suit. The helmet connects to a long hose and men on the surface pump air down the line. I will take you some time—not too deep, just enough to get a feel for it. Would you like that?"

"Is it dangerous?"

"It can be, but one mitigates the danger by being exceedingly careful. It is truly the only way to observe marine animals as they go about their business." He shipped the oars and Aurelia saw that he had rowed them into a narrow inlet that must feed the marsh. He hopped over the side and brought the boat up onto the beach.

"You will get mucky feet if you step out here," he said, scooping her into his arms before Aurelia was aware of his intention.

"I could have walked," she said, her voice sounding breathy and foolish.

"But then I would not get to carry you," he retorted, striding across the sand. "There," he said, setting her down carefully on a rock, leaning close, his eye locked on hers.

"Thank you," she murmured, her body swaying toward him without her permission.

For one long, excruciating moment she thought he was going to kiss her.

But then he smiled and stepped back. "My pleasure. We will go in this direction. It isn't far, but you will have to climb over some rather slippery rocks as the tide has exposed them. Don't hesitate to ask for assistance, Miss Burton."

Aurelia stared after him as he secured their skiff. He was flirtatious one minute and merely friendly the next. He was a frustrating, confusing, and irresistible man. She absolutely refused to fling herself at him. Not again.

Armed with resolve, she set out in the direction he'd indicated. The rocks were extremely slippery, but her practical ankle boots stood her in good stead.

The earl ranged slightly ahead of her, glancing into rockpools, and quickly rejecting several until he found what he wanted.

"Over here, Miss Burton."

Aurelia took out her sketchpad and carefully picked her way toward him.

"Right there." He put an arm around her shoulder and then pointed, his head distractingly close to hers.

She followed the direction of his finger and gasped, forgetting all about his proximity. "It is so bright! And also much smaller than I expected. That color is magnificent."

He stood up and she immediately missed the warm, hard pressure of his body. "Come over onto this rock and you can get a better look. When you have sketched what you want, I will demonstrate one of the flame scallop's most interesting characteristics."

Aurelia went to the rock he'd pointed to and dropped to her haunches to get closer. She quickly sketched the little scene—scallop, delicate seaweed fronds, and dark volcanic rock behind the bright red-orange shell of the small bivalve. Once she was finished, she took out the booklet that contained her color swatches and located the shades she would need, jotting down the numbers she'd assigned to each of them.

Once she was finished, she tucked everything away and stood.

"Done?" he asked, smiling down at her and making her realize that he'd stood and watched without complaint while she'd sketched.

"Yes, thank you for being patient."

"I have waited days to catch a glimpse of a particular creature. A few minutes is nothing." He waded slowly into the pool, stopping only when the water reached the top of the tarred boots that he had been sensible enough to wear. "Now watch this." When he leaned closer to the water and his shadow fell on the small scallop it suddenly shot across the tidal pool.

Aurelia gave a surprised laugh. "How astounding!"

"Isn't it?" he said, his expression one of pure joy. "It is a rare trick for a species that is, by and large, sedentary. So," he said with a sly look. "Are you ready to return to Crewe or would you like to investigate a few more of the better tidal areas?"

"I suppose I have time to look at a few more," she said primly, as if wild horses could have dragged her away at that point.

He grinned. "Let us explore, then."

Chapter 23

Aurelia was just finishing a sketch of a black guillemot when she realized the sky had grown darker. "Do you think it will rain?" she asked.

The earl, who'd found a relatively flat rock to sit on and was jotting down something in his small booklet, looked up and clucked his tongue. "It looks like a nasty little storm has sneaked up on us, Miss Burton."

She glanced at the water between Nesta's Perch and Crewe. The whitecaps had sprung up in a shockingly short time. "Is it safe to row back?"

"I think we should take cover and allow this to blow over."

"But will it?"

He gave her a vaguely amused look. "Eventually all bad weather passes, Miss Burton."

Why did that sound so *ominous*. And why did he keep calling her *Miss Burton*?

"We can take shelter at Walter's cottage," he said.

"He won't mind?"

The earl raised an eyebrow, the gesture managing to convey a wealth of meaning, chiefly that everything—this island, the cottage, and probably Walter himself—belonged to him.

"Come," he said, standing and holding out a hand. "Give me your satchel."

"I can—"

"Miss Burton."

She huffed a sigh and handed it over just as a fat drop of rain hit her nose.

When she began to walk back toward the sandy trail the earl shook his head and took her hand. "No. This way. I will lead you over the rocks. Once we are past the bigger ones it will be much faster."

They had both removed their gloves to sketch and poke around in the rock pools and Aurelia's pulse sped at the feel of his naked, slightly roughened fingers as his much larger hand swallowed her own. His grip was firm and she doubted she could pull away if she tried.

It is more likely that he *could not pull away from* you.

She ignored the taunting voice and paid attention to the rocky climb. By the time she reached the top, it had begun to rain in earnest. Even though it was beach grass and sand and not treacherous rock, the earl still held her hand.

Thunder cracked and she gave a startled yelp as the rain became a deluge. And then, for some reason, Aurelia laughed.

The earl glanced down at her as they splashed through puddles, his grin matching her feelings exactly.

Aurelia had no idea what was so funny—she was cold and quickly becoming soaked through to the skin—it just felt wonderful to be running in the rain with the all too fascinating man beside her.

Evidently, his lordship felt likewise because the two of them were laughing like fools by the time they reached the cottage.

The earl gave a peremptory knock on the cottage door and then opened it and ushered her into the small entry hall. "Walter?" he called out. "You have two wet visitors requiring shelter."

The house echoed emptily.

The earl turned to her. "Either he is napping soundly or he is not at home. You must get out of those wet things. I will see if I can find him."

Aurelia was shaking out her soaked, and probably ruined, bonnet when his lordship returned.

"He is not here."

Her hand froze on the buttons of her pelisse.

"He will not mind if we make ourselves at home." The earl took off his hat and hung it up on one of the pegs.

"Where could he be?" she asked rather stupidly—as if the earl would know the whereabouts of every employee.

"Probably on the mainland. His daughter lives there and he often goes to have a homecooked meal rather than his usual bachelor fare. In any event, there is a small fire already burning in the parlor and soon I will have a warming blaze." He gestured for her to come with him.

Aurelia followed, butterflies in her belly. They were alone. Completely alone. On an island. On *his* island. Or at least one of them.

Once they were in the cozy sitting room his lordship heaped more fuel on the fire and then took two ladder-back chairs and set them in front of the blaze.

"Give me your pelisse," he said after shucking off his own coat and draping it over the chairback.

Aurelia wanted to look away from his half-undressed torso but could not. At least not until she'd taken a thorough inventory of the way his dark blue waistcoat—embroidered with tiny birds—and blinding white linen sheathed his broad shoulders to his narrow waist and—

"That is soaked."

His voice jerked her eyes away from the front placket of his doeskin breeches and she felt her face heat when she met his gaze.

"I'm sorry?" she said.

"Your gown is soaked. Go to the smaller of the two bedrooms upstairs. I know Walter keeps it for his daughter's visits. There should be something for you to wear while we dry out your dress."

"Oh, surely that isn't necessary. I am not col—*ahchoo*!"

He lifted an eyebrow. "You were saying?"

Aurelia sneezed again.

"Go on and change before you catch a serious chill," he ordered, no longer smiling. "You won't be offending anyone if you borrow some clothing."

Aurelia decided it was foolish to sit in a sopping wet gown. After all, she was already on this island, alone, with a notorious rake.

How much worse could she savage her reputation?

***

Roland had spent the last six bloody weeks thinking of nothing but the woman in the other room, terrified that he might have so thoroughly cocked up his own life that he could never have her.

The fact that he had found no evidence of Rebecca in all the places he had searched was not definitive proof that she was not still alive.

But Roland no longer cared. He knew that was reprehensible. But he didn't care about that, either.

The molten desire that had bubbled not far beneath the surface since the first day Aurelia had entered his library with that milksop Talbot had finally broken through the surface and he was done being patient.

Talbot.

Roland ground his teeth just thinking about the man, who had obviously been making the most of his time with Aurelia while Roland was off on a wild goose chase.

Well, he would take care of *that* problem today.

He heard a slight scuffle behind him and turned, laughing softly at the sight that met his gaze.

"You are cruel to laugh. It was the warmest thing I could find," Aurelia said, raising one slender hand to push a lock of damp hair off her brow, the rolled up sleeves of the voluminous blue dress making her wrists look even more delicate.

The gown was amusingly short and wide, ending well above her trim ankles but hanging off her body like a big blue sack.

And yet she had never looked lovelier to him.

She was like a magnificent gem that needed no fancy setting to draw out her beauty.

"Here," Roland said, handing her a glass of the brandy he'd wisely sent over with all the other delicacies.

She took the glass and sniffed, her adorably upturned nose—the only feature on her classically elegant face that possessed a little whimsey—wrinkling. "What is it?"

"Brandy. It will warm you."

She took a sip and grimaced, but then took another before setting down her glass. Her forehead furrowed at the food Roland had set out for them, all of it expertly prepared by his kitchen at Crewe Castle. When she looked up again, he saw disbelief in her wide hazel eyes. "Walter had all this here?"

"He had it here today," Roland said dryly.

"You sent this over."

"Yes," he said. "May I fix you a plate?"

She stared, as if she could see the contents of Roland's mind if she looked long enough. He could have told her that such mind-reading took years of experience with the opposite sex. But she was certainly welcome to try out her skills on him. In fact, if Roland had his way—and he usually did—his mind would be the only one she ever became adept at reading.

"I will take that as a *yes*," he said, loading a plate with grapes, three little finger sandwiches that looked to be watercress, cucumber, and finely sliced ham, one of the cheese and salmon pastries his cook was famous for, and a cream cake with spun sugar swirls so delicate he didn't understand how they'd not broken in transit.

She took the plate without speaking.

"Would you like some tea? Or I have wine"—he gestured to the bottle he'd opened while she'd been changing. "And there is a keg of homebrew from the Laughing Hen."

She seemed to be experiencing some sort of internal struggle and Roland waited, curious, to see how it would resolve.

***

"I will have some wine, please," Aurelia finally said.

I must be mad to request a beverage that will only scramble my already scrambled wits.

You just want an excuse to be bad, a wryly amused voice accused. *If your wits are scrambled by wine then your decisions are not really your own, are they?*

The earl's voice cut into her musing. "This is cozy, is it not?" He lowered himself onto the settee beside her, his long body too big for Walter's modestly sized furniture.

She ignored his question and asked, "How long do you think this storm will last?"

They both looked out the room's only window, which was currently being lashed with wind and rain, the sky having gone a dark slate gray.

"It might blow over in an hour. Or we might be stranded here overnight." He picked up one of the decadent-looking cream cakes and took a bite, rolling his eyes ceilingward in exaggerated ecstasy. "These are delicious. You really must try one."

"I will eat my meal, first."

He wiped the cream and sugar from his full lower lip with the pad of one finger and then sucked it clean.

Aurelia felt faint.

He chuckled. "You look so disapproving, Miss Burton, as if I were a naughty schoolboy in need of discipline."

She snorted at the improbable image.

"There, that is better. Although I have developed a soft spot for that stern scowl of yours."

She ignored his comment and asked, "Do you seriously think this storm might last into the night?"

"It has been known to happen." He popped the rest of his cake into his mouth and chewed, clearly unbothered by the thought of an overnight stay on this tiny island. Together.

"If I spend the night here with you—alone—people will talk, my lord."

"People always talk. That is one of life's tedious constants, Miss Burton. And the subjects they enjoy talking about most of all are those people who lead interesting lives. So, you tell me, would you rather lead a dull, boring life whose only reward was gossip, or a vibrant, sensually rich life and tolerate a bit of envious carping?"

"Those of us who are not lord of all we survey must pay heed to all that envious carping," she retorted.

He laughed. "I like that: lord of all I survey." He smiled, his eyelid drooping. "Especially considering who I am surveying right now. Am I *your* lord, Miss Burton?"

Aurelia pursed her lips, refusing to look away from his piercing gaze.

"Here is what I think," the earl said after a moment of silent staring. "We are going to cause talk even if we are boring and do nothing. So, at least we should have the pleasure of being naughty and having fun. At the very least, we should enjoy the use of each other's Christian names, shouldn't we, Aurelia? And you must call me Roland." He smirked. "As you have once before." He picked up a second cream cake and took a bite.

Aurelia hadn't believed she could blush any harder. Roland indeed. If ever there was a man who could carry the name of a Norse marauder it was the one sitting across from her and eating his food with such *sensual* gusto.

"You are thinking Roland is a perfect name for me, aren't you, Aurelia?"

Aurelia ignored his question and nibbled on a sandwich.

"Arthur and I resemble our Norse ancestors more than our Norman ones. Can you not envision us clad only in skins and bits of hammered metal, our long fair hair braided and streaming as we descended on an unsuspecting Scots village?"

Aurelia *could* picture it far too easily. At least where the earl was concerned. Arthur, on the other hand, looked as if he couldn't conquer a village full of puppies.

"And you would like that? Raping and pillaging?" she taunted.

"I would have relished the pillaging, but there is no joy to be had from forcing a woman."

"You would have charmed your victims, instead?"

He laughed. "You know me so well." He lifted his index finger to his mouth and his mobile lips closed obscenely around the tip. He met her riveted gaze and the skin at the corner of his eye crinkled as he pulled the finger out with a wet *pop*. "Any man who uses violence against a woman doesn't deserve to have one. Here, try a bite of this," the earl said, lifting his cake to her mouth.

Aurelia reached out to take it, but he pulled it back.

"*Tut, tut*, greedy guts. I wasn't going to give it *all* to you. Just a bite." He gently nudged her lips with the creamy delicacy.

Aurelia swallowed down the moisture flooding her mouth before taking a bite, intensely aware of his gaze on her mouth and the way his prominent, blade-like nose flared when her lips parted.

"It is tender and sweet and moist, isn't it?"

She nodded jerkily and chewed, grateful for the hideous, high-necked gown since she could feel the pulse at the base of her throat hammering like a war drum.

Aurelia swallowed the sweet mouthful. "Old Walter is quite a baker, it seems."

He laughed. "Indeed, he is a man of many talents. One of the most impressive being his decision to go to the mainland today." He took a bite from the same place her lips had just been and something about the act felt bizarrely intimate.

"You planned this, didn't you?" she asked.

"I know you consider me all-powerful, Aurelia, but even I cannot control the weather."

"No. But you would have found some other reason to keep us here even if the sun was blazing. The skiff would have floated off, the oars would have been lost—" she broke off at his laughing.

He leaned closer and his warm palm cupped her cheek. "You have me dead to rights. I would have done whatever was necessary to have this time with you."

"Even though you are thoroughly compromising me by doing so?"

He nodded, his pupil huge. "Yes, even though." He lightly stroked her lower lip with his thumb. "Are you angry?"

Was she?

"Because if you truly do not want to be here with me, I can row you over to Crewe. It is windy and wet and the ride will be unpleasant, but my boat is stable enough that you wouldn't be in any real danger." He brushed her lip again. "Is that what you want, Aurelia? I am yours to command. You need only say the—"

Aurelia was suddenly tired of trying to be angry with him. And tired of depriving herself and restraining her desires.

She closed the distance between them, mashing their lips together in her haste to touch him. As kisses went, it was less than graceful.

But judging by the approving rumble that rattled the earl's chest, he did not mind at all.

Chapter 24

T he earl tasted sweet, just like the cream cake he'd so greedily consumed.

Aurelia was grateful when he took control of the kiss, tilting her head and probing her more deeply, his tongue slick and hot as it lazily jousted with hers.

His hands closed around her waist and she was suddenly on his lap, her knees straddling him. He held her hips while slowly spreading his thighs, the action causing her own legs to open wider. And then he slid an arm around her waist and pulled her flush against his body, the action causing her sex to rub on something thick and hard.

The sudden bolt of pleasure was almost blinding.

And then Roland lifted his hips and grazed her again, harder this time and her eyes rolled back.

"Lift up your skirt, darling."

Aurelia yanked at the trapped material, squirming to free it from beneath her knees. Once she had, she lowered herself, grinding against him.

They both groaned.

"Aurelia," he whispered, his hips pulsing gently, the slight friction of the soft doeskin sending jolts of pleasure spiraling through her body. "I want to be inside you, darling."

God help her, but she wanted that, too.

"Yes."

He pulled back a little so they could see each other more clearly. It felt odd to be looking down at him for a change. "It will hurt you the first time."

"I know what will happen."

Roland chuckled softly. "Of course you do."

Aurelia stared at him, rocking her hips just enough to make his jaw tighten. "I want it," she said.

He held her gaze, his normally pale eye dark with desire. "I will make it less painful." His hand nudged beneath her bunched skirts and caressed up her thigh. "I will give you an orgasm," he said, his finger grazing lightly over her lower lips. "I will give you several—until you're so wet and relaxed and ready to be filled that your body will welcome me."

A thrill went through her at his erotic words and she pushed herself against his finger and hissed in a breath at the gentle friction.

His gaze was so hooded that she could barely see the mesmerizing iris.

When he finally, mercifully, circled the source of her pleasure his eye widened. "You are drenched."

Aurelia had been aroused since the moment she'd learned he had come home. But she wasn't going to tell *him* that.

His eye burned into her as he worked her slowly toward her peak, his touch far more enjoyable than her own.

Aurelia's breathing quickened, her hips pulsing as she stared into him, letting him see the raw need that consumed her.

"Yes," he murmured, breathing through parted lips as she began to shake, a wave of want swamping her body. It was too much. It was not enough. It was…

"Come for me, sweetheart."

Aurelia exploded, her fingers clawing at his shoulders as a powerful contraction squeezed every muscle in her body.

And then he slid his finger into her convulsing sheath and she lost the battle with control, her cry mingling with the storm that raged beyond the window.

***

Wonder, joy, and sensual bliss spasmed across Aurelia's normally reserved face as her tight cunt closed around Roland's finger again and again and again, soaking his hand with her release.

Her eyelids had fluttered shut when her climax struck, but they lifted slowly, heavily, as the contractions diminished. She was breathing heavily, her face slack and sensual. All too soon she began to collect her wits and recall where she was and what she had just done.

But instead of scrambling off him as Roland had feared, a look of resolve settled on her face and one of her hands slid down his shoulder and over his chest and belly, before settling on the obscene bulge in his leathers.

Roland groaned as she did her best to stroke him, which was awkward given the position of their bodies.

Tell her the truth.

Roland gritted his teeth and tried to ignore the annoying voice.

Tell her where you have been. What you have been doing. What you have found. What you have not *found…*

"We do not need to go any further than this," he said, the words sounding as if they'd been forced from his mouth—because they had been.

Her hand stilled and her forehead creased. "You don't want—"

"Hell yes I want to," he retorted, grabbing her wrist and keeping her hand pressed against his cock. "I just thought I'd try to take the chivalric route for once."

Her lips curved faintly. "Why start now, my lord?"

Roland laughed, delighted by her cheek. "I could not agree more." He plucked at her hideous, voluminous gown. "I want this off."

Her mouth opened in surprise, but she recovered swiftly. "And I want *this* and *this* off," she shot back, tugging at his coat and breeches.

He grinned, loving this side of her. "You first," he said, eyeing the hideous gown.

She took the fabric at the loose waist and then proceeded to lift it over her head. Roland helped her with the last bit, freeing it from her arms and then tossing it to the floor.

She had removed her stays and petticoat earlier and wore only a whisper-thin chemise.

Roland's gaze locked on to the tips of her full breasts, her hard nipples thrusting at muslin that was so fine it was all but transparent. He cupped a handful in each palm, earning a whimper of pleasure as he thumbed the stiff peaks.

She gasped and leaned closer when he mouthed each nipple over the fabric, suckling and nipping until there were two damp spots.

He began to lift off her chemise but she scrambled off his lap.

"What is it?" he asked when she backed a few feet away.

She crossed her arms over her chest, hiding her gorgeous tits from him. "I have already bared myself to you once before. It is your turn. You need to take something off."

Roland laughed and then stood. First, he toed off the heavy boots he'd worn to explore rock pools. Then he unbuttoned and shrugged off his waistcoat.

Once his cravat had fluttered to the floor, Aurelia's gaze dropped to the V of his shirt, the raw yearning in her eyes making his hard cock throb even more.

Roland reached behind his neck and pulled his shirt over his head.

There wasn't a man alive who would not have reveled in her long, admiring look.

Her throat flexed twice as she swallowed, exploring every inch of him with greedy eyes, her chest rising and falling faster.

Roland's hand paused on the waistband of his breeches. A man's naked chest was one thing, but a hard cock was another entirely.

He gestured to his tented breeches. "Are you sure?"

"I have seen naked men before," she said, sounding miffed.

His hand froze, jealousy twisting in his gut. "Who?" he demanded. A sudden, infuriating thought assaulted him. "Was it that bloody Talbot? Has he—"

"*No!*" She laughed and shook her head. "Of course I have never seen Sir Gideon unclothed."

Roland grunted. At least he wouldn't have to kill the man. But he'd have to kill somebody else. "Who was it?"

Her eyebrows shot up at his tone, which Roland had to admit was a bit imperious.

"I suspect there were far fewer naked men in my past than naked women in yours," she retorted tartly.

Well, that was true.

His sexual history was hardly a subject he wanted to discuss now—or ever—so he released the catches on his fall, yanked open the five buttons, pulled on the tape holding up his drawers, and shoved down both garments in a single, practiced motion.

Aurelia's jaw dropped, her eyes going as wide as an owl's. "Oh, my."

***

Aurelia had not lied. She *had* seen at least a dozen naked male bodies, but most of those had been deceased. The few who'd still been alive had bodies that had been wasted by illness or injury.

And not a single one had been aroused.

Nor had any of them been anywhere as magnificently proportioned as the man across from her. Not just his… membrum virile, but the rest of him, as well. He towered over her, his tall, tightly muscled body like that of some scarred god of war.

A big hand slid down his flat belly and closed around the object of her fascination.

Aurelia wrenched her gaze upward. "I am sorry for staring," she blurted.

"Don't be. Your interest is charming." He stroked himself, his shoulder, biceps, and forearm flexing in a way that was mesmerizing on several levels. Not only was he sensually devastating, but his body was so hard and defined that she could actually recognize muscles moving beneath his taut skin. He was like a living, breathing, and, er, stroking, anatomy text.

He dropped his hand suddenly, allowing her to see all of him. But it was difficult to look at just one thing—no matter how impressive that thing was—

because the body it was attached to was… exquisite. Even the scars, of which there were many, added to his appeal.

"If you keep looking at me like that, I shall get a big head," he said.

"A *bigger* head, you mean."

He chuckled and yet again more muscles flexed, the ridges on his abdomen tightening until she could see the distinct line between his external obliques and rectus abdominus. Who would have believed those muscles could look so glorious?

Aurelia reached out and caressed the linea alba with one finger.

He hissed and his erection jumped, a bead of clear liquid sliding down the shaft.

Aurelia laughed.

"You think my condition humorous, do you?"

He moved swiftly, easily lifting her by her waist and putting her down on the settee, so that she was staring up at him, his erection at eye level.

"Am I naked enough for you now, Aurelia?"

"Yes… Roland," she murmured, distracted by the slick, red crown.

"How lovely my name sounds on your tongue."

Aurelia watched, fascinated, as a glistening drop oozed from the tiny slit. She swallowed and moistened her lips, which were suddenly dry, and then reached for him.

"Bloody hell!" he gasped, and then stepped back when her fingers barely grazed him.

Her head jerked up at his harsh expletive and she blinked up at him, confused.

He gave her an oddly strained smile. "You can touch it later, darling. If you put your hand on me right now all our enjoyment will be over." He stepped closer again. "Let's get this off," he muttered, taking the hem of her chemise. "Bottom and arms up," he said, and then carefully teased the garment over her shoulders and head and let it drop to the floor.

And then he stared, shaking his head, as if in disbelief. "God, you are fucking beautiful."

Her jaw dropped at the word—one she only knew because her sister Hy had taught it to her, along with every other dirty word and phrase she knew.

He sank to his knees in front of her and cupped her breasts, leaning close to suckle them, alternating until he'd made each nipple erect and Aurelia was squirming. He released them with a last tweak and then dragged his fingertips lightly down her quivering belly until he reached her sex. He nudged her thighs open and then spread her lower lips with his thumbs, casting a quick glance up at her before he leaned closer and lowered his mouth over her.

She shuddered and her lids drooped, but she never took her gaze from him.

As he had done that night all those weeks ago, he proceeded to drive her to climax with an ease that spoke of years of experience that she did not want to think too closely about.

Instead, she relaxed her clenched thighs and gave herself up to pleasure.

When she cried out and came apart, he eased first one, and then two fingers inside her. The stretch was vaguely uncomfortable, but when her inner muscles clenched around him the exquisite sensations intensified, drawing out her climax.

Roland watched her like a hawk, his lips red and slick as he caressed every part of her except that which was too sensitive. And then, after the last wave had washed over her, he withdrew from her and laid her out on the narrow settee kneeling between her spread thighs, lowering over her until his erection nudged at her entrance.

Suddenly, he chuckled. "I could have planned this seduction a bit better. This settee is a bit of a squeeze. Am I crushing you, darling?"

"No. Not… crushing… *urgh,*" she grunted when he pressed harder, his thick crown breaching her.

"Do you want to wait, my love?" he asked, smiling down at her with such warmth that Aurelia could almost believe that she really was *his love.*

And then something her mother had told her long ago came back to her. "*A man always believes himself to be in love when he is rutting in a woman. It is the best time to ask for something you want, Aurelia. Only for a short time are they ever vulnerable.*"

Roland cocked his head. "What is it? Why do you suddenly look so… sad?"

Aurelia hated that her mother's poison had invaded this moment. She shook her head and spread her legs wider in invitation. "I have not changed my mind."

Passion flared in his eye and he pressed himself against her. "Fast is better," he murmured, and then entered her in one long thrust.

The sudden stretch was startlingly sharp and she bit back a yelp.

"Breathe, sweetheart," he said, holding still inside her.

Aurelia hadn't realized she was holding her breath until he'd spoken. She took a gulp of air and waited for the stabbing pain to resume, but it didn't. In fact, there wasn't any pain at all. She was filled with a thick, throbbing erection that made the lower part of her body ache, but it wasn't unpleasant.

Roland pulled back enough that their eyes locked. "Aurelia? Are you in pain?"

She shook her head. "It only hurt for a few seconds."

He began to withdraw slowly and she caught her lower lip with her teeth.

Once he was almost all the way out, he slid back in, slower than the first time. "Better?" he asked, again pausing so she could adjust.

She nodded, her eyes drawn to his shoulder, which was scored with more black lines like the ones on his face.

Aurelia put her fingers over each groove, needing to spread them wide to fit.

She looked up at him. "You could have died."

"But I didn't. It is almost as if Fate wanted to save me for this moment." He grinned.

Aurelia laughed.

I have a man inside my body and we are laughing and jesting.

The thought was so startling that she was momentarily stunned.

There were no tears, no wishing she was dead, no shame—none of the things the countess had warned her about.

"What is it?" he asked, his voice strained as he again withdrew and then sank back in, but faster this time. "You've got that fierce look again." He stilled when he was almost all the way out.

"Don't stop." She slid a hand up to cup his jaw. "Please, Roland."

His nostrils flared at the sound of his name and he slid back in, harder this time, no longer pausing between strokes but rolling his hips smoothly, taking her deeply with each thrust. He propped himself up on one elbow and wormed his hand between their bodies, gently stroking her engorged nub.

Her sex began to tighten the way it had earlier, except this time, she had something large and hard and hot inside her. "Oh," she murmured. "That is— that is—" Aurelia tilted her hips, suddenly needing *more*.

Roland responded to her silent demand immediately, stroking harder, faster, touching something inside her that caused a deeper pleasure to build and build and—

Aurelia groaned as the orgasm swept through her body, clinging to Roland, her fingers digging into the muscles of his back. Raw, animalistic noises escaped, no matter how hard she tried to hold them back.

Roland, who'd stopped moving while the most powerful contractions seized her body, suddenly growled and resumed his thrusting, each stroke so powerful the settee gave an alarming squeak.

"Aurelia," he gasped, his hips drumming until he finally rammed himself painfully deep.

Aurelia felt his erection swell and spasm inside her. And then she felt the warm wash of his seed. Some part of her mind—a part not caught up in the sensual bliss of the moment—shrieked about pregnancy and children.

But as his big, heavy body lowered over hers, crushing her into the cushions of the settee, Aurelia could not bring herself to care. Instead, she slid her limp arms around his damp, heaving shoulders and held him close.

Aurelia could have laid there forever, regardless of how difficult it was to breathe, but all too soon she felt awareness seep back into his relaxed body, and he slowly lifted himself off her and smiled down at her, his expression languid and smug and… speculative.

"Why are you smiling like that?" she asked, suspicion prickling her skin.

"I am wondering how long it will take me to persuade you to be my wife… Lady Aurelia."

Chapter 25

While Aurelia was still too stunned to speak Roland palmed one of her heavy breasts, gently squeezing. Christ! Her skin was like silk and her tit was as soft as whipped cream. He teased her nipple until it was hard and was pondering contorting his body on the tiny bloody settee so he could take it into his mouth when she finally spoke.

"How long have you known who I am, my lord?"

She was back to *my lording* him; that was not good.

Roland reluctantly released her breast. "Since coming back from the trip I took in July."

"How?"

"I was at White's and overheard some men talking about the Earl of Addiscombe's daughter marrying Paul Needham. One of the men recalled meeting Addiscombe's oldest daughter during her Season—a Lady Aurelia—and asked whether she was the one who'd married Viscount Needham. Your name is unusual and I knew you were from Hampshire, so I put it all together."

Her lips parted in shock. "You have known all this time! Why didn't you say something?"

He shrugged. "What should I have said?"

She gave an exasperated huff and shifted on the couch in such a way that gave him more room, but also pulled her delectable breast farther away.

"I do not understand you," she accused.

Roland laughed. "Lord. I'm the easiest man in the world to understand," he protested, eyeing her breast, and dying to suck it. Something told him that would not go over well just now.

"Why do you suddenly want to marry me—because I'm a peer's daughter?"

"I do not care who your father is, Aurelia—he could be a stone mason or an itinerant tinker—it is *you* I want. And my desire is not sudden; I have wanted you for months."

"You have a strange way of showing it."

"I was trying to be less selfish." He gestured to them and the room around them. "You see how that turned out." When she didn't laugh or even smile, he sighed. "You are too young for me—too talented and with too much life ahead of you. Too… good for me, in short. I have been nothing but self-indulgent for years. If I were a better man, I would have stepped aside and left you for Talbot." He scowled. "But the mere thought of him even *looking* at you—" Roland bared his teeth. "Well, suffice it to say it makes me quite irritable." And violent, but he decided to keep that to himself.

Aurelia stared up at him, uncertainty in her gaze. "Then why did you leave me six weeks ago without scarcely a word? And right after that night in the library, when we—" she bit her lip.

Roland sighed. "There is something you need to hear—something unpleasant."

She swallowed and nodded.

"Six weeks ago I received an anonymous letter that claimed my… wife had been spotted."

Her eyes bulged. "What? But—I thought she died from the panther—oh. I am sorry. You mean your first wife."

Roland nodded. "The letter came—ever so inconveniently—after I had spent one of the most delightful evenings of my life with you in the library." He chuckled at the pink that spread over her breasts, chest, up her neck, and slowly to her cheeks.

"So lovely," he murmured, stroking the path of the blush with his hand.

"Roland."

"Hmm?" he inched near enough to lower his mouth over her nipple.

"*Roland.*"

He heaved a sigh and, reluctantly, sat up.

"What happened?" she asked, her forehead deeply furrowed. "Did you"—she bit her lip and then forced herself to say, "did you find her?"

He gave an unamused laugh. "No. I spent six bloody weeks chasing red herrings, and it all led to nothing."

"No trace of her?"

"Oh, there were plenty of traces, but never anything more. I spoke to dozens of people, but the trail—if there even was one—had gone cold. Rebecca was not an especially, er, noticeable woman." He felt a pang of guilt at the words. "I do not say that to be cruel, just to make the point that it was difficult to be sure the woman whose trail I was following was really *her*. Average height and weight, brown hair, regular features—neither beautiful nor hideous." He gave a snort of annoyance. "If she'd had a wen on her nose or a hump on her back people would have remembered. It is amazing how hard it is to track a so-called *average* person."

"What did the letter say? And who would have sent it?"

Roland inhaled deeply and then exhaled. He hated having to talk about this—today, of all days—but it needed to be said. "I don't know who sent it," he admitted. "But the letter contained one detail that only Rebecca and I knew. The writer claimed that she had a child with her." He swallowed. "A boy of approximately three-and-ten. Rebecca was pregnant when she disappeared, which is something nobody knew."

"Oh, Roland! How terrible."

He nodded. "I spent day after day searching with *nothing* to show for it." He met her concerned gaze. "I could not believe that I received a letter about her *now*—just when I had met you and—" He broke off and gave a bitter laugh. "In any case, I had to follow any lead I could."

"Of course you did."

"I paid two inquiry agents and scattered money far and wide, especially hoping to get word of the boy—if there was one." He felt a pang of shame and forced himself to meet her gaze. "But I hoped I would not find her, Aurelia. All I could think about was *you* and how Rebecca's reappearance would ruin any chance I had for happiness." He pulled his thoughts away from those weeks of frustration and caressed her face, cupping her jaw, which fit perfectly into the palm of his hand. "I love you. And even though I am probably the worst man you could marry, I want you too much to do the honorable thing and let you go. Tell me you will marry me, sweetheart."

She stared at him for a long moment, her eyes, for once, unreadable to him. And then she laid her hand over his and gently removed it from her face. "I cannot marry you, Roland."

***

Pain and confusion flickered across Roland's face. "Is it because you fear Rebecca is still alive? We looked high and low, Aurelia. That is why I followed each and every lead and why I stayed away all those weeks. I wanted to be *sure*. I found no evidence that Rebecca is still alive. She must have told somebody she was pregnant before she left—that is the only answer."

"I am not concerned that your first wife will re-appear."

"Then what is it?"

"I think it would be hell on earth to marry a man who could not be faithful."

He flinched as if she'd slapped him.

"I watched my father slowly drive my mother mad with his infidelity, and she never loved him. You have been married twice and you've had lovers throughout. Such behavior would be unbearable." *Because I love you*, she might have added, but she couldn't. Because her love didn't matter when she could never marry him.

He abruptly stood and fetched her chemise.

"You are getting goose cpimples," he said, and then he turned away while he pulled on his drawers and breeches.

Aurelia slipped the flimsy garment over her head and when she looked up, he held out a blanket.

"Let me wrap this around you. There is still a chill in the air, despite the fire."

Aurelia allowed him to bundle her up like a child.

Once he had shoveled more coal onto the fire, he said, "Your point is well taken, Aurelia. But you don't understand—" he broke off and paced toward the window, staring out into the storm.

"Then explain it to me, Roland. Tell me why you cannot be faithful. Because I must confess that I am beginning to think men are simply incapable of fidelity. At least the ones who belong to our class. My father kept mistresses and purchased fine clothing for himself and gifts for his lovers even while we, his children, remade our own garments and lived with the constant terror of being evicted from our home. He squandered not only his own wealth, but my brother's inheritance along with all the money my mother brought to the marriage. And when that was gone, he wasted his daughters' futures as well. So, I know firsthand about the selfish hungers that can consume a man and how it can wreck the lives of those around him." Aurelia bit her tongue to keep from allowing any more anger and bile to flow from her.

He lowered to his haunches in front of her, his gaze chagrined and… embarrassed?

"I have never offered excuses for my behavior because, at the end of the day, what I did was inexcusable. But if you are asking me whether I am capable of fidelity? The answer is an emphatic *yes.*"

"Why should I believe that?" she asked, unable to keep the desperation from her voice.

He snorted softly. "Given your experience with the male species, I suppose you will not accept my word as a gentleman?"

Although Aurelia's immediate impulse was to laugh, she knew how men felt about their honor.

"Never mind," he said when she hesitated. "I do not need to resort to claims of honor because I have not run out of persuasive arguments yet." He gave her one of his rakish smiles, as if to assure her that he was not offended by her lack of faith.

Aurelia nodded, trying not to hope too much.

He resumed his pacing. "I daresay you will find what I am about to say difficult to believe, but there was a time in my life when I very much believed in love and fidelity."

"I know. Nora told me how you were when you were younger," Aurelia said, loathe to interrupt him, but wanting him to know that she believed him.

Roland looked pleased. "Nora has been defending my character, has she?" He noticed her strained look and he chuckled softly. "Ah, I see. She spoke well of the boy but warned you away from the man." It was not a question.

He resumed his pacing. "Before my father interfered in my life and brought Nora to the island all I cared about was cataloging every bit of flora and fauna I could find. I didn't notice females and I didn't care if people spoke to me or ignored me altogether." His mouth twisted into a wry smile. "But once I met Nora… Well, all the passion that I'd poured into science was diverted—at least temporarily—to mastering the art of love." He snorted. "Or at least the art of sexual congress."

He stared straight ahead, lost in his thoughts.

"I don't know what she told you," he said after a moment of introspection, "but I will share my half of the story. I believed that she loved me and I fell in love with her." He gave her a wry smile. "You must think I fall in love at the drop of a hat."

Thankfully, he did not wait for her to answer before continuing.

"Nora herself told me it was infatuation, that a lad of sixteen could not know his own heart." He shrugged. "As it happened, my father took matters out of my hands. When Nora disappeared, he told me that she had run off with her lover. He said the child wasn't mine. I didn't believe him. Fights and arguments ensued and I made rash threats. He curtailed my quarterly allowance and essentially made me a prisoner in the castle. I hated him, but I hated myself more for my inability to *do* anything about my situation. But time dulls even the most painful wounds and he found ways to tempt me."

He stopped in front of her. "Can you guess?"

"He funded a journey somewhere interesting?"

Roland smiled. "You know me so well. When I showed willing to forget Nora and the child, he rewarded me. He never knew that I used my money to engage a private inquiry agent. It took several years, but I found her and Guustin and it was immediately evident that he was mine." His handsome face took on a proud, triumphant look. "I brought them home to Crewe. When my father discovered I had no interest in marrying Nora, he was amused and not angry. He said that tracking her down showed my stubbornness and determination, the *Montgomery Mettle* he called it. He was delighted that I had fallen in with his plans by becoming exactly like him."

His pale blue gaze settled on Aurelia. "And yes, I *did* become a selfish womanizer in the same mold as my father. I discovered that what he had always told me was true—that it was easier to think with my cock than to allow my heart to become involved.

"Unfortunately, when my father met Guustin he decided that I needed a *real* son—an heir—insurance if I were to die on one of my dangerous journeys." Roland shrugged. "I didn't care who he chose—what did it matter to a young man who had replaced love with pleasure?" he asked her, his smile self-mocking.

"While *I* might not have cared who I married, Rebecca, my wife-to-be, cared a great deal that our fathers had arranged a marriage without consulting our opinions. I had known Rebecca for years. Her father often brought her to stay on Crewe and I'm sure that he and my father had been plotting our union for years. The fact that Rebecca and I had always loathed each other did not matter to either of them."

He stopped and rubbed the back of his neck, staring at the floor for a moment before looking up and meeting her gaze. "Rebecca pleaded with me to intercede. She wept and stormed and begged me to convince my father to change his mind about our marriage." His lips curved into a bitter smile. "I told her I had no intention of dissuading my father, quite the reverse. You see, he had promised me a great deal of money for my next expedition if I complied with his demand. I also told Rebecca that he had offered even more money when I put a child in her belly."

Aurelia watched as he strode back and forth in the small room, mired in his past.

"I told her that all she had to do was give my father the heir he wanted and then she could take as many lovers as she wanted. She told me that if we married, she would spend her life making me regret the decision." He gave an unamused laugh. "And she continues to plague me even in death, it would seem."

He strode to the window and stared out at the rain. After a few moments during which only the crackle of the fire and patter of the rain on the window could be heard, he returned to the settee, lowering himself beside her.

He took her hand and held it in both of his.

"When I went to Rebecca on our wedding night, prepared to do my duty, she took great pleasure in showing me her bulging belly. She said as I'd wanted to please my father so much, she had decided to help me." He glanced at Aurelia when she did not respond. "You do not seem surprised," he said. "Did somebody tell you that Celsa was not mine?"

"She did."

Roland winced. "Damnation! Who told her?"

"She did not say."

He heaved a sigh and sat back, still holding her hand. "I was furious. Not just because Rebecca was carrying another man's child, but because of what would happen if my father found out. He had scattered bastards near and far—as was his right as laird—but he would never allow a cuckoo in his own nest."

"But… what could he have done about it?" Aurelia asked.

He gave her a grim look. "You never met my father."

"Are you saying he might have harmed your wife?"

"Or the child."

Aurelia stared, too shocked to speak.

"Thankfully I never had to find out just how far he would go because he fell ill not long after we married and he did not live to see Celsa's birth."

"You were not angry with your wife about Celsa?" she couldn't help asking.

Roland shrugged. "I honestly did not care whose child inherited. If my father had lived, he would have tried to force me to breed Rebecca like a broodmare until there was a son. Not because it mattered to the succession—a woman can inherit if there is no male—but because he wanted a grandson he could mold into his likeness. As he had done with me."

"He sounds… awful."

Roland smiled grimly. "You have no idea." He shook himself and continued. "I was prepared to ignore the child—I already had Guustin and he was enough for me—but something happened when I saw Celsa"—he suddenly laughed—"she was an ugly, ill-tempered baby who squalled incessantly. She was much too small and the midwife cautioned me against naming her as she did not believe she would survive." Roland shoved a hand through his hair, a welter of emotions flickering across his face. "Celsa fought so *hard* to live it was… awe-inspiring," he said. He glanced at Aurelia. "I might be a selfish arse, but I knew it wasn't her fault she'd been born in the middle of a mess. As far as I was concerned, Celsa was my heir, and if I never had a son, then she would be mistress of Crewe.

"I wasn't the only one who was changed by Celsa's birth. Perhaps it was simply a result of motherhood, or maybe Rebecca's lover—whoever he was—

had gone out of her life. Whatever the reason, she began to accept that we were married and make the best of it.

"We spent those early months after Celsa's birth learning more about each other, something neither of us had bothered to do before. No grand passion sprang up between us and we did not fall in love, but we no longer wanted to hurt each other."

He stopped and met Aurelia's gaze. "In short, we both decided to make the most of our marriage. Rebecca was delighted when she discovered after a few months that she was pregnant—or at least she made a damned convincing show of it—and so was I. For the first time, there was genuine affection and optimism." His expression turned wintery. "And then she disappeared."

"How did it happen?" she asked, even though she'd heard various versions from other people.

"I'm afraid there isn't much to tell. Her maid confirmed that all her clothing was in her dressing room and none of her valises were gone. It was fortunate that Arthur, who had worked all night as he often did and was about to go to bed around dawn, saw Rebecca leave the house. He said she was not carrying any bags or anything out of the ordinary. She took out one of the boats and never came back. The boat eventually washed up on the island about three weeks later. There was nothing in it and no sign of what might have happened." He shrugged. "And that was all."

"You think something happened to her while she was rowing the boat somewhere?"

"It depends on who you ask. Some people think she drowned, others believe that her lover came for her and then set one of our boats adrift to confuse the issue." He shrugged. "I do not know. I paid inquiry agents for more than two years and there was not so much as a whisper about her."

"Until six weeks ago," Aurelia said.

Roland nodded. "Until six weeks ago."

They sat in silence, consumed by their thoughts.

Aurelia was the first to speak. "You said she was happy after Celsa's birth?"

"Yes. She spent a good part of most days with her. She even refused the services of a wet-nurse which, as you know, is almost unheard of among women of our class."

It was very unusual. Aurelia's own mother had, like many others, sent her infants to live at the house of a wet-nurse until they were weaned.

Roland sighed. "After seven years, she was declared dead. Not long afterward I remarried." He resumed his pacing. "Which brings me to Jane, another story that does not put me in the best light. Jane was the daughter of my mentor at university. James Dickenson was England's premier naturalist. Unlike most men, it did not bother him that he'd never had a son to carry on his work. He thought the world of Jane, and it was certainly true that she was brilliant."

Aurelia felt an unpleasant twinge in her belly and was disgusted that she could feel jealous of a dead woman.

"Dickenson was certain that Jane would make earth-shaking discoveries in the world of botany and he could not countenance anything or anyone interfering with her destiny." He met her gaze and smiled wryly. "He also knew of his daughter's, er, adventurous spirit when it came to sexual matters and worried she would become pregnant outside wedlock."

He smiled vaguely and Aurelia could see that he had once again gone somewhere else—or some*time* else—in his mind.

"I had never thought to meet myself in female form, but that was Jane," Roland finally said.

"What do you mean?"

"She liked men and she liked sex. And she had as little interest in marriage and monogamy as I did." He slid her a quick look. "At least that was how I felt back then."

"You knew about her propensity for taking lovers when you married her?" Aurelia asked, hardly believing him.

"Yes, of course. She was nothing if not direct. The only reason she agreed to her father's suggestion that she marry was because she knew how vulnerable an unmarried woman could be. With the protection of my name, she could pursue both her studies—and her desires—unfettered."

Aurelia stared at him, utterly befuddled. "I do not understand."

"You mean, why I married her?"

"Was it pure altruism that made you agree?"

He threw back his head and laughed. "No, indeed. It was not altruism, but"—he cleared his throat and Aurelia swore that he was blushing, although it was difficult to see beneath his darkly tanned skin. "Dickenson had some astounding journals from when he'd been younger. He'd had the good fortune to accompany an expeditionary force into the interior of Africa. The things he brought back"—he broke off and shook his head in wonder. "Suffice it to say they were unlike anything I had ever seen before. Not just the journals, but crates and crates of specimens and—"

Aurelia gave a snort of disbelief. "You married her to get your hands on her father's journals and specimens." It was not a question.

Roland was definitely blushing. "Er, yes. You sound… disgusted."

"I don't know what I feel—not that it matters as it is none of my affair."

He turned on his heel and lowered himself beside her. "From this day forth I want all my affairs to be only yours, darling." He took her hand and raised it to his mouth, nibbling on her knuckles while giving her an adorably pleading look.

Aurelia snorted and shook her head, unable to keep a smile from tugging at her lips. "Go on with your story."

He grinned, lowered her hand, and relaxed beside her, his long legs sprawling while his arm slid around her. "You are correct in guessing that Dickenson's research was a big part of why I married Jane. It was a windfall of incredible proportions. But then there was Jane herself."

"You loved her?"

"Did I love Jane?" He laughed. "Lord no! But we were good friends and—" he broke off and cut her a sideways look and sighed. "And yes, we were occasionally lovers."

Of course, you were, Aurelia thought. Aloud she said, "Do continue."

"There was also the fact that I was fond of her father. I knew she could not do as she wished without a husband—or at least not without a great deal of danger and inconvenience. So, while it was true the marriage was self-serving, the truth was that Jane needed me as much as I wanted those journals." He smiled at her. "So, there you have it."

Aurelia struggled to digest the whole of what he'd told her.

He cocked his head. "You are looking at me as if I am a new species of vermin."

"No, not vermin. But I must admit I am at a loss."

"Why? Because I married for pragmatic reasons rather than love? You know that is done among our sort all the time."

"I do know that. And I had daily proof of what a disaster a loveless marriage can be, Roland. My family's poverty was only one unpleasant aspect of life. There was also my mother and father's constant bickering and sniping. It was… hellish."

"I understand that. But why are we talking about a marriage of convenience that went awry? Ours would not be that. I love you, Aurelia. Do you feel nothing for me?"

His words rocked her—a dream come true. And yet still she hesitated to return them.

Once you admit how you feel he will never relent. Not until you agree to marry him, Caution whispered.

Aurelia knew that was true.

But she also knew that she wanted him. And she was no coward. Love was right in front of her, just waiting for her to reach out and take it. All she needed to do was trust him.

She stared at Roland. "Yes, I love you."

His smile was gorgeous as he swooped in and kissed her soundly, leaving her breathless when he finally pulled back. "I knew it. We are in love, but we also love—I think there is a distinction."

So did Aurelia, but she was not so sure about him.

"You are regarding me with that adorably suspicious schoolmistress look again."

"I am wondering how long this love will last for you, Roland."

He frowned, the joy in his eye dimming. "Is such an emotion supposed to end? You will have to tell me because the feeling is utterly new to me."

It pained her to rip the remaining smile from his face, but…

"Since moving here I have heard many stories about you."

"I'll wager you have." He scowled. "And I'm sure Talbot is chief among your sources—but remember that he disparages me because he wants you for himself."

Aurelia gave him an exasperated look. "You do Sir Gideon a great disservice. He has never once passed along scurrilous gossip about you."

He grunted.

"But you cannot deny that you have had many lovers?"

"No, of course I would not deny that. But what of it?" He brightened. "Is there not some saying that reformed rakes make the best husbands?"

Aurelia fought her smile and lost. "There is that aphorism."

"Well, there you have it." Before she could respond, he said, "Talbot asked you to marry him, didn't he?"

"Why do you say that?"

"Do not toy with me, Aurelia." His sharp, commanding tone sent a shiver through her.

"Yes," she admitted. "He did ask me to marry him."

"You are a fool not to accept."

Aurelia gave a startled laugh. "What?"

His face was taut, the black scars standing out more than ever. "Talbot is kind, wealthy enough, and he does not possess my reputation when it comes to women or marriage. And I daresay, as men go, he is handsome enough."

"He is extremely handsome."

Roland scowled. "So, it was madness of you to reject such a paragon of masculine virtue, but I daresay he will ask you again. When he does, you should accept him."

Aurelia traced a circle around one of his tiny nipples, entranced by the way the muscles tensed at her gentle touch. "Is that what I should do?" she asked, wrenching her gaze away from the perfection of his body to steal a look at his angry face. "He told me that he would wait, and if I changed my mind I should—"

The room whirled around her and Aurelia suddenly found herself on her back with Roland leaning over her, caging her between his arms and knees. On impulse, she reached up and carefully pulled off the black patch. She looked up at two blue eyes, one burning as hot as a flame, the other as distant as the moon.

"It *is* too damned late to marry that lurking bounder. It has always been too late," he snarled, his eyelids lowered. "I wouldn't have given you up even if you *had* accepted his offer. So, unless you would have me challenge him to a duel and—"

She laid a finger across his lips, and something new flickered across his face, something… vulnerable.

Aurelia decided that she did not like seeing that expression on her arrogant lord's battered yet infinitely attractive visage. "I want you, and only you, Roland."

"It isn't just my face that is scarred, Aurelia. I have done things which do not make me proud. I have taken the wrong fork in the road more than once. I have been selfish and thoughtless and chased my pleasure and my own interests above all else. Talbot has never married and has never even taken a mistress in the area as far as I can tell." He snorted. "He might very well be a virgin and would certainly bring you his heart whole and unscathed."

"Perhaps I like things that are a bit scarred and scathed? As for the virginal part, well… it seems like one virgin in a marriage is plenty. *Somebody* should know what to do."

He gave a delighted laugh. "So, I have my uses, despite my tarnished past."

"You do. But I hope you are satisfied to demonstrate your er, *uses*, only on my person henceforth?"

"That has already been the case for a while now, Aurelia."

She lifted her eyebrows. "What about Mrs. Neel?"

"It is true she was my lover, but I have not gone to her since"—he squinted and stared up at the ceiling, as if there might be a calendar.

"I do not care when you last saw her," she lied, but only partly. "As long as it is over."

"Long over."

"What about Sadie Roy?"

He laughed. "My, that is going back a few years—decades, even. And no, before you ask, her daughter is not mine. I gave Sadie my permission to say that Dora was mine because it is better to bear the Laird of the Isle's bastard than to admit that her lover left her with a bun in the oven and no marriage lines."

"Easier for her, perhaps."

He kissed her lightly and regarded her with amused affection. "You are angry that my character has been besmirched."

"I am."

"I like that; nobody has ever defended my honor before."

"I am entirely in earnest, Roland. It is not fair that she trades on such untruths."

"Oh, it's very fair, I assure you."

The jealousy that had kindled in her belly roared to life. "What are you saying?"

"Do not be jealous of her, Aurelia, or of any woman. I have given my body often, but never before have I given my heart."

Well.

He dropped to one knee beside the settee. "I love you, Aurelia Bellamy. Say you will make me the happiest man in Britain."

A smile began to steal over her face, no matter how hard she tried to restrain it.

His answering grin was slow, sensual, and wicked and he raised both his eyebrows, the silky golden one and the tufted bits, too.

"Yes, Roland. I will marry you."

He kissed her soundly and Aurelia kissed him right back. When he pulled away, he began to lift her chemise up over her thighs.

"Roland, what are you doing?"

"I thought we might celebrate."

"Right now? In the middle of a conversation?"

"It seems a perfect time," he said, ignoring her hands, which were trying to shove the fabric back down and losing the battle. "Why are you suddenly shy?" he asked, cutting a quick glance at her before casually parting her lower lips and lowering his gaze. "I have licked and kissed this beautiful cunt before."

"*Roland!*"

He looked up, saw her scandalized expression, and laughed. "Oh, was that vulgar? But *vulva* is such a clinical term. Although I must say I rather like *clitoris*, which makes me think of a flower—or a bud, perhaps."

Aurelia gave an embarrassed laugh.

"What is it, sweetheart? You are superb at depicting anatomy. Surely you have examined your own body?"

"Well… yes, but I don't go around talking about it."

He grinned. "I am a naturalist, darling. You will soon learn that I adore talking about such fascinating subjects as sexual organs and the finer points of reproduction." He looked down and stroked his fingers through her slick, swollen folds. "*Mmm*, nice and wet." He lightly caressed her opening and Aurelia winced.

"You are sore," he said, his hand stilling. "I would love to celebrate by taking you again—making you climax until you scream my name—but…" he sighed and removed his hand. "Not today." He gave her an ingratiating smile. "You see how considerate your husband-to-be is?"

"Yes, I see that," she said dryly.

He nodded at the window and she saw the rain had lessened. "I suppose we should take advantage of this lull to go back to Crewe."

Aurelia was disappointed when he drew her chemise back down. She was terribly sore but would have gladly endured some discomfort to have him inside her again.

He suddenly caught her up in his arms and kissed her breathless. When he pulled away, he wore a smug, satisfied smile. "I cannot wait to shout it to the world that you are mine. I shall take special pleasure in telling Talbot the news personally."

Aurelia laughed. She knew she should take the opportunity to assure him that he had nothing in the world to worry about from any other man—as he had done with her—but she suspected she would be robbing him of some primitive pleasure if she did.

And perhaps she also enjoyed his possessive masculine display.

Just a little.

Chapter 26

Aurelia hadn't known what to expect from Celsa when Roland made the announcement at dinner that night.

Instead of anger or elation—either one of which would have been in keeping with her mercurial temper—Celsa merely shrugged and said in a bored tone, "I am not surprised. Anyone could see it."

Roland gave his daughter an exasperated look. "Yes, well, thank you for your heartfelt congratulations, Celsa."

"What a… surprise this is," Arthur said, a hint of sadness in his gentle smile.

Aurelia knew Arthur believed she was making a dreadful mistake marrying Roland when she could have been with a man like Sir Gideon. He would see, in time, that she had made the right choice.

"There is something else," Roland said, nodding to Aurelia.

Aurelia looked from Celsa to Arthur. "My name is not *Burton*, it is *Bellamy*. My father is the Earl of Addiscombe."

Genuine shock shone on both faces.

"But… why did you lie?" Celsa asked.

"Because the countess was not best pleased with my decision to come here."

"No, I can imagine she was not," Arthur said, looking every bit as disapproving as Aurelia's mother had.

She cleared her throat. "I also lied when I said that my father was dead."

Arthur's disapproving expression became scandalized and horrified. "Aurelia," he murmured in a chiding voice, shaking his head.

Roland reached across the table and took her hand, fixing Arthur with a flinty look. "Regardless of what name Aurelia used, she will soon be my countess."

There was a moment of uncomfortable silence and then Arthur nodded. "Of course. Congratulations, I am happy for you both." And if the words sounded a bit forced, Aurelia decided she had earned it with her lie.

"When will the wedding be?" Arthur asked.

Roland's expression softened when he turned to Aurelia. "I would like it to be as soon as possible, but Aurelia and I are going to discuss the matter this evening."

"Surely you would want to wait until you could have your family here?" Arthur asked.

"We will let you know once we've made our decision," Roland said firmly, giving her hand a squeeze.

***

Roland brought Aurelia a small portion of brandy. "Here. Drink this darling, you are chilled," he said, lightly rubbing the goose pimples on her bare arms with his hands.

Aurelia chuckled and gestured to the roaring blaze in the enormous fireplace. "I don't think you can build the fire any larger without endangering the books."

"I would burn it all down to the ground for you, Aurelia."

Aurelia gawked up at him. If anything, she got even more goose pimples at his words—and the ardent look in his eye. She hastily took a gulp of brandy and then coughed as it burned its way down her throat.

Roland chuckled and sat down beside her on the settee. "Don't look so serious, love. I won't be burning anything." He kissed the soft, fragrant skin of her temple. "Besides, fire is not the only way to warm you up." He pulled her onto his lap and spent the next few minutes doing exactly that, not drawing back until they were both breathless. He tucked a stray lock of hair behind her ear. "How long will you make me wait until you marry me?" he asked in a voice roughened with need.

"We shall have to wait at least three weeks," she reminded him.

"You have forgotten where you are, my dear—there is no waiting period in Scotland."

"Oh. That's right."

"I daresay you wish to have your family here?"

Aurelia chewed her lip. "I don't know," she finally said.

He looked surprised.

"I feel terrible saying that. I have always been so close to my sisters. And yet…"

"Yet?"

"And yet I think back to the letters I have received over the past months. First my sister Phoebe married, then Hyacinth—which *none* of us ever expected—and right before you returned to Crewe I received word that my sister Selina was to marry. They have all gone on with their lives. Why should I wait to get on with mine?" She felt a sharp pang of guilt at her words. "Is that terribly selfish?"

He caught her up in a tight embrace, covering her face with kisses. "If it is, then I am selfish too, darling. I want you in my bed and in my arms every night. And I want that to happen as soon as possible."

Aurelia gave herself up to his passion, allowing his kisses and caresses to carry her along. Allowing herself to imagine a life where she could have his love and affection every day and night.

"You have the dreamiest look on your face," he said when he released her just enough to allow her to breathe.

"I am happy."

"Does that mean that you will be satisfied by a small ceremony? Quickly?"

"Yes. But I would like to invite a few people."

"Invite whomever you like, sweetheart," he said in between kisses.

"And I also think we should wait for Guustin to return."

"On that, we agree. I will send word of our news tomorrow morning, first thing."

"The ceremony will have to be on a Tuesday because I want to invite Miss Clifford. If I can persuade her to ask for an extra day off work from her employer, might she come and stay the night before the wedding?"

"She may come and stay as long as she likes, sweetheart."

"Thank you. It will be nice for her to have a few days in comfort. She has been living in that cottage with scarcely a stick of furniture and nobody for company."

"I feel a great deal of sympathy for that poor woman and her sisters," Roland admitted.

"Me too. I will miss her dreadfully when she leaves."

"I daresay you will, but London will be a far better place for her and her sisters to go unnoticed. So," he said, "who else did you want to invite, sweetheart?" He slid a big hand around her nape and massaged the taut muscles.

Aurelia all but purred, her eyes drifting shut. "That is nice."

"Darling, if you make that noise again our wedding planning will come to an abrupt halt," he warned her in a gravelly voice. "Now, who else?"

Aurelia chewed the inside of her cheek. "Would it be too strange to invite Nora?"

Roland's hand stilled. "Nora?" he repeated, as if couldn't believe he'd heard her correctly.

"She has been a great source of company while you've been galivanting all over Britain. And Celsa adores her as well. And Guustin will be attending, so it would be cruel to exclude her. If our ceremony is very small, then surely we could ask her to come without causing too much talk?"

"We can cause all the talk we want, my love. And of course, you may invite Nora. I was just surprised."

"Why? Because I am not jealous of your past with her? As it happens," she went on without waiting for a reply, "I am horridly jealous of all your lovers." Aurelia gave him a slight shove. "You are smiling!"

"It is nice not to be the only one who feels such insecurity."

"What reason have you to be insecure?" she demanded.

"Talbot."

Aurelia huffed out a breath and shook her head. "I have never felt anything for him more than friendship."

He caressed her throat, his gaze brooding. "Not even when he rescued you from those ruffians? I know the special status a hero can have—especially when they look like a damned prince out of some fairy tale story."

"If I regarded him in any such light—and I'm not admitting that I did—it immediately dissipated the moment I saw you sitting behind your desk, looking like some feudal warrior lord."

His lips quirked up. "Oh? Tell me more."

She laughed. "You are shameless! I refuse to contribute to your already healthy sense of *amour propre*."

He grinned and kissed her hard, and for a few moments there was no talk at all. When he'd sufficiently scattered her wits, he set his forehead against hers. "I have never in my life felt jealousy like this," he confessed. "I wanted to leap across the table and thrash Arthur when he mentioned the man visiting you." He sighed. "But I trust you and I do not want our marriage to start out with depriving you of any of your friends. So you can even ask Talbot to be one of our wedding guests. You see how generous I am in victory?"

Aurelia laughed.

"I *do* love the sound of your laughter. And I look forward to hearing it often in the years to come. Oh, there was just one other thing I wanted to discuss."

"Hmm?" she murmured, tracing the fascinating curve of his full lower lip with one finger.

"Now that we are to be married, I don't suppose you would consider a renegotiation of your wages?" He lifted an eyebrow. "Perhaps a lower rate for family?"

Yes, Aurelia thought as she laughed again and pulled him down to kiss him. With a man like Roland there would be a good deal of laughter in their marriage.

Chapter 27

Aurelia woke up far later than usual the following morning and could only assume it was the excitement and strain of the prior day that had caused her to sleep so soundly.

She was reinvigorated by her long rest and her mind too busy with everything that needed to be done to lounge about.

On her list of things to do was to talk to Sir Gideon. Aurelia wanted to tell him about her betrothal in person as it just felt wrong to let him hear the news from a servant.

Aurelia decided that she would ask Roland to row her over to the mainland. She suspected he would be less jealous if she involved him in the errand.

She was just about to go down to the breakfast room when there was a knock on the door.

"Come in."

Ruby opened the door and dropped a curtsey. "Good morning, er, my lady."

Aurelia smiled at how quickly Roland had spread the news. "Yes, Ruby?"

"The master was called out two hours ago to see to some problem at the mine. He was not sure when he would return but said he would send word."

"Thank you, Ruby," Aurelia said.

The maid inclined her head and shut the door behind her.

Aurelia did not want to go to the mainland without Roland, so she composed a brief note to Sir Gideon asking if he could come over to Crewe today. Hopefully she could see him before he heard the news through the mysterious servant network.

Once she had sealed her message, she went to the breakfast room and pulled the servant cord before she poured herself some coffee.

When Beekman opened the door, she handed him the message. "Could you have this delivered as soon as possible?"

"Of course, my lady." If the butler was surprised at her sudden elevation in status, he certainly gave no sign of it.

For once, the breakfast room was empty and she was able to eat in contemplative silence. No doubt Celsa and Arthur had broken their fast at the usual time rather than lolling about in bed until eleven like Aurelia.

As she ate, she mentally composed the letters she would write to her sisters. She knew Roland felt guilty that her family was not coming, but Aurelia was relieved. She did not want a great deal of fanfare and fuss and she most certainly did not want to delay the date. Indeed, waiting the week or ten days they had agreed upon last night already seemed a terribly long time.

Aurelia smirked. Who would ever believe that serious, reserved Aurelia would be eager to marry so that she could have her husband in her arms every night?

The door to the breakfast room opened and Charles entered. "This just came for you, Miss—er, that is, Lady Aurelia."

"Thank you, Charles."

"Of course, my lady." He hesitated and then gave her a boyish smile. "I would like to offer my congratulations, if I might be so bold?"

"That is kind of you. Thank you, very much, Charles."

Still grinning, Charles bowed and left her to read her message.

Dear Aurelia,

I managed to get away today and wanted to show you something rather fascinating I learned about when I was talking to an ancient tenant farmer of mine. Can you meet me at Rock Cove? It is a very low tide just past noon—almost as low as yesterday—and I will be able to show you what I've found.

I do hope you can get away. If so, be there by noon.

Sincerely,

Gideon

She lifted her eyebrows at the mysterious message but was glad that he was on the island and she could tell him about her betrothal.

Once she had donned her heavy cloak and warmest bonnet, she recalled the note she'd given to Beekman to deliver to Sir Gideon. Rather than ring for the butler, she decided to check the salver in the entry hall on her way out of the house. A quick glance showed that it was empty, so obviously her message had already gone over.

She didn't take a horse to Rock Cove as it was one of the closer beaches. Also, a horse was more of a hindrance on the narrow trail, and she would much rather trust her own feet on the steep path.

Aurelia's thoughts naturally turned to the wedding as she walked. It would take place in the castle chapel and Roland said the Reverend Sheldon, the rather ancient vicar at the tiny church on the island, would conduct the service.

She was considering asking Roland if somebody might bring pine boughs from the mainland so she could decorate the church with a bit of greenery, which seemed more appropriate than flowers, given the time of year.

Aurelia pulled her thoughts from wedding plans and concentrated all her attention on the narrow, rather treacherous path when she reached the cliff above Rock Cove. It wasn't her favorite beach on the island and she much preferred the ones to the east which were more accessible, if far less private.

When she reached the bottom, she saw a skiff pulled up onto the shingle and looked around the small cove but saw no sign of Sir Gideon.

"Aurelia!"

She spun around at the sound of the voice and blinked in surprise. "Arthur!"

He waved her over. "Gideon has just shown me the most wonderful thing," he said when she picked her way across the rocks, which were covered in seaweed as this portion of the beach was usually beneath water.

"What is it?" she asked, a bit nonplussed that Gideon had invited Arthur as well. Perhaps she would not tell him her news today, after all.

"It is better if you see it yourself," he said. "It is just this way." He was wearing fisherman boots and quickly made his way to where the rock cliff curved.

"Wait!" she called. "I cannot go as fast as"—she yelped when her foot slipped and slid into a rockpool all the way up to her ankle. "Blast!" she hissed as she shook water off her foot, already feeling the cold seeping through the seams of her boot.

When she looked up, Arthur was gone. "Arthur? Arthur!"

His voice came from around the corner. "Over here!"

Aurelia heaved an irritated sigh and considered just turning back. But one foot was already soaked and the other halfway there, so she continued picking her way across the slippery stones.

When she rounded the corner, she paused and gaped at the huge slice of cliff that must have sheared off at some point. It had landed on one end and was resting against the cliff itself, almost like a door that had been left ajar. Prodigious vegetation covered much of the fracture, suggesting the piece had broken off some years ago.

Arthur's head popped out from between the rock face and broken slab, startling her. "It is in here, Aurelia. You need to hurry as we've barely an hour to enjoy it before the tide comes back in. Come, I've got a lantern."

"Where is Sir Gideon?" she asked, hurrying as much as she could.

"He is clearing out a path so you can get a closer look." He held out his hand and helped her over several larger rocks and then stepped aside. "You go first and I'll hold up the light to guide your way."

Aurelia took a few steps and then stared. "Why, there is a cave!"

"More than a cave—a whole system of tunnels. Go on in."

She peered into the darkness.

"Here," he said, lifting the lantern higher. "Is that better?"

"Oh my, it is huge," she said.

"You go ahead, I'm right behind you."

"The floor is rather slippery," she murmured.

"It is usually covered with water. Only at the lowest tides is this accessible.

Aurelia looked up and saw something sparkle in the gloom overhead. "I see something up there."

"Stalactites," Arthur said, his voice echoing eerily in the enormous chamber. "Go to your left and you will find the rock isn't as slick.

Aurelia did as he bade her, grimacing as her boots sank into the sort of seaweed that did not often grow in intertidal areas. "This must be underwater most of the time."

"Yes. It is a rare opportunity we have. Not much farther now," he said in a wheezy voice.

Aurelia paused and turned. "Are you sure you should be doing something so strenuous?" she asked, appalled that she'd not noticed the gray, greasy look of his skin.

He smiled, the light making his eyes glitter a preternatural blue. "I will rest as soon as you see our discovery," he promised. "Just around the next curve and you will see it."

Aurelia resumed walking, her thoughts on the obviously ill man behind her. She had meant to broach the matter with Roland but had forgotten given all the excitement of the past few days.

Her foot slipped and she put her hand on the wall to steady herself and then grimaced when she felt cold, slick seaweed.

"Careful, my dear," Arthur chided.

"The tide comes up higher than I thought."

"Indeed, it does, that is why we should hurry." Arthur lifted the light. "It is not far now, Aurelia. You need to look up high—over your head."

She rounded the corner and gasped. "It is magnificent!" Aurelia stopped in her tracks and gazed up at the figures carved into the rock walls.

"It is from the time of the Vikings," Arthur said, his voice so close she felt his hot breath on the back of her head. "They are above the waterline… for now, but I daresay they will one day be eroded by the sea. They must have been protected inside the cave for centuries before the cliffside broke off, exposing them. There are probably more, but the tunnel collapsed just ahead, so it is likely we will never see them. A pity, really."

Aurelia suddenly recalled Sir Gideon and glanced around. "Where is—" she shrieked when she saw the skeleton on the floor below the cave drawings.

"*Shhh.*" A cold clammy hand slid over her mouth and an arm like iron closed around her middle.

Aurelia's mind rebelled against what was happening. There was a skeleton chained to a rock and Arthur had grabbed her. Her brain had no answers for either of those things, but her body experienced an explosion of energy and she fought against him like a wild creature.

Arthur grunted and cursed as she squirmed. She kicked back at his legs several times, as hard as she was able, and finally made contact with something that made a sickening *crunch.*

Arthur screamed and shoved her to the ground, his body falling on top of hers.

Her head struck something hard and pain exploded, along with a thousand white stars.

And then darkness.

***

Aurelia woke to a pounding head and something warm pooling in the corner of her eyes. She tried to wipe it away but discovered that her hands would not move. She tugged harder and heard a metallic clinking. Chains.

Memories of Arthur and the skeleton flooded back to her. She lifted her head and the room spun so violently that she turned to the side and retched up her breakfast.

The next time she raised her head, she did so slowly, her temples throbbing so painfully that her vision blurred.

Arthur was sitting beside the skeleton and mumbling something to it. Or at least that is what it looked like.

"What happened?" she asked, each word like a spike through her brain.

Arthur turned from the skeleton and gave her one of his sad smiles. She couldn't help noticing that his nose was swollen and there were scratches down his cheek. "What had to happen, Aurelia."

"I don't understand." She struggled to sit up, wincing at the nausea. "Arthur, what is the meaning of this?"

"I told you to accept Sir Gideon's offer. I tried to save you, but you are willful and would not listen. You are so stubborn! It would only be Crewe for you. And I cannot have that."

"What are you talking about?" Her voice rose, even though it sent waves of pain through her skull. "And who is that?" She stared at the skeleton, revulsion joining the nausea in her belly when she saw he was holding a bony hand.

"This is Rebecca," he said, his smile loving as he stroked the skeletal hand.

"*What?*"

"Rebecca has been here alone for a long, long time," Arthur went on dreamily. "I visit her when I can, but given the tides and my other responsibilities, that is not often."

"Oh Arthur, what have you done?" Aurelia whispered, horror joining the other emotions roiling inside her.

"I had to bring her here, just like I had to bring *you* here, Aurelia." He blinked rapidly, a tear sliding down the bloody scratches on his cheek. "She was the love of my life." His face twisted into an angry mask. "Crewe never loved her! I told Rebecca that. I told her…"

"What did you tell her?"

Arthur shook himself. "I told her that Crewe would not love her the way I loved her and our child."

"Your *child?*"

He blinked at her.

"*You* are Celsa's father?"

Arthur nodded, a proud, almost sly, expression taking possession of his face.

Aurelia stared, suddenly struck. "*You* were the one who told Celsa that Roland wasn't her father."

"Because Celsa is *mine*," he hissed, his eyes glittering madly. "Not Crewe's. I cannot tell her that she is my daughter… yet. But she will know one day."

"You have poisoned Celsa's mind against Roland, haven't you? You have encouraged her to torment her governesses and misbehave so that the two of them are always at odds with each other."

Arthur did not deny the accusations. "Why should Celsa care about Crewe? *I* am her father."

"I still don't understand, Arthur. Why have you brought me here?" A revolting thought occurred to her. "Are—are—you do not think that you are in love with me?"

Arthur's eyes widened. And then he laughed, his lungs rattling as his laughter turned into a horrible hacking cough. When he could finally catch his breath, he wiped blood from the corner of his mouth and looked up at her, his eyes burning. "I tried to save you from your own lustful wickedness. I even gave you more time to see the error of your ways when I sent Crewe away and encouraged Sir Gideon to court you. But a mere baronet wasn't good enough for you. You want Crewe—just like so many other women over the years."

"You aren't making any sense, Arthur. You are ill, you need—"

"Rebecca loved me and we were going to marry!" he shouted, his voice echoing in the dank cavern. "We had planned it for years, but—but because of my birth I had nothing to offer her and her father would have cut her off without so much as a penny if she had disobeyed him." He stared, his gaze feverish and distant. "I know that I could have persuaded Rebecca's father to allow us to marry, but the earl had to ruin things for us."

"Roland?"

"Not him. The old earl." He scowled, his handsome face twisting with hatred. "He could make bastards by the score and yet he despised me." The slyness returned. "But I showed him. I put *my* daughter into his beloved son's nest. *Cuckoo! Cuckoo!*" he suddenly shrieked, and then laughed, but it quickly turned to wet coughing with blood. Lots of blood.

"Arthur, you need a doctor. Just release me from these manacles and we can leave together." Aurelia glanced at the path. She could not see water yet but judging by the water lines on the walls—and the seaweed on Rebecca's skeleton—that would change soon.

"No, Aurelia," he said once he had caught his breath. "You are not going anywhere. And neither am I." He gestured to his leg, which she only now noticed was lying at an odd angle. "You saw to that. So, we will keep each other company."

"Give me the key, Arthur and I will help you walk out of here. I promise."

He pointed to the collapsed cave entry. "I threw the key there; it is under tons of rock."

Fear stabbed at her. "No," she whispered.

He nodded. "Yes."

"You are sick, Arthur—none of this is your fault. Please… you *must* help me."

"I am sick," he agreed with a smile that made her want to retch again. "But there is no help. For either of us."

"Why are you doing this?" Her voice broke on a sob of frustration.

"Crewe cannot be allowed to marry—not again. I was fortunate the last time because Jane was an unnatural woman who took pains to prevent conception. Well," he amended, "she avoided pregnancy at first, but she changed."

"What are you talking about?"

"Jane. I had to get Jane out of the way."

"*You* killed her? But… how?"

"I did not want to do it, but if anyone deserved to die—it was that *whore*." Revulsion flickered over his face.

Aurelia recoiled at the venom in his voice. She could not believe this was the same man who had worried that she might catch a chill and had sent up a poultice.

"I went to America not realizing how I would do it," Roland went on. "But I knew that it had to be done. Jane could not be allowed to continue bringing shame to the family name." His face spasmed with disgust. "She would rut with anyone—two men at once, one night in her tent—and Crewe did not care! Of course he is no better," he muttered angrily, meeting her gaze. "I am saving you from a great deal of pain, Aurelia. Because Crewe cannot be faithful. He needs women like most men need air. He is like his father in that way, a carnal creature whose lusts can never be slaked."

His jaw worked and his eyes burned like a zealot's. "I love Crewe, and he is like a brother to me, but I can see his faults clearly." His face twitched. "Jane brought out the worst in him. She was a selfish, unnatural woman who was so mannish in her behavior that I never thought she would allow herself to fall pregnant. But then I saw her one day when we were on the expedition—bathing in a stream, naked and as bold as you please—with her belly already swelling. I doubt it was even Crewe's child."

"You murdered a pregnant woman." Aurelia's gaze slid to the skeleton and she recalled Roland's words on Nesta's Perch. "And you murdered Rebecca for the same reason. You have killed two of Roland's wives and two of his children."

Arthur did not seem to hear her. "It was so easy. Just a bit of blood sprinkled around her tent. We had seen panther scat and knew they were always prowling about the camp. I made sure Crewe's gun was not loaded—just in case—nor Jane's or her lovers." His mouth suddenly turned down at the corners. "I never meant to hurt Crewe, but he *had* to try and save her!" His angelic features shifted into a mask of hatred. No, not a mask, but Arthur's true face. A murderer's face.

Aurelia suddenly remembered what Arthur had said earlier—about luring Roland away. "It was you who sent the letter to Roland about Rebecca being alive."

His gaze sharpened slowly as he came back to himself. The look of revulsion he'd worn earlier talking about Jane was now aimed at her.

"Yes. It was me." He regarded her with disgust. "I thought you were a well-bred virtuous woman, Aurelia. But then I saw you with Crewe in the library that night and I knew then that you were no better than any of his other whores."

She recoiled. "You spied on us."

His eyes pulsed with loathing. "Yes. I saw you naked with your legs sprawled, reveling in his crude treatment. That is when I knew Crewe needed to leave the island because I needed time to plan." Suddenly, his face fell. "When you accepted Sir Gideon's request to call on you, I thought you could be saved."

Aurelia watched in shock as a tear slid down his cheek. He was mad. Utterly, completely mad, his emotions changing radically in the blink of an eye.

He had killed a woman he supposedly loved, killed another he loathed, and now he would kill her.

"Crewe has always been good to me," Arthur said in a rambling way. "He treated me like a brother. Not like his father, who thought I was lower than dirt." He swallowed. "But Crewe wanted the money—that was all he cared about. He should have argued with the earl about marrying Rebecca. He should have defied his father for once. He should never have married Rebecca. She loved me!"

Arthur suddenly sobbed. "I promised her that everything would be fine. I said we could at least be together—that I could come to her bed—if she married Crewe and lived in the castle. Crewe hated her and didn't even go to her on their wedding night. Instead, I did." Arthur's lips curved into a smile at that memory. But then, as quick as lightening, his face fell. "Something changed after Celsa was born. Rebecca said she was finished with me—that I had killed our love when I'd refused to run away with her. But how could I run away from Crewe?" Fury suffused his face. "She spurned me and went to Roland's bed!" He glared at the skeleton. "She taunted me about it—telling me the vile things she had allowed him to do to her, boasting that she was pregnant by him. I could not let her have his child. I… could not." He broke down and cried, babbling incoherently at the skeleton.

If he could kill a person he loved, he would be no help to Aurelia.

She looked at the manacles around her wrists and then glanced around her for a rock that was big enough to perhaps break one. But the only ones she could see were far out of reach.

Aurelia examined the manacles more closely. They were fastened together with a lock, and so she took a pin from her hair and poked it around inside the small hole. But no matter how much she jabbed at it, the lock stayed firm.

Aurelia squeezed her eyes shut as despair welled inside her.

Something cold seeped through her ankle boot and she gasped when she saw how fast the water had come in.

Arthur nodded as if she had spoken. "Yes, it shoots up the narrow path like the neck of a funnel. It won't be long now."

She bit her lip against the hysteria rising inside her. *Think! Think! Think!*

Aurelia looked from the manacles to the huge stalagmite the chain was attached to. Perhaps if she tried to—

"Aurelia!"

For a moment, she thought she'd imagined the voice.

"*Aurelia*!"

"Roland?" she said, the word scarcely a whisper.

"Aurelia! Can you hear me?"

"Roland!" Aurelia screamed. "I am in here!"

"I'm coming, darling," Roland called back, his voice louder.

Aurelia sobbed, almost faint with relief.

"The water is already high at the entrance," Arthur said in an eerily calm voice. "If he comes all the way up here now, he will never get out."

Aurelia's jaw sagged.

"Aurelia?" Roland's voice sounded oddly watery, as if he were—

"Go back, Roland! You won't be able to get out again. *Don't come in, Roland*!"

There was no answer.

"You love him," Arthur said, smiling that angelic smile she had once thought so charming.

"Please, Arthur—we were friends once. Help me!"

"I can't," he said sadly. "Celsa will be the Lady of Crewe. My daughter will be the mistress of everything."

She heard splashing just before Roland came around the corner, wading through water that was already surging as high as his knees.

"Aurelia! Thank God!" His sharp gaze flickered over her, the chains, Arthur, and then the skeleton. "What the hell—"

"It is Rebecca," Aurelia said, relief at seeing his beloved face warring with the agonizing knowledge that Roland might very well die with her. "Arthur killed Rebecca and your second wife, too," she said, the words tumbling over one another in a rush. "He is Celsa's father. He doesn't want us to marry. He is *mad*, Roland!"

Roland pulled his stunned gaze away from the remains of his wife and dropped to his haunches, yanking Aurelia into an embrace that almost made her pass out.

"How did you find me?" she asked when he put her at arm's length and looked her over, as if checking to see if she was hurt.

"I went to your room looking for you and found Talbot's note on your dresser. I was headed to the stables to fetch Frost and come after you, and then Talbot himself came sauntering up to the castle looking for you."

"He—he came?"

"Yes, he received your message." He took her wrists and studied the locks. "Talbot came with me and is outside in a skiff, waiting."

"Would a big rock break the chain?" she asked.

Roland shook his head. "There is no way to break this. Not in time."

He reached into his coat and took out his penknife.

"I already tried to open it with a hat pin, but obviously I did not get anywhere," she said when he started poking around in the keyhole.

He cut her a quick glance and smiled. "My resourceful, clever darling."

"You cannot go," Arthur mumbled, but they both ignored him as Roland jabbed and jabbed and—

"You did it!" Aurelia shrieked as the manacle on her left wrist fell off.

Roland picked up her right hand and began prodding at the lock, but the minutes dragged on.

"This isn't bloody working!" Roland muttered and let go of her wrist, pulling on the chain, which was wrapped around the stalagmite. "We shall have to carry it together. But it is very heavy, darling, so we have to stay close and I'll carry the bulk of it." He hefted the chain in both hands and then turned to her. "Please tell me you are a good swimmer?"

"I can hold my breath for a little over thirty seconds, if that is what you're asking."

He grinned. "That's my girl. Come on." He helped her up and the room spun. Roland caught her in his arms. "What's wrong?"

"My head," she said through clenched teeth.

He carefully lifted her matted hair and hissed. "Damnation!"

"I can swim," she assured him, her voice slurred.

"I'm afraid you must. But you need to get rid of some of this."

This was her heavy woolen dress.

Together, they stripped off her garments—needing to rip and cut them— until she was standing in her stockings, ankle boots, and chemise.

"I know you are cold," he said. "But it is better than being pulled under."

She nodded, shivering.

"Stay ahead of me. I'll give you enough slack so you can use your chained arm, but the chain will still try to pull you down."

Again, she nodded.

Roland turned to Arthur. "You had better come now, although I don't really give a damn if you do."

Arthur smiled. "I will stay with Rebecca."

Roland stared at the other man, and Aurelia could see he was torn—furious and angry and devastated.

"Be good to my daughter, Crewe," Arthur said.

Roland hesitated, as if he might say something more, but then he turned his back on the man he had once called *brother* and led Aurelia toward the water.

Chapter 28

Roland could not think about his cousin sitting back there in the cave, holding Rebecca's long-dead hand. And he could not think about the fact that Celsa was Arthur's daughter.

He could not think about anything but getting Aurelia out of this wretched death cave.

Roland put a hand on her shoulder and stopped her just before the water swallowed her hips. "You won't be able to see anything but the slightest glimmer of light," he warned. "Do you recall the general direction you took on the path?"

"Yes."

"Good. We'll walk until it's too deep for you and then I'll carry you a bit further. And then we'll both fill our lungs and go under together. We don't have long in this water, Aurelia. It is so cold you need to keep moving." He wished to God it was the time of year when the warm currents swept through, but he was already half-frozen.

She nodded, her features taut, but not hysterical. Oh, his prim, self-possessed little Miss Burton! Roland kissed her once, fiercely, and then nodded. "Go."

The water was frigid, shockingly so, and the last few inches before he took them both under were the worst.

His eye burned in the salt water, but he kept it open, staring at the small slit of light surrounded by darkness.

Aurelia swam faster than he had dared to hope and he gave her more slack on the chain and let her have room to kick, trying to stay close, but to the side of her.

They reached the cave opening quickly, but she needed to dive a good three feet lower to swim through it.

Roland's lungs were starting to burn by the time he followed her through the gap. He could see her ahead of him for a few seconds before she disappeared. He was just about to follow her when a swell of water pushed him back up against the rock and the chain went taut in his hand.

God no! I'm holding her back!

He let loose of as much chain as he thought she could carry while he struggled to free himself from the jagged rock that was tearing at his clothing like teeth.

His eye burned so badly that all he could see was a long dull rectangle of lighter gray ahead of him. Another swell hit and slammed him back hard enough that he was momentarily stunned. The links slipped through his fingers faster and he gathered his remaining strength and kicked with all his might to retrieve the heavy chain before it pulled her down.

But the next swell hit him so hard that it spun him heels-over-head and the chain was yanked from his hands.

Roland could not tell up from down when suddenly his left leg jerked and he felt the chain twist tightly around his ankle. He tried to scrape it off with the heel of his other foot, but again there was a tug, this time from above rather than an incoming swell.

His lungs were on fire and his limbs did not seem to be responding to his brain's commands.

Air.

He needed air.

The rectangle of light darkened alarmingly fast.

And then darkness swallowed him.

***

"Stop pulling on it!" Aurelia shrieked at Sir Gideon. "He must be stuck!" A swell lifted the boat and the chain on her wrist went taut, almost taking her over the side.

"He will pull you under, Aurelia!" the baronet shouted over the wind. He grabbed the chain and yanked. "He needs to come up or he will drown."

Aurelia realized she was crying because her tears were the only hot part on her body. "I need to go back in," she said, pushing off Sir Gideon's coat, which he had wrapped around her the moment after he'd lifted her in the boat."

"No!" he shouted. "Crewe would have my head if I allowed you to go back in. Now, help me pull!"

Weeping openly, Aurelia grabbed the chain and they both pulled, almost tumbling out of the skiff when it suddenly went slack.

"He has come loose," Sir Gideon said as he pulled hand over hand. "Take the oars, Aurelia. We're drifting close to the cliff."

She shipped the oars awkwardly, her entire body shaking from the cold, her arms like jelly as she tried to row.

"Here he is," Sir Gideon said, and leaned over. "You must stay where you are or we shall tip over." He groaned as he grabbed onto something heavy and then heaved.

One arm flopped over the side and Sir Gideon heaved again.

Roland slid into the boat like an enormous, landed fish.

Sir Gideon quickly turned Roland onto his side.

Aurelia inched closer but already felt the skiff beginning to unbalance, so she stopped. "Is he—"

Roland convulsed and water spewed from his mouth.

"He is breathing," Sir Gideon replied tersely. "But he had water in his lungs; we must get him inside as quickly as possible. Keep rowing while I wrap him in his coat."

Aurelia pulled for all she was worth, spurred into a near frenzy by the knowledge that Roland's life might depend on her rowing.

Chapter 29

Roland's mouth tasted foul—as if he had eaten old straw—and his head felt as though somebody had stuffed it full of rags. As for his eyes, the one that worked burned like lantern oil had spilled into it and the other felt as if somebody had packed it full of sand.

He tried to open his functioning eye and groaned at the stab of pain.

"Thank God! You are awake," a familiar, much-beloved voice said beside him. A cool, soft hand stroked his forehead and arm.

"Your hands feel so good. Why is it so bloody hot in here?" He forced his eye open a crack, hissing at the stinging. "And where is *here*?"

"We are in the home of Mr. and Mrs. Temple. It seemed advisable to treat you here rather than move you up to the castle. But if you feel better today, Dr. MacMillan says—"

"How long have I been here?"

"Just over a day. Dr. MacMillan said you took in a great deal of water and must be careful of your lungs. And—and your leg is broken, just above your foot."

Roland was about to ask which one but then tried to move them and yelped like a kicked cur. "How unmanly," he muttered.

She chuckled and the sound was a balm that numbed the myriad of aches and pains in his body.

"Are you in pain, Roland? Dr. MacMillan left me laudanum and—"

"No laudanum." So that was why his head felt like a desiccated gourd. He squeezed her hand. "Are you—"

"I am fine. I made it to the boat unscathed. It was you who suffered. Do you recall what happened?"

It all came back to him, the excruciating pain of having his foot torn from the rock. "Got stuck. Couldn't get loose." Each word was like chewing on glass, but he had to know. "Is my leg bad?"

"The doctor was able to set it swiftly enough that it should heal nicely. It will take some time, but you will walk just as well as you always have."

He heaved a sigh of relief and then immediately groaned at the burning pain in his chest. Sleep pulled at him, but he needed to make sure of one last thing.

"Do not tell anyone about Arthur and Rebecca and—"

"*Shhh*," she murmured, kissing his cheek. "Gideon and I have told everyone that Arthur was showing me some rock pools when we were caught by the tide."

He felt an almost crippling sense of relief that was instantly swamped with sorrow.

Christ! Arthur. His dearest brother—or so Roland had believed for more than three decades. It hurt as badly as his leg to think about his cousin and what he had done to Rebecca and Jane.

And what he had almost done to Aurelia.

***

Guustin returned to Crewe three days after Roland and Aurelia escaped the nightmare in the cave.

They sat down with Guustin his first evening home, after dinner, and told him the truth of what had happened that day.

"It is impossible to believe," Guustin kept saying, shaking his head in wonder.

Aurelia knew what he meant. She had been there—had heard Arthur's mad rambling—and had almost died because of him, but she still found it difficult to accept.

"He must have had a sickness in his mind for a long time," Roland said. "I should have guessed there was something wrong."

Aurelia shook her head. "You cannot blame yourself for what happened, Roland. He might have looked ill recently, but he did not look sick fifteen years ago when he killed your first wife, did he?"

Roland frowned but nodded. "You are right."

"Do you think his sickness might have had something to do with the mercury or arsenic he used?" Guustin asked.

"I truly do not know," Roland said. "Perhaps the sickness goes back even earlier. He was a reclusive and shy boy—very insecure—and my father was not kind to him."

"Will you tell Celsa about him?" Guustin asked. "I mean, that he was her father?"

"I don't know," Roland admitted. "Aurelia told me that Arthur was the one who told Celsa she was not mine."

Guustin nodded. "Yes, she flung the information into my face several years ago when I made the mistake of referring to her as my sister. I was shocked that Arthur had told her such a thing. I wondered if I should tell you about it, but I did not like to run and tattle on him, especially when he already disliked me so much."

"I should have simply asked Celsa what was wrong," Roland said. "Her behavior changed so fast—like night and day—I should have guessed there was something amiss."

"There is no use in looking back on what you might have done," Aurelia said, not just to Roland, but to Guustin, too, who was looking guilty. "Why would anyone guess that Arthur was so sick? I never saw it either."

"Oh, there were glimpses—I see that now," Roland said. "He could be so very... puritanical and often became extreme in his criticism of what he considered ungodly behavior."

"Which is somewhat ironic given that he also fathered a child out of wedlock and passed it off as yours," Guustin said wryly.

"I do not think he did it to hurt you, Roland. He seemed to feel your father deserved to have a *cuckoo* in his nest, as he termed it. I believe he saw his revenge as biblical in nature." She shrugged. "But we could go mad ourselves trying to understand the thoughts of such a man."

"You are right, my dear," Roland said, taking her hand. He turned to Guustin and said, "You said something earlier—that Celsa told you she was not your sister?"

Guustin nodded.

"You must realize that she does not think of you as her brother?"

Guustin laughed. "I doubt there is a person on the island—or in Balcrewe—who is unaware of Celsa's infatuation with me. But that is all it is, sir: an infatuation." He sounded far more certain than Aurelia felt. "She will grow out of it."

"One never knows with Celsa," Roland said.

"I think you should tell her," Aurelia said quietly.

"You mean tell her about what Arthur tried to do?" Roland asked, his eyebrows high.

"I do not think that is necessary. It would only hurt her. But she already knows you are not her father, Roland. It is cruel to keep the truth from her at this point."

"I agree," Guustin said.

Roland nodded slowly. "I will think about it."

***

To say that Roland was a terrible patient was an understatement. He was a relentless nag when it came to getting out of bed. If somebody was not with him every moment, he would be found hobbling the corridors on his crutches— which they eventually had to hide from him—instead of obeying his doctor's orders and resting.

Aurelia, Guustin, and Celsa divided up the days and took turns as Roland's gaoler. Every day it became harder to keep him off his feet.

Today marked the four-week point after the bone had been set and Aurelia suspected it would be impossible to deny him his crutches for much longer.

Aurelia had worked in her studio that morning, but it was now her turn to sit with Roland until late tonight, when Guustin would take over.

When she approached Roland's chambers she heard laughter. She set her ear to the door and heard a delighted female giggle, joined by one of Roland's distinctive bellows of laughter.

Aurelia could not help grinning at the sound. One good thing to come out of Arthur's murderous behavior was the new relationship that had grown between Celsa and Roland.

Six evenings ago, Roland had told Celsa that Arthur was her father.

Celsa had not been as surprised as they had all feared. As Guustin had feared, Arthur had been manipulating the girl for years, controlling her in subtle ways and encouraging her to act out against Roland.

It would likely take years for Celsa to get over the damage Arthur had inflicted, but Aurelia was glad she at least knew the truth about her heritage.

Already Celsa was a far less combative, prickly young woman to everyone around her. And she and Roland were greatly enjoying their time together.

Another burst of laughter came from beyond the door and Aurelia tiptoed away; Celsa needed this time with her father. Aurelia would come back in an hour and relieve her.

In the meantime, she could get to work on the letters she had yet to send to her family. With Roland recuperating, there was little chance of accepting her sister Phoebe's invitation to come home to Wych House for the last half of December.

Aurelia would have loved to spend Christmas with everyone, but even if Roland was better what about Guustin? If she invited him—not as odd as it sounded as Phoebe's husband's illegitimate daughter lived with them—then what about Nora? If her son left, she would be all alone for the holiday.

It was a conundrum. But she had to write something, even though there was so much that she simply did not want to discuss in a letter—if ever.

Aurelia sighed and sat down at the desk in her room and took out a sheet of paper. She would simply say the work was at a critical juncture and she could not come home at this point. Maybe, after Roland was better and things had been sorted out here, she could tell her family the truth.

She dipped the quill into the inkwell and drafted the first of the five letters she would need to write.

***

"Look," Roland said to Aurelia a week later, tugging the blanket off his legs, lifting his foot, and wiggling his toes. "I am better," he said, biting back a wince.

"I am certainly well enough to stand beside you in the chapel and get married." He lowered his eyelid. "And I am *more* than well enough to lie beside you, or on top of you, or beneath you, or—"

"Roland," Aurelia said, her lips pursing in that prim way that did nothing to alleviate the constant erection he had been suffering for weeks.

Roland had repeatedly attempted to convince his stern, serious lover that a broken leg did not mean his cock was not functioning, but she had been remarkably firm on the subject. A firm Aurelia was almost as arousing as a chastising, scolding Aurelia.

He was utterly captivated by his betrothed and thoughts of her consumed his days and nights.

Although being in love was thrilling, Roland was grateful that he had not been struck by Ero's arrow twenty years ago. If he had, he never would have looked at another insect or animal again. Never had anything interested him more than nature. Never.

"We are getting married in two days, Aurelia. Two."

"How in the world will your friends get here in two days?"

He muttered a curse beneath his breath, mulling over the possibility of *not* inviting Lampton and Shield and their wives. Roland had known both men for years and had gone on more than one expedition with them. He'd not had even one guest of his choosing at either of his prior weddings and had looked forward to introducing Aurelia to the men and their wives, who were delightful, intelligent women.

Roland looked at Aurelia's patiently waiting face and sighed. "Fine. We will marry in a week. That will give Lampton and Shield plenty of time to get here."

Aurelia looked dubious at that claim but nodded.

He gave her a stern look. "We are getting married in seven days even if I have to carry you to the chapel." He paused and smiled. "I like that thought."

"Of course you do, it harkens back to your primitive Viking heritage."

He laughed.

"As it happens, I agree with you that seven days is as long as we can wait or two of my guests will be gone."

Roland took her hand in his and lifted it to his mouth, kissing the tips of her fingers. "Oh no. Is Talbot going somewhere? Perhaps we should wait two weeks, after all?

Again, his words earned him a chiding look. "You are very ungrateful to the man who saved your life, Roland."

Roland grunted at that.

"And grunting is not the same as having a real conversation."

He laughed again, something he did a great deal with his betrothed. "Very well. I will thank Talbot *again* when I see him—in *seven* days. Where is he off to at this time of year?"

"Evidently he has family in Edinburgh and will spend the holiday with them."

Likely to lick his wounds after losing Aurelia, Roland reckoned. He could not fault the man for his excellent taste in women but did not care to have him hanging about like a dog in the manger.

"And Larissa will be leaving shortly after Sir Gideon," Aurelia said.

Unlike Talbot, Roland was glad that Aurelia's friendship with Larissa Clifford had flourished.

"So, you are ready to marry in a week?" he asked, and then tugged on her hand, pulling her closer to his chair, where he'd sat with his foot up on an ottoman for far too many days.

"Yes, my lord."

He smiled. "Why do you sound so naughty when you say that?"

"You think I am naughty no matter what I say or do."

"True. Kiss me," he commanded.

She looked around the library, as if somebody might be hiding among the books, and then offered up her mouth for plundering.

"Ahh," Roland murmured happily a few minutes later. His Aurelia had become a skilled kisser over the past weeks. Largely because it was the only activity she would allow. No fondling, no… frottage. And she refused to allow him to pleasure her with his mouth, even though it could hardly harm his bloody foot in any way.

Perhaps he should just demonstrate how well his foot was functioning by using it to sneak up to her chambers tonight. The same thought occurred to him every single evening, but he was trying to be a better, more thoughtful, and less selfish lover.

And it was hell.

"I will send a message to Sir Gideon and Larissa today," Aurelia said. "And you must write to your friends immediately."

"*Mmmm*," he said, his mind still on a nocturnal visit. Was it really so selfish?

"Guustin can let Nora know when he sees her tomorrow," she said.

"Yes," he agreed.

She sighed.

Roland frowned. "Why the heavy sigh?"

"It is nothing."

"No, there is something wrong. I can see it in your eyes. What is it?"

"Really, there is nothin—"

"No lying to your lord and master," he said with exaggerated sternness.

She snorted. "Lord and master? If you recall, that position is still vacant. It might *remain* vacant if you—"

He kissed her, swallowing whatever she'd been about to say. She melted against him, making those soft little whimpery sounds he adored so much. Roland suspected she was not even aware she was making them. His prim Miss Burton would be mortified to know she *whimpered*.

Roland gave a groan of protest when she pulled away. He allowed her to break the kiss but kept her close and looked hard into her eyes. Yes, there was a shadow. "Tell me what has saddened you?"

"My family will be reuniting at Wych House for Christmas and I will miss them."

"Have they not invited you?"

"Of course they have, but there was all this"—she gestured to his leg and vaguely in the direction of Rock Cove and all that happened there—"to be dealt with."

"Darling, if you wish to go to Hampshire for Christmas, we must go."

She caught her lush lower lip with her teeth. "I do not want our first Christmas together to be spent without Guustin."

Roland felt an unpleasant twinge at her words. "I will not hide my relationship with him. Not for anyone."

"No, no, it's not that," she hastily assured him. "It is just… what about Nora?"

"Nora?" he repeated, utterly befuddled.

"She will be so lonely if Guustin is not here."

Roland's eye widened. "You cannot be suggesting that we take my ex-lover with us?"

Aurelia continued to chew her lip.

"You *are*!" He gave a disbelieving laugh. "Darling, even if Nora agreed to make such a journey—which given the state of her health I am not sure about— what in the world would your family say?"

"Viscount Needham moved his former mistress and illegitimate daughter into my family's ancestral home, Roland. And then my sister Phoebe agreed to marry him. And then," she paused, giving him an impish look, "Phoebe and Needham's ex-lover became quite good friends."

Roland didn't think much could surprise him anymore, but *that* certainly did.

"*Hmm*," he said. Because, what else could a person say to that? "So, you believe your sister would not be shocked about Nora, then?"

"Phoebe is very practical. My mother would be horrified, but…" She stopped and gave a very slight shrug of her elegant shoulders.

Roland suspected Aurelia's relationship with both her parents was something that would plague her for years to come.

"Well, darling, all you can do is write and tell your sister what you have in mind and see what she says."

"What about my work? I shall never finish the last of the paintings if I spend a month away. I will be hard pressed to finish them even if I *do* stay."

"I have already written to the publisher to move the date back a year. He was glad to do it. I think he overestimated how easy it would be to find enough competent people to finish the plates. I know you've been so busy caring for me that you've not been able to keep to the schedule," he said. "Another year will not harm anything. And it would make a Christmas trip far more pleasurable for you."

"But I have already written to say that I am not coming. Not just to Phoebe, but to the others, as well."

He chuckled softly. "Is there some law that says you may not change your mind?"

"Well… no."

"Then write to your sister Phoebe and tell her whatever you think she needs to know. She is our hostess, so it is her opinion that matters. As for your other siblings, let our visit be a surprise."

She cupped his face and looked at him with so much love it robbed his breath. "You are so good to me."

"I know," he said with exaggerated modestly, making her laugh.

"That is exactly what I will do, Roland. But first I must ask Guustin and Nora if they will come."

"No," he corrected, slipping his hands around her waist and lifting her into his lap. "First you must give your brilliant lord and master-to-be a proper kiss and cuddle for coming up with such a perfect idea."

"Hmm. A *proper* kiss and cuddle?" she asked, wiggling her bottom on his lap in a way that was destined to leave him in torment. "But is this really proper, Lord Crewe?"

He laughed. "Oh darling, not if you do it correctly. Not at all proper…"

And he proceeded to show her exactly what he meant.

Chapter 30

Aurelia's heart swelled as she looked around the drawing room at the small gathering of friends and family who'd come together today to celebrate their wedding.

The ceremony and breakfast had passed in a blur and soon everyone would be leaving. She wanted to brand the moment into her mind so that she could enjoy it later at her leisure.

Celsa was sitting next to Sir Gideon and the two were engaged in what seemed to be a heated argument, at least on one side. The handsome baronet looked amused while Celsa was incensed. Aurelia could not help feeling a little relief that her new daughter was not, for once, casting languishing gazes at Guustin, who was chatting with his mother and Larissa. Whatever the three of them were talking about was causing smiles all around.

Viscount and Viscountess Lampton and Baron and Baroness Shield—who had, on surprisingly short notice, made the journey from their estates just south of Edinburgh—were chatting with Roland.

They had arrived the day before and stayed last night at Castle Crewe. Aurelia had been concerned about how they would react to the presence of Nora and Guustin at the festivities and had been pleasantly relieved when both women had been civil, if not effusive, to Nora, who'd arrived shortly before the ceremony that morning. If they thought it odd to have the mother of Roland's illegitimate son at his wedding, they were too well-bred to comment on it.

"You look happy."

She glanced up at the sound of Guustin's voice and smiled. "I am. Very happy."

"I am glad," he said, sitting down on the settee beside her and lowering his voice to say, "And I am also very grateful for your generosity toward me and my mother, not just for today, but for Christmas."

"I am so delighted she is willing to make the journey, Guustin. For a while I worried that we would never be able to convince her to go to Wych House."

He chuckled. "There was no possible way she could hold out when you, me, Celsa, and my father all weighed in. We are both looking forward to it and it will certainly be an interesting Christmas."

"My brother and sisters will adore you," she assured him. "As for my mother and father?" She shrugged. "They are generally too involved in their own affairs to take much notice of anyone else."

"It really does not bother you to see my mother and father together?" he asked, a wrinkle of concern between his green eyes as he turned to where Roland had joined Larissa and Nora.

"I adore your mother," she said, meaning it. Every now and then Aurelia felt a twinge of jealousy that Nora and Roland shared a child, but there was nothing left between Nora and Roland except the mutual love of their son.

Roland and Aurelia had both agreed that they would all travel to Hampshire together. They would leave in Roland's traveling coach tomorrow, even though that only left them one night to celebrate their wedding. But they were already getting a late start and would be arriving at Wych House a week after all the others, so they did not want to delay.

Aurelia was so happy that she had done as Roland suggested and had written to Phoebe telling her about Nora and Guustin and asking her sister if she thought it would be alright for all of them to come for the holiday.

Phoebe's reply had come back immediately. She had been delighted by Aurelia's marriage and had insisted that Aurelia bring whomever she wanted for Christmas. Regarding ex-lovers and illegitimate children, Phoebe had amusingly written, *Paul and I will welcome _all_ your family with open arms. And he says it will be your new husband's duty to draw our mother's fire as Paul has already had to do so for six months.*

Aurelia's only regret was that she would miss the first week of the celebrations. But fortunately, several of her sisters would be going to London right after the holiday, so she would see them in town, as well.

All too soon the small party began to break up and their wedding guests began to take their leave.

Nora and Guustin were the first to go. "I still have a bit of packing to do," Nora said, her eyes tired from the day's exertions but amusement glittering in them. "I am so excited about our journey tomorrow that I doubt I'll get any sleep at all tonight."

The next to depart were the Lamptons and Shields, both of whom reminded Aurelia and Roland that they had promised to visit their estates—which bordered each other—next summer.

"You can take a look at my collection when you come to stay," Viscount Lampton said, sliding a sly look at Roland. "And perhaps you might consider doing a spot of work for me. I can offer wages far more generous than Crewe."

Aurelia lifted her eyebrow at Roland. "*Hmm*, higher wages?"

Roland laughed ruefully and shook his head. "Lord, Lampton! Don't be giving her any ideas. She already has plenty."

Last, but not least, to leave were Gideon and Larissa.

"If Crewe does not behave himself, remember that assistance is only a short boat ride away," Gideon said, embracing Aurelia and kissing her soundly on the lips before stepping back and smirking at Roland.

Aurelia blushed, Larissa laughed, and Roland smiled sourly.

Larissa threw her arms around Aurelia. "I hate that I am leaving here now that I have met you." She lowered her voice and added, "And thank you so much for all you have done for me, Aurelia."

"I have done nothing but write a letter to a friend," Aurelia chided, guilty that she could not have done more for the other woman. "I shall miss you terribly."

"But you will come to London, won't you?" Larissa said. "The earl mentioned you would arrive sometime after the New Year?"

"Yes. He has agreed to deliver a talk at the Royal Society so we will go there directly after visiting my family."

"I will be living at the academy by then, so please do call on me," Larissa said, referring to the girls' school where she would soon be teaching. "Be well, my newest sister," Larissa whispered, giving Aurelia one last hug.

Aurelia blinked back tears as Larissa and Gideon climbed into the carriage that would take them the short distance to the pier.

Roland slid an arm around her and pulled her close to his side as they stood and waved. "Alone at last," he murmured, kissing her temple.

She laid her head against his shoulder as she wiped away a tear that had sneaked past her guard.

Roland squeezed her tighter. "Don't cry, darling. You will get to see Miss Clifford in less than a month. As for Talbot," his voice changed to a far less indulgent tone. "I daresay he will plague me like a burr in my arse for the next thirty years."

Aurelia gave a watery laugh.

"But come," he said, "I don't want to think about him or anyone else but you, Aurelia. You are mine, mine, mine," Roland hissed. "Now. Let us go up to bed."

"Roland!" she gasped. "We cannot. It is barely five o'clock."

"The doctor said I needed to spend more time in bed," he reminded her as he limped along, using only one crutch.

"Somehow I don't think he had in mind what *you* have in mind."

"Good Lord, Aurelia. The man is ancient, not dead. Of course he knows what sorts of plans I have in mind for my wedding night. Besides, we need to take advantage of your comfortable bed because it will be the shortest honeymoon in history. We will be closeted with Celsa and Nora inside a coach for the next six days." He thrust out his lower lip. "I still think I should be allowed to ride alongside like Guustin," he said, his voice amusingly petulant.

"The doctor strenuously advised against that activity—unless you want to risk permanent damage."

Roland scowled.

"You will have a lovely time inside the carriage with us. Nora has the latest fashion journal from Paris and you would not believe the new fashion for sleeves—"

Roland whimpered. "Oh, God."

"And then there are the bonnets—"

"No bonnets, Lady Crewe. I beg of you, no bonnets!"

Aurelia laughed.

***

Roland gave his new wife thirty minutes to prepare for bed but opened the connecting door when only twenty-five had passed.

Fortunately, the maid had wisely buggered off and Aurelia was alone, brushing her hair in front of the looking glass.

Roland paused to admire her, smiling when their eyes met in the mirror, and a pretty flush colored her cheeks. "You get lovelier every time I see you."

"You only saw me"—she glanced at the clock— "twenty-four minutes ago."

"It feels like a lifetime."

She pursed her lips and set down her brush, but he could tell she was pleased. She turned away from the mirror as he crutched his way over to her.

"How is your leg?"

"Fit as a fiddle," he lied. It ached like the bloody dickens, but he had no intention of sharing that fact or he knew she would hustle him back to his bedchamber and pack him in cotton wool for the foreseeable future.

She gave a skeptical *humm*, but he ignored it.

"You will have to undress me as I'm still a cripple," he told her as he set his crutch against the nightstand.

Her warm gaze dropped to the V of his banyan. "I thought you were *fit as a fiddle*."

"All the important parts of me are extremely fit," he assured her.

She laughed and stopped less than a foot in front of him, her lips twitching as she studied his red silk robe.

"Why are you smirking like that?" he asked.

"That is quite a, er, *flamboyant* banyan."

Roland grabbed her around the waist and tossed her onto the bed, only hurting his leg a little in the process. But it was worth it to hear his stern, serious wife giggle.

He shrugged off his robe and climbed up onto the bed.

"I thought undressing you was my job," Aurelia protested, propping herself up on her elbows to stare at him. Her lips parted and her eyes widened. "Oh," she said, an adorable flush rising in her cheeks as her gaze settled on his arousal.

"That is for you," he said, rolling onto his back and shamelessly exhibiting his body to her.

She gave a breathless laugh, staring in a way that made him throb with need.

Roland laced his hands behind his head and smirked as her hot eyes caressed up and down his body. "As you neglected your job, you will now have to undress yourself instead." He clucked his tongue when she merely stared. "Focus on the task at hand, Lady Crewe. Time is wasting."

"We have all night. And a good part of this afternoon," she added wryly. But even as she spoke her hands went to the devilishly tiny buttons on her night rail.

"Trust me, it won't be nearly long enough."

She pushed her lower lip. "Poor Roland."

"You little witch! Are you mocking your poor crippled husband?"

"You like it," she said, her gaze sliding to his cock, which was bobbing and drooling. "Or at least part of you does."

"When I am fully mended, you will pay dearly for this," he promised her.

She laughed.

And then, thank God, she lifted the night rail over her head.

Roland groaned at the sight of her perfect berry-tipped breasts and tiny waist. Her hair was a shiny tawny river that fell all the way to the triangle of darker hair at the apex of her long, slender thighs.

"You are… perfection," he said in a voice rough with need. "I have been dreaming about this for weeks." He held out his arms. "Come here."

Rather than obey him, she cocked her head to the side, as if she were considering the matter. *Teasing* him.

It was adorable.

Roland lunged for her, catching her around the waist as she squeaked with surprise. "Roland! You will hurt your leg if you do that. Lie down," she ordered, straddling his legs and then lowering her lush bottom onto his thighs.

He smiled. "Much better."

The slightly anxious expression that flickered across her face reminded him that for all her self-possession and teasing, they had only made love that one time.

Roland set his hands on her thighs and gently stroked her. "Look at me, darling."

She pulled her gaze from his prick with obvious reluctance.

He smiled up at her and gently pulled her down for a long kiss before saying, "I would like nothing more than to take you the way I did the last time, but that really would be bad for my leg. And so, my dearest love, you will have to be in charge tonight."

***

In charge.

The words caught Aurelia's attention. Looking down to where he was jutting up at her it wasn't difficult to discern what Roland meant, but Aurelia had to admit it surprised her that men would hand over control in such a way.

"It is the same principle as before, but you set the pace," he said, as he caressed the skin of her thighs, kneading and stroking the muscles and moving up and up, until the pads of his fingers traced the tender crease between her legs and sex. "I might be flat on my back, but that doesn't mean I can't still give you pleasure," he said, his pupil swelling as he parted her lower lips.

Aurelia gasped when he circled the sensitive bundle of nerves, his slick finger sending jolts of arousal to her womb, belly, and breasts.

"You are already wet," he said. "Have you been thinking about this evening, Aurelia?"

She had no intention of confessing just how eagerly she had been anticipating this night.

She frowned as his clever finger moved in the wrong direction and away from the source of her pleasure. Aurelia shifted her hips to follow him. And then noticed his smile.

"You are doing that on purpose."

He didn't deny it. "Answer my question. Have you thought about tonight?"

"Yes."

He began to stroke her the right way and her eyelids fluttered. Why did it feel so much better when he did it than when—

"Did you touch yourself?"

Her eyes snapped open when his finger stilled. Again.

"Did you touch *yourself?*" she retorted.

He laughed. "At least once a night, sometimes twice."

Her sex clenched at that mental picture and his smile turned into a grin. "You like the sound of that, hmm? You would like to watch me, I think?"

God save her; she did. What sort of deviant enjoyed thinking about the sins of Onan and wanted to watch? Her sort, apparently.

"Yes and yes." She said the words quickly, before she could come to her senses.

His hand resumed its magic. "I will want to see that at some point, Aurelia. You spread out on the bed, your legs wide open, your dainty finger—"

"Roland!"

He laughed, the sound satisfied and wicked.

Thankfully, his hand did not stop. Instead, his other hand joined it.

"Eyes on me, sweetheart," he murmured as her body began to shake, the pressure inside her so intense it almost hurt.

His hot blue gaze burned through her, his lips slack as his own breathing sped. "Yes," he urged as her tremors became shudders, the pleasure inside her suddenly unfurling.

Aurelia cried out, her eyes closing no matter how hard she tried to keep them open.

Roland slid a second finger inside her, easing the emptiness, but not giving her enough.

"Roland," she murmured. "I need—"

"I know what you need, darling. Rise up on your knees."

Her legs felt boneless and it took effort to push up. And then she felt the blunt heat of him at her entrance and her body knew what to do. She slowly slid down his length, the sensation of fullness heavenly.

Roland's hips lifted off the bed, filling her until he could penetrate no deeper. "Bloody hell," he muttered.

The sight of her normally self-possessed lover struggling for control made her inner muscles clench.

He groaned and met her gaze, his face hard, no sign of the humor that usually lurked. "Ride me, Aurelia."

Aurelia began to post him—*hard*—earning more groans and mutters and crude words.

Roland flexed and thrusted, sweat building on his abdomen and chest. She leaned forward to tease his tiny nipple and realized instantly the benefit of such an angle. The next stroke made her moan as his shaft rubbed against her sex in exactly the right way.

Beneath her, he gave a breathy chuckle when she nipped him. "Naughty. Now make us both come, Aurelia."

She shuddered at his filthy command, not needing to be told twice, concentrating all her effort on where they were joined, experimenting with the way she rolled her hips to get the most friction. Aurelia lowered herself harder and harder with each stroke, her hips becoming difficult to control, the pleasure yet again spiraling out of control until her climax overwhelmed her.

Roland grabbed Aurelia's hips when they stopped responding to her commands, thrusting only a few times before his body stiffened and his thick shaft spasmed inside her, filling her with jet after jet of heat.

Aurelia's head rested against his chest and she marveled at the erratic but strong pounding of his heart. The sense of completeness that filled her was so profound that it startled her. She had experienced moments of complete contentment occasionally when she had painted something she was entirely pleased with, but never had she felt it with another person.

"I love you," he said, as if he could hear her thoughts. And then his arms tightened around her.

Aurelia felt his breathing gradually become more regular and gloried in the fact that he was still inside her even though he slept.

Her sated, sluggish thoughts wandered back to that dreadful, endless coach ride from Little Sissingdon to Balcrewe that she had endured half a year ago, when she had left behind the only life she knew and all the people she loved. At the time, Aurelia had worried that she and her sisters and brother would never be together again—and she'd feared that she had only her work and a subsistence future to look forward to.

But rather than losing her family, she had found a brand new one.

She kissed Roland's chest, unable to resist his small nipple, nipping and sucking it as he did hers.

He jolted beneath her, his eyelid heavy as he glanced around the room. "Is it morning already?"

Aurelia laughed softly. "No. I doubt you've been asleep for even a quarter of an hour."

He gave a groan of relief, the corners of his mouth slowly curling into a smile and the tiny lines at the corner of his eye deepening. "Ah, then we've still got plenty of time, hmm?"

"Yes, my love. We still have plenty of time." Aurelia took his face in both hands and rubbed their noses together, the way that he'd taught her to enjoy. "All the time in the world."

Epilogue

December

Six Years Later

A*argh*, how on earth have you done this twice before?" Celsa moaned.

Aurelia chuckled at the younger woman, who'd been shifting unceasingly on a chaise longue for the past few hours, unable to get comfortable.

"I have never been two weeks past the doctor's predicted due date as you have," Aurelia pointed out.

"Where is Gideon? I sent him for strawberries ages ago," Celsa groused.

Aurelia did not point out there were no strawberries to be had at this time of year, not even in the hothouses. No doubt poor Gideon had gone to hide somewhere and avoid another tongue-lashing from his waspish spouse.

Celsa had been in a vile mood since well before she had passed her due date. Now, two weeks later, she was inconsolable.

Aurelia could not blame her. She could not imagine carrying a child past term. It was possible that Dr. MacMillan had mistaken how far along Celsa was—he was, after all, on the far side of eighty—but everyone in the village swore it would be the first time if he had.

"This is the only child I am having," Celsa said—not for the first, or even the thirty-first time. "If it is not a boy, I do not care. It would serve Gideon right for not allowing a girl to inherit."

"I don't think the entail is Gideon's fault." Aurelia felt compelled to defend her dear friend, who had been a model husband to a wife who had been less than model for the past several months.

Celsa gave a piteous groan. "I am being dreadful to him, aren't I, Lia?"

Aurelia smiled at the nickname, which she loved hearing from her stepdaughter who was more like a sister. "Yes, Celsa, you have been quite dreadful. Luckily for you, Gideon has already forgiven you."

"He is a darling, isn't he?" Celsa said, her voice suddenly dreamy.

Aurelia decided that was a rhetorical question.

The door opened and Roland entered, a child holding each hand.

"Mama!" her daughter Judith shrieked, and then tore across the room and flung herself on Aurelia.

"Ooof!" Aurelia grunted as the small body scrambled into her lap.

"Judith demanded to see you. And you know I cannot deny her," Roland said, looking proudly at his hellion of a daughter's wild tawny curls.

"Mama, Erik ate an insect," Judith said, scowling at her little brother.

Erik, at barely three, merely regarded her with his serious hazel gaze, clinging tightly to his father's hand.

"What sort of insect, Erik?" Aurelia asked her son, who rarely spoke more than five words a day.

But Erik pressed his lips together, almost as if the insect might still be in there.

Aurelia glanced up at Roland who knew what she was thinking and shook his head. "I checked. Whatever he had in there, it is gone."

"It was an *xestia alpicola*," Judith informed them, her slight lisp making the Latin name sound adorable.

Roland grinned proudly at his daughter, who had inherited her father's fascination with wildlife, while his son evidently preferred to eat it.

"At least Erik did not eat anything too rare, darling," Aurelia said philosophically. "There is no shortage of *xestia alpicola* on the island." Aurelia smoothed back her daughter's riotous curls, which were the same color as her own hair.

Unfortunately, neither of her children had inherited their father's guinea gold locks or his icy blue eyes. Indeed, except for their tall, lean bodies they both resembled Aurelia so closely that it appeared—at first glance—that nobody else was involved in their creation.

Judith scrambled off her lap as quickly as she'd scrambled onto it, darting across the room to something that had caught her attention.

"Papa? Have you seen Gideon?" Celsa asked.

Roland gave his oldest daughter a wry look. "He has locked himself in the dungeon."

"No, he hasn't." She paused and narrowed her eyes at Roland. "Has he really?"

Roland laughed. "No. But I would not blame him if he had."

Celsa's lower lip trembled. "I have been awful to him."

"Yes," Roland agreed. "But Talbot is so besotted with you that he does not care. He has rowed over to the mainland to see if there is even one berry left anywhere in Scotland.

Celsa's eyes became glassy and a fat tear slid down her cheek. "He is *such* a darling."

Roland's eye-roll showed what he thought of that.

Aurelia and Roland had been pleased when Celsa had come home after her year at finishing school—which she had loved—having shed her infatuation with Guustin.

They had taken her to London where Celsa had enjoyed a successful Season without giving her heart to any of the young men who had pursued her.

You could have knocked Aurelia down with a feather when three years later, just when they'd begun to believe Celsa had no interest in men or marriage or children at all, the girl had decided that nobody would do for her but Gideon.

Although Gideon had remained one of the most sought-after bachelors in the area, he'd become more set in his bachelor ways with each year that passed, until Aurelia had begun to fear that her dear friend would never marry. But when Celsa set her mind on him, Gideon had not stood a chance.

Roland had been delighted that Celsa had settled so close to Crewe and the two had become closer than ever after he had purchased land not far from Gideon's home as a wedding gift for Celsa. Enough land that Celsa could indulge her dream of breeding horses. A dream which Aurelia quickly discovered her husband also shared.

Roland spent hours every week with Celsa, the two of them making such a roaring success of the modest operation that they had doubled the size of the holding only the year before. It had been Roland who had been managing the stud these past few months when Celsa could scarcely walk, her feet were so swollen.

The pregnancy had been hard on Celsa and Aurelia hoped there would be a long lull before the next child.

As for her, it seemed that bearing children was something Aurelia had been born to do. While she had suffered aches and pains and discomfort just like any woman, she hadn't vomited nonstop like Celsa nor had her labors been more than a few hours each. She'd had such easy pregnancies that she had worked all the way through both, illustrating not only for Roland but also for a select few friends.

Roland's book had been a great success and was going into its third printing. He was not resting on his laurels, however, and the two of them had taken a necessarily brief journey to Portugal last year where he had begun the process of documenting the birds of the Peninsula. They would need to make several trips rather than one long one, but Roland's wandering spirit seemed to have gentled these past few years. Between the children and the horse breeding business with Celsa he was less driven to explore new frontiers.

Christmas was less than a month away and Aurelia and Roland would make the journey to Wych House, they were just waiting for Celsa's baby to arrive before they departed.

Aurelia and her siblings had decided last Christmas they would begin taking turns hosting the celebrations after this year, so this would be the last time they met at Wych House for another six years.

They had drawn lots to see who went first and Aurelia had won, which meant next year they would host the holiday gathering at Crewe Castle. She could not wait to welcome her siblings and their families to Crewe. While Doddy and Katie had both visited, her other sisters had not yet made the journey to the island.

Aurelia felt a light touch on her hand and pulled herself from her musing to see that Erik was holding out his little hand. She glanced at Roland, but he had pulled a chair closer to Celsa and the two were deep in a discussion about some horse or other while Judith's legs stuck out from beneath Celsa's chaise lounge. Doubtless, her daughter was searching for insects. Unfortunately, Beekman still ran the household with an iron fist so poor Judith was destined to be disappointed in her search.

Aurelia turned back to her son and patted the cushion beside her. He solemnly climbed up and then looked at her before holding out his tightly closed fist.

"Do you have something for me?" she whispered.

He nodded and opened his hand.

Aurelia was relieved that it wasn't a mangled moth on his palm but a piece of paper that had obviously been folded and re-folded many times, until it fit in his hand.

"For me?"

He nodded.

She unfolded it and her eyes widened. "Did you draw this, Erik?"

He nodded.

"Is it… Papa's horse?"

Erik flashed her one of his rare smiles and nodded.

"It is a very good likeness," she praised. "Are you going to be an artist, like mama?" His answer was to burrow in close to her, sigh happily, and promptly fall asleep.

She glanced up from the three-legged gray smudge on the paper he'd given her to find Roland looking at her.

I love you, he mouthed.

I love you.

He grinned and turned back to his conversation.

Aurelia sighed, utterly contented and happy. Life on an island might not be exciting, but there was something to be said for peace. She closed her eyes and settled in for a nice nap.

"Aurelia!" Celsa's sharp voice jerked Aurelia instantly awake.

"What is it?" Aurelia asked, bolting upright.

"I think it is time to call Mrs. Brown. I believe I am finally going to have this bab—" the last word turned into a scream.

Roland, who was a coward in such matters—an odd reaction in a man who was a naturalist, Aurelia always thought—snatched Judith from under the couch and tucked a still-sleeping Erik under his other arm. "I shall summon the midwife and find Gideon," he tossed over his shoulder, one foot already outside the door.

Several long hours later…

Roland and Aurelia stood together beside the small cradle, admiring the red-faced but healthy little bundle who was currently resting after making her long-delayed entrance into the world.

"How does it feel to be a grandmother?" Roland whispered in Aurelia's ear, having to bite his cheek to keep from laughing at the look she turned on him. He held a finger over her lips, took her hand, and towed her from the nursery.

"You are a wretched man," she accused once they were out in the corridor, but he could see she was fighting back a smile.

Roland laughed. "I am, I admit it. Grandmama."

She snorted and they made their way toward their chambers.

"What a relief that this is over and both Celsa and little Ursula are healthy," Roland said.

"Yes, we will be able to go on our journey with no concerns. I'm sorry they won't be joining us on our trip south, but they will appreciate this time together."

"You will still have me," Roland pointed out.

Aurelia gave him an arch look. "Are you volunteering to accompany me, Judith, and Erik _inside_ the coach instead of riding Frost?" she taunted.

Roland's jaw dropped. "Er—"

"No. I thought not," Aurelia laughingly said, and then stifled a yawn.

"You must be exhausted, darling." Aurelia had stayed with Celsa almost the entire nine hours of her labor, taking only short breaks to eat and have a nap.

"It has been a long day," she admitted. "But a very good one."

"Indeed, it has." Roland had been hoping to end it in her bed, in her arms, buried deeply in her body, but sometimes being a good, caring husband required personal sacrifice. This, he suspected, was one of those times.

And so, Roland stopped outside her chambers and tilted his wife's face toward his before kissing her lightly on the nose. "As much as it pains me, I will allow you to get your rest tonight, my love."

"You needn't stay away. I am not so tired as"—she yawned hugely.

He chuckled. "Yes, I can see how *not tired* you are." He kissed her again, opened the door, and laid a hand on her lush bottom to propel her into the room. "Good night, my love."

"Good night, Roland," she answered groggily as he shut the door behind her.

Roland had hours ago sent word to Jenks, his valet, telling him not to wait up. And so he undressed himself and quickly washed his face and body in water that had long been cold.

As he slipped between the blankets, he gave a pleasurable moan when he realized that Jenks had put not one, but three bedwarmers beneath the covers.

Roland glanced at the book on his nightstand and then decided he, too, would get some rest.

He had just blown out the candle and closed his eyes when a noise came from the direction of the connecting doors.

"Aurelia?"

"I could not sleep."

"You will catch your death of cold. Get under here immediately," he ordered, lifting the blankets.

The mattress sank and he lowered the covers and slid an arm out, giving a pleased growl when he encountered her naked body. "*Mmmm*, no night rail. I have taught you well, Lady Crewe." He pulled her small, cold body close.

She ran a hand like a block of ice over his bare hip and Roland bit back a yelp. "*Mmmm*, no nightshirt. I have taught *you* well, my lord."

He laughed and took her freezing hand in both of his, rubbing it to bring some warmth to it. "I want to point out that I was a model of self-sacrifice earlier to let you go to your bed alone." He nuzzled the soft, fragrant skin beneath her ear. "As much as I want to importune you, you should rest, darling. Tomorrow will be the first of several very long days."

"I know it will. And I also know you were being a generous husband to let me sleep. And I appreciate your effort, Roland. But I wanted to be with you." She leaned forward and he hissed when her soft, hot mouth closed over one of his nipples. His naughty wife had discovered how sensitive they were and took great pleasure in teasing him.

He groaned when she slid her newly warmed hand over his belly and then closed her fingers around his cock.

She laughed. "Are you *always* erect, Roland?"

"That would be rather inconvenient, darling," he retorted, subtly thrusting his hips and hoping she would take the hint. She did, and her strong, cool hand commenced pumping him with firm, tight strokes just the way he liked.

"I need something to make me sleep, Roland."

"I might have… something," he admitted.

He heard her give a half-snort, half-giggle—truly one of his favorite sounds in the world.

"I think you deserve a reward for your selfless behavior earlier," she said, rising up on her knees. "Spread your legs, husband."

Christ, yes! Roland wanted to cheer.

When she sank down between his thighs and engulfed him in the hot, wet heaven of her mouth Roland had to admit that there just might be something to the whole *self-sacrifice* thing.

The End

Dearest Reader:

I hope you enjoyed my gothic homage! If you are a fan of Victoria Holt, Dorothy Eden, Phyllis Whitney, and Mary Stewart then you might have recognized some popular gothic elements.

And if you love Victoria Holt then you might have noticed my nod to several of her novels:

Mistress of Mellyn

The Shivering Sands

Shadow of the Lynx

Lord of the Far Island

Just to name a few.

The world of romance has changed a lot since those authors wrote and one of the biggest changes is the modern emphasis on getting the hero and heroine together RIGHT AWAY. While I can sympathize with the desire to get right to the romance (and the "bangziety" this delay often causes, LOL) sometimes the story requires a bit more background and build up. Oftentimes in the older novels the protagonists wouldn't really meet until half the book. Victoria Holt, especially, spent far more time exploring the heroine's life and story.

And of course those older books never showed the story from the hero's POV, a change that dramatically impacts the tone of a story.

Yes, the Isle of Crewe is fictitious. Why? Because I wanted to do things like have a palatinate that was a Scottish island. I also wanted to play with the various waves of conquest in the area—Viking, Norman, and eventually English—and creating my own private island allowed me to have exactly what I wanted.

Naturally, as I edited and re-edited and re-re-edited I cut out a great deal of the history that was originally so important to me, LOL. In any event, there is the reason for the fictional island.

The illustrated book Aurelia and Roland are working on in the story is based loosely on John James Audubon's famous work, which was released a few years later than the one in AURELIA.

I had tons of stuff about the painting process, but that hit the cutting room floor. I also researched a lot about the flora and fauna in the Hebrides as well as the issue of trees and why they don't flourish on those islands. All that precious information was cut, cut, cut.

Another part I had to cut due to space constraints was a great deal about the character Larissa Clifford and her family. In the first draft I introduced ALL the Clifford sisters—as secondary characters who would provide Aurelia with some much-needed sisterhood—but they immediately tried to hijack the book! There was a big masquerade ball in Balcrewe and all sorts of shenanigans occurred with the Clifford sisters hogging the limelight.

Again, that had to go!

Never fear, the poor, disgraced Clifford sisters will get their own books… soon, I hope, because they have a lot to say and want to say it all NOW. But they will have to wait, although I am very excited about their stories.

Are you surprised that Aurelia and Roland will be joining the other Bellamy sisters for Christmas? Well, so was I! What can I say, these characters just want to tag along for the fun. Also, I developed a bit of a soft spot for Guustin and wonder if he might find his love on this journey to the south. Who knows?

A VERY BELLAMY CHRISTMAS will probably not be a novella, but more of a novel—or, at the very least, an extremely loooong novella.

What am I working on now, you ask?

Well… I have been naughty and wrote another story simultaneously along with AURELIA. Yes, I do that sometimes. I write the story that is scheduled during my workday and then write even more at night as a reward for working hard. That, my friends, is when you know you LOVE writing, lol.

This next story was a complete surprise to me and is a new addition to my VICTORIAN DECADENCE series. It features a hero and heroine I never saw coming, so that was fun. The book is called HER VILLAIN. Right now I'm in the editing process, so look for that in late May 2024.

I am currently beavering away on IO: THE SHREW and I'm just LOVING Lady Io and Corbin Masterson, who fight more than any other characters I've ever had. I really hope to finish the book by the deadline, but I'm not sure that will happen.

Why am I such a disorganized mess you ask? No, not more health issues (knock on wood) but we are trying to sell our house and that will be taking up a great deal of my in April and May (cross your fingers that it sells fast!). I have high hopes for my writing schedule, but I am also trying to be more realistic.

Speaking of delays in my schedule… I want to apologize to the thousands of you who had your pre-order cancelled for A STORY OF LOVE, book 6 in THE ACADEMY OF LOVE series.

I HATED doing that, but I got Covid and it was awful. It was truly the sickest I have ever been and there were two visits to the emergency room during December and January, so finishing my book on time just wasn't going to happen.

Rather than bump AURELIA I decided to reschedule A STORY OF LOVE to December 2024. Hopefully I will release book 7, THE ETIQUETTE OF LOVE in March 2025. It would be nice to have them both come out back-to-back.

As for Katie & Doddy… Yes! They will get books of their own. I'm not sure what the schedule is for them, but it will probably be mid-2025.

So, there is your newsy update.

I just want to give my heartfelt *thanks* to those of you who've sent me such lovely, supportive emails over the past months. Those emails really, really make my day and I always appreciate people taking the time to reach out.

Until next time, happy reading!

Love,

Minerva/S.M.

Who are Minerva Spencer & S.M. LaViolette?

Minerva is S.M.'s pen name (that's short for Shantal Marie) S.M. has been a criminal prosecutor, college history teacher, B&B operator, dock worker, ice cream manufacturer, reader for the blind, motel maid, and bounty hunter. Okay, so the part about being a bounty hunter is a lie. S.M. does, however, know how to hypnotize a Dungeness crab, sew her own Regency Era clothing, knit a frog hat, juggle, rebuild a 1959 American Rambler, and gain control of Asia (and hold on to it) in the game of RISK.

Read more about S.M. at: www.MinervaSpencer.com

Follow 'us' on Bookbub:

Minerva's BookBub

S.M.'s Bookbub

On Goodreads

Minerva's OUTCASTS SERIES

DANGEROUS

BARBAROUS

SCANDALOUS

THE REBELS OF THE *TON:*

NOTORIOUS

OUTRAGEOUS

INFAMOUS

AUDACIOUS (NOVELLA)

THE SEDUCERS:

MELISSA AND THE VICAR

JOSS AND THE COUNTESS

HUGO AND THE MAIDEN

VICTORIAN DECADENCE: (HISTORICAL EROTIC
ROMANCE—SUPER STEAMY!)

HIS HARLOT

HIS VALET

HIS COUNTESS

HER BEAST

THEIR MASTER

HER VILLAIN*

THE ACADEMY OF LOVE:

THE MUSIC OF LOVE

A FIGURE OF LOVE

A PORTRAIT OF LOVE

THE LANGUAGE OF LOVE

DANCING WITH LOVE

A STORY OF LOVE*

THE MASQUERADERS:

THE FOOTMAN

THE POSTILION

THE BASTARD

THE BELLAMY SISTERS

PHOEBE

HYACINTH

SELINA

A VERY BELLAMY CHRISTMAS*

THE HALE SAGA SERIES: AMERICANS IN LONDON

BALTHAZAR: THE SPARE

IO: THE SHREW*

THE WICKED WOMEN OF WHITECHAPEL:

THE BOXING BARONESS

THE DUELING DUCHESS

THE CUTTHROAT COUNTESS

THE BACHELORS OF BOND STREET:

A SECOND CHANCE FOR LOVE (A NOVELLA)

THE ARRANGEMENT